THE HOTEL GENOVIE

SHANE M RYAN

First paperback edition 2025
979-8-9924885-0-0

For Kayla

I

Such a misfortune it was when the previous manager under the employ of the Hotel Genovie lost his head. It was a ghastly affair. The poor chap was seeing to the gears of the lift—which had just that morning lent itself to malfunction—when suddenly a belt snapped loose, and his shoulders soon felt quite a bit lighter.

Oh, to be sure, there wasn't much of a mournful disposition among the staff, owing to his proclivity to disagreeableness. But it still came as quite a shock to the guests. We, at the beautiful Genovie, are not inclined to pride ourselves on the grim affair of decapitation along one's route to the dining hall. We rather try to avoid it, when possible. But, as our French friends tend to say, such is life. I, myself, if one were to insist on my putting it into proper words, would suggest the minor alteration of the phrase to read: such is death. But we at the Genovie do not ascribe our business to that of death, but rather to life. So perhaps the French had it right after all.

It seems I have lost myself in all this talk of life, death, and fine accommodation. As your host, I should like to keep my identity to myself. For the time being, at the very least; you will indulge me in that, I trust. All you must know, as my dear reader, is that it is my duty to know everything that goes on in the hotel. Whether that be concerning the staff, the guests, or the walls themselves, I am charged with the record-keeping of the ins and outs of day-to-day life of our dear hotel. While it is of little consequence who I am, I have the pleasure of introducing our new manager and proprietor of our esteemed Hotel Genovie, Lawrence Theodore Erlik the Third. It is his duty, as manager, to see that our guests have a stay that is unlike any earthly accommodation available. One that—with the risk of indelicacy due to the passing of our late manager—could be labeled as to die for.

By no means a man of calm nerves, Lawrence Erlik often allowed his frantic sensibility to bounce about the room—perhaps not the first attribute that one might list when searching for the perfect man for the job. However, our dear Mr. Erlik saw things differently than many of us, naturally due to his chaotic composure. In fact, the way he saw it, it was exactly this quality that made him into the excellent figure of the manager. It was precisely because he knew how to control the internal hysterics that he was such an exceedingly respected head of the Hotel Genovie. After all, patience found within the depths of one's own haunted spirit exudes through one's exterior life.

It would surely not enter the mind of one attempting to describe the manager to say he was a tall man, though he was not a short man either. Lawrence was right in the center of the pack, creating a sense of ease for our guests—not being made to look at a man too small, nor screw their eyes up too high. His hair was a chestnut brown that was always slicked back to one corner with grease. He wore a set of grey pinstripe slacks, a matching double-breasted waistcoat, a stark white shirt with a stiff collar, and a blood-red tie, all covered by a black jacket with a peak lapel and a white kerchief stuffed into the breast pocket. He also made sure to keep a timepiece in the pocket of his vest at the end of a silver chain. When the clasp was opened, the viewer would be permitted to tell the time. When the clasp was closed, the viewer would be granted the serenity of ponderance amongst the etched gaze of a snowy owl.

Reception, as Lawrence liked to call the beginning of every morning, always began with a good deal of nerves plaguing the back of the throat. It was not uncommon for him to find himself purging in the bathroom of the manager's suite of the hotel in the early morning, for the simple reason of overwrought anxiety over the desire to make sure incoming guests had the perfect first impressions of the hotel and its staff. As it was Lawrence's station in life to lead the charge for that aim, he often felt pulled thin by the pressures that came with such a position. However, he was a wise enough man that he saw fit to hold these apprehensions and squeamishness to himself, braving a stern face for the good people under his charge.

On this particular reception day, it was the hottest day of July during the year 1919 when our good manager looked about his station for an early start. The beginning of the day was filled with a proper measure of pacing to and fro through the suite, making sure he was prepared for the coming of fresh souls.

"Ten chimes of the clock's toll," he would mutter to himself. "Nine. Nine caws of the morning dove. Yes, yes. And eight. Eight steps from the door to the lift. Seven seconds down to the first floor and six clicks of the lift gate upon opening. Five clicks of the heel on marble before the carpet. Four yards to the front desk. Three bellmen, two glass doors, and one deep breath." And with that, our good manager was off.

"A fine day and a good morning to you, sir." The old lift

operator shuffled his feet to provide ample room for his boss as Lawrence made his way onto the lift.

"A fine day, indeed, Arthur. I hope you find it to your satisfaction. I can't help but feel a tinge of excitement on mornings like these. Receptions are often filled with such hope, don't you find?"

"Indeed, I do, sir. Though I dare say there is not much difference in the day for a man such as myself. The crank needs turning whether the guest is fresh or not. Er, so to speak, I mean."

"Yes, so to speak."

The lift—whose gate still had a chink in it at the bottom where the unfortunate prior manager saw his neck meet a bitter end—came to a halt at the first floor where Lawrence would begin preparation for the reception.

"See to it that we have that disagreeable chink fixed, dear man," Lawrence ordered upon exiting.

"I shall," Arthur croaked, embarrassment stretched across a wrinkled face.

Ordinarily, stepping onto the marble floors of the lobby was met with a serenity of mind. Lawrence had a profound appreciation, perhaps even an adulation for the grand maiden. After all, she was the height of luxury. I have on more than one occasion found Lawrence pontificating over the wonder and amusement that a guest might have upon first entering the Genovie. "The blacks of their eyes widen to the rims at just the sight of her!" he would say. "Her grand entrance decorated with gold mosaic stretching along the archway that cup the beautiful glass doors. The pillars that wrap around the veranda shine in pearly magnificence that surely reflects the sun into their faces. Not too bright, of course, otherwise they'd miss the rows of arched windows leading into the grand foyer. Or the upper balconies, layered as icing and sponge upon a cake on the second and third floors. And what a tragedy if their eyes were kept from viewing the breathtaking round bays on the top floor, two sprouting from each corner and one larger placed in the middle. And my personal favorite, the dome roofing resting overtop it all."

You might be wondering to yourself, dear reader, whether any man could really find himself talking with such romantic sentiment over the architecture of a hotel. I assure you, strange though it may seem, he often would.

And how can I blame him? The hotel truly was remarkable. But it did not stop at the old girl's façade, I can attest! Upon climbing those wonderful stairs and entering through her large glass doors, held open by the finest bellmen the world had to offer, one might have a tear brought to the eye at the sight of marble flooring polished to glass. The eye would not linger low, however, as the reflection of light from above would naturally drift the guests' eyes to the chandelier. One might be forgiven for thinking it was floating of its own accord in the grand space above the lobby. A glimpse of the heavens, made of only the finest crystal ever to grace the eye.

To the left of the chandelier, one would see the balcony to the second floor, hoisted in the air by grand pillars and archways, decorated with stone carvings of snarling lions' heads plastered overtop the voussoirs. The black carpet against the white marble steps of the grand staircase was often looked upon with a peculiar eye, though one that might become forgiving after vision came to appreciate the beautiful painting adorning the wall of the large landing.

Many a joyous occasion began at the Hotel with a guest standing on said landing—typically a woman in a dazzling ball gown being adored by a young suitor dressed in tails from the bottom of the grand staircase. Eyes would gravitate to the intoxicating spark of young love brightening their faces. Of course, where would we be without the inexorable juxtaposition of the macabre? Yes, our fine landing knew the opposite fashion of sensibility all too well.

I believe I am not mistaken in recounting the unfortunate evening where bouts of lightning illuminated the shaking young lady's hand wielding a knife to her own throat. Oh, it is difficult to erase the sound of her wailing over her misfortunes, the timbre of her scream as the blade beckoned blood to fall on our fine floors. It was quite a shame to have to replace them the following morning. I believe it was a Miss Callawood who caused the unfortunate stain. Or was it Hallawood? Fallwood?

Stepping further into the hotel—if a guest had not already been swept away by the sheer beauty of the architecture—the front desk would act as the ferryman, crossing the guests away from the troubles of their lives and toward the delicate ecosystem of a stay at the Genovie. Much of this fell to the esteemed talents of the manager, to whom we shall presently return.

The silence of the early morning left little to be desired. The good manager might make time for a cup of tea while getting settled upon his high throne of the front desk. He might stop in to check on the maids, walk over to the tea room to ensure there were no problems he could sort out for the wait staff, or perhaps make his way to the boiler room to ensure the handymen had their fair share of breakfast.

On this day, however, Mr. Erlik arrived on scene to a bit of a ruckus being made toward the front of the lobby.

"That's it, lads, a little to the left. Ho! There she goes again. Going to be a bit of trouble, this one is." A familiar voice echoed through the lobby walls at high volume. The voice belonged to the young Dorian Berus.

We have always had three bellmen under the employ of the hotel, though we have not always had the pleasure of triplets operating under our great roof. The Berus brothers have become world-renowned for their service. Baptiste will be the gentleman at the door, ready to greet guests with the most charming smile. Everyone seemed to find his boyish face, youthened by the curl of his raven hair and the freckles spotted upon olive skin, quite the charming visage. The second encounter one might have with a Berus would be with Dorian, who might be so obliged as to take your bags to your room. A natural wavy-haired blond, Dorian never found trouble persuading a young miss to adorn a smile. And of course, one could not forget Adrian—the frizzy brown-haired Casanova himself. Adrian would be pleased to take care of any odds and ends that might come about through the process of checking in and settling within the halls of our hotel. Whether that be finding your room, seeing you to the bar for an early refreshment, or lending his ear for the pleasurable conversation of a man most interested in anything you had to say. He was also one that might feel so inclined as to sport a good joke or the odd limerick if a guest gave him the chance, which they often did given his vivacious disposition.

The Berus brothers were a sight to see in the glory days of our hotel, the very days that I am pleased to share with you in this esteemed record. In fact, there was one particular occasion I can recall—the messy business of a poor young woman who found herself unexpectedly in labor. The unfortunate soul would have been in quite a sticky situation given the lack of doctors we had staying with us at the time, if it weren't for our fine bellmen who were ready to sweep her away to a more private location and help her through the process of delivering the child safely between the walls of the Genovie. I daresay there is no finer place to take one's first breath. If I remember correctly, in honor of their efforts, the mother was inclined to assign the child the middle name of Berus—something that truly tickled all three of them.

"Gentlemen, gentlemen, please! Keep the voices down, I beg of you. My lord, what seems to be the issue here?" Lawrence asked, rushing to the scene with stealthy haste.

"Sorry, sir. We meant no harm, sir. It's just—there's been a bit of an accident. It seems that Adrian let in a bird when he was sweeping the lobby floors and kicking the dirt out to the curb."

"Steady on! I did no such thing. Baptiste let him in when he was polishing the glass, he did!"

"Oh, that's a lie!" Baptiste snapped.

"Gentlemen!" The three brothers, who looked very much as if they were about to start slitting one another's throats, spilling a river of red over the shining floors, came to a crashing halt and stood at attention. Adrian held on to an absurd-looking net that the three of them fashioned from a broomstick and a pool skimmer.

"Now," Lawrence straightened himself into the tallest figure he could embody, pulling his waistcoat by the bottom in a stiff tug, "it appears the three of you, in your infinite wisdom, have seen fit to go about this poor creature's capture with this…contraption. Shall I leave you to it, or shall we call in the brigade?"

Threatening to call in the handymen, who always had a disagreeable way about them in the mornings, caused the brothers to straighten themselves and shake their heads in disagreement.

"No, that won't be necessary sir," Adrian responded. "We'll have her safely flying to the trees here in no time, promise."

"That's a good lad," Lawrence said. "Do be so good as to straighten that tie when you've finished, Master Dorian."

"Yes, sir!"

"Thank you. And Adrian, I expect that dirt you've swept outside will be removed from the curb before our guests arrive?"

"Absolutely, sir!"

He turned to leave them to their devices, but hearing a rather hushed, "Alright lads, she's just over the grandfather clock," he spun around in exasperated tension.

"Gentlemen! No netting around the grandfather clock; she's older than the three of you combined!" At that moment, the culprit fluttered her wings to land on the top of the beautifully carved clock that stood off to the side of the lobby just beside the grand staircase. She caught Lawrence's eye, and he became transfixed by the sleek black feathers of a raven. Three caws sounded, reverberating through his chest with a melancholy pulse. His eyes were entranced by the bird's dark display, rapping one foot against the top of the clock's carvings. "How curious," he whispered to himself.

The trance was broken by Baptiste taking a small coin and tossing it toward the raven, causing it to jump in fright and take to her wings toward the front door.

"Here we go, out with you, my lady fair! Sing sweet poems to us in the night!" Dorian called as he opened the door while Adrian chased the bird with the net. Erlik stood frozen in the center of the hall, finding a bit of his breath had been taken from his lungs during the whole affair. The three caws echoed through his ears as he turned to continue on his path toward the front desk.

"Three," he murmured under his breath. "Three caws of the raven. Two black eyes. One somber beak. Three caws. Three caws." Another tug of the waistcoat and a crack of the neck were needed before our fine manager made his way to the desk. Lawrence was ready to receive his guests.

We have often found through the years that our dear staff have ushered in an experience for our guests that has changed the way they see the world. That may be a bit of an exaggeration on their part, but I suppose anything is possible with fine accommodation. One might say that all those who enter the halls of the Hotel Genovie have something that needs a little adjusting before they are able to check out. One might even say that this very adjustment is why our guests book their stay to begin with. I myself know very little about such things, but if I were to be so bold as to have an opinion on the matter, I would say that such a characteristic of a stay at the Genovie is quite veritable.

Some who have heard stories of our hotel—I imagine it is only those who have heard stories, as it could not possibly be the opinion of a soul that has had the pleasure of staying with us—have gone so far as to allege that our grand halls are haunted. Could you imagine? Staying at one of the—no, *the* finest hotel in the world only to find a deranged apparition floating in the lobby? The scandal that would create! No, our grand hotel is not, by any means, haunted by ghosts and ghouls and poltergeists.

Since the hotel's opening in the year of 1827, we have ushered in thousands of souls through our grand doors and seen to the care and transition from one state to another for each of them. Surely each and every one of them carries an important story of their own that could make up countless pages of record. However, while it is quite an expected feature of the hotel that our guests are left changed from when they first walked in, it is a rare occasion indeed that the guests change the staff.

In this record, I see fit to review a handful of guests that our dear friend, Lawrence Erlik, found himself a changed proprietor over having seen to their stay. It is this very experience that a manager's career at the Hotel Genovie aims toward. After all, if the hotel were only fit for guests, what type of establishment would we be?

II

"Good morning, Aurelia."

Aurelia was a petite, nimble woman of fair complexion. She wore her fiery red hair pinned back in a bun and dressed in a black skirt and jacket combination that showed the flirtation of a bright white slip flashing through when she turned her arm at the proper angle. The smell of the latest French perfumes that reminded the nose of wild day lilies wafted around her atmosphere, dancing alongside the scent of a freshly lit cigarette, despite her protestations of partaking in the fiendish habit. Lawrence had a fondness for Aurelia. Not the same fondness that our young Baptiste could be seen to sport through the eyes of a man infatuated by the gentle curve of a young lady's tantalizing allure, but the fondness of a man who enjoyed the company of a proper working partner. Aurelia offered very little in the way of speaking. Instead, she asserted her prowess through the noble effort of ensuring all manner of accommodations were available to the guests without so much as a cinch. Just as Lawrence preferred.

"Good morning, Mr. Erlik," she responded. This tended to be one of the few times in the day Aurelia would speak, aside from the possible "Good evening, Mr. Erlik," or "Have a good night,

Mr. Erlik." All other forms of communication with the young manager's assistant were simply nonverbal. That worked out quite well for our dear manager, as having to speak nonstop and grow bored with the unfortunate affair of listening to others made for a tiresome day. The two understood each other perfectly.

"Three caws," Lawrence breathed as he opened the guest log for the arrivals, making sure the pen had the proper amount of ink within its converter and a nib that was sure to last the signatures of those who might have a more forceful fist. "Very good. One, two, three, four, five rooms are opening today. Hmm. Keys?"

Aurelia glided from the other side of the desk to arrange five solid gold keys fastened with merlot ribbons that held leather tags with room numbers pressed into their hide. Spreading them out in the order the guests were expected to arrive, Aurelia silently made sure each key was aligned perfectly with the one before it, with equal space placed between each one.

"Splendid," he said in thanks. "Five rooms, four rotations of the stagecoach wheel, three bellmen, two concierge, one raven. No. That's not quite right, no. Simply will not do. One... One... One guest book. Yes, that's better."

After he calmed the nerve on a singularly dreadful count, his eyes met something altogether despicable. "Heavens!" he shouted. A defiant march over to a pedestal in the center of the space between two pillars aside the hotel lobby brought Lawrence to stare at a vase. Within said vase was a bouquet of what ought to have been freshly cut and misted white roses. "Adrian! I believe your service is required."

"Yes, sir?" The young Adrian had stepped with light over to the good manager, wasting no time.

"These are not acceptable. We cannot carry on with these in our lobby."

"I am sure that I agree, sir. But if you would permit me…"

"Permit you to what, Adrian?"

"Well, pardon sir, permit me to ask the nature of their unacceptability?"

"Really, dear boy, must I even say? Clearly, I must. The little one in the corner of the group there, you see? He has fallen quite ill. Pedals are withering away with our very breath. No, take this." Lawrence reached into his pocket and pulled out a single coin. "Take this and run down to the florist shop, make sure you tell the old toad that we are *not* in the fashion of displaying dying roses. Collect a new dozen and return straight away to replace this…mess."

"Should I not just remove the withered one, sir?"

"Really, Adrian, this habit of yours of not seeing the whole picture is growing rather tiresome. The ill flower has *touched* the others. Will it not be long until the plague spreads? No, we must start anew. Fresh flowers, off with you then! Fresh flowers."

Adrian nodded and took off at double speed, holding the coin up with one hand and his hat firmly upon his head with the other. "Fresh flowers," he whispered, snarling at the offending plant.

Just before the perplexed manager took up his favorite pastime of counting down—this time beginning with twelve long-stemmed roses—he heard a sound that brought him to a state of disarray at his unpreparedness. The striking of the grandfather clock. It had already turned half-past ten, and here he was messing about with flowers and ravens! This simply would not do. There were, after all, guests that would be walking through the door at a moment's notice, expecting to be greeted in the utmost manner of high regard. His station awaited.

Of course, the front desk was where Lawrence felt most comfortable in the grand hotel. Surely, there were plenty of times where he would retire to the manager's office just behind the wall that he held his back to, or on the very rare occasion, he would find himself sipping on the indulgence of a bold whiskey when guests weren't looking and the bartender had a slick hand. But more often than not, one would find the good manager dutifully displayed at the hotel's front, keeping watch over the lobby and positioning himself at the ready for whatever lay ahead.

Our manager found himself back where he belonged, and not a moment too soon as the beginning of the receptions was nye. Though his state was not much improved owing to the decaying flower within his vision, Adrian's triumphant strut through the hotel doors with twelve beautiful roses just one minute prior to the three-quarter hour surely aided in quelling his vexation.

Precisely at the striking of the three-quarter hour, the doors opened again, only this time Mr. Lawrence Erlik was met with the visage of a portly man dressed in a day suit of a bright shade of tan, a blue shirt, and a red tie that was spotted with blue dots. Though Lawrence never much agreed with such a casual mode of attire, owing much to the heat of the sun on the hottest day of July, one might be forgiven one's indulgences.

"Good morning, Mr.—"

"Don Cherry, radio newsman from—"

The reader will forgive the interruption of the narrative for my explanation of Mr. Erlik's doubtless frustration in the nature of his first guest of the morning. We at the hotel have found that waiting for the guests to provide their names themselves hinders the exhaustive effort of ensuring each guest feels personally respected and welcomed. Best to start with a bang. That said, when our good Mr. Erlik greets his guests, he makes sure to know their names, the relations they bring with them, where they have traveled from, and how long they plan on staying. So, it is only natural for Lawrence to have felt rather perturbed at being interrupted at the first of his aims, and even more natural that he should take the risk of interrupting his guest in order to carry out the rest of them.

"Atlanta, yes, Mr. Cherry, we have been expecting your arrival. I am terribly sorry about this frightful heat we are experiencing this day. Not even noon and one would be forgiven for ordering up a bucket of ice."

"Not much one can do about the state of the weather, even a man such as yourself."

"Perhaps, Mr. Cherry, perhaps."

The Genovie's first guest of the day gave a puzzled look to the manager's response, as if he were to imply that the hotel simply was so accommodating as to be able to change the weather at the request of the guests. Though the manager might, had he the ability, Mr. Don Cherry shrugged off the idea and stood at attention before the front desk.

"She's a beauty, Mr. Uh…"

"Erlik, my dear man, Mr. Erlik."

"Right, well. As I was saying, she's quite a beauty you've got here. I would not be surprised if you told me I was hit over the head with a club and taken to France while I was knocked out cold. Ha ha. I'm only joking, Mr. Erlik; don't worry yourself."

"Have no fear, Mr. Cherry, you are right where you belong. I have a single sleeper room for you, view of the waters, though I do apologize at the state of the evening view. I'm afraid a good deal of rain will be clouding our usual spectacle of the evening stars. But not to fret, there is plenty of beauty to indulge yourself with in the walls of our humble establishment. While you enjoy your stay here, the hotel would like to gift you this bottle of brandy, fetched from France just this week. It is such a coincidence that you should bring our good sister to our attention this morning, don't you find?" Lawrence produced from the opposite side of the desk, a polished bottle of cognac and extended it to Mr. Cherry.

"Courvoisier," he said with a bewildered expression, "But, this is my—"

"Favorite bottle? I had thought as much. I am glad to see you still enjoy a little dip in the old caramel here and then."

"Why, yes…well. I'm sorry, sir, but how did you know?"

"Sneaking suspicion, my good man. A sneaking suspicion." Mr. Cherry looked to the bottle before screwing his eyes back up to his host. After a few stilled seconds, he broke into a hearty laugh.

"Well, who am I to turn down such a gift, eh? What a nice touch, Mr. Earlick. What a nice touch indeed."

"That would be Erlik, sir."

"Oh, my apologies; I meant no offense."

"And none has been taken! How might I, a humble hotel manager, be anything but joyous to be in the company of a man with such an infectious laugh?" Mr. Cherry's face colored at this compliment, forcing him to fall into himself for a second before eyeing Lawrence and breaking out once more into a laugh. It thundered about the room as if heavy grey storm clouds crashed together above the lobby floor. "Ah, here is our good Dorian now to take your bags. Thank you, Dorian."

"Oh, Christ! There's two of them!" Don let out with a start.

"Actually sir," Lawrence heard Dorian explain as they shuffled toward the lift together, "I am the second of three. The brothers Berus, you might call us, at your service should you need anything along the course of your stay. Oh no, don't trouble yourself; I'll get all the bags. This way, sir."

If a guest was in no great hurry—which it might be said that Mr. Cherry certainly was not—they might look around the back of the lobby to see the stone pedestals that lifted the immortalized busts of our esteemed managers of the Hotel's past. In honor of their service to the hotel, each bust labeled with the owner's name and years of employ. Percival L. Harrington, 1827-1839. Thomas J. Loathine 1868-1881. On the event of the prior manager losing his head, a particular facetious little hoaxer saw fit to fill his empty pedestal with the unbeatable likeness of the severed crown. We had the luck, and indeed good sense, to have that spot of ill-mannered nonsense swept away and taken out of the view of the lobby before our good guests had the opportunity to catch a glimpse of the harrowing visage of the inauspicious ornament.

Incidentally, the bellman who found himself in the unfortunate position of being the one to discover the frightful display, found something altogether more peculiar than the bloodied head perched on the pedestal. Upon the golden plaque, just as all the others before our late manager, his final year of service was etched in only moments after his passing. Therein the inscription read: Markus D. Alexander, 1905-1919. To this day, the source of this morbid manifest is unknown, but there are some members of the staff who have their speculations.

A tinge of pride pierced Lawrence's tough heart as the young prodigy guided Mr. Cherry to his room. But it lingered none too long, as there was another opening of the grand door to let in a timid-statured man. Sharply dressed in army greens, the young man fixed his posture and walked with a confidence that looked unnatural to him, owing to its having been drilled into his psyche by a stranger shouting abuses at him day and night so that he might be fit to serve his dear Uncle Sam.

Private First-Class Michael Goodman stood at attention in front of the desk, looking about with careful, searching eyes. There was something within those eyes, when Lawrence took a brief second to examine them, that exuded a profound sadness into the beholder. Like a deep pond in the center of a dense forest—once untouched by the evils of man—where a heart-wrenching death of an innocent child was swallowed by her bosom. "Good morning, sir," the soldier spoke with practiced grace and composure. "How do you fare?"

"Hello, my good private," Lawrence responded. "On a day such as this, I find myself in the mood to sit amongst the old library and listen to our maestro play a tune of a lost love."

"That is awfully specific, sir. Though, I cannot say that it doesn't strike the heart, myself."

"Indeed, it does, does it not? I think you will find that our library may be the place for you to spend some time this afternoon. Private Goodman, I take it?"

"Yes, sir. Private First Class."

"Not that it is any of my business—indeed it is a rare thing for me to ask, but I find you something of a kindred sort, so perhaps you will pardon my manners—but what brings you to stay with us at the Hotel Genevie?"

"I should not take offense in any way, sir. I am here on a halfway point, you see. The army has seen fit to send me to an institution of healing. The journey is long, and I find myself weary in long bouts of travel. This is simply where the army has provided lodging. You will forgive a soldier for saying so, but this is quite an unexpected level of accommodation, certainly grander than anything my tired eyes have had the fortune to rest within."

Lawrence paused and felt his posture loosen as he held to the soldier's key. A great, slow exhale added to the melancholy of the moment before he said, "You, sir, are most welcome in these halls. Most welcome. I think you will find everything to your liking. I have had your rooms freshly cleaned, of course, and they are ready for your stay. Oh, dear me. I had almost forgotten. It is custom for our hotel, or rather custom for myself, to provide a small gift to the guest on arrival. I hope it isn't too much of an intrusion to presume that you might find this to be a handsome gift, but do accept this on our behalf. Careful, it is quite delicate."

The young soldier gracefully held out his arm in order to receive a package covered in brown paper wrapping, held together with a piece of twine that looked as if it had been tied for a decade. Little that affected its ability to slip loose, as a gentle tug from Pvt. Goodman proved all that was necessary for it to come apart. The wrapping unfolded with a warm crinkle that reminded one of opening a parcel from a loved one who had spent far too long abroad. Michael stood in astonishment. In soft forest green leather binding, he held a copy of *Great Expectations* by a Mr. Charles Dickens.

"I'm sure you'll forgive the subject matter, though I have found that this particular volume can be a great comfort in times of ill-thoughts and sharp pains," Lawrence added. "It was always a favorite of mine."

"It was my mother's as well," Michael said without removing his eyes from the handsome edition. His fingers thumbed through the pages that were worn to a soft, feathery touch. The leather felt of his grandfather's old traveling coat that he used to run around in, pretending he was a pirate on William Kidd's galley. "She used to read it to me when I wasn't well. I was always particularly fond of Joe Gargery. Old Joe. How did you know, sir?"

Michael looked up to his gifter's eyes with a welling tear

before receiving the peculiar response, "Ever the best of friends, Private Goodman. Ever the best of friends." Lawrence's sentiment was accompanied by the starry shine of a wink before he broke out in a full-throated voice, "Ah, that'll be Mr. Berus to accompany you to your room. Here is your key; all is quite in order. Dinner is served promptly at seven. Good day, sir."

If Lawrence had enough time to pay attention to his second guest, he would have seen a look of astonishment painted across his face as his arm was taken by a winded Dorian, who had rushed back down to ensure his duties were well taken care of. As it was, he had heard the voice of Baptiste welcoming another guest into the lobby.

We have thus witnessed the reception of the first two guests, conspicuous arrivals if ever there were any. In just the same manner two more guests came through the arrival gates of the hotel, ushered in by our obliging manager and shuffled to situate themselves in their rooms. A charming widow named Doris Applebaum was absolutely tickled by the service rendered in such a seamless fashion. Furthering her state of elation was the bestowing of a box of chocolate-dipped pineapple along with a bottle of German Riesling.

The fourth reservation to enter the lobby was a pair of youthful, angelic-looking faces, Thomas and Sarah McKenna, who glowed with the ray of newlyweds. Their honeymoon suite had been made out for them during their transition from one destination to the next. While the brilliance of the Gonovie was only to serve as a pit stop for the young couple, that did not stop Lawrence from seeing to it that their experience was just as luxurious as the others. They were sent to their rooms along with a set of crystal champagne flutes that had been engraved with Mr. And Mrs. McKenna and a chilled bottle of Bollinger, vintage 1914.

As one might expect with newlyweds, not much was seen or heard from them outside of the general vicinity of their room.

It was only when the fifth and final reservation entered the lobby that things went awry.

III

"How is a five-year-old meant to have a registered booking at a hotel?"

The words were sharp and cutting. But that was nothing out of the ordinary for Lawrence, who had seen to the comings and goings of many a disgruntled guest. Granted, if he were to have it his way, the Adonis family would not have had any reason to complain, and certainly not upon arrival. As it were, however, somewhere along the well-oiled machinery of booking a stay, something or someone had obviously been very confused.

"I am so terribly sorry, Mrs. Adonis; I of course had no intention of implying that your daughter was meant to stay here alone. Only that—and I do hope you will accept my apology in the matter—our record of booking states that a one Rachel Adonis will be staying with us. It appears to be a clerical issue and one we will rectify straight away." Rachel, for her part, appeared rather imperturbable. The curling chestnut locks of her hair bounced as she spun her torso left and right, gripping onto a fluffy teddy. Her attention in the matter seemed rather distant, as children often are. It was more likely that she was dreaming of faraway lands where pixies and princesses danced under the rays of the morning's sun than her having any concern of her name being written within the guest log.

"I should hope so. Imagine that, a child staying in a hotel by herself with no guardianship. What a ludicrous thing to say!"

"Now, Angela," the tall, slender man standing beside her said in a cooling, albeit condescending tone. "Haven't you heard what the good manager has just said? A clerical issue. One he will rectify. I find no reason to fret in all this confusion; we will be enjoying our suite in no time." The silkiness of his voice worked like a magnet, drawing listeners in, causing them to lean forward and fall into that trance that his voice inevitably drew.

"Just so, sir! Only—and again, your forgiveness—in the midst of the confusion, it seems we only reserved a single studio with a double mattress. Not to worry, not to worry! We do have our penthouse available, only it will take a moment's time to prepare for the lovely family. Er, will that suit the madam?"

The woman gave a humph followed in short order by an annoyed yet consenting nod. Angela Adonis could be called many things. Manic, anxious, prone to rumination, cautious, and endowed with the sort of cleverness that often-overwhelmed men in conversation to name a few. But the first thing one noticed when setting eyes on her was her beauty. With radiant blonde curls that flowed to shoulder length—always topped with a charming cloche hat—fair skin, deep red painted lips, and wide blue eyes, she was the enchantress Circe come back to haunt the realms of men.

Angela had chosen as permanent victim to her charm, Dr. Frederick Adonis, whose physical qualities were as desirable as those ascribed to his genius. Many eyes were drawn to the perfect pinstripes on his dazzling navy blue suit, the shine of his patent leather shoes, and the stone chisel of his jaw.

"Very, good," Lawrence responded, shooing Aurelia off to find the maids to ready the penthouse for the most honorable family. "We have a gift for the young lady. It is customary for our guests to receive a...token of our appreciation. Regrettably, due to the nature of the clerical issue, it is specially fashioned for her."

Lawrence produced a small box covered in black velvet. Upon opening its clasp, a beautiful blue hair ribbon was curled in a neat bow.

"Look at this, Rachel," Angela said, her tone softening at the prospect of her daughter being doted upon. "Stand still for mommy, that's it." With a flick of the wrist, Angela tied the ribbon around her hair and fashioned her chestnut curls into a tail. Rachel hardly seemed to notice, continuing in her silent swaying back and forth.

Though it would not be discernible for the Adonis family, searching though their hawkish eyes were, Lawrence felt his skin burn with embarrassment. As it primarily fell on him to ensure bookings were properly taken care of, he felt enraged that someone would have taken it upon themselves to secure such a booking. It is not every day a family walks into a hotel and finds their reservation was made for a single bed for a five-year-old. Even rarer still was the idea of this happening at the Genovie.

Even so, through his embarrassment and his contempt for whoever the wrongdoer was—and Lawrence assured himself that he would, indeed, get to the bottom of that—something else plagued his mind. While Adrian shuffled the happy family into the sitting lounge, and while the clinking and clattering of crystal could be heard from the bar, echoing down the marble hall, Lawrence's mind was fixed on a singular vexation. A bird. And not just any bird. A raven.

It would not, on the face of it, appear that anything

extraordinary had happened in the event of a bird mistaking the open doorway for an invitation to stay at the Genovie. Surely, it had happened before and would indeed happen again. And it was not particularly worrying that this bird was the largest raven he had ever seen. What was most troubling to our dear manager was the way in which the bird stared into his eyes. Those cold, black eyes.

Not only that, but the manner in which the bird cawed, as if whispering to him in another language. As if…warning him of something. Such a notion was, of course, preposterous. Yet, in the flickering of his frantic thoughts, he couldn't help but entertain such a senseless idea.

Once one has entertained the possibility of such nonsense, it is only a natural regression to ponder what was being communicated. Perhaps it wasn't a warning, but a simple "hello, how are you?" But for some reason, such an innocent intention felt more ridiculous than a sinister one.

One also had to consider—if one were to insist on expressing these possibilities—the manner in which the blood felt upon the bellowing of the caw. Oh, it was not an unusual thing for the manager to get in his own head about simple matters such as this. But seldom were thoughts accompanied by physical symptoms. The blood turning cold as those black glossy eyes stared into his soul was not something in Lawrence's power to ignore. Rather, it was this very fixation that chiseled away at the hardly solid encasing of his conscious. It had become such a central point of obsession that the poor manager began to break away from his statuesque posture and give in to the ever-abominable habit of fidgeting. His thumb began to drum on the counter, his toe tapping on the floor, his eyes frantically searching every inch of the lobby. Searching for imperfections, for roaming guests, for lazy employees, for the raven.

All thoughts, no matter how distracting they might have been in another moment in Lawrence's proud life, would inevitably revert to the raven. The shimmer of its shiny black wings catching the stream of sun from the grand windows flashed before his eyes, as if the bird were flying right in front of him. It haunted his very soul. Speaking of which, that haunted soul felt as if it were being crumpled and forced up his throat as if he had a rotten egg for his breakfast. This was, of course, an absurd possibility, given that Lawrence made a point to never indulge in the vanity of eating eggs for breakfast. Whatever that meant.

At that moment, when the hysteria had begun to cause a pressure in the air surrounding his ears and a deafening ring, he heard it. The caw. A bead of sweat dripped down the reddened temple as he tried to get ahold of himself, but it came again. It was different this time, however. Softer, as if a whisper from the damned. Yet they mocked him all the same.

It wasn't until Aurelia nudged him after the third clearing of her throat that Lawrence realized he hadn't been hearing the bird at all, but the thick phlegm coming from the back of his assistant's throat, no doubt exaggerated by the cigarette she would deny having snuck out to smoke. The tunnel vision that had built like small scopes around his eyes began to clear. His breathing calmed. His chest loosened.

"Yes," Lawrence said inquisitively, "yes, what is it, Aurelia?" But when he turned, Lawrence was met with an accusing, searching look from the young woman. Given her proclivity to silence, Lawrence had grown used to reading her facial expressions. The funny thing about humans, Lawrence often thought, was that they needn't use words most of the time at all. There was plenty that could be said in the expression of the face, the countenance of the astute. The flicker of a brow, the curl of a smile, the moistening of the eyes, all little clues that one might use to ascertain the thoughts of the individual standing on the opposite end of the room. Aurelia had a myriad of such expressions. This one held concern and fear. It was as if she was saying, "I can see something is wrong with you."

"Enough from you," Lawrence said in response, causing her to wipe the look of consternation from her face. "What's this about booking a room for a child? Do you know anything about it? The mother was beside herself when she found that the reservation was made under her daughter's name."

Aurelia, used to the antics of an overly-prone-to-stress manager, simply nodded and blinked her eyes closed. Had Lawrence not been disposed to the demands of accommodating such an unforgiving class of society, he might have read in her face that she meant simply to say, "What use is there in getting worked up over such a small issue?" However, Lawrence had the nature of a servant, and if his guests were displeased, it was then his duty to take up their cause in their name.

"Well, someone had to have booked it!" he said, as if demanding she reach into the abyss and report back to him a list of heads that might be suitable to put on pikes. Instead, Aurelia shrugged her frail shoulders and glided past Lawrence with a face that told him it was best he work it out on his own. Aurelia, being Lawrence's favorite for her silence, was the only employee that had the ability to dismiss herself from his call. Such as it was, however, Lawrence had a word or two more he would like to get out on the matter of incorrectly reserved rooms. He would have spat those words in a thunderous rage too, were it not for the unexpected happening of the front door being held open by Baptiste in an effort to oblige a portly framed shadow that was quickly sweeping across the lobby floor.

Lawrence looked with a furrowed brow as the stranger walked carelessly with a suitcase visibly too heavy for his strength. "You said five bookings, if my memory does not deceive me, madam," he whispered, glaring toward Aurelia. She nodded her head with the utmost confidence as if to tell him that it was no use challenging her, the business of her craft was well documented. Five reservations there were; this was not a reservation.

It was an unusual thing, a soul wandering into the hotel in search of an open room. And while the unusual is certainly not synonymous with the unheard of or the impossible, Lawrence was growing rather tired of it, nonetheless. Even still, he straightened his posture with the appearance of a man that was not at all put off by the surprise and feigned the warmth of a charming smile as the scuttling man arrived at the edge of the counter, breathless, hardly able to lift his tongue to speak.

"'Scuse me, sir, excuse me. Let me...just one moment," the stranger spoke before wiping his head down with a hidden handkerchief tightly gripped in his luggage-free hand. The coughing fit aside, the state of the poor devil was enough to repulse our composed manager. Sneering with disgust while the stranger's eyes remained downcast, Lawrence elected to breathe through the corners of his mouth, lest he inhale some unpleasantry that he could not help but assume was wafting from the direction of the stranger.

"Excuse me, sir." His voice was deep and raspy, thick with an eastern accent. Slavic in its origin, or as far as Lawrence was able to surmise from the few scratchy syllables he had heard. "I have not the honor of a reservation," the old man said, for now that Lawrence was able to look his stranger in the face, he saw that he was indeed old. "But I was hoping...you see, sir, I am in a bit of a bind. I am in need of lodging for the night, sir. The honorable gentlemen will forgive my abasing myself so as to say that I am in *desperate* need of accommodation."

"Well," Lawrence began, wanting more than anything for this old fool to take his desperation elsewhere. After all, emotions such as desperation were far too close to the animal for his comfort. "If that be the case, there are a number of inns and hotels in the area that might be so good as to accommodate you. You see, I am not sure that I have an open—"

Lawrence's insistence on his disinclination was cut short by another clearing of Aurelia's throat. Her eyes burned when he looked up at her, and she gave a face as if to say, "Do not turn this poor man away."

"You will forgive my assistant, sir. I have often requested she step into the lavatory in order to address her throat," he hissed with wild eyes. Aurelia shot a fighting glance at him but surrendered her objection, nonetheless.

"No, sir. No, it must be here. It must be the Genovie. I have made it a point for it to be the Genovie, sir. Please, be so kind as to see whether there will be a room available. I should take a broom closet if I must, but please, do see."

Lawrence's huff of annoyance was internal, so as not to disgruntle a potential paying customer. As it was, and as the manager well knew before his little tirade of protest, there were two rooms open. The reader will be well aware of the first being that which was originally reserved for the innocent child, Rachel Adonis. But, as such a room would, in Lawrence's eyes, befit the old man's exasperated description of a "broom closet," he could not in good conscience leave out the second option. After all, though Lawrence found himself repelled by the old creature, pity was well ingrained in the life of a man of in his position.

"Actually, sir," Lawrence said after pretending to search his records for any scrap of availability in order to keep from any hair of suspicion, "it seems we have two rooms available. We have a small single studio, but," he said, seeing the opportunity to draw money from a man in desperation, "we have a very nice suite available with a sitting room and master's quarters. How does that sound?"

"That sounds capital, old man," the foreigner relayed, his rumbling voice fragmented by the incessant interruptions of coughing. "Capital!"

"Yes, very good then, sir. Er, might I have the honor of your name?"

"Name, yes, how silly of me! In all my antics I had nearly forgotten. Well, not a moment further, sir, not a moment further. Roman Pavlovich Kosorukov, sir. At your service." The old Russian bowed low, dipping so that his torso was parallel to the ground. Such a feat impressed Lawrence as he would have guessed that such a kind of gymnastic enterprise would cause the man to fall into further fits of coughing and hacking.

"Lawrence Theodore Erlik. The Third. At yours, sir."

"Charitably, done, Mr. Erlik, charitably done."

"It is the pleasure of the Genovie that we might find ourselves to be of service to a man such as thee, Mr. Kosorukov." Lawrence bowed as he extended his pale hand which grasped the key to room, "319, you'll find it to the right of the lift, sir. Oh, and I may have failed to mention in all the hubbub, but dinner will be served promptly at seven."

"Seven?" Kosorukov asked.

"Seven," Lawrence confirmed indignantly.

It was not an unorthodox sight for a man who has been so obliged by a manager of the Genovie to nod or bow in return for his kindness. Nor, in fact, was it so uncommon for such a guest to be swept off their feet and taken by the mirage of comforts and splendor as the Berus brothers saw to their accommodation. What was uncommon, and indeed altogether worrying, was the sight of the black raven that stood on the pavement just outside the entrance of the hotel. What was further unorthodox, and one might say unnerving, was that raven's insistence on pecking against the beautifully set glass that made up the adorning windows, particularly when it happened as an especially peculiar guest made his way to the lift. Just such a guest made a man of propriety stir in his freshly polished Oxford wing tipped shoes, as Lawrence thus found himself doing.

The second appearance of such an ominously feathered creature within such a short amount of time left Lawrence Erlik in a state of sweating. Of course, in such moments where fear begins to shape the imagination, one might be forgiven for letting one's thoughts run away without so much as a doubtful eye. It was just in this way that the manager shivered and began to wonder what his creator was attempting to tell him through such a foreboding courier.

With closed eyes, he muttered through strained breath, "Four trunks, three bellmen, two parents, one little girl." However, the incessant tapping of his polished shoe kept his usual method of calming himself down from its normal potency.

Unnerved as he was, Lawrence decided it best to remove his thoughts and body from the moment. Calling over Adrian to "remove that foul pigeon from my porch," he retired into the back office in order to gather his nerves through the medicinal benefits of a warm spot of tea.

IV

"I've always found mornings to be positively insufferable, wouldn't you agree?" was the first thing Lawrence was met with upon entering the manager's office, situated just behind the wall of the front desk. The room would, in theory, be the perfect place of solitude for a man troubled by thoughts of a possible haunting through birds. There was the comfort of the roaring fire within the stone fireplace, set with two roaring lions at either side of the hearth. The large wooden desk adorned with decadent hand carvings made a fitting home for one's elbows to hold up one's sunken head. The tapestries, paintings, and protruding pillars created a scholarly atmosphere that made one feel rather aristocratic.

There were all the makings for quite the little sanctuary. One could indeed find solace within those walls. That is, if they weren't always inhabited by Cyrus.

Cyrus was a man of the old breed. He wore his pitch-black hair greased straight back. Such as it was, his hair was unseasonably dark for a man of his years and contradicted the other signs of aging he wore about his face. His neck was always clean-shaven, though the prick of peppery stubble seemed to keep the habit of breaking through the line. The scent of his perfumes were of the fashion of his day, well before the young men of that time would have been able to catch a ball in their little hands. Alongside their sharp aromas was the dulling of the stale tobacco he insisted on smoking out of his ridiculous meerschaum pipe. A white piece of art, as he saw it, featuring the visage of a rather sinister-looking billy goat whose horns wrapped up and around the bowl. Black was his chosen suit color, and though he had several of them, the motif of his wardrobe made it appear he never changed out of what he had been wearing the day before. Not that it took away from their luster. Each suit was fashioned by the softest of wools that had been rendered to a shine so as to make one think it was stitched with silk.

Seldom was the day when Lawrence retreated from the lobby to the office to not find Cyrus lounging on the chair behind the desk, as if it were his own. It was little known what Cyrus's responsibilities at the hotel really were, though there were plenty of rumors spinning about Lawrence's head. The truth of it was likely less ominous than anything he could dream up, perhaps a relation of ownership that spent his days spying on the staff. But he had been with the hotel for far longer than any soul currently under employ. Indeed, now that it has been made mention, the writer finds himself searching his own memory for how it came to be that Cyrus inhabited that regal manifestation of comfort—and what precisely his responsibilities were—only to come up short. He simply came with the fine furnishings.

"You look absolutely dreadful, my dear!" Cyrus exclaimed, rising from his chair to meet Lawrence at the entrance. He raised his hand to Lawrence's shoulder, using the other to guide him to take a seat. "Come, this way Lawrence; it will do you no good to break your strength and fall to the floor now. You really must take better care of yourself, Lawrence. What would ownership think?"

Cyrus had an incredibly swift sense of movement that allowed him the power to glide about the room as if floating on a cloud. In such a manner, he drifted over to the fireplace where a kettle was hanging over the flames. Cyrus insisted on brewing his leaves in the old manner, none of that stovetop rubbish all the frivolous young men and women of the day so gracelessly adopted. Earl grey with two sugars and a splash of milk to calm the nerves, as he always said.

The truth of it was, Lawrence thoroughly detested having any such disgrace as a splash of milk in his tea. Cyrus never seemed to hear any of his complaints.

"Here you are, my dear, just as you like it. Yes, drink up, drink! It will do you well. What is this all about? How was the reception?"

"What?" Lawrence looked over to Cyrus, who had placed himself upon the small settee by the adjacent wall, attentively nursing the steaming cup held by his two pinched fingers. "Oh, yes. Quite an interesting show this morning, I'm afraid." And then he whispered under his breath, "Four caws, three pecks, two sugars, one splash of milk."

"Hmm? Interesting? Oh yes, reception. How should such a thing be interesting? Really, you do let your pride get the better of you. I would hardly call a few guests—"

"Do you believe birds have the ability to latch on to someone?" Lawrence interrupted, his eyes glazed over and staring at the floor just beyond the edge of the desk. "To try to get to them? I mean to say, can an animal have the power to infiltrate the mind of a man? To mutter about in their head as if making grand nests in their thoughts? No, that's all a bit ridiculous, isn't it? But, then again, it is often the ridiculous where man finds answers to life's mysteries, isn't it?"

"What? What is this? Are you wandering into fine talk? I am not so certain I am in the mood for philosophy, Lawrence. Drink your tea; it is getting quite cold."

"No, I do not mean in the way of fine talk. I mean, do you think an animal, a raven for example, could see a person and decide them to be a mortal enemy?"

"A raven? Mortal enemy? Lawrence, have you hit your head? What is next, the trees are going to start growing just to spite you? Really, all this is making me quite concerned for you, my dear. I won't have it. Drink your tea." Such was the way of Cyrus' speech, somehow leaving one with the inexplicable feeling of losing a sparring match and wondering how they had entered into that match altogether. Cyrus was often given to brazenness in his mannerisms and mocking in his tone. The man approached nearly every subject dealing with matters not quite concrete with an overt air of suspicion.

It was, however, just the sort of talk that Lawrence was in need of hearing in order to dispense himself with such ridiculous notions as being haunted by a raven. Condescension could be medicinal.

"Nevermind," he said, forcing a large gulp of the now-chilled tea down his throat. "It's all a bit silly, I suppose. I must be on edge from the booking error."

"Booking error?" Cyrus noisily flapped the newspaper he had just opened onto his lap and looked to Lawrence with concern. This was of course a false emotion. Apathy was carved deep into Cyrus's bones, inscribed by a creator who found passion to be the death of intellect.

"Yes, I'm afraid so," Lawrence persisted, his eyes cast upon the milky surface of Earl Grey. "It appears someone made a booking for a one Rachel Adonis."

"What a travesty," Cyrus gasped through a wicked smile.

"Just so, Rachel Adonis is the five-year-old daughter of a Frederick and an Angela of the same surname."

"Surely, not the same surname. How unconventional."

Lawrence felt his cheeks flush and the outermost layer of skin burn. He hadn't the slightest idea what brought him to state the words "of the same surname" in such a manner. The truth of it was Lawrence was feeling altogether unwell owing to the confusion of the morning. He even began to feel that confusion in his own mind, allowing it to pour into his speech.

"You know what I mean," he said.

"Such a simple error. I'm sure you made right by the charming family. Not to worry, my dear." Cyrus had returned to his paper in an attempt to signal his distaste for discussing subjects pertaining to the operations of the hotel.

"Yes, that was simple enough. But the sharpness with which that woman spoke to me, you would have thought I had threatened her family. Quite the strange malevolence in her voice."

"Who, the child?"

"Have your jokes, Cyrus. I don't know what it was that had caused her to take a simple error as an offense, but she could cut through my skin with her eyes."

"Sounds like the woman I divorced."

"You were married?"

"Of course not, Lawrence. Keep up."

"One often feels inferior to your wit, Cyrus."

"How can that be my fault? I have only worked to reconcile my thoughts with the world surrounding, nothing more." Cyrus paused to pull his horn glasses from his breast pocket and flicked them open with a definitive motion of the hand before gently placing them atop his ears. He returned his attention to the news of the day before retorting, "You mustn't worry yourself with these things, Lawrence. A mother has a tendency to become absolutely unconscionable when faced with opposition to her children, intended or not. There is nothing one can do about it, and it does one little good to labor under any illusions to the contrary, my dear."

Lawrence sat, silently reflecting on this explanation for a moment before standing up to throw a small log into the diminishing flame. This action felt so automatic, so routine, that Lawrence had not even stopped to think of the oddity that was a rolling fire in the middle of a hot summer's day. Granted, the office had always been one for growing chillier than the rest of the hotel, but a fire seemed a bit morbid in this heat. Even so, our manager thought little of it. Instead, he meandered over to the opposite wall where a large tapestry hung.

The surveying of his eyes over the subjects dancing in a formed circle around a fire had some quality that further unnerved his already excitable state. In the stitching, at the center of the flames, he could swear that he could make out a screaming figure tied to a post. He squinted his eyes and leaned forward. There, in the work of a few pieces of thread, his suspicions were confirmed. *Is this some witch sentenced to the stake?* But he found that hard to believe given he had never seen any like work where the spectators were dancing around the condemned. Further, the figures appeared to be without any sort of dress. Stark naked, each holding onto the hand of the one beside him, they danced.

"I have never noticed the detail in this piece, here," he said, turning his head in a tilt akin to a greyhound hearing the high pitch of a kettle.

"What is that now, Lawrence? Finding yourself to be a

romantic gazing at art all day, are we?"

Instead of pushing further, Lawrence decided to let the matter drop, though his eyes had a hard time falling from the scene. The dancers sent a worrying chill down the edges of his fingertips. A lesser man might have felt it to be a phantom hand stretching out to his own, beckoning him to join the dance.

"We had the most curious old man come in and nearly beg us for a room today," he said, trying to break himself from his thoughts.

"Is that so?" Cyrus feigned interest, flipping his page.

"Yes, I don't know what it was about him, but he was quite off-putting."

"You know old men, they often give the younger generation the shivers, Lawrence. It all boils down to fear."

"Fear?"

"Yes, dear. Fear of inevitability. That death comes even for them. The old and the decrepit are nature's sly reminder of such an inescapable fact. I wouldn't read much more into it than that."

"Yes, yes perhaps you're right."

"Of course, I'm right, Lawrence. I am always right."

"What news today?" Lawrence said, managing to twist himself around to face Cyrus and stuff his fidget-thirsty hands into his pockets.

"Nothing terribly exciting, I'm afraid. Looks that a bit of a scrap has broken out in Ireland. It seems the king has seen fit to engage. They always have something to bicker about over the pond, don't they? One might have thought they had enough of that after all that business concerning the old Kaiser."

"I suppose so," Lawrence answered, not having paid any attention to what Cyrus had said. His mind had inevitably returned to the raven pecking at the freshly cleaned glass. Perhaps Cyrus was right about the feeling that he had gotten from the old man. Death was a worrying prospect to a man who worked so hard to perfect a pristine image. Perfection tumbling down in a rolling crash at the fault of mortality seemed a bit vulgar whenever he thought about it. But that only further disquieted his thoughts about the raven.

In the way that often comes rushing through the blood of men who know not what to do with their confusion, Lawrence took to anger. It would have been impossible to tell from looking at him, as he was a man who had become adept at emitting a sense of composure, but an internal feud broke out in his mind. The feud of whether all of this was a silly, boyish fright, or if there was merit to his hysterics.

Spite entered his mind for the manner in which Cyrus waved him off and returned to the dullness of the morning paper. Though it was mixed with relief. In a way, Lawrence wanted nothing more than to be told he was acting silly. Given to fantasies. But another part of him—indeed, so much as half of his consciousness— demanded to be taken seriously. Not a dichotomy, rather, but a contradiction of the mind. It only served to intensify his discomfiture in the realm of supernatural terrors.

Confusion gave way to a startling rap on the door. Disgruntled and a bit dizzy, Lawrence pinched the bridge of his nose with eyes tightly shut as he raised his voice to say, "Come in!" The tone of annoyance must have leaked its way through the fibers of the oak door as the knocker opened it with the speed of a snail. An eerie breeze slipped through the crack as a bellman's hat peered through.

"Yes, Baptiste," Lawrence said, "what is it? How can I help you?"

"I'm frightfully sorry to disturb you, sir," he stammered in reply.

"It is a waste of time to feel sorry. Come now, what is it?"

"You see, sir, that fine gentlemen, Er Korosov—, Koloto—Kosolv—"

"Kosorukov, yes, yes?" It might make itself plain as to why Lawrence was in a perpetual state of aggravation. Constantly being surrounded by the ineptitude of his subordinates made for a dreadful time.

"Right, Mr. Kosorukov called down. He said he was having trouble with his radiator."

"And? Have you sent Joel up to handle it?"

"Well, no, sir. He requested you help him."

"What? That's absurd! I am no handyman. Why would he want my assistance?"

"I don't know, Mr. Erlik. All I know is that he quite insisted on your seeing to the radiator. Said he would let no one else through the door."

Lawrence stood astounded for a moment. Never in all his time at the hotel had a guest insisted on a manager beleaguering himself to the status of handyman for their amusement. There was no doubt in his mind that this was meant to be a fun game of abasement, something the old fool would take home with him and laugh about with all his acquaintances.

"A joke, no doubt," Lawrence insisted. "Just send Joel up to fix the damned thing. There's no use in my seeing to anything only to require Joel to come up after I've had a useless look at the hunk of metal."

"Now, Lawrence," Cyrus said, folding the corner of his paper, "is that any way to treat a guest at the Genovie? The honorable man has given a command; rush off to his service! Go then, my dear, go and be the hero he is calling for!"

Lawrence closed his eyes and exhaled in an exaggerated manner before speaking through gritted teeth. "Fine, fine, Baptiste. Tell Aurelia I shall be gone for a moment. What are you doing standing about? Ought you be finding something that needs cleaning? Surely there is plenty work that needs doing. Where are Adrian and Dorian? We haven't given ourselves to idleness I hope?"

Ordering about the Berus brothers in such a way had always proven to be a great comfort to Lawrence. This instance was no exception.

"Oh, no, sir. Idleness is a great injustice, as you always say, sir. Dorian has just returned from seeing to everyone's luggage. I trust he will be with Adrian in the lounge, ensuring there are no guests in need of anything."

"And you, ought you to find yourself back to the door should we have any further surprise guests? Go on, off with you then!" Lawrence's sharp bite in his words sent the young bellmen running, either from fear or relief to no longer be in the presence of an annoyed manager.

"Do be careful," Cyrus mocked, "radiators can be tricky things. So easy for one to burn a finger or cut one's hand on a sharpened edge. We wouldn't want that, would we, Lawrence?"

V

Sweltering heat was the first thing Lawrence was greeted with upon the swing of the door leading to room 319. *A radiator problem, indeed.* The room was just as it ought to have been, overwhelming temperatures set aside. Windows were ornately decorated with thick velvet curtains that many felt were too heavy to rearrange to their liking. The main suite featured a salon of two oxblood leather couches facing one another. The leather itself was so soft that one often forgot they were sitting on a chair and not a cloud. The oriental rug placed in the center, featured deep blues, bright ivories, and crimson reds twirling in the most wonderful decoupage of Persian artistry. The bouquet of tobacco that curled around Lawrence's nose reminded him curtly of his father.

It was not entirely a curious thing that the guest's bedroom was sporting a closed door; it would not befit a man of Lawrence's station to snoop on his guests. Still, there was a curiousness surrounding this strange guest that could not quite be accounted for, closed doors and gloomy personage aside.

Roman Pavlovich Kosorukov, whom we had the pleasure of meeting in quite a disgruntled state in the lobby, was a port man of about seventy or seventy-one years of age. It was quite a difficult thing for one to come to a precise number, as a man of Kosorukov's childhood lent himself to mystery surrounding such origins. In fact, Kosorukov himself would not likely feign to guess.

"Yes, yes," Kosorukov said with a warmth that was not at all matched to his temperament during their prior meeting. "Come, good man, come in. No, no need for formalities, my good sir. But what am I saying? A man of your station is not quick to dispense with them. We are, after all, creatures of habit, men of our lot. Are we not?" The old man's was more of a wheeze than a voice. Its timbre was not so pleasing to listen to, though there was a homeliness about its somber intonation that beckoned one to hear what he had to say. However boring his topic of conversation was.

"And," Lawrence began in a tone that did not hide his annoyance as well as he might have hoped. Clearing his throat in order to blame the presence of his impudence on a cold, he continued, "What kind of man would you mean by your phrasing: 'our lot,' sir?"

"Why, men of dedication to our craft. Certainly! Oh, I hope I have not offended in lumping you in with myself. You see, I am so very fond of coming across another man of dedication. They are often so hard to come by these days. After all, perfection is a lofty goal. Many men look up to the stars and are discouraged. Why not settle for the clouds? they ask. Indeed, why not? Because a cloud does not shine, that is what I say. How do you respond, eh, eh?" Kosorukov chuckled, his chubby, stubble-infested cheeks turned rosy with satisfaction in his own wit.

"I am afraid I do not know what you mean, sir. I am merely a man of accommodation; it is my pleasure to provide you with the service you require." Lawrence gave a questioning look that made the stranger take a reserved step backward, realizing he was not yet on the familiar ground he had hoped to be. "This is where the problem lies, then?" Lawrence asked while pointing to the copper radiator.

"What? Oh! Yes, yes thank you, old man. Thank you. So, a man of accommodation. Has a nice ring to it, though I am afraid I am not sure what it means. A Russian by birth, as you probably well know, it is not in my—how do the French put it— repertoire, such a phrase, eh?"

"Ah, a man of travel, no doubt?" Lawrence said, happy to move on to a new subject. The nervousness of his task was getting the better of him. He had not been one for fixing mechanical issues in all his life. It rather created a natural perturbation within him that this Kosorukov insisted on him being the one to come and play handyman. What on earth were employees for? Unless, as it now began to seem to Lawrence, the radiator was more of a guise to pull him up to his room. *What the devil for?*

"Travel? Oh yes, indeed. Travel is something to take the mind away from old haunts, don't you find? Hehe. Yes, I have indeed traveled from St. Petersburg to Virginia, from Virginia to Paris, from Paris to Constantinople. Such wonderful traditions in the lands of the ancients, hehe."

Problems caused by sheer incompetence were often the reason for Lawrence's having so many migraines. A proper disdain he had for that foible. Such was the case this evening. The radiator was not, as our lovely guest so admirably worded it, "busted," but rather working in proper order. The issue, were one to call it that, was simply a matter of it being turned on and dialed all the way up. If Kosorukov was interested in getting on equal ground with the fine manager, he was off to a rather embarrassing start.

"Here you are, Mr. Kosorukov, all fixed," Lawrence lied in order to save face. Whether for his sake or Kosorukov's, Lawrence did not care to determine.

"Ah! Splendid, splendid, old man. Oh, you do me a great disservice, however. Roman Pavlovich, if you please. Or, if you'd like, Romik as I prefer to be called by my friends."

"Very well, Master Romik. All ought to be quite in order. Now, if you won't be needing anything else." Lawrence made for the door, reaching his arm out to twist the brass handle before it was interrupted by a measure of sound coming from Kosorukov's voice. It was just enough to call Lawrence to pause, but not enough to actually say or mutter anything intelligible.

"Is there a problem, sir?" Lawrence asked, this time better able to mask his annoyance.

"Problem? No, not a problem at all. But won't you sit and have a drink with me? Now, it will do no good to protest. You are renown for your services, are you not? You would not deny an old man his indulgences?" The smile on Kosorukov's face was worn and tired, but warm and welcoming all the same. It was then Lawrence noticed the glass of brandy in the old man's hand. There was another glass and an old dusty bottle sitting on the table next to one of the couches.

"Really, sir, I must be seeing to the guests."

"I am a guest, am I not? Right, then you will see to me. Come, it will do no good to refuse. There we are, have a seat, yes. And take this, now I insist, old man. Take it, go on."

Lawrence reluctantly reached out and grasped the crystal glass that Kosorukov had just finished pouring a hefty amount of brandy into. The old man crashed himself onto the couch with a loud sigh that made Lawrence think of the way his grandfather used to take up rest.

"You see, Mr. Erlik, I am in need of confession."

"Oh, Mr. Koso—" Lawrence stopped himself as he saw the old man's reproachful face on resumption of formalities. "Romik,

I am not a man of God, at least not in the proper way. We have a priest staying with us this evening, I believe. A withdrawn chap, but seems to be intelligent all the same. I am sure he would oblige us with his services."

"No, no," Kosorukov waved a hand at Lawrence and shook his head. "No, I am not looking for a godly confession, old man. I am looking for a confession of equals. Men of equal station. Men of dedication. We understand each other, eh?"

Lawrence stirred, not understanding him quite at all.

"Good, good," Kosorukov said in response to the awkward fidgeting of a man who didn't see a clear way out of his current situation. A captive audience. This was, after all, what the old man was after. It was no great consequence that Lawrence be the man for the job, but he had set his mind on it and there would be no changing it, as far as could be surmised.

"What is it you would like to have confessed, sir?" Lawrence asked in as polite a tone as possible. He allowed himself the indulgence of a sip of the old man's brandy. The hints of oak singed his nose hairs in a way that reminded him of youth and carelessness. Caramel and vanilla swirled over and under his tongue in an intoxicating dance that eased his shoulders and pressed his back against the tufted cushion of the leather couch. Whether he had been annoyed or not a few seconds earlier, he no longer remembered. Peace seemed to creep itself into his bones.

"A fine thing, isn't it?" Kosorukov asked, nodding to the brandy. "If men aged like liquor, I think we'd be better for it. Wouldn't you? After all, we men are too short-sighted. Oft we squander the days of our youth, unknown to us how vigor abandons the bones to frailty. Wisdom and youth do not dance together, my friend, wisdom and decay. Wisdom and decay. Hehe, I have been thinking a lot about my youth these days."

"It must not have been all that long ago." As Lawrence said this, his eyes followed the sands of the man's wrinkles. Grooves like trenches dug into the wet sod in order to prepare for war. Liver spots hid behind well-starched cuffs, skin so thin the blue of his veins drew the eye like following rivers breaking across a field.

"Yes, you are kind, you are kind, old man. A man in your station ought to be. But it is no use, I am too sharp to fall for such a flattery," Kosorukov laughed and wheezed before taking another sip of brandy. The glass had hardly moved from his wet lip before he sputtered out, "She comes to visit me at night, you know."

"Who does?"

"Sonya Ivanovna Zomitov. She was the daughter of the esteemed councilor Ivan Zomitov. Not only that, she was a woman of sharp wit, great pride, and unforgettable beauty. Even further, sir, even further. She was my wife." Kosorukov's eyes beamed with pride at this last statement. He flushed and smiled. The color could have come from the alcohol, but Lawrence knew that not to be the case.

"Yes, my Sonya. My Sonechka. She could have had any suitor that offered his hand, and I will tell you old man, there were a great many in number. But the young daughter of a councilor had eyes for me. *Me!* The son of a poor coachman. I didn't have two kopeks to rub together." The man burst into a rolling scratch-like laughter. Something about it sent shivers down Lawrence's spine. Nothing that a small swig of excellent brandy could not remedy.

"But we were happy together. I knew not at the time whether I made her happy or the idea of her father's rage at marrying me made her happy. Alas, we men will take what we can get, eh? It was all the same. I suspect love had to be part of it for her. It takes more than childish defiance of one's father to abase oneself into the station of the Russian peasantry. Yes, we were happy together.

For those few years.

"We rented a room together; it was a small room out of a tailor's apartment. I don't know if it was the state of the room or the chill of the winter that gave her the consumption." Kosorukov's eyes glazed as they turned to the carpet. "Yes, it was a terrible sight, that consumption. Did you know they begin to cough blood? Yes, it is a terrible sight, old man. The tailor, Mikhail Fyodorovich, was a kind man. He retrieved a doctor for her, a friend of his. But a man can only work for free for so long.

"I had no money, my friend. Her father had arranged for a clerkship at the council office, despite his hatred for me. Fool that I was, I was unable to hold on to it. You see, the drink is a nasty habit. Yet here I still am, hehe." He raised his glass and swirled the brandy around, bidding Lawrence to take another drink.

"I'm terribly sorry, sir, but I have responsibilities to the oversight of the hotel—"

"Oh yes, yes. Of course, I will get straight to it. Yes. It is not a rushed business, getting to the substance of a man's confession. Patience, my dear, and we'll get right to it." Kosorukov was looking directly into Lawrence's eyes as he spoke, denying Lawrence's urge to protest. Lawrence stared at the old man searchingly. His shrunken eyes were shot with blood, as if he had spent the hour before their meeting in dreadful tears. The lines surrounding the corners of his lips and resting atop the furrow of his brow were deep, as if etched with chisel into mahogany. Some spoke whispers of profound sorrows; others sang muted tunes of joy—joy long forgotten.

"Yes, right to it. Mikhail Fyodorovich was a kind man, but kindness cannot feed children. It was to the cold, wet streets of Petersburg for us. My poor Sonechka."

"He kicked you out?" Lawrence was surprised to find himself

interested in this story, even crossing one leg overtop the other and leaning into the couch. There was a pull, a clouded feeling that left Lawrence ignoring the ticking clock in the back of his mind telling him to get back to work. "And you call this man kind?"

"It is as I said, old man, kindness does not feed children. The man had four hungry mouths to feed. What am I to fault him for when I could not hold a job? No, sir, drink is a filthy habit." As he spoke these words, he lifted the snifter of brandy to his shining bottom lip. After swallowing the remnants in one gulp, he refilled it and rose to offer Lawrence the same courtesy. There was little use in refusal; before Lawrence could open his mouth, the caramel-colored elixir was already splashing to the bottom of the crystal. As he lifted it, he came to the realization that these glasses were not the hotel's. The old man had brought them for the occasion.

"So it was to the streets," Kosorukov said with a sharp exhale that filled the room. "I begged for work, shops, restaurants, even the Neva had little work for me! Some days I would get lucky, but most went wageless. And I had the shame to drink half those wages, sir. Can you believe that vileness? My poor Sonechka lay dying while I settled into stupor. For a time, I cleaned myself up, seeing her in desperate condition, and found work as an organ grinder. Can you believe that? A councilor's daughter married to an organ grinder. What darkness surrounds the unfortunate souls of His creation? Ah, but what do I know of salvation?

"I vowed to earn a living, not drink it, but to spend it on medicines. But it was too late. Every day her fits grew worse. Blood sprayed the cobblestones when she coughed. Each night I held her in my arms, held her tight, praying for a miracle.

"Then the madness started," he said with a croak in his voice. "She had these visions, or at least she told me she did. Of her father, of her mother, of strange demons chasing her. One night she told me that Christ came to her, told her it was time for her to jump into the Neva. I had to restrain her from diving into the freezing cold waters. Such profound strength she had mustered that night! It took everything in me to keep her in our little alley.

"The following morning, she did not wake up. A man knows not sorrow, nor regret, nor shame, nor disgust—not truly—until he sees the love of his life, laid to waste at his ineptitude, sir. I am sure you know something about that, eh? Eh? Oh, don't tell me then, sir. Keep it to yourself, sir. This is my confession, after all. Hehe." The old man wiped the sweat from his brow with a folded handkerchief, bright red in color. Lawrence's heart pounded while he tried to surmise the old man's meaning behind his words. *I am sure you know something about that, eh?* Echoed in the expanse of his racing mind.

"Her father didn't come to the funeral." Kosorukov continued his incessant staring into Lawrence's eyes as he spoke. The manager returned to his previous state of discomfort and began to fidget and squirm on the leather of the sofa. That discomfort pleaded with him to find an excuse to leave, yet there was something deeper, something graver that held him to that couch. "It wasn't much of a funeral, you see, more just a burial. I spent my last Kopek putting her in the ground. That was the day I met him."

Lawrence shot his glance, which for the last few moments had been avoiding the eye contact of the old man, back to the blacks of his eyes. They were wide and intense. "Met who, sir?" he asked. It was a curious thing to our good manager, how he was pulled, almost forced to speak those words. He had no will to utter them, yet sure enough they were leaving the quiver of his lips without so much as a second thought.

"Aye, who indeed, sir? He never told me his name. Dressed all in black. I had managed to scrounge a bottle of vodka from the parlor down the street from where she died. I had nearly soiled my breeches from drunk when he found me. 'Roman Pavlovich?' he said in that crooked voice of his.

"'What do you want with a man in mourning?' I spat. 'Is there no pity in St. Petersburg left for the dead? Leave me to stew in pain, sir.' But he did not move. He stood over me like a devil. A grim smile curled on his face. It was enough to send shivers down my spine. It surely pulled me out of that stupor.

"'Your fate does not become you, Roman Pavlovich,' he says. 'How have you succumbed to such squalor?' There was a hatred in his eye, sir. I tell you as God as my witness, there was a hatred in his eye. They shined yellow. You don't believe me, eh? I suppose that's right of you, not to believe. But of all the wretched things you can call me, I have never been a liar, old man."

Lawrence averted his gaze while Kosorukov emptied his glass for a third time and refilled it. The painting on the wall caught his eye, one he had never quite taken the time to inspect. It was of a shipwreck. The sails blazed with fire as the man-of-war was already halfway swallowed by the depths in the background. In the foreground, a small lifeboat was overcrowded with terrified-looking survivors. Several more seamen were treading water by the lifeboat, clawing their way on board. At the boat's bow, a man held a long oar, using it to cudgel the desperate and the damned in order to keep what little chance they had of the boat not capsizing alive. The fury in the man's eyes struck Lawrence. There was luck involved in his being the one on board, of his holding the oar. And yet the righteousness of choosing who lived and who drowned flared in his eyes.

"I'll never forget those yellow eyes. They haunted me for the rest of my days. But it was they that pulled me from the gutter, you understand? The man spoke with icy words, telling me of a fortune that he would bestow upon my name. 'It is cruel to play with a man in mourning,' I said. 'I have buried my—' but he cut off my rambling by guessing the singular word that was at the end of my vodka-steamed breath. 'Sonechka, yes,' he said. 'And it is the price that has been paid. I have looked upon your price and found it suitable. Your offering has been accepted, and so you will now be a man of means, Roman Pavlovich.' You can only imagine the terror in my heart at these words, sir.

"What causes evil to torment the souls of the innocent? Was I innocent? Pah! Perhaps that is for the creator to judge. But this I tell you, there was darkness in this man. Yet still, I believed him. I don't know why I believed him, but I believed him. I was drawn to it, like a moth to a flame, you see. And he was honest!"

"Honest about what, Mr. Kosorukov?" Lawrence wiped a spec of saliva that flew from the old man's ramblings to land on his pristine lapel, growing rather annoyed at the old man's delay in "getting straight to it."

"Please, please, Mr. Erlik! Roman Pavlovich. Honest about the fortune, dear lad! Do keep up, will you? Hehe! So it was, for he pulled from his breast pocket, two hundred thousand rubles. Can you believe that, sir? Out on the streets of St. Petersburg, in the cold of November, no less! Thieves and crooks about, sir, thieves and crooks. He stuffed it in my hand, telling me to buy myself some clothes that didn't stink of piss and vomit. A bitter insult, but perhaps deserved, hehe. Still, my eyes deceived me. 'An account has been set up in your name,' he says, not stopping to explain himself, or even tell me his name as I've already told you. 'In America,' he says."

"America?" Lawrence asked. "Surely this was a trickster, a

fraud."

"As sure as the day is dark and the night is light! But you are right to be suspicious, as was I, as was I. But I was delirious in my grief. There was no telling what I would believe and what I wouldn't. But here I was, holding those rubles in my hand. The most money I had ever had my hands on at once."

"You mean to say, you went with him?"

"There was nowhere to go. No, I did not go with him. Instead, he gave me instructions. Told me that the condition of my acceptance was to never set foot in Russia again. Or I would die a humiliating and painful death. The look in his eyes, sir, I believed that. There was to be a train, November the 23rd, that would take me to London. From there, I would wait four months till I received a ticket for passage across the Atlantic."

At this, Kosorukov had a great fit of coughing. It was so fierce that his face turned the color of his bright red handkerchief he held to his mouth, veins rising in his forehead. When he finally settled and took the handkerchief away, Lawrence noticed a dark stain on the inside of its fabric.

"But you mean to say that you did as he asked?" Lawrence prodded a bit more. It was at this time, or right around the first mention of the mysterious benefactor, that our good manager forgot about the responsibilities awaiting him downstairs. He made no more insistence on his being needed elsewhere, gave up his fidgeting, and even began to lean forward in anticipation of the old man's every word. This was well noticed by Kosorukov who— coming all this way—had no desire to speak so heartedly to a man feigning interest under the guise of polite society.

"Can you blame me, sir? Does a soul surrounded by darkness not thirst for the sun? Eh? Does it not hum at its core when it catches a glimpse of its first ray? Do not feign to suggest that you would not have done the same. We are all creatures cursed with the desire for comfort, are we not?"

"I suppose so," Lawrence conceded.

"Suppose so, indeed." Kosorukov continued in his drinking. He washed his mouth with brandy, not in the aristocratic way of pretending to enjoy the notes of different flavors, but in the way a poor soldier washes down the fear of going up over the edge after already having full acquaintance with the bitter sting of the hell that awaited him.

"I still remember the caw of the raven," Kosorukov interrupted Lawrence's lost thought. Our good manager's heart skipped a beat.

"I beg your pardon, sir?"

"Indeed, I had been counting the rubles, you see. I hadn't quite trusted that they were real. But when I looked up to inquire his reasons, he was gone. No sign of his shadow remained, save the raven that stood on the cobblestones. You would laugh if I told you the raven looked deep in my eyes, sir. Would you not? Eh? Pah! It matters not, I know what I saw."

"I believe you," Lawrence said, harkening back to the raven standing inquisitively upon the wood of the grandfather clock.

"Do you? Yes, it would make sense that you would. Have some haunts of your own, then? Hehe, it is like I said sir, men of equal station." Lawrence felt the blacks of Kosorukov's eyes widen as they searched deep into his own. Another shiver ran through his spine. It took him aback that this was the third or fourth time in the last hour that such a shiver would rattle his bones in that stifling room.

"And you came to America then?"

"Hmm? Yes, indeed. I came to America. However, I never saw my benefactor again. Not that I am complaining, sir. I should be grateful to him, but alas, men avoid those whom they fear. Or perhaps children do, it is all the same."

"What did you do with it, with the fortune, I mean?"

"I ran," Kosorukov said.

"Ran?"

"Ran."

"For what purpose?"

"I thought I was running from my benefactor, the evil look in those yellow eyes. I was afraid he would find me and take the fortune from me. Or perhaps accuse me of stealing it, have me thrown in prison. I became a very cowardly animal, Mr. Erlik, very cowardly. I traveled from city to city, port to port, never staying longer than a month or two at a time. I saw the world, twice over, in fact. But I was not running from my benefactor, sir."

"No?"

"No…no, no. I was running from her."

"From your wife?"

"From my Sonechka." The old man emptied the snifter once more, offering Lawrence another fill for himself. Now, ordinarily, dear reader, our good manager would not allow himself the indulgence of a third glass of brandy before the clock struck one on reception day. There was certainly the excuse of it being quite a finely polished vintage. However, the young manager felt himself ashamed of the desire—nay—the need to take the edge from his nerves in the presence of Kosorukov. The old man was beginning to feel like, not a stranger, but a familiar ghost that had watched him grow from childhood from a faraway distance. Never daring so much as to make a friendly introduction, but catching a mysterious glimpse every so often. And so, Lawrence reached out his glass in acceptance.

"She followed me to every city, to every port. She sits in every train car, every ship cabin, and every hotel room." Lawrence shot a glance around the room with searching eyes. "Yes, I see your eyes looking for her. She is here. And she was here that first night."

"First night, sir?" Lawrence asked, attempting to ignore the old man saying a ghost was in the room.

"Yes, yes. The first night. This is the very hotel my benefactor put me up in my first night in your country. I must say, I am surprised to see it in much the same state. You all must have had a fine time during the restoration." Kosorukov reached over to the side table, giving his snifter a momentary rest beside the dusty bottle of brandy, now nearly empty from the pair's exploits. Sitting next to the bottle were two leather packages, one short and wide, the other skinny and long. Kosorukov reached for the short package, opening its clasp to reveal a quartet of sweet-smelling cigars. Lawrence waved off the old man's advance, who in turn contented himself to smoke on his own, lighting the taut cigar with three puffs of a match's burst of light. "It was then I made her a promise. A promise I knew I would have to keep. She stared at me with those cold, dark eyes. Black eyes of the dead. Did you know they turn black when they leave this world?"

"Promise, sir?" Lawrence said through a crack in his throat.

"Yes, I promised her, I did. I promised her I would return here, to this very hotel, on the day I am meant to die."

VI

Up until the harrowing words "I am meant to die" left the old Russian's lips in an apathetic whisper, Mr. Erlik's remaining within the parlor of Kosorukov's room could be blamed on the singularity of his unbridled curiosity. Now fear kept him. Not the fear of danger—for our manager seemed quite sure of his own safety—but fear of responsibility. Both of these emotions were of the nature that men of Lawrence's station often avoid falling prey to whenever possible. Duty demands a certain performance in stoicism. However, the manager might be forgiven for allowing a momentary crumbling of his honorable expression of imperturbability.

It was in this moment of curious conundrum that the manager of the Hotel Genovie cleared his throat and fixed himself with several tugs along his waistcoat. Ordinarily, Lawrence's shaking fingers would have slipped into that waistcoat pocket, retrieved that scintillating timepiece, and noticed an hour had passed. But in this instance, his hand held still, his mind focused on the abstract, and he attempted to bring himself back to a proper state of mind.

Smoke curled in shimmering ribbons. The silver stream caught the light of the lamp as it rose from the ash of the cigar resting between Kosorukov's fingers. It twirled and swayed in a macabre dance. Lawrence found his breath was tight, his chest inflamed. There was, of course, the minute possibility that he had not heard the old man correctly. But Lawrence had no illusions of this being a simple matter of misunderstanding, which made it all the worse. He was unnerved by Kosorukov's calm demeanor. There he sat, staring back at Lawrence, as if two university professors were discussing the qualities of a young student—trivial work.

"I'm sorry, sir?" Lawrence coughed, setting his snifter to the side.

"We really are the most abominable creatures, men. It is true, I tell you, it is true." Kosorukov kept his eyes fixed on Lawrence, the small smile remaining. The softness of his expression was somehow more unnerving than if it matched his words. "Yes, we destroy the best of things, don't we? Yes, indeed, we destroy the best of things."

Lawrence stood at once, stiffening his waistcoat and taking three steps toward the door, then three steps back to where he began. He sat back down and put his shaking hands on his knees. "How do you know?"

"How do I know what? That we destroy the best of things? Well, I am a capital example, aren't I? I destroyed my Sonechka. Sonya was the sacrifice laid upon the altar of my dominion. What can be a better example?" Kosorukov puffed at his cigar. He had pretended not to notice the nervous jitters Lawrence was unable to keep himself from. The old man was so good as to politely ignore the manager's fitful rise and retreat as well.

"No, Mr. Kosorukov—"

"Roman Pavlovich, sir."

"No, Roman Pavlovich, I do not mean your hypothesis—

sound though your defense in its truth is." Kosorukov bowed his head in thanks, bending his cigar-wielding hand toward his listener. "I mean your proclamation. Of…death."

"Yes, that unfortunate abyss that reaches for us from behind since we enter this frightful world. The power always at our tail, unshakeable. Death. Such a sweet sonata for an old man such as myself."

"But how do you know this is the day you are meant to die?"

"Why, that is a matter really quite simple, sir. I will it."

"You will it?"

"I will it." Kosorukov gave a second cough into his handkerchief. This time, he made little effort to hide wiping the blood from his lip. "Oh, you think this is how I am to go? No, Mr. Erlik, not as such. Though, there is something poetic about leaving this world in the same manner as Sonya Ivanovna. No, I cannot bear the look in her eyes for that long. It must be quick, you see. It must be quick."

"How can a man dispel the manner in which the torments of death shall reach out to him?" Lawrence turned cold as he spoke these words. His eyes slowly screwed back to Kosorukov, convulsing him to a sharp shutter.

"A capital question, sir. A capital question," was all Kosorukov wheezed in response before taking another drag from his cigar. The smell of its burn filled Lawrence with a slight edge of comfort, the kind that comes for only a second before its fleeting warmth runs from its shivering subject. Lawrence placed his eyes on the polished wood of the bedroom door. Madness began to play with his thoughts.

Was that a shadow under the door?

Without another word, Kosorukov reached over to the side table, where the long and skinny stretch of leather-wrapped box rested. Picking it up, he held it hovering above his lap, as if methodically assessing its weight. "This belonged to her father," he said. "Awarded to him for his valiant service to the empire in Warsaw. 1831, I believe. A very proud man. Very proud. I could not understand as a young man how his pride left him to abandon his daughter. Yet my own evils are enough to contend with, sir. They are enough." The creak of the tiny brass hinges lining the edge of the box pulled Lawrence to the edge of his seat. Something inside the box reflected the light from the lamp to shine on Kosorukov's face, a mournful smile stretching his lips.

It wasn't until the object had been removed from the box that Lawrence was able to understand what it was. His stomach split in two. The shine came from the blade of a knife, steel polished to look as brilliant as a blade of silver. The hilt of the knife was a sparkling cross, a dark blue stone glistening in its pommel. Lawrence struggled to swallow the lump that had formed in his throat. He loathed to hear the answer to his next question.

"What is your meaning with this?" The words came out choppy, nearly imperceptible. But the old Russian heard. For a moment, not a word was made in reply, only the solemn nodding of his head while his eyes remained glued to the edge of the blade. He twisted it around several times, desire beaming in his face.

"Meaning, yes. A swift end, sir. A swift end."

"You don't mean…"

"Why, of course I do. Do you take me for a man weak of will? I trust you know the truth in that matter, sir. I made a promise to her, a promise that we would return together to this hotel. It was this very room, in fact, where she made her first appearance to me. I knew then that I would never escape those eyes, try though I did. I never escaped them. Her and the raven."

"The raven?"

"Aye, the raven. It always followed me, always came first. Whenever I saw the raven, I knew she was close by. I knew she would soon find her way to me. I knew I would have to look in her eyes again."

"Sir, I cannot allow you to…"

"Me? No, not I, sir. You." Lawrence's heart fell to the floor. The pressure of the room compounded and popped in his ears just before the feeling of a cold finger crept down his spine. For the unending plague of a few sharp seconds, Lawrence could hear nothing but the ringing in his ears and the echo of the old man insisting, "You."

"What is the meaning of this?"

"Well, that is not altogether accurate. It will be both of us, together. I need a little…a little reinforcement, hehe." The dusty laugh was at its most chilling, especially given its rolling into another fitful cough.

"I don't understand. This is ludicrous! I won't have any—"

"My good man, I must apologize for giving any indication that you had a choice in the matter."

"What?"

"Choice. A cruel thing to be taken from us, I do know, but I am afraid in this instance, such deprivation is warranted."

"This is madness!"

"Madness? Yes, perhaps madness lurks in the corners of the room, as it often does. But I speak to you from a position of clarity, sir. No, it is madness to continue on in this way. To allow her haunting. Perhaps when I am in the ground, she will finally find her rest."

"This is not the way."

"It is the only way, Mr. Erlik. It is the only way." Kosorukov sat quietly for a moment before reaching over for the bottle of brandy. This time, the old man found it an inconvenience to pour his poison into a carriage of crystal, electing to swig directly from the bottle. Lawrence was perplexed as to whether to spring for the knife, run to the door, or call out the window for help. He ran through each possibility, noting the likely length of time one of the Beruses would take to come to his aid in each instance. But something—a force not unlike that which holds a man pinned to his sheets at the conclusion of a night terror—held him in place, shaking on that lovely, tufted leather.

"I am guilty, sir," Kosorukov said in a tone so low it was nearly a grunt. His eyes did not lift from the ground, his lower lip sagged, and his breathing nearly stilled. "I am guilty of such wicked thoughts."

Lawrence's ears resumed ringing. The sight of the dejected old man buried his sense of propriety, of what was wrong and what was right. It took him to the brink of sanity and yanked him back to fall on the floor in confusion.

"I'm afraid," Lawrence's voice shook in strained effort, "that is not a crime punishable by death."

"Perhaps," Kosorukov responded, "though I have often dreamed of the release." A final swig from the bottle gave the old man the courage to stand up and place the tip of the knife to the edge of his throat.

"No, no, sir! Please!" Lawrence jumped to his feet. His hand wrapped around the old man's and attempted to pull the knife away. He found, however, that though he had a considerable advantage in the way of youth, the old man seemed to be a bit stronger than him. "Let's not be rash," he insisted. "Lower your hand."

"Raise yours," Kosorukov said with a haunting smile. "It is okay, old man, it is okay. All we need, is just a little...push." The blade slid up through the wrinkly neck, piercing through the bottom of the jaw and up into the man's skull. Lawrence looked into those eyes, stretched open from the excruciating pain. Dread poured into his heart as he felt the blood drip down his fingers, nearly hitting his starch-white cuffs before curving around the pad of his palm.

It was at this grim moment when our good manager remembered he had forgotten to breathe. And not a moment too soon. The color of his lips had begun to purple before he let out an exasperated gasp.

The sweet taste of oxygen mercifully returning to his brain, he could contemplate the smooth fashion wherein the hilt of the knife slipped from the grasp of his fingers as the old man fell swiftly to the ground. A worrying thud must have sounded in the room below. Pity. But as for the manager, his thoughts were not quite concerned with the accommodation of the other guests—a rare lapse in his life's pursuit. Every thought rolling around in his practiced brain concerned the nature of the dead body sprawled on the floor, soiling the elegance of the Persian rug with a slow and steady stream of red ink.

Just when he was contemplating whether phoning the police would hurt or help his sorry state, a sound emitted from the other end of the room. The sound of a door latch. In his agitation, Lawrence screwed up his eyes toward the suite's bedroom to find that its handle twisted downward, and the smallest of slivers cracked, the light from the main suite stabbing through the black of a dark room.

Eyes. They were the only thing Lawrence could see. Not the door itself, nor the bleakness of the room it barricaded, but those eyes. They were black and caught the light of the lamp with a hellish shine.

"It isn't what it looks like," the manager said through panted breath. He straightened his back and gave a tug at the waistcoat in order to put on a more accepting facade for the soul watching from the other room. But still, no movement. "There was nothing I could do, I tried...I tried to stop him. But his will was impregnable." Nothing. Staring eyes. They were beginning to make a mockery of the hotel manager, a man who had never been made a fool of in all his life. For a moment, he forgot the harrowing scene displayed below his proud posture and gave way to vexation.

"Enough of this childish game. Stop hiding your face behind that door. Show yourself!" It was a rather unusual thing, Lawrence raising his voice. Particularly more unusual was his doing so to a guest, or potential guest. The truth was he had no idea who was behind that door, and he feared discovering it. Whoever it was, they had witnessed what had transpired. If not in vision, then certainly by sound. "Come now," his voice faltered, "I said show yourself."

The minute hand on Lawrence's timepiece seemed to move faster than this curious individual had in opening the door. It was at such a pace that the hinges lent themselves to the nasty business of squeaking like an old floorboard.

When the obstacle was removed, our dear friend froze in place, his heart skipping a beat. Standing in the frame was a figure wearing a loose woolen dress, stained with crusted mud toward the hem. The pinafore, which in some time or other may have been passable as white, was a decayed grayish-yellow. The headscarf was loosely tied, with strands of hair falling from her pins. Lawrence felt an avalanche of cold when she entered the room, as if he were thrown out in the dead of night during a rapturous blizzard wearing nothing but his skivvies. Though the room was now one person fuller, it felt a great deal emptier than it had seconds ago. It was as if—despite Lawrence's insistence in not putting stock into such silly superstitions—all the life had been drained from the room. Even his own. But that was not the worst part. The worst part, the detail that had caused him to freeze in place and weigh his own measured breathing with the utmost care, not knowing if he should speak, sit still, or run at all speed, were the eyes. The woman's eyes—for indeed, the figure the writer is describing was, or at some point in time was, a woman—were a solid, glossy black.

Through the numbing terror that had stricken his bones, Lawrence managed to swallow the lump in his crusted, dry throat. The figure stood still, unwavering in her obstruction of the door frame. In the stillness, in the stifling air that turned to ear-popping pressure in a crescendo of dread, panic, and sorrow, Lawrence Erlik was only fit to mutter a few syllables from his quivering lips. So soft as to be imperceptible to the living ear, he muttered, "Sonya Ivanovna."

The reader will forgive the writer for his previous description of the Hotel Genovie as to the question of its being haunted. It would behoove one to recognize the contrast between the haunting of an individual and the haunting of the particular place or the location. Such was the case for our late friend, Roman Pavlovich and his dearly departed wife, Sonya Ivanovna. It is with regret that the writer shared that the record of specters and ghouls be abysmally low. After all, perhaps the presence of such fabulous attractions would be favorable in the way of guest bookings. However, all that aside, the manager of the hotel was resting his eyes on something he had, up until this point in his respectable life, never seen: the sickly pallor of a ghost.

Sonya Ivanovna gave little in the way of confirming her

identity, apart from the infinitesimal measure of a nod. In so doing, she kept her eyes gazing directly into Lawrence's, further intensifying the rattling of the poor man's bones under his lively skin—a feature he was alone in enjoying despite being in such meritorious company.

Upon reflection of the now fully-restored credibility of the old man's tale—for truly, until this very moment of laying his own narrowed eyes on the woman herself, Lawrence had not believed a word of the old man's insistence on his seeing his dead wife everywhere he roamed—he began to convince himself of the virtues in leaving the dead to rest. There would be no need for phoning authorities, no need for alerting the press and ruining the summer bookings, and no need for pressing further the idea that Sonya Ivanovna was not, in fact, signed into the guest log downstairs. After all, an obliging manager might be willing to overlook the impropriety in such a transgression.

Instead, Lawrence Erlik—with his wits beginning to recover, the ice in his veins starting to melt—slowly stepped toward the door. The whole time, without ever moving to see where his feet were stepping, he kept his gaze on those black eyes. They, in turn, kept their gaze on him. They stayed with him until the final moment he opened the door, stepped into the hall, and drew the door close. As it came to a click, he could hear a raven cawing at the window.

With the utmost care and attention to detail, Lawrence dusted himself off, drew a kerchief from his breast pocket and wiped the blood from his palm, let out a considerable exhale, and walked mournfully down the hall.

"Five glasses of brandy," he muttered under his breath. "Four windows, three unlit cigars, two black eyes, one pale ghost."

A MEMORY

The image of a doctor with a cigarette in his hand was never one that made much sense to Angela. Still, the curls of smoke in the dinge of the desk lamp had a sort of calming effect. Had Frederick been so obliging as to accompany her to the office, she might have received serenity through his presence. Such as it was, she would have to make do with smoke dancing in the light.

It wasn't an easy thing to be comfortable in a doctor's office. What was it about framed degrees that made one want to retch? It was as if they were a pompous symbol to those who walked in the door, screaming something akin to "I am better than you." Angela detested the whole thing. She insisted on Frederick clearing his office of the terrible things. Waste of good wall space as she saw it. He had been good enough to allow her to make his office a welcoming environment. Warm tones of paint, soothing landscapes hung in beautiful frames, plants that Danielle promised to water every day before tidying the nurse's desk. Doctor Hampstead did not seem to have the luxury of a wife with such a keen eye.

"Let's see what we are dealing with here." Doctor Hampstead wiggled his thick set of mustaches as he formed that smile. That false, disingenuous, crooked smile. Perhaps he had some success with his bedside manner at some point in his long career, but such a skill had long been forgotten. Or perhaps ignored, cast out, dispensed with, labeled as a waste of time. Just the same, Angela had grown rather bored of the whole sympathetic train of woes. Doctor Hampstead at least had the decency to treat her like an adult. Not like a child who didn't understand why her boo-boo was not healing.

"It appears that we are in a binding state, Mrs. Adonis."

"Yes, Doctor, I believe you have gone and hit the head there," she said, keeping her composure calm and icy as usual. Appreciation was not quite the correct word for how she was feeling about this little charade they had formed the habit of performing. Angela would arrive, exchange pleasantries with the nurses, be shuffled into a cold dark room, and be made to take off her clothes and spread her legs while Dr. Hampstead poked his little balding head between them. How they managed to sit across from each other only moments after, fully pretending such a show had not just concluded, was beyond her. She sneered at the memory of a jittery young thing she had first come to visit before she landed on Dr. Hampstead. The sniveling little tyke who had just started under his daddy's practice. How precious he was.

"This is now the fourth miscarriage since you have been under my care," Hampstead continued, not looking up from the manila file that had worn thin and grimy from all the visits that always began with him pulling it from his file cabinet. That same old file that was passed from doctor to doctor. Angela could hardly remember when it still looked fresh.

More than the ruddiness of the file, more than the apathy of the cigarette, more than the usually searching eyes that failed to make their way to Angela's neckline as they always had, the tone told her everything she needed to know. It wasn't the words, though they were filled with attempts at making it seem as if there was a possibility of Angela's having a child if she kept trying. They seemed to invoke a higher power's will of some sort and how faith might bring about a miracle. Men with all the luck in the world loved boasting about miracles. Not for themselves, they had their industriousness and their ingenuity to thank for their successes. But for the others, for the less fortunate. Miracles would do for them, if they were lucky enough to find them.

But he could not hide that tone. Faith was a fickle thing, something Angela ought not mess about with. The tone Dr. Hampstead used said plenty to confirm that. Angela would never carry a child; she would never have the family she had spent her honeymoon daydreaming about. Hell, ever since she could remember, she had wanted this, desired this. Ever since she played about with a doll house taller than her six-year-old frame. But the fates were cruel creatures.

She let the doctor continue his tirade of symptoms and findings. Something about a misshapen uterus, damage to the ovaries, it didn't matter. Not a scrap of it mattered. What mattered to Angela was she had finally found someone who could give her the release she needed. The release from hope. Such an exhaustive thing, hope was. Every soul around another's tragedy might repeat words of hope. How ironic it was that such words only carried darkness with them. An increase of the weight of reality. All this time, seven years' worth of suffering and hope, she just wanted to be cut loose. And for his tone, for the scissors that his words created to cut the cords that bound her to hope, she was thankful. She could have kissed him. But instead, she nodded, feigned a tear and a shake in her voice, and picked up her purse to leave.

"Of course, I can phone everything to your husband's office. His practice is on 3rd street, is that right?"

"Yes, that would be most kind of you, doctor. Thank you for your care. Perhaps we will meet again under better circumstances."

"Yes, er, perhaps we shall," he said with a twinge in his face. It was clear to Angela that there was no need to carry on with their visits, though Hampstead had not actually dictated that. Instead, she would take it upon herself to leave the office without scheduling any follow ups. In the future, she would have Celeste dodge the office's calls should they reach out.

"Oh, you've just missed the lady. Her and Mr. Adonis have gone out to tea."

"Sorry, the lady and Mr. Adonis are lunching at so and so's estate."

"The lady will have to call you back; she is simply too busy to come to the phone at the moment."

Such would be the way of the next few months, dodging calls and requests for follow-up by the skill of the housemaid until they simply gave up trying. Hopefully, they wouldn't ring up Frederick's office and inquire there. There was that damned word again! Hope.

"I am dreadfully sorry, my love." Frederick entered their bedroom while Celeste finished brushing Angela's hair. A quick curtsy and a wordless dismissal shortly followed. "Easily frightened little dove, that one. Are you sure she's the right fit for you?"

"She is the perfect fit," Angela said, pursing her lips to apply a luscious shade of red lipstick that matched her dress. "I will have no other. You hear me, Frederick? No other."

"Alright, my love, alright. None but Celeste, as you wish."
He stood there with his hands in his pockets, transferring his
balance between his heels and the balls of his feet in a way that
made him look like a bored schoolboy. All the same, the man
looked irresistible in a tuxedo. So irresistible, in fact, that during
the occasion of a charity dinner, such as the one they were to
attend that evening, she had stumbled into an empty hall in search
of a bathroom. Unbeknownst to Angela, another woman had
found him just as irresistible. Enough so that when Angela had
turned the corner, she found her tongue down his throat and her
leg wrapping around his thigh.

She often wondered if forgiving him was the right thing to
do. After all, there were no children to worry about. But the
gossip. The dreadful gossip of it all—that was enough to keep her
tied to the brute. Yet, that wasn't all. The truth of it was, she loved
him. And for all his faults, of which there were many, she saw the
genius in him, and would not hear of separation. Despite his
imperfections, she also knew that he loved her. After all, love was
required to see through such hardship.

"About the doctor's visit," he said. "Hampstead phoned me
the moment you left. Said you left in a bit of a storm-off. I don't
suppose you were wrong to do so, such terrible news. I know it
hurts, but—"

"I do not wish to discuss this, darling," Angela said in an
undercut tone, one sharp enough to silence him. Angela was the
only person on earth with that ability. It baffled him that she could
still him with a look in her eye, with a cut from a word.

"Are you sure?"

"What good is it? It's all terribly boring, isn't it? I would
sooner fall off a cliff than have to march through all the incessant
well-wishes. Let's drop it, Freddie, I mean really drop it. Let's go

away, far away, and forget all about it together."

"Why, what a charming notion. I rather think this is a splendid idea!" he said after a moment's reflection. The light in his eyes confirmed he was just as tired of it all as she was. "Where shall we go?"

"Paris, Cairo, Glasgow, anywhere. Anywhere but here."

"I should like to see you in a bathing suit with a Rickey in your hand."

"We could make love on the beach."

"The beaches aren't private, my love."

"Just so, let them watch, they can all watch. And they'll say, 'There is Angela Adonis, a goddess laying claim to her Zeus.'"

"So, they shall! Not a word more. I'll call in to the office and we'll be off tomorrow!"

"Isn't that too soon? Shan't we order suits, some new clothes? What about Charlie?"

"We'll phone it all in. Celeste will watch Charlie; she's very fond of the little pup! Yes, what a splendid idea."

"It's settled then, you mean it?"

"Quite settled."

VII

"Great heavens, you look as if you've seen the devil himself, dear boy!"

Lawrence might be forgiven for missing the irony of Cyrus's exclamation, though it shook him, nonetheless. "Come, have a seat. Really, Lawrence, you are starting to make me suspect that you are altogether unwell. How are you feeling? Did you awake this morning with a fever or something?"

"What?" Lawrence shuddered as he took a seat. Even though the fire continued burning in the fireplace, even though the room would have been considered sweltering by any sane man's standards, Lawrence felt deathly cold.

"A fever, my dear, have you got one?"

"N-no. Not a fever, no."

"Well, then for heaven's sake, what has gotten into you?" Cyrus asked with a high pitch in his tone. He had moved back to perch upon his settee and opened up an old and cracked leather-bound book.

"I don't know," Lawrence lied. He had decided on this lie far before he reached the office. He decided on it before his feet entered the lift. After all, the way he saw it, he was culpable for murder. That wasn't the way of it, surely, but what did that matter? The only witness he could call on was not a viable one, given the terrible misfortune of her lack of pulse.

Sonya Ivanovna. Each letter of her name was etched into the wrinkles of Lawrence's brain. He contemplated each syllable, let them roll around echoing in the voids of his consciousness. Sonya Ivanovna. Seared in the backs of his eyelids, her face materialized as a foggy apparition. The gloss of her eyes, the pallor of her visage, the ice of her presence—all served to drown Lawrence in a stupor of fear.

The tea he had neglected an hour prior, now an undrinkable cold temperature, sat staring at him. Flecks of leaves taunted him as his eyes fixated on their floating around the little cup. It felt to Lawrence as if they were laughing at his fear, as if they were telling him they could read his thoughts.

A ridiculous premise, of course, tea leaves reading one's thoughts. But all the same, Lawrence was in no state to understand the ridiculous from the respectable.

Screwing up his eyes to look at Cyrus, he found the pompous man adorning a devil-may-care expression while reading the ruddy old volume he had just picked up. It angered him to look upon his apathy. Had he really no idea of what Lawrence had just witnessed? No, he knew; he was teasing him with his inattention. Waiting for an outburst where he would smile and contort his face before calling in the police. The devil with him! That was at least how Lawrence saw it.

Perhaps this is what enraged Lawrence the most, that it was in fact quite possible that he could suffer so, all the while Cyrus sat lost in his book.

The pulsing desire to free his mind from the vision of Sonya burned in his chest. It even flamed hot enough for him to turn his gaze over to the tapestry that had given him so much pause before. There it was, and there they all were. The dancers and the condemned. Or the sacrifice. Or the volunteer; Lawrence was still quite perplexed as to what was happening. But something new caught his eye, something that caused his stomach to split in two.

The teacup was nearly knocked to the ground. The chair made an ear-splitting scratch upon the marble flooring. "What is this?" Lawrence demanded, his finger shaking as it pointed to the tapestry.

"Still on about that tapestry, are you?"

"Was this there before?" he asked, narrowing his eyes on a particular stitch.

"There before? Lawrence, you asked me about it once already, remember? Anyway, how did the radiator business go? You were an awfully long while up there."

"No, not the tapestry, the woman in the tapestry."

"I haven't the slightest idea of your meaning."

"Look, here!" But Cyrus continued scanning the worn pages of his book, pretending not to hear the insanities of an exasperated manager staring angrily at a wall.

For Lawrence's part, his bloodshot eyes became fixed on a central point. A woman who was not with the other subjects of the work. She was not dancing, she was not naked, and she seemed flatly disinterested in the burning figure yelling out in pain. Or ecstasy. It all remained unclear. What was clear was the loose-fitted dress, the filthy pinafore, and the headscarf which showed loose hair miraculously through the stitching. What was most worrying to Lawrence's weak temperament were the black, staring eyes that looked not at the ongoing scene, but out toward the viewer. Those ghastly, wicked eyes that happened to match the raven perched upon the figure's shoulder.

"My god," Lawrence whispered. "Sonya Ivanovna." Her very name felt like ashes in his mouth, rolling over and under his tongue in a putrid wave. Swelling clogged the back of his throat as the blacks of his eyes widened and contracted.

"What is that?" Cyrus asked with piqued interest. "What did you say?"

"What? Oh...nothing. Sorry, I must be beside myself." Lawrence attempted to sort himself out with the tug of his waistcoat and a few steps about the office. All the while, he could feel Cyrus's burning, judgmental eyes follow each inch of movement. He wondered at what Cyrus was thinking. Surely, he was quickly convincing himself he was in the company of a madman.

As it turned out, the throes of his pacing was the very reason why Lawrence was unable to see the curl of Cyrus's lips form a twisted smile as he watched the manager walk about the room. Before Lawrence had steadied himself, however, that same twisted smile had turned back to its original apathetic expression.

"Cyrus?" Lawrence questioned while slowing and attempting—quite unsuccessfully it might be said—to keep his gaze away from the tapestry.

"Yes, Lawrence?" Cyrus said, failing to lift his gaze from the book.

"Do you believe, I mean to say, do you consider it *possible* that the dead come to visit the living?" There was an uncomfortable pause after the question was posed. So long was Cyrus's stalling, that Lawrence, for the second time that very day, gave way to fidgeting.

"What? More fine talk! I thought I told you I was in no mood for philosophy. Really, you need something to calm the nerves. Perhaps a spot of brandy?"

"No!"

"Alright, my dear, alright. No need to get testy, Lawrence. I'm only looking out for your health, you know. Someone ought to do it."

"You're right, I'm sorry. I'm just having a little vertigo is all. Yes, that's it. I'll be fine."

"I should hope so, Lawrence. What would the hotel do without you?"

"Have your jokes," Lawrence chided.

"What good is there in jokes, my dear boy?" Cyrus had returned to his reading and was hardly paying attention to anything Lawrence did or said. For Lawrence's part, he was primarily concerned with his inability to shake the frightful images spinning around his mind. He could see that quivering, lifeless eye of Kosorukov before he fell to the floor. He was in desperate need of something, anything, to take his mind off it.

"What are you reading?" Lawrence snapped.

"'Within the hollows of the trees, and the whispers of the breeze, through the babbling of the brook, and the harshness of her look. Evermore would her haunts be mine, for the pain and the death of Adeline.'"

"What? What are you blathering about?"

"It is poetry, my dear. Really, you must soften up a bit. This new rattled state of yours is very unbecoming."

"Poetry?"

"Indeed."

"Look who has succumbed to fine talk now," Lawrence said, feeling triumphant in his retort.

"It is not fine to listen to the rhymes of the dead, my dear. Their words give little meaning apart from the comfort of their rhythm, that is all. "

"I think you hide your feelings behind a mask," Lawrence said, his temper growing.

"I wear no mask, Lawrence There is little need. What have I to hide? I pity the man who walks his whole life without the sun ever touching his face for being hidden behind the mask he wears for the world. Such a pity."

"This is all very fine," Lawrence insisted.

"If you say so, Lawrence," Cyrus replied, burying his nose into his book. But before Lawrence could breathe his well thought out and articulate response, which he was sure would win the debate, a rapping came at the door. With it, the cleverness and the jeering fluttered from his mind.

"Yes, come in!" Lawrence called, this time quite welcoming the distraction.

"Morning, sir!" Dorian called. "How's it carrying on for you?"

"Very well, Dorian," Lawrence lied. "How can we help?"

Dorian's face scrunched as his eyes darted around the room, his head turning to land on the fireplace. "Er," he began, tugging at his collar, no doubt from the heat.

"Yes, out with it boy!" Lawrence nearly shouted, rolling his hands in a circular motion to coax the words from the young man's mouth.

"There is a Mrs. Adonis at the front desk to see you, sir."

"Very well," he said, stepping forward and placing his hand on Dorian's shoulder, giving it a firm squeeze. "Did your brother clear the entryway of that infernal crow?"

"I think it was a raven, sir. Crows are quite a bit smaller. And they run together, sir. Ravens are often—"

"Enough, my boy, that is enough. What of this raven, is it gone?"

"Cleared out, sir. I helped him do it. Chased him off with a broom and a bucket."

"A bucket?"

"Er, for the noise sir. I clambered about while he jabbed at the little devil. Clever as they come, ravens. They can live up to thirty years and—" He was cut short by a wave of his manager's finger and closed eyes. Not chancing his luck any further, Dorian bowed his head before turning to walk out the door. Lawrence could hear a cheery, "He'll be right with you, ma'am!" from around the corner.

Before braving the wrath of Angela Adonis, Lawrence took a final glance to the tapestry. Much to his surprise, the stitching that previously bore the likeness of Sonya Ivanovna was nowhere to be seen. Instead, where she had stared out to the viewer moments ago, there stood the raven that had been perched on her shoulder.

VIII

"A pleasure to see you again so soon, Mrs. Adonis. How do you find your rooms?" Lawrence had nearly begun speaking before he rounded the corner to the front desk. There he found the complacent stature of Angela Adonis, her long, red-painted nails thrumming on the desk's marble top.

Such clattering of nails on stone somehow drowned out the shuffling of guest feet, the whispering and laughing of old friends, and the stroke of noon on the clock. Perhaps it was detestation for the prideful woman that made Lawrence hone in his attention on her every move. Perhaps, but something else seemed to take detestation's place. Something akin to obsession, but its lesser cousin. Distraction. Her presence distracted him, something he was desperate to hold on to, no matter the source.

"The room is fine," she said. The word pierced through his heart. Fine. The penthouse suite at a most prestigious hotel as the Genovie. Fine.

"I'm glad to hear it," Lawrence forced himself to say. "How might I be of service?"

"I thought I might come and ask you for a bit of stationery."

"Stationery, madam?"

"Yes, I'll have to write a letter."

"Not a problem, Mrs. Adonis. I am sorry you made the trouble of coming all the way down. I would have been more than happy to send you—"

"It is not a problem, Mr..."

"Mr. Erlik, madam, or Lawrence, if it pleases you." The false smile began to tighten his cheek into a cramp.

"Very well," she said drily. "It is all the same. As it happens, I felt that I owed you," she took a large breath before speaking her next words, "an apology."

"An apology, madam?"

"Yes, Frederick tells me I was rather curt with you. The way he sees it—and he has brought me around to agree with him— there is little use in being upset over such trivialities. After all, no harm done." The way she said the words seemed as if they tasted of poison on her tongue. Her eyes darted around the room, never making contact with Lawrence's. The truth of it was, Angela felt she was well within her right to be upset. Even so, keeping the peace might be a more suitable alternative to a highly contested stay at the Genovie.

"Aurelia," Lawrence called. Much to Mrs. Adonis's consternation, the phantom of the manager's assistant popped out, standing by his side. *Funny little bit of a thing,* she thought, casting her from her mind in one swift notion.

"Aurelia," Lawrence continued when she approached. "Please be so kind as to fetch some stationary for Mrs. Adonis and be sure to include a complimentary pen with the package."

"Oh, that won't be necessary; I have my own."

"I do insist, madam. Parker has just sent us a shipment of their new Duofold line. They are simply a dream to write with. I think you'll find it satisfactory. Call it a peace offering between two high-spirited individuals."

One can only fathom the sharpness of the look given by Mrs. Adonis at the transgression of Lawrence placing the two of them on equal footing. However, the luxury of the gift was enough to assuage such prickly temperament.

"Very well," she said, turning her head to look about the lobby while Aurelia darted off to retrieve the stationary. "Is that..." she began, squinting her eyes. "Is that Donald Cherry?"

Lawrence followed the line of her eyes to the lounge area across the lobby. Sitting in an old and cracked brown leather chair was Mr. Cherry. He looked to be reading the morning's paper while enjoying a steaming cup of coffee and a smoldering cigar. Tactless as men of his lot tended to be, the cigar's ash had been drifting down, landing on the chair's armrest like a grim flurry. This disturbed Lawrence, and he had half a mind to march over and make an example of the brute. However, being the accommodating man his station required, he calmed himself with the work of a breath.

"Yes, we have the pleasure of his staying with us for the evening. All manner of celebrities and personalities make their way through our doors. Would you like me to introduce you?"

"No," she snapped in a quiet, cutting voice. "No, that won't be necessary."

"Do you already have the pleasure, madam?" Lawrence asked.

"I am unsure whether I would call it a pleasure, Mr. Erlik. But yes. Donald is a distant relation of sorts."

"Fancy that!" Lawrence exclaimed with intent to slightly perturb. It would appear to the well-versed in the whims of hotel managers that he had not quite forgiven Mrs. Adonis for her razor-sharp tone earlier that same morning.

"Do keep your voice down!" she hissed.

"Yes, ma'am, I do apologize. I regret that I should be put in a position to cause any consternation."

"That is quite alright, Erlik. Do me a favor, will you?"

"Anything in my power to do."

"Do not mention my name to Mr. Cherry."

"Madam?"

"Please. If I can get through the stay without him noticing me, we would all be better for it, I should think."

"If the madam thinks it best, I shall oblige." Lawrence raised an eyebrow and looked toward Don Cherry. His lips were drooling so profusely that his cigar was no doubt limp at the end.

"I'm afraid I must insist," she whispered. Oddly enough, Lawrence felt he could hear a tinge of playfulness in her tone. Quite the whiplash, in his opinion.

"Very well then," he whispered back. "Though, I must ask, shall I take certain precautions for you and your family in regard to lunch or dinner? Room service, perhaps?"

"No, no, no. That will not do. We had plans for a luncheon with some old friends around the neighborhood, but they have mysteriously canceled. I think we will take our lunch in the tearoom, if that is permissible."

"Perfectly, madam, perfectly! I will alert the staff of your arrival. Er, shall we say, one-fifteen?"

"That would be agreeable, I should think." It was at this moment Lawrence realized Angela was bent at an angle, a hand pressed against her stomach with a wince in her eyes. He raised his eyebrows again, this time not in curiosity but concern. When he made to speak, Angela gave him the sharp eyes of a snake and the ever-so-slight jolt of a headshake. It was enough to ward him from the pry.

"Splendid, we look forward to being of service." As he spoke these last words, in a seamless motion, he grabbed the package of stationary from Aurelia—who had, like a shadow, returned silently to his side—and swiftly handed it to Angela. "Oh, and one more thing, Mrs. Adonis."

Angela paused as she turned away. The raise in her right eyebrow was all that was needed to bid the manager to continue.

"Should you need it, one of the Berus brothers would be delighted to run your letter to the post and see to it that it is treated with the utmost priority. Courtesy of the Genovie. We do have a flourishing relationship with the fine men and women couriers."

A small, sly smile adorned Angela's lips, her eyes turning away from Lawrence. "That won't be necessary, Mr. Erlik."

Before the idea was ushered out of his head by fighting off his own inner demons, Lawrence thought he could see a hint of flush fill her cheeks.

As to those bothersome demons that seemed to plague the good manager's sensibilities, it seemed as though they had gathered a new favorite form. As Mrs. Adonis was stepping away from the front desk, so then did Sonya Ivanovna sweep over the lobby floor, her black eyes cast on Lawrence's quaking pallor.

It was odd, in Lawrence's view, how nobody present seemed to notice her. Nobody shivered at the sudden plummet in the hotel's temperature. No one cast their eyes to the fixtures as they flickered and lowered in their luminance. No one noticed the cold sweat dripping down Lawrence's forehead.

The chief concern, beyond the frightful implications of a wraith haunting the halls of the grand hotel (not at all a luxurious experience), was understanding why. Why had Sonya stuck around after Roman Pavlovich slid the point of his shimmering blade through his skull? Why had she decided to torment a manager of a hotel in return, especially one so dedicated to his craft and so wanting to ensure his guests have the finest stay imaginable? It was all very disconcerting. Further, and a question of profound significance for the manager, was why his heart slowed to an unimaginably lethargic beating when she set her eyes to his. It nearly stopped. It soon became a question as to whether or not he would be able to go on living under such duress.

"Old man!" He heard in a muffled tone, as if he were submerged in cold water and a voice shouted from above the surface. "Can you hear me, old boy?"

Lawrence felt as if he were yanked by some force from one plane to the next. His head lightened, his spine tingled, and the overwhelming aroma of sulfur filled his nose. It was one that could not quite be explained. It wasn't something that could be pinned, located. It was as if the very hairs of his nose were coated with the stench. After what any attentive man would have noticed as a great too many blinks, Lawrence came back to himself.

"Ah-hem, hmm. Oh, I'm frightfully sorry, sir. Is there some way I can be of service?"

Standing in front of him was the sweaty visage of Mr. Don Cherry. Cigars did not seem to agree with him. The complexion of his skin turned rough and sickly green, his usual dopey gold-toothed smile was particularly nauseating at that moment. A quick flicker of the eye above Cherry's shoulder led to the uncomfortable realization that the lobby floor was empty. It was not inhabited by Sonya Ivanovna, not haunted by a drifting specter or cawing raven, and not even bustling with the chatter of exuberant guests. Empty.

Aside from the inconvenient visage of Mr. Cherry, of course.

"Well," Mr. Cherry began in the tone of a man who felt he

was about to take advantage of an opportunity. "I was wondering if you would clue me into something, old fellow."

"Anything in my power to enlighten, you shall have."

"What a sporting man you are, Erlik. Just a fine old fashion boy! Haha, happy to be in your company. But on to business! Would you be able to identify for me that tall glass of water that was just standing where my humble feet now trample?"

"Oh, you are too modest, my dear man," Lawrence lied. "Just so, it is the official policy of the Genovie to withhold the identity of our guests without their explicit permission to the contrary."

"Oh, come my lad," Cherry grumbled in the manner of men who are used to getting their way. "Would it be such a breach of conduct? You see, I have a sneaking suspicion that I know the little lady. I believe we were...well, we were, in a manner, acquaintances. If you like."

"Just so, sir, I am afraid I haven't the power to oblige."

"Haven't the power? Well, that sounds like nonsense to me, while I—"

Mr. Cherry's grumbling was interrupted by the call of the quarter hour from the grandfather clock. Lawrence took a bit of pleasure in seeing the man start and dart his eyes around the lobby as if he were under some sort of threat. There was something about the smoke-induced rasp in his voice and the sourness of his breath that caused Lawrence an intense aversion to the man. Or perhaps it was the squirrely smile that said, "We men can trust one another."

"Ah," Lawrence said, disallowing Cherry's rebuke to continue, "Luncheon will be served momentarily. You are looking rather peckish, if you don't mind my saying so."

"I do? Ah, well I suppose I have been feeling rather famished now that I think about it. Perhaps I'll head to the tearoom and—"

"Nonsense, dear man, nonsense." Lawrence walked from behind the desk and wrapped his arm around Cherry's shoulders in feigned friendship, stepping away from the lobby. "It'll be the café for you! Trust that I am cluing you in on a little secret of the hotel. The service is much better, the pours much heavier, and the food…well, I should think it best to have you judge for yourself. But I doubt you will be disappointed there, sir."

"Humph," Cherry chortled, "I suppose you may be onto something there. I believe I spotted a pretty little thing light on her feet as I was walking by. Perhaps I'll pay the café a visit."

"Ah, yes, that'll be Anastasia. The best waitress in the world, I would bet the house on it, sir. Run along then."

It might concern the reader that Lawrence shooed away Mr. Cherry from Angela's tail only to set him loose on Anastasia, an employee no less. Out of the frying pan and into the fire, one might say. But one would then not have been educated in the sharpness of Anastasia's eye, the power of her right hook, the joy she took in picturing the tip of her knife gliding across the neck of a drooling imbecile. As it would often occur, she and Lawrence would likely meet in the evening to chuckle at the absurdities that a man such as Don Cherry would abase himself to in order to gain the young lady's favor.

As soon as Lawrence found himself alone again, he realized every inch of his body was shuddering in a frigid cold. It was as if he had crashed into a lake at the end of winter, ice caps still bobbing in the calm waters. There was also the inexorable feeling of a slender, poorly dressed peasant girl lurking behind his shoulder. The fear paralyzed him.

But only for a moment, for fear often gives way to curiosity. That is to say, Lawrence felt a stronger urge to ensure there was nothing lurking in the broad daylight, causing consternation for his guests, rather than to cower over something he had been so strongly convincing himself wasn't actually there.

As it turned out, the proof of the matter seemed to corroborate with his denial. When he turned around—and indeed, it was a vigorously executed whip of a turn—he found nothing but the floating particles of dust illuminated by the sunlight shining through the grand window.

Such a reaction, only to prove no one was actually there, convinced Lawrence he had given in to paranoia. Perhaps there was merit to Cyrus's aversion to fine talk and philosophy. Lawrence was just working himself up, allowing his mind to roam into the fanciful and the paranormal.

There was, of course, the dead body in room 319 that needed dealing with. No amount of paranoia, fanciful thinking, or philosophy would change that fact. A lump formed in the back of his throat. Just as he managed to swallow it, fighting through the pain of its meaning, a terrible thought plagued him. It was the type of thought that screams in one's ears, blaring so defiantly that all others pale in comparison. The type of thought that pulls a man to action from the abyss of fear.

"Aurelia," he called. "Aurelia, do come here. Have you seen Margarette lately?"

Aurelia's eyes turned to the upper right corner of the room, then returned to Lawrence. She shook her head.

"Damn it all!" he said, going red in the face. "Well, if you see her, will you point her in my direction?" A closed-eyed nod. "Thank you, Aurelia. Off with you then."

It was too soon, too raw in his heart. It crawled under his skin and danced upon the tender meat of his lungs. He could not go back up to the room. There was the horror of it all, but even further, he hadn't the slightest idea of what he would do if he did.

But what was most pressing was ensuring no one else went up there. Certainly, there would not be an attempt by Margarette until the morning, but one could never be too sure in these matters. He let out a morbid guffaw. What was he thinking? One ought not mess about with the delicacy of a corpse. What might he do, drag it through the halls? To think of the stains upon the carpet! Even still, it was imperative he drum up some sort of plan. It was getting to the point where police would begin to question his hesitance in calling them. Did he even feel that he should? How had this hellish game started?

Such were the questions coursing through the spiraling manager's frantic mind. An onlooker might have had cause for concern. There he stood, in the middle of the lobby, lightly rocking back and forth as if his ankles were on axles. One might even be forgiven for thinking he was stammering to himself.

In the end, it was duty that pulled him out of his trance. After all, he had to see to lunch. The first step is always the hardest when faced with such excruciating circumstances, and so it was for Lawrence. But as he lifted his heel, his feet fell to the floor in a rolling rhythm, set in time by the clinking of the first few drops upon the windows as a thick gray cloud drifted over the Hotel Genovie.

A MEMORY

"You've always been a little whore, haven't you? Just covered it up to lure a good man in, eh?"

"I don't know what you are talking about, Jed, please! Michael will hear you."

"Let the little freak hear! It's time he learned what a slut his mother is. Going about town, embarrassin' his Pa!"

The crash was as loud as the thunder sounding from a crack of lightning in the yard when Michael was only two years old. It had always stayed with him, every time his father lost his temper. He heard the crack of thunder, saw that blinding flash of light, and shivered under his blanket with his hands clamped to his ears. Eyes tightened, tears squeezed past, and Michael prayed to God to send angels to calm his father.

But this sound was no lightning bolt. Pa had gone mad with drink again, flipping the table on its side in his stupor. Michael's heart sped and rose into his throat. It was Thursday. Pa always got his wages on Thursdays, always came home in the dead of night reeking of whiskey and stale cigarettes. Some nights they were lucky, lucky not to provoke what Michael called Shadow Pa.

Most weeks it was harmless, though terrifying, nonetheless. Pa would come home, scream for an hour about how he was owed a better lot in life, how he had Michael and Mama to blame for it. In short order, he would wear himself out and fall to the bottom corner of the bed and pass out with the sound of a steam ship snore.

It was the nights after he had gotten reprimanded by his no good, son of a bitch, pig-fucking, ass-sniffing foreman where he would feel the need to show his prowess as a man. Usually that meant giving Mama a close-eyed look of the back of his hand. Once. One terrible lash, Mama falling to the floor in tears, and Pa marching into the bedroom, slamming the door in a jealous rage. But it would be over. Mama would come and sleep curled up with Michael on his tiny, lumpy mattress. If it weren't for the cause of her being there, Michael would have actually preferred those nights. But life has a funny way of sticking the good with the unbearably evil.

This night was worse. A new smell was in the air. Fear.

"The devil has come into my house! This woman has taken me for a fool! Satan! Satan laughs at me now! Do you hear 'em? Do you hear the devils scream? What evil have you done?" Michael was shaking under the scratchy cloth he used for a blanket. He felt something in the air, someone, something whispering in his ear telling him, "Go look." Shuffling to the very edge of the blanket, his eyes fixed on the glow of the keyhole.

"I done nothing, Jed. I told you already, I done nothing!"

"I saw the look in his eye, Mary! I saw the devil grinning at me! No good piece of shit foreman. Takes my wages, now he takes my wife! You stupid slut, the devil can have you!" Another crash and a tumble echoed through the walls; Michael was sure it was something slamming into his bedroom wall. In the corner of his eye, he saw something move in the shadows. Were they the demons Pa was yelling about?

Therein lied his trouble. Should he stay hidden in his room, trapped with demons lurking in the shadows with no protection outside of a ruddy blanket? Or face what was happening outside? Shivering steps pulled him to peek through the door.

"It wasn't enough, you forcing me to live in this shit hole, come home every night to *this?*" Another crash. Michael's eye was apprehensive, but it approached the keyhole, nonetheless. Through the tiny hole, through the blur of the sharp light, he saw a raging mountain of muscle and sweat, draped in a filthy workman's shirt. Pa's braces had fallen to the side of his trousers. He staggered back and forth before stepping out of Michael's line of sight.

"You had to go and fuck him, didn't you?"

"I dint, Jed, I dint!"

"Shut up! Shut your filthy mouth. Satan may listen to your slithery tongue, but I am a man of God! My ayeng— my angels are with me!" There it was; Michael heard that all too familiar *thwap* of Pa's hand crashing into Mama's cheekbone. Pa would stumble away, and Mama would open his door soon, and she would take care of these demons he was avoiding making eye contact with.

Only Pa didn't stumble away.

He didn't get up from where he was, didn't quit his screaming, and more *thwaps* came raining down on his ear. Each one sent his stomach closer to splitting in two. He shut his eyes and cupped his hands over his mouth, begging that phantom voice to still. But the whisper only returned. "Go," it said.

There may have been not a single thing on the face of God's Earth that Michael feared more than opening his door at that moment. But the sound of the *thwap, thwap, thwap,* intermixed with fiendish screaming. "Should have known you would embarrass me, should have known you were a whore. Did you give yourself away on the first try or did you make him work for it?" *Thwap!* "I bet you made him work for it. Had a little fun, did you? While I was out working, breaking my body for ye? The devil can have you!"

Michael opened the door.

For the rest of his life, he would never forget. He would never forget the blood streaming from her broken lip, the swell of her eye, the tear in her floral dress. The thick drench of sweat and dirt coming together to form a crusty mud on his yellow shirt.

Pa's hand was raised in the air, ready to fall down on Mama when Michael whimpered.

"Jed, please. Mich—" His hand fell swift and heavy.

"Let him watch! It's time he became a man!" Another one, swift and heavy. Eyes stung with the salt of his tears. He could taste the snot bubbling above his upper lip. Then the whisper.

It was a scary whisper, but perhaps it was right. Perhaps it was time that Michael became a man. Without another thought, he stormed with heavy feet into his parent's bedroom. Michael was able to fly through the shack of a house before Pa had finished slurring, "Where you going, boy?"

The crack of the lightning in the yard was identical to the crack of Pa's six. The rolling of the thunder was akin to the thump of Pa's body on the hardwood floor. The puddling of the rain was the same as the pool of blood inching toward the edge of the rug.

"What have you done?" Mama asked. "God in heaven, what have you done?"

"I—"

"You devil! You've killed him, what have you done? Jed! Wake up, Jed! Wake up! Oh my God, my Jed! Oh! Oh!"

"Mama…"

"Put that wicked thing down, now!"

Michael did as he was told, letting the gun fall to the floor.

"He was hurting you, Mama."

"I was fine! Oh God, what have you done? You are unclean! We have to go. Now. Before it's too late."

"Where?"

"To the river."

Before Michael could think, Mama was already on him, grabbing him by the wrist and pulling so hard as she walked, Michael could hardly keep up. They were out the door and into the cold of the night—Michael in his paper-thin pajamas and Mama in her torn and bloody dress. There was no one to witness their clambering but the crickets and the field mice.

It was about a fifteen-minute walk at a normal pace, but the devil was at their backs, prodding them with his trident to move faster. Mama kept saying so. That is, she said so when she wasn't repeating the phrase, "My God, what has he done?" to herself over and over. Michael was confused; he thought he had done a good thing. He had saved his mother from a thunder of abuse, from death even. Shouldn't they be grateful to be together, safe?

"They're calling to you. I can hear them. The damned are calling out, reaching from the rage of their eternal fire. You can't take their hand, Michael. You mustn't take their hand!" Her voice was breathless. She tugged wildly at his arm every other syllable. "They'll take you and let you burn. You don't understand, Michael. They are laughing, can you hear? They are laughing at you. They are going to hold you, pretend everything is alright. That's what they want you to believe but you just can't. You'll burn, Michael, you'll burn!"

It wasn't until they got to the river's edge that Michael felt the bite of the cold. Or heard the coo of the owls, the snap of the brush, the rolling of the water against rocks laid to rest centuries ago.

His eyes were mesmerized by the curl of the current. A million shimmering stars formed in the ripples from the moon's dazzling reflection. The river carried them to faraway places where the troubles of the living were left far behind. Michael begged them to take him with them. He yearned to leave the dread that was filling in his stomach like a pile of rocks weighing him down to where he stood.

"Take your clothes off," Mama said in a voice broken by tears. "Take them off, Michael. Do as I say."

"Mama?" Michael asked with a quiver of his lip. All the warmth in the world seemed to emit from his two small arms wrapping around his torso. "I'm...scared."

"The devil knows it," she said. "We have to wash you, Michael. We need to make you clean again. We need to make you clean."

Those words served as Michael's only warning. Once his clothes were torn from his pale skin, he was dragged by his mother's vice grip into the flow of the river. His head bobbed in and out from the surface, water splashing in his ears. "Mama!" he tried to say, but the current washed his words from his mouth.

"You need to be clean, boy. You need to be clean. Jesus, please cleanse him of the filth of Satan! Bring him into the holiness of your kingdom, and forgive him his wickedness. Cleanse him in the river. He was wrong! God help me! God save me! He was wrong!"

Michael danced on the edge of life. One moment the water was rushing through him, pounding at his mouth as if it willed to reach his lungs. The next he was stabbed by the needles of the chilled air. His vision was ruined by the sting of the current, but he could still see his father's rueful eyes clear as day. He was wrong.

"Do you hear them, Michael? Do you hear?" Mama said, pulling Michael out of the water. But Michael could not hear anything but the water leaving his ears. His lungs burned from coughing up the sediment.

"They have forgiven you, Michael. They have seen that the devil had you in his wicked hands, but we have washed him away. You see? We have washed him away. You are clean, Michael. You are clean again."

Michael stared at his mother, not daring to utter a word for fear of his saying the wrong thing. He felt little in the way of cleanliness. Instead he was shivering in the soak of piety. Confusion compounded as the weight of what waited for them at home pressed into his chest. The crack of the gun rang in his ears, echoing through the planes and waking the meerkats and the coyotes. Tricks played with Michael's eyes as he felt he could see shapes dancing in the pitch of the night.

"Can you hear them, Michael? They sing for you; they sing to welcome their child back into the grace of their kingdom. Listen, Michael, listen to the angels sing! We are clean again!"

Michael struggled to get to his feet, shivering all the while. He staggered, gained his balance, and felt the breeze tickle his naked skin. The look on his mother's face turned his blood colder than the river water. Her panting, almost laughing breath scared him more than his father's fist.

Catching his own breath and closing his eyes, he froze where he stood. Lightly, no louder than the whistle of the wind, Michael began to hear a faint choir hum the most beautiful melody.

IX

One might be forgiven for pondering the idiosyncrasies of our beloved manager. In fact, he was wont to do so himself from time to time. But, as the author has written from the onset, it was precisely his temperament that made him perfect for the role of overseeing the madness that ensues in the line of fine accommodation. It was not, however, quite so fruitful in the ways of coping with murder.

Now, let us be fair. It was not Lawrence's will that slid that shimmering blade into the throat and pierced the skull of the late Kosorukov. However, his hand was in fact on the hilt. A bothersome detail he had become rather engrossed in.

Once the shock had worn off—though perhaps it is better to say subsided—the question of guilt began to surge. It is this question that was accompanied by the clinks of silverware against china, the low hum of polite chatter, and the bustling of feet from service to table. Quite an inconvenient consumption when one is pressed to oversee the swiftness of a proper lunch service.

However, fear not. Our manager was a professional. After all, it was just in this way—that is, the splitting of the mind—that Lawrence had dealt with his mental afflictions all his life. The interior was on fire, while the exterior was sculpted from a block of ice.

The appearance of the Café Genovie, in many respects, likely resembled that of other bistros and cafés found in many luxurious hotels. The stark white linens freshly pressed every morning adorning each table, the crystal glassware polished to a radiant shine, and the two-story windows with high draping velvet curtains were cordially welcoming to guests. There was something about the café, however, that led to a different sort of feeling that many of the guests were not keen to until they left. The air was lighter, the food kept warmer, the coffee stronger, and the champagne bubblier. In accordance, the laughs were heartier and the chatter more interesting. Indeed, the manager knew the last detail all too well. Resting off to the side, just next to the swinging doors to the kitchens, was a small podium where Lawrence fancied a perch and a dropping of eaves in order to gain the upper hand.

No, the reader mustn't misunderstand. Not the upper hand in the way of gaining some sort of advantage over the guests themselves. That would be altogether iniquitous and vile. Rather, the manager was looking to gain the upper hand in the good fight. That is to say, the fight against an un-enjoyed or insufferable stay at the Genovie. After all, a man fit for such ends must abase himself to the means, wouldn't the reader agree?

"Ah, Father Callione, how is your stay treating you?" Lawrence did well to greet incoming guests as they filtered through the café. The old priest was a comfortable looking man, permanently bent forward with a worn smile stretched across his face. There was something about his countenance that left one inclined to trust in the comfort of his presence.

"My," Father Callione said, "I must admit, I have been thrown for quite the imbalance in my sentiment, my son."

"I'm sorry?"

"You see, it is not a common occurrence for a man of my profession to be surrounded by such...earthly comforts. I have not the familiarity with their richness. They do me a disservice, almost, with their obliging nature."

"Perhaps," Lawrence said after pondering his words for a moment. "But we have received all manner of priests and men of the cloth in our humble walls. Do not bequeath yourself to the guilt of enjoyment, for it is the splendor from on high that puts our lodgings to shame. Fear not, dear Father, we hold ourselves not in comparison with your benefactor."

"My benefactor? Is that right? Then He is not, as you put it, your benefactor as well?"

"Perhaps, perhaps not. It is for Him to decide. In the meantime, I am honored to entreat his servants with the accoutrements of the Kingdom of Earth, having not within my reach the stars men have praised since looking to the heavens."

"One ought to be careful with the Kingdom of Earth, my lad."

"Just so, Father, one ought to be careful reaching for the stars."

"Perhaps the clouds, then," the old priest said with a raspy chuckle.

"Ah, Father, but the clouds do not shine."

"Perhaps not, perhaps not."

"Forgive me, I am keeping you from your lunch. Shall I set a place for you over by the window? The garden is quite beautiful this time of year. I've always found the blooming of the white roses particularly heavenly, if you'll forgive the comparison."

"There is nothing to forgive, dear boy. I expect the gates of St. Peter will be lush with roses. But no, I must forgo their splendor for the time being. I might ask, if it is within your power, to entreat that young man a few tables over to do me the honor of lunching with an old man?" Lawrence turned to see a silent soldier sitting square-postured in a chair, looking awfully befuddled at a menu.

"Ah, the young Private Michael Goodman," Lawrence confirmed. "He has only just arrived this morning. I suspect he will be happy for it. Allow me to put the offer forth." Bowing to the priest, Lawrence approached the young soldier who shuddered at the shadow of the manager's presence.

"Good afternoon, Michael. Oh...I do hope you will excuse the familiarity. I am not altogether certain as to why, but I feel as though there is a bond between us. Forgive my transgression and allow my recompense of beginning anew. Good afternoon, Private Goodman." Lawrence was altogether flushed with heated embarrassment at forgetting himself in such a way. As for Michael, however, there was very little on his mind other than the overwhelming menu and the old leather-bound book sitting on the table's corner that he had been obsessively reading through since arrival. There wasn't a thought as to the familiarity with which the manager addressed him.

"There is nothing to forgive," Michael said. "I would prefer you call me by my Christian anyway. I've never been one for the formalities that come with the uniform."

"As it is," Lawrence began, "I'm afraid there may be one formality connected with your uniform that may cause you to view me in a dark light. But fear not, my friend, for I believe it might meet you rather agreeably. You see, the good priest standing over there, Father Callione, has requested the honor of your company at lunch."

"The honor..." Michael trailed off.

"Of your company, yes."

"But, why?" His voice turned to the innocence of a child who is first asked to help his father in the garage.

"I am afraid I am not clued into that exact answer, though the good Father has stayed with us these past two nights and has, on the whole, been very well received. I trust you will get on famously."

"Well," Michael said, looking straight ahead as if deep in thought. "Alright then. Send him over, I should be glad for it. It is terribly lonely traveling alone."

"Straight away," Lawrence bowed. The young private might be forgiven for having been startled by the sudden appearance of two waiters setting a place in perfect harmony for a second diner. It was without any visible instruction from Lawrence, at least not from what he was able to ascertain. And before he knew it, he was listening to the kind, aged voice of Father Callione, thanking him for allowing the intrusion on his lunch.

For Lawrence's part, as the father walked over to the table, he had half a mind to fall to his knees and weep into the black cassock. The impulse to confess the haunts that plagued him, to shout for all to hear that he held the knife that killed Roman Pavlovich Kosorukov was overwhelming and filled him with a sense of foreboding that he could hardly shake. But that would not do, not there, not at that moment.

Instead, he drifted over to his podium where he found interest in the conversation between an old priest and a young soldier to be enough to take his mind from the ill-nature of the sins that awaited his return to room 319.

"I must confess," Michael began, though immediately fumbled over the awkward faux pas of his wording. "I mean to say," he recovered, "I must admit I have little earthly idea as to why you would see fit to lunch with a mere soldier, sir. Er, Father."

"Either is fine, as is Francis. Though, I must confess myself," the priest gave a glistening wink and an emphasis on the word confess, "I have grown so accustomed to Father that sometimes I forget my own name." He chuckled and accepted a small menu that was laid before him by a breathless waiter. "You need not concern yourself with the reasons for my desire of your company, for they are quite innocent, I assure you. Two there are. The first, and probably the one owing to my own patriotic sensibility (though, I admit, such as it is, I ought to dispel myself of that sentiment), I should like to dine with a man who pledged such a noble sacrifice in service to his country."

"I should not call it that," Michael muttered.

"No? Then what shall you call it, if not a sense of duty to one's neighbors?"

"Perhaps an inevitability, a condemnation, a frightfulness. There is little honor in it, sir. I gave no blood for my country."

"Though witnessed the blood of your countrymen before your very eyes?" Callione insisted.

At this, Michael was silent, reflective. It looked to Lawrence, who remained clued into the conversation from a few adjacent paces, that Michael's eyes welled red and watery. It was, however, not to be the case that the dam blocking the tearful river should break.

"There is no nobility in war, Father, I assure you," he said at nearly a whisper.

"Perhaps you are right, though to subject oneself to its horrors is no small thing, my lad."

"What is the second, Father?"

"The second?"

"Yes, sir, you mentioned two reasons, but named only one."

"Ah, right you are, young man. And so, I'll get to it presently. The second reason is that we are brethren, familiars in a strange land."

"Sir?"

"Why, we are the only two that don't belong. Not in this society. You will forgive my assumption, of course, but men of wealth—that is to say, men who have the type of wealth to afford a stay at the Genovie—and who are simultaneously finding themselves in the service of their country are often officers bred in West Point. It is also my experience that such men sing songs of the glories of war, the romance of battle, without ever having seen one."

"You are a master of puzzles, Father Callione. Though I must point out a bit of an error in your reasoning."

"Oh?"

"Yes, on your final point. Before wishing to dine with me, you had not known my views on the war."

"No, you are correct. Your views on the war cannot be credited in the column of my judgment. But they *can,* and indeed ought to, serve as proof of my judgment's cogency."

"Yes, sir," Michael said, returning to his prior squared posture.

There was something within the boy that kept him reserved. Beyond the order of a regular serviceman. Something deeper, suppressing a demon in his stomach and keeping him a docile mouse wandering in search of a scrap of food, though not daring to trespass into dangerous territory.

"Well," Father Callione said after the waiter came by to take their order of cheeses, caviar, and grapes. "Now that we have gotten motivations out of the way, I should like to ask you how it is you came to be here yourself. And in return, I shall give you my own little story. Perhaps it will be a bit of fun."

"Oh," Michael said, his face flush, "it is not a very interesting story."

"Nonsense, my lad. I spend my days hearing of the transgressions of poor schoolboys who had not the tact to evade the eyes of the sworn sisters of St. Joseph's school. Your story will be a Dickens tale."

"Strange," Michael said, placing a hand over his book.

"Something I said?"

"Yes. Oh, no. At least, not in that way. You see, I was given this book. It is strange that the name should be mentioned twice in one day. I have not thought much about Dickens since I left my mother's house. She used to read it to me as a boy. Er, *Great Expectations*, that is."

"How very curious indeed. Our Lord works in mysterious ways," Father Callione said while crossing himself very slowly and compassionately. "All the more curious for our arrival together. Do go on."

"Well," Michael began, "like I said, there's not all that much to tell. I was sent across country by the army. They said I was to go through evaluation and a short stint at a place of healing, as they call it. I am here on their orders. As a humble soldier, I have little say in where I lodge. Though I must admit, most of my lodgings in the army have been quite less luxurious to say the least."

"A place of—what was it that you said?"

"Healing, sir. Some of us were..." Michael cut himself off, his eyes drifting into a misty glaze.

"That's alright, lad," Father Callione said in a voice as smooth as warm milk. "That's quite alright."

"I'm sorry," Michael choked, his cheeks reddening further.

"Some of us were...in a bad way. When all was said and done. It's a hard thing, war. There's no glory in it, sir, no glory at all."

"No," Father Callione whispered knowingly. "Glory is for the poets, my lad. For the poets and the drunkards."

Michael blinked, looking abashed and unsure of what to say. It was the face of a man who had been used to other's patting him on the shoulder for a service he felt he had failed to commit. A man that had little pride in himself despite the thousands of strange voices speaking in the contrary. Yet, he found a dissenting voice in an unexpected corner of the world.

"Ah, Mr. Erlik!"

The voice was loud and came from the back of the throat like a smooth bullfrog. It was the opposite of the meek and humble vibrations of the soldier and the priest. Lawrence turned, taken from his concentration on their conversation, to view the ghostly figure of Mrs. Doris Applebaum.

The writer labels her as ghostly, for at certain angles she looked as if life had left her altogether. She was a wasted enterprise of a former lavish life. Tall and withered to the bone, she stood with dress that didn't quite grip her, but fell loosely as a child playing dress up in her mother's closet. Her voice, as has just been likened to a croak, did not fit her appearance in any way. It may have been off-putting to the manager to hear the strange juxtaposition, if his mind were not plagued with other ghostly affairs.

All the same, Doris seemed to be a perfectly splendid spirit—or at least, she resembled the remnants of a splendid past. One with pink champagne bubbling in Chrystal glasses, fine caviar and late nights in the cigar rooms of the stuffiest clubs. Simply put,

Doris was a woman of society aged to the foundation.

"Mrs. Applebaum," Lawrence managed to compose himself quick enough to say, "I was beginning to fret you would not join us! How pleasant it is to be proven wrong."

"Oh, you wretched man! You do me a disservice. By the time I leave here I will have a head that has tripled in size. Not exactly the growth my friends would like to see in me, I assure you."

"Nonsense," Lawrence protested. "It is with utter humility in your heart that you fight back with sword and shield. Come, let's find you a table. You are no doubt famished."

It was while Lawrence guided his guest to the center of the café that she stopped in her tracks and said aloud, "I know your voice!"

Lawrence turned to discover the source of the disturbance and found Mrs. Applebaum centered on the carpet, staring at a guest who had just finished ordering a cup of black coffee to round out his dining experience, taking good care to address Anastasia as "pumpkin" as he did.

"Ah," Lawrence said, walking over to meet her. "I see you have found our guest—"

"Don Cherry, radio news man out of Atlanta!" Mr. Cherry nearly shouted with pride, much to the annoyance of a scuttling, eye-rolling Anastasia. "And what beauty have I the honor of meeting?"

"Oh, Mr. Erlik, it seems that I have spoken of wickedness too soon, for it appears I have the devil and his flatteries before my very eyes!" she said with a laugh that Lawrence recognized to encourage further embellishment. To this transparent consent, Cherry—a vulture in his own right—bowed. Before rising, his hand floated underneath the unsuspecting palm of Mrs. Applebaum, raised it halfway between her waist and his chin, and pressed his lips against the paper-thin skin of her knuckles. The obviously entranced Mrs. Applebaum flushed and used her other hand to press her fingers into her chest just below her collar bone. Her eyes glistened as bright as the shine of her lipstick—the shade of which, the writer does not mind admitting, was much too bright for a woman of her age, though seemed to suit her in a way quite indescribable without witness. Perhaps it was her youth of spirit.

Not wanting to risk the ever-compounding possibility of their making him ill with their flatteries, Lawrence pronounced an ignored, "shall I leave the both of you to become acquainted?" and took up his position at the podium. Much to his consternation, he found that the conversation between priest and soldier had progressed far enough that he was unable to become more enlightened on Father Callione's journey for having been disposed to the whims of vanity from his other guests.

However, just as he was about to turn his mind's eye back toward the darkness of the day—which, consequently, was only growing darker with the unexpected storm—a few shaken syllables caught his ear.

"Father," the young soldier muttered.

"Yes, son?"

"Do you believe, well, do you think that one can truly leave the past behind? Or is the truth closer to the premise that the past will continue to show itself, as if in a mirage of torment and remembrance?"

"Well," Father Callione chuckled, "I expect I would be in the wrong line of work if I were to believe in the latter. I would be more willing to concede that the past ill-penitent is a past ill-remembered. Perhaps the man that has not sought forgiveness is doomed to be haunted by his transgressions in this life. I will not harp on the teachings of the life that follows."

"I am unsure, myself," Michael went on, unbeckoned. "I am unsure a man can do anything to dispel the haunts of the events that wound him."

X

Salt stained the threads of Mr. Erlik's lapels as he contemplated the young soldier's hypothesis. The singular tear that fell from a flushed cheek pulled him from a hypnotic spiral of panic, screaming in its wake to pull himself together. He could hear it, as if Sonya Ivanovna were standing beside him. Not only was he roused by such a bone-chilling, infernal cry that seemed to echo in the depths of his perplexed mind, but there was a sharp tug at his jacket sleeve.

"You were looking for me, Mr. Erlik?"

"Huh, what?" he said, spinning himself out of view to clear the moisture from under his eye and compose himself with a slow-drawn breath.

"Miss Aurelia came to me; she never speaks to me. Such a silent little squirrel, that one. So, when she speaks, I listen. And she comes right up to me, nearly knocking me down, and she says, 'Miss Margarette, Mr. Erlik is looking for you!' Just like that. It scared me so. I thought the worst, that I had done something wrong. So, I ran right over, that is why I am so out of breath, sir. So please, if there is something wrong, I demand you tell me at once. Do not hunker about; has there been a complaint?"

Once Lawrence had gathered himself and processed the long-winded tantrum of the old maid, he saw that she was, in fact, out of breath. Poor Margarette. Sweet Margarette. She may not have been held as high in regard by Lawrence as Aurelia, but she took a close second place. It was her insistence on perfection that awarded her such a high-prized position on the managerial roster.

Many years had passed since Margarette came to work at the hotel. Or at least, that is how she told it. "Been here since I was little Meg! I had nothing but the clothes on my back and a little dolly. One day, the manager at the time, God rest his soul, took the dolly and replaced it with a feather duster. I've been cleaning ever since. God bless that man, instilled purpose, he did. Did not let my life fall to idleness." She was a natural favorite.

"No, Margarette. There has not been a complaint."

"Thank heavens! I said to Miss Aurelia, I said, 'Just you wait! Some guest will have it out for me, and I'll be cast out of here, my bottom skipping on the pavement.' Haha, I cannot tell you what a relief it is to be wrong, Mr. Erlik. Such a relief."

That is what kept Aurelia above Margarette. Margarette rambled.

"We would have been the worse for it, Margarette."

"Oh, you jest, you jest! But silly me, here I go blathering and have forgotten to ask what it is you needed. Go on then, I am all ears!"

It was at this moment that Lawrence himself remembered just why he had called the old woman over to his aid. A shudder ran through his bones before he was able to speak. His eyes lowered back to hers after drifting for a moment, only to find she remained staring at him with an inquisitive and suspicious look. *She knows*, he thought. *She knows all about Roman Kosorukov. She knows about Sonya Ivanovna; she's seen her. And she mocks me with her false ignorance.*

"Yes, right," he said, shaking the wickedness from his skull. "Yes, I meant to inform you that we have a very important guest staying with us. A last-minute arrival, one very unexpected. As such, it is important that we do not bother him. That is to say, I should like you not to enter room 319 until I have given you explicit permission to do so.

"But sir, 319 was not in perfect condition. You put a man in a room that has not been properly accommodated! I must go; I must ready it! Can he not have a drink while I—"

"No!" Lawrence nearly shouted, arousing the suspicion of Father Callione. "No," he then whispered. "That is quite alright, Margarette. I have informed the esteemed guest of the state of the room, and he has waved off the need for full accommodation. In fact, he insisted on access now and a strict policy of non-disturbance. I assure you; the state of the room is satisfactory for him, and he will in no way look at its condition as a reflection of your good work, Margarette. Ah! I will have not a word of protest. Trust in your manager, and do not go into that room until he has left, and I have given you word of allowance."

"I do not like this business, Mr. Erlik. What cause does a man have for locking himself in an ill-prepared room?"

"I am afraid that is not for us to concern ourselves with. Our duty is to the guests and what this guest requires, we will see done. Do me the honor of handing me your maid key for room 319." He held out his hand, which had gone visibly clammy.

"Oh, Mr. Erlik, you insult me! If I am given an order, there is no disobeying the directive. What need is there in such petty precautions?"

"I am afraid I must insist, Margarette. And again, I beseech you not to view this as a reflection upon you and your efforts, but rather an acquiescence of the highest degree toward the satisfaction of the guest."

"Yes, well, I suppose. But Mr. Erlik, as you can see, I have come straight to you, leaving my cart behind. I have not the key to the room with me at the moment."

"Run and fetch it. Straight away, I must insist. Consider it the highest importance, my dear Margarette."

"Yes, sir," she offered solemnly.

"And Margarette," Lawrence interjected as she was walking away.

"Yes, Mr. Erlik?"

"You really are among the best of us. Not a single complaint in this universe could cause me to forget that. Your home is here."

These words of kindness (which, it should well be said, were hardly ever uttered by a manager such as Mr. Lawrence Erlik) served to throw the maid off balance and nearly knock her off her feet. However, she was able to remain standing and bowed in a nervous curtsy before fluttering off to accomplish the strange task Lawrence gave her.

There, he breathed to himself, with a slow, methodical pace back toward the front of the lobby. *That is one loose end that has been tied.*

Splattering drops of rain on the windowpanes served to spin the mill wheel of inner dread as Lawrence stood with his hands clasped together around his back. The blur of the running water presented him with the ability to fall into his thoughts with full discretion. Breathing calmed, his heart rate slowed.

"Four lunching guests, three menus, two tables, one storm," he whispered, trying desperately to forget. Forget the dead body rotting into the fibers of the rug in room 319. Forget the looming apparition of a woman Lawrence had never met, brought here to plague a man no longer breathing, transferred through her undying will to torment Lawrence.

The rain had turned from a light spit to a howling thunder in the time that Lawrence had spent lunching—or rather, seeing to the lunch of his guests. By the time he reached the entrance, he could hardly see the road leading to the hotel. Ordinarily, it was a brilliant path to behold. Strange exotic trees grew along the sides of the road, masking the hotel's beauty until the very moment when transportation turned the corner and showed the building's beauty in an instant flash of radiance. Cut off from society, the hotel made itself into its own secluded island, aiding in the serenity of a stay well accented by precious anonymity.

The front gardens would blossom from March to November; unseasonably resplendent was the phrase most often uttered by guests who took notice. And many guests took notice.

But now, during the wrath of Poseidon's temper, the exterior of the hotel was a grizzly grey mire.

"It's almost haunting, isn't it?" Cyrus's voice was a low raspy whisper behind his ear. Lawrence was too transfixed on the fright itself to confound his inability to pick up on the click of Cyrus's approaching heel on the marble floor.

"Steady on," Lawrence started.

"Now, now, Lawrence, it doesn't do good to abandon one's wits. I did not mean to startle you, my dear."

"Well, perhaps you should have refrained from hissing in my ear."

"Hissing?" Cyrus laughed. "Yes, I suppose it was rather slithery of me. I do apologize. Such an unexpected turn of events with this storm. The day is turning out to be beyond expectations altogether it seems!"

"What do you mean? What is unexpected?" Lawrence snapped. *He knows.*

"Calm down, Lawrence, I am only repeating what you've told me yourself. Something about a frantic guest, is that right? And what was the other thing, a booking error? And now this storm. It's all quite an interesting coincidence, haven't you thought? But you know what they say."

"No," Lawrence calmed himself with a long, silent breath. "No, what do they say?"

"Why, bad things come in threes. I don't know if I much believe that myself, but the minds of people are funny in that way. So creatively superstitious. They often find the white hair on a black horse and cry for the devil's hanging."

"I don't understand you, Cyrus."

"Me?"

"The very same. You go on about your contempt for fine talk and philosophy and yet you stand here with your grand statements about the people of the world. People you've never met or spoken to or even seen, I gather." Lawrence was nearly breathless from his exhaustive rant.

"That is where you are wrong, dear Lawrence. Before my time in our good hotel, I spent much of my life wandering the sewers of the cities of the world. Breaking bread with the destitute and the hopeless, sharing in their torment."

"Yes, I suppose you did," Lawrence chided. "And did you dine with the pope as well?"

"No," Cyrus said, gazing out into the drudge of the storm, not taking heed of the sarcasm spitting from his companion's mouth. "No, far too much vanity. Not like the old days, not how I remember it."

"Remember what?"

"Hm? Oh, nothing, Lawrence. Look at me, rambling in the rain. Just what I need, another excuse for babble." Cyrus took to leave, but Lawrence turned toward him, furrowing his brow.

"Remember what?'

"It's nothing, my dear. Speaking nonsense of history books and wives' tales. I really must be returning to my work."

"And what work is that, exactly?" Lawrence spat. But Cyrus walked away passively, as if to announce he had not heard this remark, or if he had, he had not cared to dignify it with a response.

For Lawrence's part, he was left feeling rather uncomfortable with the way in which Cyrus's eye had gleamed in the light of the chandelier, now lit bright to pierce through the darkness of the storm. His heart began to compound with a sickness of mind, brought on by the whole affair. Just being around Cyrus bothered Lawrence. It was as if he really did know what had happened in room 319. He knew and he was willing to torture Lawrence with that knowledge.

Lawrence had half a mind to storm over to him. To march right up and shout, "Yes, he's dead. There was nothing I could do to stop him, and there is nothing I can do now that he is gone!" In fact, he had nearly taken the first step in such an action before there was another, familiar tug at his jacket sleeve.

"Mr. Erlik," the timid voice remarked. "Oh, are you alright? You are giving me a fright, sir. I am sorry to have disturbed you, I only—"

"That is quite alright, Margarette, quite alright."

"Oh, but you look, bless me, you look like the Devil himself has been playing with your head. Are you sure you are alright, sir?" At the word devil, Margarette made sure to cross herself several times and nod in an attempt to ward off any contagion that might be found from being so close to an afflicted soul and daring to utter the word.

"I assure you, Margarette, there is no need for concern." Lawrence found himself growing rather annoyed as the conversation continued. His eyes surveyed the lobby to distract him away from his aggravation.

"Bless me," Margarette muttered and swallowed a dry lump, looking him up and down as if she were faced with a malevolent shadow.

"Alright, enough blessing, Margarette. What is it you want? That is quite enough of that as well," he added as she raised her hand to sign the cross for what Lawrence had no earthly guess as to how many times it had been. "For goodness' sake, there is enough superstition roaming about these old halls without all that nonsense."

Lawrence turned red and felt the heat rise in his cheek as his inferior was demonstrably offended by his outburst. Two tugs of the waistcoat cooled his temperament enough to dispel hesitance from the quivering maid. "I am sorry, sir," she said, but dared not continue in her apology at the sign of Lawrence closing his eyes and twitching his head in an attempt to fight back the steam that was wanting to burst through his ears. "Anyway," she continued, "here is that key you asked me for. I am sorry for the delay in getting it for you. But, as I told you, I left my cart right away when Miss Aurelia called for me."

"Key?"

"Yes, room 319, like you said."

It came rushing back like a motor car. "Yes, that is right. 319. And you are sure you found your cart quite as it was? No signs of tampering of any kind, no missing keys?"

"What? Oh, no, sir. Should there have been? Is there

something—"

"No, Miss Margarette, no. There is nothing. I am sorry I bothered you with asking. Run along to the rest of your duties, then. You have been made aware that the penthouse is occupied, I trust?"

"Yes, sir!" She nodded, clearly happy to be back on familiar footing. "Right away." She turned to leave, but before she did so, she stopped, and a look of consternation scrunched her face to half its size. "There is something that maybe you should know…"

"Yes, well?"

"Well, it's just, perhaps you already know. And, you know, it is none of my business what guests do in their rooms and who comes and who stays. I look down and try not to notice these things, Mr. Erlik, you know that. But it is that you've only just yourself brought the room to top of mind, and as it happened my cart was on the third floor."

"Yes…"

"You said there was a gentleman staying in that room."

"I did."

"And that gentleman was alone."

"Quite alone."

"And that he wished not to be disturbed."

"Yes, yes this is all as I said."

"Very well, sir. So, you see, I remember everything. Well, I'll tell you what I saw, then. Not that I am in the habit of looking for anything, mind you. It is only that—"

"Yes, only that I brought the room to your attention. Yes, yes, go on."

"Right to it, then. Well, I saw someone enter the room."

"You mean earlier today, before you came to see me?"

"No, sir, just now. As I was getting the key for you. I saw

someone walking down the hall and open the door. It seemed as if it were unlocked."

Lawrence felt his stomach split into three equal parts before dropping to the floor. Zeus struck three titans dead to the ground with a triumphant volley of lightning just outside the front of the hotel, startling even poor Miss Margarette.

"You are...quite certain?" Lawrence muttered.

"Yes, sir. Ordinarily, I would not say anything even now. But you see, it was so curious because you said he was alone. But I am speaking of a woman."

"A woman?" His lips were numb as he spoke. The haze of shimmering light coming from the chandelier felt as if it were attempting to blind him, as if it carried a will and malice of its own.

"Yes, sir. A woman."

"What did she look like?"

"I cannot say much, exactly. I did not get a look at her; my eyes are not very sharp these days. And I was at the end of the hall. But I know it was a woman; she was wearing a dress."

"What color dress?"

"It is hard to say from that distance. Beige, maybe grey. I do not think I can say for certain."

"Very well," Lawrence said sharply. "Thank you for telling me, Margarette. Keep your watchful eyes on the evils of dust for me, would you?"

"Oh, yes, sir. Of course, sir. Thank you!"

"What for?"

"I am not quite sure, but thank you all the same." She gave a nod and, for the second time, made to leave. Again, for the second time, she stopped herself mid-turn and moved her eyes questioningly toward Lawrence.

"Yes," he said quite contemptuously. It would have appeared the news of this inauspicious occurrence involving a mysterious woman entering room 319 had rather erased Lawrence's ability to be calm in the face of overzealous hotel maids.

"I am sorry, sir. It is only that there is a scrap of paper trying to break free from your pocket. I wouldn't want you to lose anything important."

"What? Oh, so there is. Thank you, Margarette." With this final thank you—and it was indeed forcibly put in such a way that Margarette dared not utter another word, nay, another syllable until she had seen to the clearing of every speck of dust in the whole of the hotel—Margarette made her leave on the third and final attempt.

When he ensured she made it a suitable distance so as to no longer be at risk of a third turning and a further insufferable blathering, he pulled the slip of paper from his pocket. A queer thing, it was. It was a strip of paper that looked as if, at some point in its life, it had been folded several times over. To the point where the creases grew fuzzy with tiny fibers breaking away from the initial sheet. It was a piece of paper Lawrence had never seen before, and as such had no earthly idea when or how it had ended up in his pocket. Yet there it was.

His attention was stolen away for a brief second as his ears picked up the faint sound of a harsh gurgling croak that had echoed in the chambers of his mind for hours now. Yet as he looked around in the pouring rain, his eyes were unsuccessful in finding its source. There was no raven staring at him in the downpour, no pair of beady eyes watching his every move. Though that did not stop him from walking out of sight, over to the corner of the lobby, where he returned his attention to the scrap of paper.

It burned in his hand as he lifted it within sight. Crediting that sensation to his newly rogue imagination, he ignored it and proceeded to inspect the bit of parchment. The first side—that is, the one wherein his eyes settled first—was barren. Worn thin and nearly snubbed out with grease. Turning the devilish scrap over, however, Lawrence was able to make out mysteriously faded writing. So faded, in fact, that it looked as if it had been written centuries ago and had somehow managed to survive the harshness of that inexorable femme fatale who names herself Time. One word.

Murderer!

XI

Sulfur is often a worrying thing when the nose picks up its scent. No less so when one is surrounded by the beauty of a fine hotel. Such as it was, it was not precisely the smell of sulfur singing the manager's nose hairs. In fact, he had altogether ignored his sense of smell, not questioning the source of the strange odor. Nor was it the echo of the raven's caw, nor the shadow and applause of rolling thunder that sent Lawrence into a conniption of frantic counting and quivering as he teetered back and forth on the edge of sanity.

The writer fully concedes that it is impossible to ascertain the exact state of the manager's so-called sanity, as one never really knows if oneself is secure in the safety of a proper mind, let alone the status of others. But suffice it to say, it was, at the least, worrying to the casual onlooker, who would be well within his or her rights to be concerned over the state of mind the nervous manager seemed to be fighting. It was all in the pallor.

But where was I before I lost myself in talk of pigmentation? Ah yes, the source of our dear friend's vexation. The reader might well guess that it was the scrap of paper that caused the shivering bones to rattle through his frame.

It was now his prerogative to ferret out the offender of this macabre message. Who was speaking to him in such an ominous fashion? While that question was certainly top of mind for Lawrence, what was forming a deeper sense of malaise was the motive. The sender's knowledge on the subject.

Certainly, as he saw it, whoever sent the message belonged in one of two categories. It was either that the sender had full knowledge of the events that occurred and decided to untruthfully accuse him of a ghastly, unforgivable sin. Or—and this Lawrence feared more than the former possibility—the sender had only partial awareness of the events that took place in room 319 and was genuinely accusing Lawrence of the suspected crime.

The reason—or perhaps I should say reasons—Lawrence found this possibility more dreadful than the last, was the danger of such a rogue inquisitor. For, as it may well have been the case, if our mystery sender was under the impression that a murder was to have taken place, then surely that accuser could not have bore witness to the events as they unfolded. Which meant, much to the consternation of the disheveled manager, the sender had found him out in another way. Why did this matter? For if the sender had not borne witness and instead found out another way, the only singular possibility of that having happened would be through the passage of the sender through the door of room 319. A calamitous affair.

This was even further unsettling because if a man were to have known precisely what had happened and was simply sending this foul note in order to stir a fanciful reaction—well, Lawrence would know how to handle that. Men of extortion were predictable. It was a man of honest intentions that he had the most concern for. Their insistence on doing the right and proper thing would prove inconvenient. There was no way to prove his innocence against a man who had not witnessed the crime. And he *was* innocent, according to his own logic.

"I had nothing to gain," he muttered to himself in the fashion of a man who has long forgotten the comforts of a well put together existence and given himself to drink and wild illusions. "Of course, I am innocent. I had no quarrel with Kosorukov; I had no envy, nor malice, nor ill-content. This writer, this coward who sends his accusation in ink, knows nothing.

"Or perhaps he knows everything. An honest man would not send his accusation through covert inscription. He would phone the law, send a telegram, and have them here by the dining hour.

"Or he wants me to sweat while I await their arrival. What will I say? How will I explain all this? They'll ask why I haven't called; they'll ask why Kosorukov would call me to the room to witness his suicide. They'll say I contrived the whole of it. The absurd stay, the long-winded confession, they'll even convince themselves that *I* broke the radiator, that *I* brought the knife. I must do something, but what?"

If a guest were to have seen the way in which Lawrence began pacing and muttering to himself back and forth under the glisten of the chandelier, they would have figured he had given himself to lunacy. It was even a thought that had crossed his own mind; one he was able to dispel on proof of the fact that if one had gone mad, surely the evidence of one's madness would be found in one's inability to conceive of said madness. Since Lawrence was able to concern himself with the mere possibility of madness, he must have been in his right mind. It was decided. Of all of Lawrence's concerns, of which there were many, he could not discount for himself the fact that he was not mad.

With that out of the way, he turned himself back to the problem of who the sender was. Here, there were two separate questions to be tackled. Who was the sender and did the sender do the deed of placing the parchment in his pocket himself? Or had he employed the hand of another, further tainting the pool of likely suspects to this crime against his sanity?

The most likely scenario was, of course, that the sender was the same as the courier. The simplest solution being the most likely, as Lawrence saw it. But if that were the case, who had done it? Cyrus liked to play games with Lawrence, sure, but he liked to bear witness to the torment. He enjoyed the battle of will and wit. His was not such a sinister ploy.

Margarette was too innocent a creature. Her suggestion that he keep the scrap from falling on the ground itself proved her ignorance to the scrap's contents. Cherry. The little frog stinking of ash and brandy. Perhaps it was him. Perhaps. But Lawrence was far from certain on any aspect of the whole affair.

The one thing he felt sure of was he had to return to room 319.

Taking off at a bit of a run, Lawrence attempted to step with light feet out of the lobby and in the direction of the lift. It was just when the gate was in sight that he heard a hurried, "Mr. Erlik!"

Lawrence stopped in his tracks with an air of defeat, his eyes bouncing back and forth between the offender of his delay and the chariot that was meant to take him toward the solution to all his problems. Whatever it was the manager had stressfully decided that solution was.

"Yes, Baptiste?" Erlik gritted. It was a most curious thing for a manager so attentive as Lawrence to have missed a flushed Aurelia scurrying from behind the desk where, up until the point of Lawrence's halt, Baptiste had been leaning over.

"I think there's a bit of an emergency." The way Baptiste scratched the back of his head and scrunched his face, as if feigning simplicity of the mind, irked Elrik to the point of tapping the tips of his shoes in a vain attempt at expelling the annoyance from the depths of his chest.

"You think...there's an emergency?" he asked, his mind half screwed into the matter and half running away from him to room 319. *Of course, there's an emergency. There is always some emergency unfolding in this God forsaken building.* "Well," he said aloud, "what is it then?"

"I'm not quite sure," Baptiste said. "It's just...Joel. He called up here a moment ago, wanted to speak with you. I told him you were busy with the guests at lunch, but he said it was urgent. He said you should join him in the cellar."

"The cellar?"

"That's what he said, sir."

"And in hearing that this matter was urgent, you felt the most pressing task ahead of you was to lounge about the front desk rather than find me presently?"

"Well, no, sir. It's not that way. I went to the café first, but you weren't there. Most of the guests had left, so I figured you'd be at the front desk. I was just asking Aurelia where I could—"

"Alright, Baptiste, stay your stuttering. Please. Now, to the cellar."

"You want...me to come with you?"

"Naturally, my boy. It is high time the two of us rolled up our sleeves. After all, I am having an awful premonition that this has something to do with the storm. I suspect that we will find ourselves in need of great haste, and I cannot waste time running about looking for you."

"Right, sir. Right." The twisted expression of fear that paled the young man's face gave Lawrence a spot of pleasure. Perhaps that is not the right term, and the reader will forgive me. It must be understood that Lawrence was not a cruel man. No, not even in the slightest. I have claimed since the onset that the staff did very much prefer working under his leadership than any prior management. Seeing the fear on the boy's face did not give him pleasure so much as it gave him relief. Relief that he was not the only soul shivering within the shackles of fear, binding them to the animal-like state of childish trepidation.

The objects of their fears were, in one way, quite opposite. Or perhaps one might think they were very much the same. Baptiste was terrified of ghosts. It was among Lawrence's first few weeks on the job that he found Joel had been spreading rumors of ghosts lurking in the corners of the cellar. He told them to the triplets in an effort to get them to "shite their breeches," as he so eloquently described it. It also seemed to give the old man pleasure to witness the exasperation of the young ladies that found employment at the hotel. Primarily the waitstaff. Lawrence believed that Joel would have continued his tyrannical terror of stories until he succeeded in getting so much as a wince out of young Aurelia—who, the reader might well have guessed, was reluctant to give him the satisfaction.

So it was that both Lawrence and Baptiste carried on toward the cellar, their fears of the supernatural haunting their steps. It pleased Lawrence, or rather comforted him, that he was in the intellectually superior position of fearing his own experience rather than the fear of a superstition. Of a wives' tale.

But that comfort did not last long. For as soon as that thought entered his mind, it was pushed out by the all too real possibility of having another run-in with Sonya Ivanovna. In fact, that was precisely his reason for dragging the poor bellman along on this journey. The fear of the specter of Kosorukov's greatest sin.

Naturally, no one else had borne witness to her presence. Lawrence felt there were two distinct possibilities in having Baptiste accompany him. The first being that if he were with another soul at every waking moment, the spirit of Sonya Ivanovna would leave him alone through the guise of not wanting to reveal herself to the innocent of heart. The second—and much to the manager's shame, the possibility that he rather hoped for in a cruel and twisted sort of way—was that Sonya did show herself. If this were to unfold, as Lawrence saw it, Baptiste would then be a living testament to his account of what happened in room 319. That is, if the sender of the formidable little scrap of paper were the honest type as mentioned previously. In such a happenstance, those who wished to see the downfall of the manager could not blame his accounting of the tale as the blathering of a raving lunatic. He only hoped the young man had the capacity to keep his sanity intact long enough to provide such a critical testimony.

"What's that smell?" Baptiste could not help but spew as he raised his wrist to his nose.

"Good heavens, boy. You'll get snot on your uniform. Take this." Lawrence produced a small white handkerchief from his pocket and handed it to Baptiste.

"Rat shite," an old croak of a voice called from around a corner. The pair stood perched at the midway of the stairs leading down into the cellar, Baptiste clutching his newly acquired handkerchief in one hand and a torch in the other. Lawrence was beginning to regret pulling his handkerchief out for anyone's use but his own and fingered around his pockets for anything else that might be of use. Just as he was about to give up, he felt in the right breast pocket of his jacket, the lump of a small cotton square. Reaching in, he felt his luck increase for once and pulled out a second handkerchief, pressing it to his mouth.

The cellar was more of an underground cave than a functional storage space. The walls looked as if they were carved from the earth with large rotting beams plastered to their sides to keep them from falling. The beams inspired little confidence, the rocks little comfort. Ownership—no doubt, in an effort to pinch a few pennies in one of the few areas of the hotel that did not concern the experience of the beloved guests—elected to refrain from having the cellar properly lit when fitting the hotel for electricity in 1902. One dismal bulb flickered in the center of the cellar. Any hope one had of sight came from one's foresight to bring a quality lamp or torch. Joel preferred his lighter.

Worse, on this particular occasion than the hollow lighting, the worrying rot, or the ghastly smell, was the sound of flowing water.

"It's all gon'ta hell, Mr. Erlik. All gon'ta hell! Uh can't help this storm, she breachin' ar castle like cannon on stone!" Joel came waddling from around a stone wall and, much to the manager's chagrin, his grey trousers had gone dark from the hem up to the kneecap.

"What is this all about, Joel? What has happened?" Lawrence stepped down the stairs, not quite sure whether the squeaks he heard came from the rickety steps or from excited mice. Enshrouding himself in the darkness of the cellar felt almost as if he were being pulled by some force. An unwelcome force. Had the manager let his imagination get the better of himself, he might have concluded that Sonya had grabbed ahold of his collar, pulled him down the steps, and slammed the door shut.

Baptiste didn't much care for the sound of the creaking door hitting the latch himself. But the door was installed on an angle, one of the very few architecturally incorrect features of the hotel. So, it was often given to closing against the will of its opener. All the same, it being a normal occurrence did not much comfort Baptiste—nor, for that matter, Lawrence. The only living soul unbothered by the whole affair was the old handyman that stood with soaked trousers and spat a hunk of tobacco juice from his mouth onto the stone floor.

"What on earth?" The offense was enough to pull Lawrence from his bitter thoughts. "What have I told you about that disgusting habit? Spitting on our own floors, I'll have you know…"

"Awright, Mr. Erlik, awright. I won't be doin' it a second time, I tell ya that. Sides, the water'll be warshing an' polishing yer precious floors in no time."

"Water?"

"Aye, the storm, sir. The storm is breachin our walls." It was commonplace for Joel to make a bigger deal of things than they actually were, though Lawrence always appreciated the urgency he tended to show all things concerning the hotel. He was the perfect infantryman. "The Lord's a-comin, I tell ye. That Babylonian whore'll be 'ere too. Bout time if you ask me. Thought she was going to throw herself upon us during the war. The end is comin', that's what I've been sayin' all these years. Time's at hand, it is."

"Yes, alright Joel. Alright. Are we able to stick to the matter at hand before we trouble ourselves with…with…"

"That Babylonian whore."

"Yes, that's the one. We'll get to her next. First, what's this about water?"

"She's flooding, sir."

"The hotel?"

"The cellar. Been fillin' her belly with the drink of Noah, she 'as. Can't do much to help her, she has a fierce thirst."

"Does he mean the storm is causing the cellar to flood?" Baptiste asked with a shake in his voice.

Joel simply looked at him and nodded with a short grunt.

"But the storm is not *that* bad, is it?"

"She's a bad one, sir. God's throwin' something' fierce at us, I tell ye."

"Alright, Joel. I understand. Are you able to fix it?"

"Aye, fer now. I don't know how long she'll hold, but I can at least plug the leak. Might not stop it, but maybe slow to a trinkle. 'At way we can pump her dry in the morrow."

"Tomorrow? Would it not be better to take care of this now?" Lawrence protested. As he uttered the final word, something brushed the back of his ankle, ruffling the perfect drape of his slacks. A jump and a sharp whip around came at too slow a pace for him to catch sight of the offending party.

"Today's no good, sir. She'll just keep stormin'. I tell you, mark my words, the Lord hath spoken and he spake of terror and vengeance!" Ordinarily, the simplicity of Joel's ecclesiastical fervor made it easy for Lawrence to roll his eyes and carry on. However, there was something about this unexpected storm, the chill of the dreadful cellar, the lurking memory of Sonya Ivanovna that made this particular sermon most stirring. Perhaps there really was a fearful fire in the sky, condemning the misdeeds of those he—or it, for all Lawrence knew—oversaw. "Terror and vengeance," Joel repeated at more of a whisper, looking down at the ground.

It was at this point that the water began to flow from around the corner and seeped toward Lawrence's toes. As the cellar was at a frightful slant, the creeping of the small pond had remained out of sight.

"Right, then," Lawrence said, stepping slowly backward until his heel found the first step of the creaking staircase. "Do what you can, Joel, and see to it that I am kept updated on the situation."

Expecting a brisk nod and a "yes, sir," Lawrence was perplexed to find the old handyman standing idle, his hand scratching the back of his head, his eyes fixed on the incoming water. Teetering back and forth, he repeated in a soft, low mumble, "terror and vengeance, terror and vengeance."

"Should we tell him about the radiator?" Baptiste, who had chosen the virtue of the silent attendee up until that point, asked.

"What? No, no. That is not—no." He tugged at his waistcoat as the color drained from his face. "Keep quiet, Baptiste!"

"Yes, sir. I was only trying—"

"I am well aware, and I thank you. But please, let me handle it." Lawrence did his best to tone his temperament to an unsuspecting level of annoyance. His attempts were futile.

Turning back to Joel, Lawrence was relieved to find the old man had not overheard Baptiste's inconvenient suggestion. He continued to stand, as if a haunted statue of ivory, looking thoughtlessly toward the abyss. Or perhaps deep in thought.

"Joel!" Lawrence shouted, clapping his hands to gain the handyman's attention. The effort was fruitful, producing an animated start from the poor sod. "I'm sorry," Lawrence said, resuming an air of disinterest. "Will you please—"

"Keep you updated. Yes, sir. What's this about a radiator?"

Lawrence felt a lump form in the back of his throat, the kind that alters one's voice when one attempts to choke out the words. "Nothing, Joel. It's nothing. Only a guest who thought it was broken. I saw to it."

"It's best to leave the handiwork to me, sir."

"Yes, Joel. I meant no breach of conduct, it was only—"

"Otherwise, people could get hurt. Ye coulda' burnt yer finger or cut yer hand!"

"Yes, that is true," Lawrence conceded with a prickly feeling creeping up the back of his neck. "I am sorry; next time I will make sure to inform you."

"Thank ye, sir."

"Carry on, Joel. Baptiste," Lawrence said, hissing into his handkerchief, "come with me."

The pair marched up the stairs and spoke not a word until they reached the light of the first floor.

"Is there…anything I can do, sir?" Baptiste asked, handing the borrowed handkerchief back to his manager. "That was something else, I tell you. That place gives me a proper fright, every time. You know, I once heard that a pair of guests went down there, a husband and wife on their honeymoon. The husband, in a rage, drew his saber (one of those military types, or so I was told) and lopped her head clean off! They say she roams the cellar, looking for her head at every corner. They say you can hear her weeping late at night. Supposedly, that's when it all happened, you know."

Lawrence was too caught in his own thoughts to interrupt the spirited retelling of the most ridiculous story he had ever heard. Perhaps if he let him get it all out, it would be the last of this nonsense.

"And who are *they*, exactly?" Lawrence asked with a hint of contempt. Not for the boy, surely, but for whoever filled his ears with such fairy tales.

"Well, er, Joel is the one who told me."

"Ah, and has Joel been recognized as the authority of hotel

history since I last checked?"

"Is there such an authority, sir?"

"What? Of course not, Baptiste. Try to follow along. That is just the point, isn't it? If there is no such authority, then surely Joel cannot be your source of information."

"But, sir, if there is no such authority then wouldn't Joel be a perfect, unchallenged source of information?"

"No, that is not correct. That he is unchallenged, you have right. But you have forgotten that the absence of challenge does not prove the validity. In fact, it must make one be more on one's guard than before."

"But…why?" Baptiste twisted his face in confusion, trying not to be rude but clearly wishing to leave the conversation.

"Isn't it obvious? If there is no authority to challenge the validity of a speaker, one must be less willing to take what one hears as gospel for the simple matter of not having the safety of the authority. As such, even the most confounded foolishness can run amuck without the slightest interference."

"And so could the truth, sir."

"Indeed, so could the truth. And that is where it is important to keep one's wits about them. Tell me, how does one learn the truth?"

"I don't know, sir."

"Well, it seems a bit silly to take everything at face value, does it not?"

"I dunno, I guess you could say so."

"I would. I would say that looking for facts is where virtue lies, would you agree?"

Baptiste loosened his posture and tilted his head, as if pondering this question before concluding: "Yes, I suppose I would."

"*Précisément*, dear Baptiste. So, perhaps it would behoove you to search the records for this heinous act whose truth you so willingly believed."

"The records, sir?"

"In my office, you will find records of notable events of the hotel in the cabinet. Third drawer." Lawrence handed him a small, insignificant looking key. The look of astonishment on the young boy's face gave Lawrence a moment of pleasure as he nodded consent to rummage through the managerial office.

"Do not make me regret allowing this one slackening of the rules."

"No, sir. Not at all, sir!"

"Remember, third drawer." Baptiste hardly stuck around to confirm the drawer that contained the information he had renewed interest in. He twisted and began at a bit of a run. But what a dutiful bellman he was. Before he got too far, he stopped himself, quickly walked back, and asked, "Will you be needing anything else before I go?"

"No, that is quite alright. It appears Joel does not need our help at the moment."

"Thank you, sir!"

With that, he disappeared from the manager's sight.

In consequence to the small distraction, Lawrence had nearly forgotten the lucky occurrence of having a second handkerchief on his person. In the cellar, when his nose was in desperate need of reprieve, he hadn't quite worried himself with how the handkerchief got into his pocket.

However, now that he was released from the clutches of the wicked smell, he found himself overcome with curiosity. Was it an old bit of cloth he had forgotten to remove upon last wearing this jacket? How long had it been in there? Had he swiped a handkerchief thinking it his and placed it in the most unusual location as the right breast pocket?

Looking down, meaning to inspect the object for any such clue that might answer his little inquisition, he found—with a nasty spell of horror—the fabric was covered with a large splotch of red that he could only identify as blood. Worried, he touched his hand to his nose, checking for any sign of a hemorrhage he had somehow not noticed. Finding it quite dry, he returned his gaze to the peculiar article to further inspect and found an embroidery stitched into the corner. Three lonely letters. RPK.

The handkerchief was immediately dropped on the ground and Lawrence's feet backed up against the wall. His breath turned to a huff; his mind scattered. Finally, he spoke, forcing himself to utter the words drifting to the surface of his consciousness.

"Roman Pavlovich Kosorukov!"

XII

Just about the same time Lawrence was busying himself with excessive pacing in front of the front doors, Michael had come to the end of his lunch.

It was with the utmost respect and cordiality that he saw fit to excuse himself from the old priest's company, thanking him for a lovely conversation and the comfort of companionship. However, there was something settling in the pit of the young soldier's stomach that set him in a fit of unease. Something restless. Owing to this unfortunate humor he found himself in, Michael decided that returning to his room, lending himself to idleness while awaiting the next opportunity to dine, was an ill-advised notion. Best to take a bit of a walk.

But where to go? Certainly, the hotel was a grand old maiden, but a man of Michael's sensibilities did not crave adventure. In fact, all the adventure he had ever had in his life was involuntarily hoisted on his shoulders. Uncle Sam even did him the disservice of claiming it a gift. To see the world on the nation's dime. All Michael ever saw was downed trees and immeasurably large shell craters.

As it was, the feeling rising in Michael's chest, as he looked out to the grandeur of the marble pillars bearing the integrity of the Genovie on their shoulders, was one that inspired confidence. A fruitful adventure. That's what this was going to be, was destined to be.

However, Michael did not know the way. That is, once he had set his mind on the destination, narrowed from the limited clues given to him by the hotel's staff during the short duration of his stay thus far, he had little idea of where to find it. But the young soldier had a fond memory of the twinkle in the manager's eyes when he had winked and uttered the heartwarming line that Mr. Dickens had scribbled down all those decades ago. Ever the best of friends, Pip.

Surely, the obliging manager would see fit to set him about in the proper direction of his aims. However, fortune did not seem to favor this chance meeting of two souls. Michael felt Mr. Erlik and he were connected in some way—the manner in which two souls happen upon each other and feel the tender warmth of familiarity even before sampling the taste of one another's names falling from the tongue. Even though Michael felt such a serendipitous connection, one could not find fault in the young soldier for his pause when he discovered the manager pacing about the entry to the lobby, muttering vexatiously to himself in a way that reminded one of an old hound with a cough. Such a picture could be reliably labeled anything but approachable.

Instead, our dear young soldier found it fit to find the help he so desired within another source. A gentler source.

"Er…" Michael began. However, finding himself gravitating toward the front desk as if being pulled to it, Michael found he was more likely to choke on his spit than to force his simple question from the back of his throat. And how could he be blamed? For standing behind the prestige ivory of the front desk was the most unimaginatively beautiful flower. Dazzling red hair gleamed in the light of the chandelier. A fair complexion gave way to a painting of freckles, and the grace of her gait was such that Michael could hardly believe she was of the vileness of such a sinful species as man.

Her face seemed to do all the talking for her. There was something in the way she raised her brow and curled her lips and narrowed her eyes that made one feel an ease of comfort. Any other conveyor of such an expression might leave one feeling condescended. But not from this fair creature.

The reader will have doubtlessly guessed that the fair creature mentioned was our very own Aurelia. And indeed, Michael was not the only one made better for this chance encounter. The reader might well have assumed, knowing what has been conveyed thus far in this record, that Aurelia was beginning to feel a bit flummoxed from the sight of her employer. As it was, her heart felt a bit of a flutter at the handsome young soldier's gawking gaze.

It is true that Aurelia had gotten used to the male eye finding its way to her soft features. But it was seldom the case that she found herself enjoying the admiration. As in this sense, those rare occasions were often met with a delicacy in her demeanor.

"Li—library," our young Montague so eloquently began.

And yet our lady Capulet found him charming just the same. To give him a second chance, she tilted her head slightly and softened her lips.

"S-sorry, miss. I meant to say," Michael began anew, his courage rising, "that Mr. Erlik made mention earlier of a library. I was only wondering if I could be pointed in that direction? If it's not too much trouble, that is."

Aurelia nodded her understanding and stepped down from

her tower of the front desk to level herself with the inquiring soldier. As she began to lead the way, waving her hand for him to follow, Michael interrupted her progress by saying, "Oh, I wouldn't bother a lady to show me the way. I mean, you must be so busy. If you were to just...point me in the right direction, I might find my way on my own."

Aurelia's expression started tight and pursed, but as he went on, she dulled its edges and let out a deep breath before taking his hand in hers. Turning the palm to face the heavens, she placed her index finger on the flat of it just where it met the wrist. Then, through a quick succession of points, she indicated this to be where they stood. She then traced across his palm a long line, two right turns and then a left, followed by another line and a final right turn.

When Michael nodded his understanding (perhaps prematurely) she closed his hand gently and squeezed it twice with her own. It is difficult for those of us too far removed from the charms of the unspoken throes of love and youth to understand the flush that coursed through Michael's cheeks. Yet we may rest assured in the virtues of his desire and the gentleness of his manners. He harnessed the strength to nod his thanks, and a quick grin sent enough charm to warm even the heart of our stone-faced Aurelia to a melting point.

From that point on, whenever she saw Michael roaming about the lobby or heading toward the lift or marching toward the promise of a drink at the Golden Swan, Aurelia had an eye watching over him.

Now, our Aurelia is nothing if not fastidious. Her

directions, followed by Michael to the detail, brought him precisely to the doorway of the grand library.

Perhaps grand is not an unerring descriptor for our library. But for a man of Michael's upbringing, it might have been the grand halls of Alexandria before her perilous dance with the devil to the symphony of crashing spark and flame. Poor Michael Goodman had seldom seen a stack of books together, let alone a collection as plentiful as the Genovie's.

It is proper and true that a hotel ought to have enough reading material on hand should a guest have forgotten their copy of *Crime and Punishment* or *The Woman in White*, or even *Madame Bovary*! Are we to expect our guests to pick up some random volume for the duration of their stay, muddling the memory of the story they had been working through? Nonsense. So that our guests may pick up where they left off, the Genovie subscribed to the notion that a copy of each classic must be on hand at all times. In some cases, for the more popular of stories, two were kept. Such was the case with the copy of *Great Expectations* that Michael held tightly in his grasp upon entering the library. While Mr. Erlik had seen fit to relieve the library of such a treasure (in fact, it was a first edition!), the librarian was not aware of such intentions. It was with no small amount of luck that young Michael was able to sneak it under her nose.

"Can I help you, dear?" The librarian was an old maid, the type one considers when imaging a lover of dusty pages and leather bindings. She was prim, she was proper, and she knew every location of every volume without so much as having to reference the chart so exceptionally put together utilizing the indexes thought up by the ingenious Dewey and his decimals.

"Oh," Michael muttered, caught embarrassingly off guard. He seemed to have been making a habit of falling victim to the charms of maids behind tall desks, young and old. "I'm sorry, I just thought I'd...walk among the stories, miss."

"Ah, I'm afraid the books are kept under my care, but if there is a certain volume you are itching to read, I would wager I could find it for you. Or perhaps a recommendation? A strapping young lad like you no doubt likes tales of adventure! Pirates and gold and dragons and battles!"

"No!" Michael snapped, though not sharply enough to cause offense. Only enough that Margery found herself taking a new course of action.

"Perhaps philosophy then! I believe we have works of Mr. Freud, or perhaps a little more ancient. I'm sure your schooling has taught you Cicero, Aristotle, Plato?"

"Er," Michael stammered, never feeling more ashamed of his lack of education. "No, ma'am. I'm afraid I've never had proper schooling."

"And who is to say what's proper, dear boy?"

"I'm afraid I don't know, ma'am."

"Ah, so afraid, this one. What are you afraid of? Nonsense. What is it I can get for you then? A romance?"

"No, ma'am. I think I should be well serviced with what I've already got. I just felt like settling in amongst the books is all. I shall get out of your way."

Michael had begun to take his first step out the door when the old librarian cleared her throat and asked, "Is there anyone in the hallway then?"

"What?" Michael asked, confused, but looked out to collect the requested information. "Er, no, ma'am. There is no one, not a soul, it seems."

"Souls are funny things," Margery replied, "often lurking long after they should. Come, don't tell anyone I let you in.

There's a nice chair in the corner over there. Just come on out when you're done and don't mind me scuttling about."

"Thank you, ma'am!" Michael said, too relieved to find a corner of seclusion to go through the necessary "oh are you sure" and "but I can always find somewhere else" routine.

"Off with you then." The Librarian's warmth reminded him of his grandmother on warm Georgia nights, sending him back home. The only difference was, here he wanted to arrive at the destination.

For a brief moment, Michael felt as if the clouds of paradise had parted for his benefit, welcoming him into a world that had been kept away from him. He felt dirty in its presence. Unwashed, unworthy, but welcome.

His welcome lasted but a few moments.

Nestling into what might have been the most comfortable wingback chair he ever had the luck to sit upon, he opened his new copy of *Great Expectations* and continued reading of young Pip encountering escaped convicts and imagining the sight of prison ships in the fog of the water.

"Where've you been, boy?" a grunt of a voice demanded.

It was a deep voice, a slurred voice, a voice that Michael had pushed from the recesses of his memory years ago. A voice he had washed from his skin in the river on a cold night, replaced by the melody of the angels.

"I says, where've you been? Answer me, boy!" The growl turned to a full-throated shout, causing Michael to start. *Great Expectations* fell to the ground.

"Wh-what?" Michael couldn't believe what he was seeing. The man appeared monolithic in size. The rag of a shirt stuck to his skin, drenched in sweat, suspenders draping down his legs. In his hand dangled the neck of a glass bottle with the label torn off.

The dark brown liquid only reached the first fifth of the bottle.

"I says, where've you been? I been lookin' for ye all day! No good, lazy piece of shit."

"Papa, I—"

"You are no son of mine, boy. I've always known it." The man took a step forward and Michael collapsed into his own frame, holding a hand up and preparing for a blow, praying his assailant didn't think to use the bottle as a weapon.

"Yer whore mother must have pennied her legs out and some other bastard squirted you into her. I'd bet my soul. You're a good for nothing little prick. Thorn in my ass. A shit stain on my bed." The man took a three-gulp swig of the liquor, emptying the bottle.

"I tried to make you proud, Papa. I tried to—" Michael was cut off by the crashing thunder of the glass bottle hitting the library floor. Tears fled from the corners of his eyes; his heart nearly beat out his chest.

"Proud? Who would be proud of you, boy? Who would be proud of a son who came from that whore? You think those medals make you a soldier? You think you could be a killing machine? The honor of your country? A hero? Is that what you are? Most pitiful fucking hero I ever seen. Most disgraceful piece of shit hero. We're all doomed now, aren't we?"

Michael's instinct to curl into a ball with his arms cradled around his face to block any wild blows from his drunk father left him blind. So blind, in fact, that he not only could no longer see the red-faced, snot-nosed, vein-popping exasperations of his father, but he also didn't see the blood soaking from his stomach, slowly expanding in its stain across his already mud-drenched shirt.

"Oh, we're supposed to put our faith in this? This shit eating, sniveling little child? You are not a man; you could never be a man.

You are worthless!"

Michael rocked gently as the abuses rained over his ears like thick balls of hail. The thunder clapped in the gardens on the opposite side of the library wall. He braced himself for a blow that never came.

"Private Goodman?" A calm and soothing voice echoed from the other side of the room. A haze of leather and old oak swirled in a confused vision as Michael unspooled his arms, feeling a chill from the lowering of his guard. A tall man, different from the presence of his father, stood in the center of the room with a look of concern. Warmth radiated from his person. He was well dressed in a tuxedo whose lines were sharp and elegant. The oil that kept his hair pushed back reflected in the cool ambience of the dim lighting, presumably kept low so as not to disturb the slumber of stories of centuries passed.

"Private Goodman, are you quite alright?" The gentlemen, for Michael knew of no other word to describe him, took a step forward. One hand was folded around his back with the other held out in front of him, clearly hesitating on whether it ought to extend and offer the soldier a helping hand. "I'm afraid you've gone rather pale, my dear."

"Yes, er, I mean…yes." Michael felt about his torso as if his fingers needed to ensure he was still in one piece. In the meantime, his eyes darted across the floor in search of the thousands of glass shards that ought to have been there. But alas, the floor was barren. Nothing but an ocean of finely finished hardwood in the calm of a storm-less night.

"I'm very sorry to have…stumbled in on you. Sometimes Margery allows me to take a little stroll back here. We have an understanding, her and I. Go way back, you see, further than either of us would care to admit." The stranger laughed as he rounded his free hand behind his back and bounced on the balls of his feet, taking care to avoid eye contact with the confused soldier.

"Do I…I'm sorry, do we know each other?" Michael asked, regaining a margin of his senses as the stranger spoke. There was a certain rhythm to his voice that recalled a dulled memory, the type that seeps into the bones and reveals itself over the taste of a particular vintage or the notes of an old sonata. For Michael, it seemed, the timbre of this old man's voice broke through the shell of repression to reveal a young lady, French, swaying to the rhythm of an old man's violin in a dusty basement tavern somewhere south of Alsace. Before the rattling of gunfire disrupted his dreams, before the blood and the shit and the stench.

"Know each other? My, I should think not. I'm afraid the time of my being acquainted with young men, much less young soldiers," he said with a chuckle, "is long past. You'll forgive the familiarity, Private, but I am a member of the staff. The good manager has seen fit that I ensure you are alright. Is everything living up to your expectations? I must say, it looks like you've had a bit of a fright, though I don't imagine that's rare in these old halls. Guests seldom find themselves back here."

Michael strained to pay what attention he could to the stranger, still wondering whether his father would round the corner and hurl more abuses in his direction. Would he offend this man as well? Or would he simply embarrass Michael and make him feel even smaller than he already had?

"Miss Aurelia," Michael started, but was hardly permitted to get even those few syllables out before being interrupted by this strange man.

"Aurelia, yes. Charming creature, would you not agree? Oh, there's no need for blushing, Private, I assure you. Your secret is safe with me. I'm afraid I've plenty of secrets that I stow away in the old vault. Yes, I've found that my seniority lends itself to a certain level of...remembrance for what these walls witness. Yet I never tell. It's in a man's best interest to keep his secrets well kept, don't you think?"

"Yes, sir," Michael said unknowingly. The truth of it was all this talk of secrets and memories had Michael feeling rather confused. A piece of him attempted to latch on to that memory, to that girl in the tavern south of Alsace, the drape of her skirt swaying with the violin. But the more he tried to concentrate on it, the more the look on the girl's face shifted. Before long, it was Aurelia dancing in the tavern, nervously catching his gaze with her own.

"Well, I'm sorry to have disturbed your afternoon; perhaps I'll be on my way."

"Sir," Michael interrupted, not quite understanding where the inclination was coming from. "Is there something...strange about this place?"

"Strange?" the stranger asked, twisting his body in such a casual way as to not give away his increased interest in the conversation.

"What I mean—well, perhaps I don't know what I mean. But I get a strange feeling that..."

"That you don't belong, that you're being watched by several eyes, no matter how gently?"

"Yes, I suppose that's it. Watched, followed, haunted almost."

"My dear lad, I don't know much about such things, but I can tell you this: the world of the Genovie is small, yet expansive; beautiful, yet horrifying. There is not a concrete reason why, and I am sad that you should have been troubled with experiencing some of its...charms. Truly regrettable. But I can assure you this, you'll be well enough in the end. The stay is brief, the pain swift. And if there is anything that our staff can do in the meantime to heighten your stay, you know where to find me."

"I do?"

"Of course, just ask for the old man at the front desk; they'll know who you mean." The stranger gave a wink and made to leave.

Before he rounded the corner, he turned to look at a confused Michael, scratching the back of his head and searching the floorboards for something or other. Before he made his final disappearance, the stranger gave a bit of a sigh before saying, "I am frightfully sorry, young man. It was never my intent that you should be here."

XIII

Gratitude would not be the word the manager would ascribe to having held the bloody cloth to his face—unbeknownst to him—for the span of several minutes. And perhaps it would be considered indelicate of the writer to use such a phrase. But, indeed, Lawrence ought to have at least considered the fact that, up until that moment, his mind had been distracted from the pressing situation of room 319. So, grim though one may find it, the soiled linen served as a reminder to pull his mind from the trivialities that distracted him.

Within the span of a breath, the word scratched in faded ink on folded parchment ran across his eyes with a shudder straight down through the bone. Murderer.

It would not do to dally. Stuffing the unfortunate token of his late guest into his pocket, Lawrence made with full haste for the lift. "Arthur," he said, upon arriving breathlessly at the edge of the gate. "Arthur, I must get to the third floor, if you please."

"Right away, sir." The old man had been startled by the sudden panting and exasperation of his manager. He had, at the manager's earlier request, suffered himself to bear down on his knees with a hammer and a pair of pliers and was working to remove the chink from the elevator's gate. The same chink that served, in the earlier part of the morning, as a reminder for Mr. Erlik of the perils of the office. Only now, it seemed inconsequential when compared to his own troubles. At least the prior manager had only been troubled with the mechanical failure of the elevator and not the failure of the reasonable separation of the supernatural and the natural.

"Oh," Arthur muttered under his breath, his brow moistening with sweat.

"What is it?" Lawrence nearly snapped.

"I am quite sorry, sir; it seems something is wrong with the lift. Something has jammed the lever."

"Well, unjam it. Hurry up, man!"

"I am very sorry, sir; it is not intentional, I assure you. It seems I haven't the strength to loosen it. Perhaps you should give it a try?"

The suggestion annoyed Lawrence, but he was in no mood to risk his being seen by a guest or another employee and being pulled into another fool's errand when he had business that needed tending to. Try as he did, however, the lever gave Lawrence just as much struggle as it had given the poor lift operator. When he had stepped over to the corner in order to give himself the maximum available leverage, he found the small space to be frightfully cold. It was as if he stepped out of the summer and straight into a blizzard. He attempted to ignore it and set to work. Three violent tugs were enough to send Lawrence into a panting fit, restoring his frame to the heaving, sweaty mess it had been seconds before. "See to its fix, Arthur. Call for Joel. We would not want this embarrassment to hinder the guests should they require your service, which I could only assume would be at any moment. I will suffer the stairs."

"Yes, sir. Straight away." There was a small fraction of

Lawrence's heart that felt vaguely sorry for the harshness of his speech toward the old man. It was observable how hard he was trying to please Lawrence. He filed that away for a later time, one in which he might be inclined to award Arthur with a chocolate or perhaps a free drink, if he so desired.

To the stairs.

The stairwell was a wretched thing. The kind of place that finds itself a misfit when surrounded by such splendor. No doubt, it would suffice as a suitable mode of transportation in the hotels that operate today, classless hovels they are. But the Genovie had a standard to upkeep and the stairwell seemed to fall short. It wasn't in the trappings of the staircase itself. It was still adorned with fine carpet, shining wooden handrails, and polished console tables on each landing. They were wide enough to accommodate two rows of upward-bound travelers and two subsequent rows of downward-bound.

The problem lay, not in its appearance, but in its air. One never felt quite right stepping through the double doors into its stale atmosphere. It was barren, a vacuum, a hole void of the happiness and majesty of the surrounding construction.

Perhaps that is what took the wind from Lawrence's chest before extending his foot to the first step. The lack of majesty. Or perhaps his thoughts were clouded by the doom of his errand. One foot in front of the other; one step climbed at a time. That was the only way for the frightful disposition to calm itself.

"Six rooms, five reservations, four cracks of thunder, three nineteen, no. Three floors, two dead Russians, one flooding cellar." Mr. Erlik had nearly dispelled from himself the inconvenience of a chattering inner schoolboy, daft with freight, by the time he rounded the final landing. There, the frigid air returned in the form of a resounding wall, smacking him in the nose as he traversed through its gate. For a moment, he paused. Frozen in place by the feeling of being watched, of being hunted. In stillness, he stood. It felt, if only for the brevity of a moment, that the hotel itself stood in judgment. Some hellish breed of malcontent seeping through its very walls, counting his sins and tallying his qualities with faint, scratched marks.

If he had let his imagination get the better of him—which, it must be said, is a highly inadvisable habit for one of Lawrence's office—he might have surrendered himself to the notion that he could feel breath on his neck.

Not the warm, lustful breath of a woman in tender arms, but a cold, harsh, brutish breath. A fiendish air thirsting for the break of goose-bumped skin. For a moment, it lay in sync with his own. The thought had occurred to him that he might turn around, find that it really was his imagination, and go about his not-so-merry way. But his next thought, beginning before the prior had even concluded, opened the possibility of the reality of the fear; the possibility that there actually was someone lurking close to his back, bringing their chin ever so close to his, so that the hair on his neck began to stand straight up.

And so, it was a stiff, relentless step forward. Not a turn, not a revelation of the truth, but a march of ignorance until he had walked through the door and heard the click of the latch. That would have been the end of it, if there hadn't been the sound of relentless pounding from the other side of the door as soon as he took his first step into the hall.

"Enough, you devil, you vixen! Show yourself." That is what dear Mr. Erlik had been diminished to. A frantic, stammering, pale, shell of a man given to lunacy. But how can we blame him? The pounding was, after all, sounding as if it were meant for him specifically. As if it were meant to torment him, to goad him into becoming transfixed upon a singular idea meant to cause him harm. And for a moment, only a brief moment, he had begun to allow it.

Three tugs of the waistcoat. A clearing of the throat. Three steps back toward the stairwell door.

Lawrence half expected to see Sonya, half expected to see his cruel tormentor. The very same that had sent him that damned note. But the rectangular pane of glass on the door gave no indication of either possibility. No clue as to the source. In fact, its emptiness had even emboldened him to open the door. A cautious hand placed on the handle, a slow turn, and peering creak and...

Nothing. The stairwell was empty, mocking him with its vacancy. Perhaps he was going mad after all.

No such stupefying sensation had ever creeped into the muscles and tendons of the young manager as did the image of that door. Room 319. He willed himself to forget it, to turn around and never come back. They would find what hid inside at some point, whoever "they" usually were in these situations. Lawrence was not one for crime novels or murder mysteries. Perhaps it would be poor Margarette after all. Or one of the Berus brothers. Or Aurelia. No, he could not allow such a harrowing, ghastly mess to be discovered by the lovely Aurelia.

If one were to ask Lawrence what he was waiting for— standing in front of the door, his hand stuffed deep into his trouser pocket, fingers fidgeting with the cold brass of the maid's key— he would not have been able to give a proper answer. Perhaps he would have blamed it on the drifting mind, wondering who it was Margarette had seen enter through this threshold of his darkest thoughts. Was it Sonya Ivanovna? Had someone else borne witness to the single most terrifying figure he had ever laid his eyes on? Had Margarette felt the warmth leave her body, had she found herself incapable of recollecting any moment of happiness, of bliss? Was she instead forced to relive the most wicked moments of her life, flashing before her very eyes as if seeing them on a theater house stage?

But Margarette had not said anything indicating that she had witnessed anything beyond this life. If she had seen a phantom of a woman, rather than an actual living, breathing woman, would she not have said so? Margarette had always prized herself with the capability of a higher connection to these sorts of things. Lawrence had taken it for granted that she was a highly superstitious woman who allowed herself to get lost in her own fantasies. *Who was lost now?*

Lawrence fully understood that it was necessary to continue, to stifle the hesitancy of cowardice.

The key offered resistance. Not in the way of it being the wrong key, how he would reprimand such a mistake on Margarette's part when he had been so perfectly clear with her. No, this was a different form of resistance. The kind that a dog gives before stepping into a cold, dark, and unfamiliar room for the first time. A wariness, a vigilance of spirit.

Then rushed the heat.

Lawrence, in all his troubles, had nearly forgotten the state of the room before everything had transpired. The reason he had come in the first place. A broken radiator. Not broken, simply on in the middle of a hot summer's day, twisted to full blast at the behest of a wicked operator who feigned trouble to lure his prey into his lair.

There was a staleness to the room. He could still smell the

wafts of tobacco smoke, though it felt different, distant. There remained the burn of the brandy on the tip of his tongue. Sweet, warm, homely. The mass in his throat, growing and choking him, had returned upon setting sight to the thick, velvet drapes.

Lawrence was sure to keep his eyes straight forward, not yet daring to drift to the ground and find what was resting in a sticky crimson puddle, seeping into the fibers of the rug upon which it spread. Instead, his eyes turned to the painting that had sent a shudder down his spine. All he could then think was how he would gladly trade places with the oarsman at that very moment. Or even the poor souls who found themselves at the opposite end of his oar.

The door to the bedroom had been closed again. Or perhaps it was Lawrence that closed it. Had he? The memory of the whole affair had blurred. No, certainly not. He stood sternly on the other side of the room while the door creaked open. The only door Lawrence closed was the main door on his way out.

Finally, he mustered the strength to look. The mass of it was hidden by the sofa. But he could see the legs. The polish of his patent leather wingtips, the perfect crease in his trousers. Lawrence began, almost immediately, to fall into a fit of hyperventilation.

The heat left the room. Much in the same way that it had on the stairwell, the following wave of cold air burst onto his face with such force that it nearly knocked him off balance. Perhaps that would have been the easier thing to do. To fall, his knees hitting the ground and his shoulders sagging to a discontented slump. The truth of it was, beyond the fear, the trepidation, the worry, Lawrence was tired. He was weary of the day's entanglements, and how it made him yearn for the comfort of a consoling hand. Of a proper bout of rest.

But such was not to be his fate.

The lobby grandfather clock's hour hand might have seemed as if it were moving faster than Lawrence Erlik's feet shuffling toward the confrontation he had been loathing to encounter. Seconds felt like hours.

The closer he got, the tighter his throat felt. A pressure in the air mounted around his ears, causing them to pop and ring relentlessly. Before long, the scent of tobacco was replaced by the sickly smell of blood, the way it begins to waft through the air when it has been spilled from its former temple for too long, left to stale in the open air. The sensation could have caused him to retch, and nearly did.

But it was the sight of the old man's lifeless face that sent Lawrence toward the abyss. The eyes were the worst of it. Still open, they pointed directly toward Lawrence's own, as if Kosorukov had heard Lawrence enter and turned his gaze in expectation of his guest. They were frozen in an image that blended horror with tranquility. As if in the darkest of his moments, Kosorukov found his peace. Such a peace did not pass on to Lawrence. His vision tunneled and inspected the body.

The glint of the knife's hilt, born from the still-lit table lamp, reflected in the blacks of Lawrence's eyes. The skin had turned a sickly grey, the whites of his collar dyed a deep crimson. The air began to fail in Lawrence's lungs, his arms began to quiver and shake. He swallowed the lump in his throat and some of the watery saliva rising around the sides of his tongue, filling his mouth with a coppery taste that usually preceded something more solid making its way to the surface. What had he decided on doing, once he arrived in the room? He knew he couldn't just let the situation fester, like a wound open to the elements.

The flickering of the lights was the first sign that she had come. Come to witness the pathetic heaving and frantic gasping for the right inspiration to strike Lawrence into action. This time, she did not come from the bedroom, but stood silently in the corner of the room.

He could see the drape of her dress from the corner of his eye. He dared not confirm any further than that. "Damn you," he whispered. "Damn you both." But that was the only indication he offered to let her know he saw her. There was something imperative in his mind about keeping his eyes from looking her straight on. Just being near her made things fuzzy. Not quite like the haze of something as corruptible as a stiff whiskey. More like static on a radio that struggled to receive waves properly. That was the right word. Static.

His eyes remained fixed on the body, wondering how he was to move it, where he would move it. Was it wise to act now, in the middle of the day? Or should he wait for the dead of night, when the guests were all likely sound asleep? Perhaps that is precisely what his tormentor would expect of him. Perhaps he was waiting, ready to catch him in the night.

Even more worrisome than being caught by the sender, was being caught by the guests in full daylight. Or worse, the staff. The pounding of water on the panes of glass set just beyond the velvet drapery reminded him it wasn't exactly full daylight, but the effect was all the same. What would Aurelia think of him? What would Cyrus have to say in his usual sneering tone?

Murderer.

"Why have you done this to me?" he whispered, arching his back, as if inching closer to Kosorukov's ear would penetrate that impregnable wall between life and what came after. "Why have you saddled me with this hell? With...with *her?*"

He knew she heard him invoke her. The room turned even

colder; the faint sound of a rapid click broke the silence. Was she angered? If she was, she need not quarrel with Lawrence, not as he saw it, anyway. Her feud was with the dead, and as she was unmistakably of the same kin, she ought to leave this place and take up her grievances with the one who caused her offense. Not with Lawrence.

But still, she stood in the corner, goading him into looking in her direction. The closest he came was a second glance at the hem of her dress, now gently swaying as if settling back down after a few steps of movement.

Even the suggestion of her leaving that corner to come another inch in his direction was enough to send him into a stuttering mess. Not words. Words were too refined, too civilized for the fear that was crippling him. Just syllables, beginnings of phrases, and grunts. He was allowing her to get the better of him.

In his wish to look at anything but the dead, his eyes fluttered to the side and behind him. The cigar case still rested on the cushion of the couch; the box that once held the dagger strewn about to its right. Lawrence sat. Knowing she was likely still standing in her corner, staring at the back of his head, his neck locked in place. He wanted nothing more than to leave. Perhaps not only leave the room but rid himself of the whole affair. The room, the lobby, the Genovie herself. But something bound him to the hotel. Most days it felt as if his ankle bore shackles that chained him to the building. And like a beast in the dark, he learned to love his cage, to see the beauty in it.

He would not leave. He would simply have to insist that Kosorukov check out, in whatever way he could see it come to pass.

"The devil jeers at my pain," he said. In the mix of it, he almost pulled out the bravery to look at Kosorukov again, instinctively wanting to plan the removal of the body. The thought then dawned on him, that Kosorukov had said she might rest when she had found him lain in the ground. Yes, that was it. *Perhaps the gardens would need fertilizing; perhaps a brandy-soaked Russian would do perfectly.*

Brandy.

His eyes slowly panned to the table to his right. Still standing with abject pride was the dusty bottle of brandy. His own snifter resting on the table opposite. One drink couldn't hurt. He could almost smell the caramel from there. In one fell swoop, he lifted himself from the couch, reached for the brandy with one arm, the snifter with the other, and returned to his seat before he could be mistaken to have any foul intentions from the ominous spectating specter to his rear.

The golden elixir curled in a tiny, splashing wave as it hit the curve of the bottom of the glass, rippling back into the body of the surface. The way alcohol sounded pouring into a glass always made his heart flutter. The hairs of his nose were nearly singed from its heat as he lifted it to his mouth. It was a heavy drought of the stuff, the last of the bottle, enough to warm the chest and settle the stomach. Kicking it back, he felt the tingle of its properties dance like fairies to the tips of his fingers and back to the center of his heart.

His eyelids began to close. Too heavy to hold.

Within a moment of his drinking the last of the brandy, he felt the overwhelming desire—nay—the need to sleep. He had hardly the chance to think of how ridiculous such a proposition was before he felt his body slipping down the soft leather. His knee hit the floor as his back was caught by the seat cushion, slowly sliding to his right and onto his side. The tips of his hairs reached out for the fibers of Kosorukov's slacks.

The light felt as if it were dimming; he could hardly lift his arm to feel his face, let alone hold himself up. Consciousness flitted like the dying embers of a fire as he blinked to stay awake.

The last thing he saw before surrendering to the unstoppable slide into sleep was the pallor of Sonya Kosorukov, standing over him, her beady black eyes staring directly at his—lifeless, as if looking through his soul.

XIV

While it might go without saying, a man such as Lawrence—
that is, a man wholly dedicated, body and spirit, to the service of
others—was not in the habit of indulging in such a vanity as
dreaming. Dreams revealed too much of the self, what lurks
beneath. Then again, Lawrence was also not in the practice of
consuming what he thought was a simple splash of brandy only to
find himself reeling to the floor in an uncontrollable stupor while
the ghost of a dead guest's wife lurked above, smiling as his eyes
faded to a fuzzy hue of black. It appeared to be a day of firsts.

Lawrence might not have even felt he was dreaming. At least
not at first. Not when he found himself in the third-floor hallway
of the hotel, looking around to decide which way he ought to carry
himself. He knew for certain it was the third floor. The painting
directly opposite the lift gate depicted a Roman goddess weeping
at the steps of a throne where sat a man Lawrence had always taken
for Zeus. But in this haze of a dream, he might have thought the
seated man was less deity and more mortal. A strange thing, he
thought, that the divine might throw itself at the feet of the
mundane.

There was an insatiable urge to leave the space where he

stood. But where to go? The third floor, as all floors, split in two directions with an equal number of rooms to the left as there were to the right. One of these rooms, though Lawrence was unsure which, was exactly where he needed to get to.

The caw of the raven was enough to keep him from going left. That way lay trouble. It wasn't quite clear to him as to what exactly lay in wait down that path, but the curiosity of a raven standing on the carpet was in itself a worrying thing. How had the raven come to be there? Was it speaking to Lawrence? Was it warning him?

Right it was.

The funny thing about dreams, when one doesn't know one is dreaming, is that everything seems quite correct. No matter what is put in front of one. Just so, Lawrence did not question that it felt closer to trudging through the dirty waters of a mire, rather than strolling through the hall of a high-end hotel. Nor did he question the rain falling from the ceiling, soaking through his suit coat that he appeared to be wearing inside out. All quite normal, all quite correct.

The sense of dread did not seep into his bones until he realized which room he was heading to. There was only one room it could be. Only one handle would move in this parade of thick, heavy, dark oak doors. Lawrence had that knowledge. It didn't matter how it came into his head; what mattered was that he knew it. He knew how the handle would feel in his palm, how it would burn, as if set under a blowtorch for hours before meeting contact with his blistered skin. He knew how the numbers would glisten with their polished gold, reflecting their script onto his soaking-wet face. 319.

That dread stilled him, halted him in his tracks. How could he move on through this raging storm when he knew what followed? Looking back, he saw the raven. It had followed him down the hall, as if knowing he would need further encouragement before the end. What would that wicked bird do if Lawrence simply turned around and rode the lift? It was only a bird, after all. Could he not leave of his own will? But as Lawrence was thinking this through, weighing every thought as if it might be his last, he saw the bird's talons, as sharp as daggers. He could feel the edge of their blades swipe across his neck at the first sign of disobedience.

Obedience. Yes, that is what was happening. Lawrence was trudging through the mud and the water of the third floor in order to obey. What gods instilled themselves into the pitch-black feathers of the formidable bird that stood in watch behind him? Whoever—or whatever—it was, Lawrence was here at its behest. There was no turning around, no will to leave. He would enter that room. Room 319. The room, that for reasons he was not in that moment aware of, he loathed to enter.

The handle seared his palm as he knew it would. Like cattle suffering a branding. Yet, screaming though his skin was, begging for relief, he kept his hand pressed to the handle. The muscles refused to turn until the branding set into a permanent melt.

The door opened with a familiar creak—one he had heard before, one that had turned his bones to a shudder. But on this occasion, the shuddering swelled at the behest of a new proprietor. The resident of room 319. Standing in the empty chasm of the hotel room, somehow dry from the pounding storm, her dress flowing as if heavy gusts of wind were bursting through the closed windows. There was beauty in her face. A soft curve formed her cheek, the kind that drives a man to endless means to graze with the backside of their cupped fingers. A few strands of hair fell from their pins, drifting carelessly in the breeze in front of her dazzling blue eyes.

Reserve held her in the middle of the room, like an expectant sweetheart patiently awaiting the return of a lover long traveled. Fingers intertwined in a gentle clasp, held just under the scoop of her waist, the curve of which was hidden by the exaggerated protrusion of her belly.

He spoke the words, not in his own tongue, but one with a looming rasp of old age and battered lungs. The tang of blood filled the sides of his mouth as if sharp teeth broke skin in a frustrated fit. The words tasted of blood mixed with ash, rolling around in a wicked elixir to remind the speaker that they were not his words to utter, but those of another.

"Oh, my Sonechka!"

His expectant outstretched arms toward him, beckoning his steps toward her embrace. He heard the slam of the door as the tips of his fingers met the bare skin on her back. It was cold, as if life had left her long prior, and there she stood in relentless mock of the living.

He attempted to squeeze her, a folly effort to instill passion and love into her veins, to replace the blood that no longer flowed. Sorrow and regret in place of a beating heart. But she simply went limp. Not a word spoken, dead flesh being held by faltering strength that brought him to the ground, whimpering as if he lost something that never belonged to him—not in this life or the one that preceded.

Snot ran from his mouth as the first flame caught the drape of the velvet curtains hiding the hell storm from their funeral. Lawrence felt the smell of burning oil singe his nose, causing him to break into a fit of coughing and blubbering. Lamenting the loss of the lovely Sonechka.

The flames grew in their rage and hunger, devouring first the curtains, second the wooden furnishings, until the wild winds blew enough sparks to catch the rug. It roared in its fury, cracking and burning as old wood hidden behind plaster moaned for a strength lost in the decades of humidity and rot. They would soon know dry.

It was when the flame first caught Sonya Ivanovna's hem that her eyes snapped open, as if forced by the mechanics of a spring and small wires. They were so wide they looked as if her lids had been ripped from her sockets. No longer radiantly blue, they glossed and faded to a forgetful black, mourning the beauty of a life left in the shadows of despair. To love and trust, to put faith and stock, only to feel the bitter sting of betrayal.

Lawrence forced himself to stare into their void. In his gaze, he found that the abyss looked back at him, pulsing from the guilt in Lawrence's heart, gifted with the force to extract the tears and the vulgarity from his sniveling mess of a visage.

"I am sorry," he cried, barely audible above the crackling of the fire. "I am sorry, Sonya. Forgive me, Sonya. Oh, God, forgive me." His own voice had not yet returned to him, leaving that aged rasp to pierce through the galaxy in her staring eyes.

He didn't feel the heat of the flame. Not when it caught his own jacket, not when it ate through to his bones. Pain was something long forgotten, left behind or perhaps sitting in another room, drowning from the river of melancholy coursing through the hotel.

As he was consumed by the flame's starving appetite, he saw Sonya Ivanovna fade into ash, a dry cut of wood thrown on a hot pyre.

When the mound of ash moved, Lawrence gave it little thought. When the dull black beak emerged, cracked along the midway point as if bashed into a heavy stone, the heat overwhelmed every inch of him. As the Raven emerged, black eyes replacing the penetrating stare of Sonya Ivanovna, he felt the skin from his jaw melt and drip like a cone of Italian ice in the summer's sun.

Behind him, creaking under the pressure of the swallowing storm, Lawrence heard the boards of the sinking ship in the painting hung on the wall. He could feel the breeze of the hollering wind coming to ease the pain of the splintering fire. Men shouted from their pathetic life boat, cheering for him to extend an arm that they might offer him safety, while the oarsman shouted, "Back you devils!" to the pitiful creatures treading through the mountainous waves. When Lawrence turned back to look to the painting, he heard a final crash of thunder and an ocean of water poured from the frame onto the pristine floor of room 319. Just before the water's edge doused him and the fire ravenously eating the curtains, he shuddered awake.

As his desperate breath faded from a world of fire and flood to the present, the inhaled soot coated his throat. But the place he was returning to was no less dark, filled equally with evils brewing under the manager's nose.

The dream would have been enough to send him into a fit of panic, a frantic, panting mess. It was not necessary for his plunge away from sanity for him to find himself, not slumped over next to the couch, nearly rubbing against a lifeless Kosorukov, but laying in the trappings of an elegantly dressed bed of the hotel's fame. Further tantalizing his mind's flirtation with lunacy was the writing on the wall, smeared as if written with a red soaked hand, the crimson message no doubt composed by the sender of the little note still stuffed in the bottom of his trouser pocket.

You'll burn, too, Romik.

"No," he said to himself, patting his chest, hips, legs, and dragging a sweaty palm over a contorted face, dirtied with stubble. "No, not him."

This was the moment the manager saw fit to expound his descent into madness and begin playing logic games. Perhaps to soothe the aching heart that still felt as if it were engulfed in flame.

"Sonya," he said aloud, as if daring her to challenge his conclusion. "Sonya Ivanovna did this."

He was sure of it, but when? Had she painted these words on the bedroom wall while he was sitting on the couch with Kosorukov in the other room, nothing but polished oak separating them? Or had she waited until there was a body. Yes, that had to be it. Where else would she have gotten the ink if not for Romik's neck?

The realization swelled in his throat like a rotten dinner surging to the surface. It wasn't a conscious realization. Indeed, if one had the opportunity to ask Lawrence at that very moment, he wouldn't have been able to answer to what it was that vexed him. But the door that closed him into the bedroom of room 319 began to buzz and vibrate as if alive. Rising from the sheets, tugging on his waistcoat, he took three morose strides to open the door, his hand flinching as the skin touched the handle in memory of one much hotter.

When he swung the door open and stepped into the sitting room, the already overwhelming dread compounded to a crescendo when his eyes surveyed the ground to find that Roman Pavlovich Kosorukov was no longer lying on the floor where he had left him. Nothing but the pool of blood that had gathered beneath his corpse remained, enveloping around the glisten of the knife that had somehow been pulled from the dead man's neck.

XV

"Lawrence, every time I see your face you look further and further from health. What is going on with you?"

Lawrence had grown rather perturbed with the casualness in Cyrus's condescension. For some reason, he grew particularly disdainful at the presence of that little leather book he gripped in his hands, freshly snapped shut at the entry of the manager into his office.

On an ordinary afternoon, the condition of the managerial office would have put Lawrence in a state of utter disarray. The strewn about papers—some folded, some stacked in frenzied piles, others discarded into the corner of the room as if to indicate their uselessness to the organizer's efforts—were hardly even noticed by Lawrence. He simply stood in the doorway, muttering words under his breath that were hardly perceptible to the casual listener. If one put in an honest effort at bending an ear in his direction, a few words might have broken through the silence. "Gone, vanished, who, how." But one word repeated most often, sliding between fragmented whispers like a phantom grazing over the pines in a darkened wood. "Sonya."

"At this rate, we are going to run out of tea, aren't we

Lawrence?" Cyrus said, shuffling Lawrence through the forest of papers. "I wonder if it's even doing you any good."

As Lawrence took his seat behind his desk, his bloodshot eyes staring at his hands shaking violently in his lap, he caught a glimpse of the mess's culprit. An excitable bellman was walking back and forth, his nose buried in a handful of old-looking records. Newspaper clippings, manager reports, booking logs. A boyish smile twisted his crimson cheeks, expressing the age of innocent curiosity.

"Amazing!" Baptiste said, shaking his head as if in disbelief of witnessing some inexplicable phenomenon. Romance stirred in his eyes; pride expanded in his chest. "Oh, Mr. Erlik! You'll never guess what I have found."

Lawrence barely moved his eyes toward the boy, a look akin to disgust tainting his face. Not having the breath in his lungs to answer, he turned his gaze to Cyrus, who carelessly tended to the kettle.

Lawrence found his mind racing. What had happened to Kosorukov? Had his tormentor followed him into room 319? No, not followed. Preceded. He had snuck into the room somehow, slipped something into the last of the brandy, knowing Lawrence would find himself overwhelmed and in need of encouragement found at the bottom of a bottle. All he had to do was wait, move him into the other room in order to cause a stir when he awoke, and steal away the body to hide somewhere in anticipation of the police. *What a foolish man. Does he not realize he has tampered with the evidence? Does the fool not see he is now just as culpable as I?*

Or was he overthinking it? Was the answer simpler? Had Kosorukov risen from the dead like a profaned profit? Had he slid the deadly needle from his own neck, let it fall to the ground in a wet thud, walked down the stairwell and out the front door as if he had never come to stay at the hotel? Lawrence would have recognized the insanity of such a notion when he awoke in the early morning. But it would behoove us to observe, Lawrence had yet to witness the pulsing pallor of a ghost until after he awoke and started his day.

What a difference a day makes.

"You see! It's printed out right here, just as Joel said! In 1852, 'the young couple had checked into the Hotel Genovie just that morning. Owing to a particularly grievous argument, the couple excused themselves from dinner. According to Mr. Kosorukov's confession, he had beckoned her to the hotel's cellar under the guise of wanting to enjoy a more private venue where they could air their arguments and sort out their troubles. It was when the conversation turned particularly foul that the young general unsheathed his scabbard and struck the fatal blow to his newly named wife, Catharine."

"What? What did you just say?" Lawrence snapped, his first acknowledgment of the young man's presence. A fire burned passionately in the center of his heart. "Repeat that name to me. Go on, what was the cursed's name, boy?"

"Ca-Catharine?" Baptiste stuttered, fear draining the color from his face.

"No, not the damned victim. What did you say the general's name was?"

"Callaghan, General Callaghan."

"That's not..." But Lawrence forced his voice to die off before risking his own insanities coming to light. He was allowing Kosorukov to get the better of him, allowing Sonya Ivanovna into his head, swirling around like an unwelcome insect. Outside, he heard the tolling of the grandfather clock, only there was something different about the sound of its chimes. Something unfamiliar, something sinister. Lawrence almost convinced himself they sounded akin to the cawing of a raven.

"What is the matter?" Cyrus asked, seeing the contortion of the manager's face. Lawrence, in the meantime, could not help but notice the faintest hint of a smile twisting Cyrus's words in a dim and devilish scorn. Hatred burned in his chest, causing a boiling acid to rise through to his throat and nearly choked him. Cyrus knew. Cyrus knew everything. He knew what Lawrence had been through, what he had witnessed. He sent the little note to tease him, to watch him squirm. He moved the body, poisoned him enough to ensure he would have the time to do it. And worst of all, he was enjoying it. Enjoying watching Lawrence suffer, watching him burn with the distaste of the day, the acrid swill sloshing in his mouth like a scrap of onion left to rot. "Is it something the boy has said?" Lawrence wanted to spit in his face at the question.

"What is it he has said that is meant to upset me?" The words were as good as phlegm, cutting Cyrus's grin in two.

"Well, I haven't the slightest idea. I only noticed you are looking rather morose and wondered whether it is something we might dispel ourselves of, hm? After all, we do have a hotel to run. Ownership is counting on us, my dear."

"Yes," Lawrence replied, "ownership, indeed."

"By the gods, you are acting awfully strange."

"Gods? So, you've taken up religion now?"

"I have no fight in the sparring of gods, neither real nor imagined. It is not for me to say. But enough of this, it is all beginning to sound—"

"Like fine talk?"

"Well, perhaps, yes. I was more thinking we were coming up to a hint of the ravings of lunacy, myself. Should we spare ourselves the discomfort of odds? Come, let's leave the clouds of the gods and return to the realm of man. Things always seem much more concrete that way, don't you think?" Cyrus returned to his favorite settee as he spoke, and while he adorned his usual devil-may-care exuberance, Lawrence could tell his shortness had rather cut the old man. Perhaps he had been too harsh. Was it not in his own admittance that he just concluded that the Kosorukovs were getting to him? This was merely his imagination running wild, wilder than the poor bellman who stood reading newspaper clippings, seemingly unaware of any disagreement happening in the meantime.

"I am sorry, Baptiste, what was it you said about the married couple? Something about the cellar?" The whole affair had rather escaped him, seeing as he had plenty to distract his thoughts since he had visited the flooding tomb with the young employee.

"Hm? Oh, yes! See, it's just as Mr. Joel said. The murder, that is. It really happened, Mr. Erlik. A murder, right here in the Genovie! What an odd thing. I should think I would be rightly shocked if it were to happen to us these days. Rightly shocked."

"Yes," Lawrence admitted with a shudder, "but that does not prove the existence of ghosts, young Baptiste."

"Who are we to discourage one's belief in the supernatural? Let the boy dream. After all, a proper measure of fear instilled in one's subordinates might be a useful commodity." Cyrus spoke as though reading lines from the faded leather book he had resumed his dead-pan stare toward.

"Well," Baptiste muttered immediately after Cyrus's words trailed to a halt, as if not hearing him at all, "it proves that it happened. And that's one step closer, don't you think? You were down there, sir. You saw how…creepy it is. So cold and dreary."

"The proof is that men live, and men die, Baptiste. There is nothing further to discuss. You needn't worry yourself with the silly antics of an old handyman, bored from monotonous work and looking to have a little fun with an unsuspecting mind. Remember that. There are no ghosts roaming the halls of the Genovie."

"It would be bad for business," Cyrus chimed.

"Indeed, it would be bad for business," Lawrence confirmed. He sounded as though he were more interested in convincing himself of this truth, the very truth of which he had evidence to the contrary.

"But you do believe in ghosts, don't you?" Baptiste sounded closer to a child asking his father not to spoil the fun of haunted campfire stories than a bellman asking his manager a philosophical question.

"What business is that of yours? Damn it all, Baptiste, haven't you made quite the storm in here? Why don't you stop this childish nonsense and tidy up the place? I have too much on my mind to sit in this mess!"

Baptiste nodded his freshly colorless face in acquiescence and began tidying the papers he had so clearly been meticulous about stacking into piles of different categories.

"You aren't saying you don't believe in a life after this, surely?"

Lawrence might have thought better of this question and its suggestion of innocence and susceptibility if it had come from the naive young Baptiste. As it was, it came from the snide lips of a menacing looking Cyrus. He asked it in order to carve his way under Lawrence's skin. Toying with him, twisting his already plagued mind in some wicked display of superiority over him. A false superiority.

Before he could open his mouth to answer, however, Baptiste let out an unexpected yelp. The offense of a man freshly discovering a new clue after hours of investigating.

"Mr. Erlik," he said, not waiting for Lawrence to lift his head from his palms before he continued, "did you know about a fire?"

"Fire?" Lawrence asked, craning his neck. The word fell from his mouth with a sour taste. His own voice sounded fuzzy in his ears, faded, weak. It was as if the word itself was a sin to speak. A cursed word, a word that if spoken, might ignite into spark upon kindling.

"Yes, look. I must not have seen it before. 'Hotel Hell,' it says. 'Late in the night on June the 15th, a fire broke out and charred the west wing of the Hotel Genovie, killing several guests and a handful of staff. Local responders fought through the night and were unable to quell the hunger of the flames until dawn. The hotel has been a well-known den of accommodation, being a favorite place of lodging for traveling celebrities and individuals of repute, including six presidential visits since the first visit of President Lincoln in 1863.' It then goes on to talk about how beautiful the hotel is and what a shame the fire was."

"What year is that paper, boy?" Lawrence snapped. The red streaks looked as if they were carved into the whites of his eyes, permanent fixtures of distress.

"Well let's see, er, 1883."

"Does it say how the fire started?" Cyrus peered over the cover of his book.

"Yes, yes, how did it start?" Lawrence was nearly drooling like a famished beast moments before the kill. It would be of little surprise to those present if he took one step further in his hunger to hear more by letting his tongue wag from his shimmering bottom lip.

"Let me look."

"Come on then, come on," Lawrence insisted.

"I'm getting there, sir. Don't rush me now. Let's see, well-known den of accommodation, right, presidential visits. Oh, apparently Roosevelt stayed here as well. Right, the fire. Ah, here we are. It says that a member of the hotel staff was thought to have snuck away with a guest to their room. Officials spoke of the matter in such a way as to only provide a working theory of how it all transpired, though current speculation would have it that, owing to a disagreement, the hotel employee wounded the guest with a hammer blow to the head before setting flame to the curtains and committing suicide. The murd—" The bellman stopped himself before letting the last word leave his innocent lips.

"Murder! Another murder, Mr. Erlik! You don't think that Joel is correct about this place, do you?"

"What room?"

"Sorry, sir?"

"What…room? Where was the fire started? Where was the murder?" Lawrence could feel sweat glue the edge of his shirt to his collarbone. A pencil, which he had grabbed with the intent to take note of what he was hearing, was in mortal danger of snapping under the tension of his grip.

"I don't know, sir."

"Well, perhaps you ought to read and find out!" Lawrence was on the verge of a shout, enough volume and menace in his throat to give the young bellman a start before his eyes began to dart from left to right, desperately scrambling to find the answer.

"It appears, well…yes, that's it. 'The room wherein the flames began, being on the third floor, allowed little time for guests to escape to the stairwell as its proximity to room 319 lent itself to falling an early victim to the fire's rabid hunger.' That's worded awfully strange," Baptiste opined, "does that suggest—"

"The fire began in room 319 and burned into the stairwell,"

Lawrence explained, hardly letting the words settle in his own consciousness before letting them roll off his tongue. "That cursed room." The last four words were said at such a volume that Lawrence could hardly hear himself utter them into existence. It was then a wonder, to Lawrence and to the writer, how it was that Cyrus came to hear them. Not only had he heard them, but he found that they were in themselves worthy of comment.

"What was that?" Cyrus said, under the heat of Lawrence's blood shot eyes. "What was that about curses?"

Lawrence thought it best to ignore him, darting his eyes away from the old man's penetrating gaze. After all, what good would a confession do without a body?

Where are you hiding him? Lawrence asked in the silence of his thoughts. *What have you done, Cyrus? What have you done? What have I done?*

His hands began to shake, the heat of the room disappeared; it felt as if it were the dead of winter, a blizzard howling in the wind instead of a fire crackling in the hearth. Perhaps he ought to surrender. Not to Cyrus, the gaiety that would permit the old man to indulge in would not do. Perhaps to the guests. He could apologize for the inconvenience and ask that all those with information as to the whereabouts to the wretch's body would be compensated for their entire stay. But that would not do. Many would simply laugh at a lunatic dressed in proper suit and waistcoat. Or perhaps fill themselves with impenetrable fear, and he wouldn't want that. Lawrence may have been on the edge of his own sanity, but he would not want to be the direct cause of an unsavory stay at the Genovie.

Perhaps he ought to burn it down. Burn the whole lot to cinders, laughing as his raving eyes admired the shower of sparks. Burn the body, burn the drapery, burn the raven, burn...burn

Sonya Ivanovna.

But she wouldn't burn. The flames would rip through her as if she were flesh and bone, but still would she stand, flickering in their devouring hunger, staring. Mocking. He could not burn Sonya Ivanovna.

"What was his name?"

"Sorry, sir?" Baptiste was not the only one in the room who found the manager's question interesting, if not a tad confusing. Cyrus, for the first time since perching himself on the usual place upon the settee, lowered his book. The color of his skin—which had always, as far as Lawrence could remember, been rather pale—turned the color of ash. One might have thought he loathed to hear the manager's question answered. Fear. There was fear in his eyes to hear it.

Or perhaps it was the tone with which the manager asked the question that concerned Cyrus. It was nearly spat, as if Lawrence were of royal blood speaking to a gutter rat. One could barely see the colors of Lawrence's eyes as they rolled back toward the other end of his scalp, the skin over his cheeks stretched thin by bony fingers pressing down.

"I said, what was the cursed's name? The one who lit the fire?"

"Er," Baptiste began in the tone of a man who knew what he had to say would displease his audience. Shaking, falsely amplified. "I don't know, sir. It doesn't say."

"What do you mean it doesn't say?" he hissed, slamming his hands down on the desk.

"My, my, Lawrence. We wouldn't want to give the poor young man a fright, would we? Perhaps it's best for us to allow this charming gentleman to get on with his responsibilities. You have been missing long enough; should we not see to it that two hotel employees aren't left unserviceable?"

"What do you know about my missing?" Lawrence snapped, though he began to feel better for it before brushing off his venom and turning to Baptiste to say, "It is best you return to the lobby and your brothers, Sir Berus."

"Sir?" the young man said, his face filling with the light of ample color and vigor. "Well, you do me an honor, si—Mr. Erlik. We'll get straight to work! Sir," he said to himself as he trailed from the office over to the door, "Sir Berus, I like the sound of that."

Before the young bellman had the opportunity to open the door, it was swinging in front of him, and his brother, Adrian, appeared panting in a hint of a fervor.

"Mr. Erlik, Baptiste, where have you been? Something—" He interrupted himself, finding his startled brother standing amongst such admirable company.

"That's Sir Berus to you, brother."

"If you're a sir, I am."

"Are not. You couldn't tie your own shoes this mornin'. How do you expect to be called sir?"

"It wasn't that I couldn't tie them; it's that they kept falling loose!"

"Sounds a lot like a problem with the one doing the tying, if you ask me."

"Why, I have a mind to knock that sir back into your throat with the nobility of my knuckles, you little—"

"That is enough, lads," Lawrence said, beginning to look quite himself again. Indeed, it had appeared the presence of petty arguments, those of which he was quite able to sort out, brought him back to himself. The role of manager did have some healing qualities after all. "What is it, Adrian, that I can be of service to?"

"Right, I'm afraid something is wrong," he panted.

"Yes, that much I had assumed." Lawrence stared, an arm wrapped around his back, his toe melodically tapping in anxiety to hear what the young man had to say. The brutishness of clearing one's throat was required when the bellman looked as though he struggled with the words in his stomach, not wanting to let them boil to the surface. "Ah-HEM."

"Yes. Sorry, sir. It's Mrs. Adonis."

"Does she find the tearoom unsuitable?"

"What?" Adrian said, looking to his brother for a clue. When Baptiste shrugged his shoulders in reply, Adrian continued. "No, sir. It's just. I think you'd better come. She's a right mess."

XVI

Sniveling and snot corrupted the graceful beauty of Angela's desirable features. Lawrence, for his part, had already exhausted whatever remnants of energy he had left in room 319. As such, his ordinary proclivity toward doing anything and everything within his power to right whatever wrongs had befallen a guest was substantially diminished. Setting eyes on the weeping damsel, an exhale of contempt escaped him rather than his usual empathetic rise to action.

"Is there something wrong, Madam?" He had the sharp tone of annoyance to thank for the jab in the ribs given him by the silent Aurelia, who had just that moment come to stand next to him. He could nearly feel the heat fuming from her ears. "It is with great displeasure that I find you in such a state of...duress, Mrs. Adonis."

"My poor Rachel," she whimpered, holding a white handkerchief stained in several tones of charcoal, no doubt from the running of mascara as she blotted her eyes. Lawrence felt too distracted by his own woes to feign a guess as to who Rachel was. Memory was like a shadow in the night—fleeting, barely visible without a sharp squint.

"I'm sorry, Madam?" Another sharp jab in the ribs, this time in response to Lawrence holding his hand to his face, two fingers pinching the bridge of his nose while he clasped his eyes tightly shut. The pain pounded at his side. Aurelia had elbows made of steel, rolled into a deadly blunt force. This particular affront came with her sharp "Humph," that Lawrence detested so much.

"Here," Lawrence began, reaching for his own handkerchief. Thinking better of the ordeal, owing to his lapse in memory as to which handkerchief was in which pocket (and a sudden fear that he would pull the tainted piece of cotton from his jacket), he reached for a small drawer that included several toilette enhancing effects. Toothbrushes, colognes, perfumes, and of course, handkerchiefs. "Take this, Mrs. Adonis. Now, what might I be able to offer you aside from a fresh kerchief? If we work together, I am sure there is no problem we cannot solve." He attempted to stretch his least conspicuous smile across his lips. It somehow felt over-fawned.

"My Rachel," she continued in her blubbery utterance. "She's gone, just gone."

"I—did you say gone?" Lawrence leaned in, the hotel lobby bending into a tunnel around the edges of his eyesight. "Your daughter?" The memory of just who this Rachel was came flooding back with the pounding of the rain on the glass windows. The little one, the silent miniature of Angela who resembled Aurelia in her insensibility for speech. A charming little tyke.

"Ye-yes." There was a glisten in her sorrowful eyes as she finished clearing them of the salt-spattered tears. Soft. Her gaze turned from the sharpened dagger to the softness of a millpond in the morning air. Lawrence felt a mending throb in his heart from the look of her. There was warmth there, under that cold exterior, under the vicious metal plating meant to protect soft and penetrable skin from the evils of the world. There was warmth, and her name was Rachel.

"Come, now. Let's have a seat, that's better." Lawrence guided her over to the wall opposite the grand staircase, its insatiable power looming over their broken figures, to a bench where they sat together. "Let's see, what has happened, exactly?"

"I don't know, Mr. Erlik."

"Lawrence, please."

"L-Lawrence. Rachel wanted to run along and play in the garden, but when Frederick told her it wasn't safe during the storm, she threw a fit. She ran off and said she would play in the lobby instead. Frederick went to collect her about an hour later, but she wasn't here." Angela stopped to sniffle into the fresh handkerchief before she continued.

"She wasn't in our room either; I've checked. We were still in the tearoom when he went to gather her, so I would have seen her come back in. Oh, tell me you've seen her. Tell me she's been running along the lobby, and she's just playing hide and seek!"

During her pleading, Angela reached out her hand and pressed it into the shoulder of her listener. Lawrence shivered as she squeezed her perfectly painted fingers around the curve of his arm. Not from chill, but from the surprise of warmth. It radiated from her fingertips, pulsing and massaging into the fibers of his muscle. It was the first warmth he had felt since that morning, walking into the swelter of room 319.

"Er," he muttered, turning toward Aurelia. The look on her face was grave, solemn. With a brief shake of her head, Lawrence had enough information to deliver the bad news. "I'm afraid no one on the staff has seen her."

Angela went into a fit of tears. The look on her face had pleaded more than the words she used. There was desperation there, something deep and insatiable, even for a woman so obviously used to self-control.

"I shouldn't worry, Madam. You have the full weight of the hotel's staff within your armory. There will be little cause for concern once I rally the troops to your call!" The truth was, and Lawrence shuddered to think it, he loathed to help her. Not for malice or malevolence of any kind. But because he enjoyed this version of Angela. The version without daggers, the version where she was a damsel that needed his help. In the light of the hazy chandelier's gloom, the softness of it bouncing off her cheek, he even felt something lift in his stomach.

Of course, love is a silly thing altogether. Does it not drive men to madness and women to sorrow? But for some reason, beyond the base urge of desire, Lawrence felt something deeper for Angela. Something so vile in his blackened heart, frozen from the moorings of the day, that he was glad for the absence of her husband, that the visit of her hand upon his arm might linger a little longer.

"Oh, do you think? Tell me, Mr.—tell me Lawrence, tell me you'll be able to find her! She is such a sweet little girl; she never runs off or does anything without our knowledge. I cannot imagine what has gotten into her head. Oh, you mustn't judge her, Lawrence, you mustn't!"

Each time his name left her lips, still lusciously coated with red lipstick, Lawrence felt something stir within. He felt the back of his scalp begin to itch when she squeezed his arm tighter. Warmth.

Her eyes screwed up to his, and in the flash of a moment, he saw something that ignited a fire in his chest. He had a vision, one of a different life, one where his passions were dedicated to a woman rather than a hotel. One where they were together, happy, in love. I confess, I know not why the dream took the form that it did—perhaps it was the sole misfortune of Mrs. Adonis sitting next to him in a momentary display of vulnerability. That is, the woman in question transitioned from a hazy figure of an ideal, into something more concrete. This phantom woman was, in a sense, Mrs. Adonis herself. Lawrence, in his lapsed mind, leaned into his desire, yearning to make it a reality. A wave of infatuation flared in his eyes, though propriety did well enough in taming his base desires. The reader would be forgiven for any judgment in Lawrence's forthright illusion.

How could he keep her there a moment longer? How could he let the warmth wash over him and take away the pain and fear and cold?

"Of course, Mrs. Adonis." Angela, he wept to call her Angela. Would he not yearn to be familiar with her, to reach his own arm out and touch her? In that moment, as her eyes locked on his, he would submit to pain, to suffering, to damnation, all for her. Perhaps that was her way, he thought, that it was how she suffered all those in her presence to worship her. The warmth of a goddess granting you stay. Granting you the grace of her presence. "Of course, we'll find her."

Lawrence felt a rush of cold shoot up from the ground and charge with a jealous rage toward the warmth in his shoulder, clashing at it with splintered spears and dented daggers. Angela's eyes, their softness and safety, transformed in a flash, pooling in a pitch-black abyss. But when Lawrence blinked and rubbed his eyes, they were the shimmering blue they had been seconds prior. Only now her brows were furrowed.

Still, though she had clearly felt the stir of fear—not only for her daughter—but for the sanity of the man sitting beside her, Angela expressed her thanks. "Oh, Lawrence, you are too kind. Please, please hurry and make fast work of it. A mother is nothing without her daughter. Please hurry." She rose, prompting Lawrence to follow suit.

"With great haste, Madam," Lawrence bowed as he spoke, not daring to look her in the eye for fear of finding their color might have changed a third time. He preferred to remember them as blue, glistening like a pool on a hot afternoon.

"What a darling man. And to think of the injury I might have caused with my venom. Do forgive me, and I pray you not to punish Rachel for my wickedness."

Lawrence stalled at this, not knowing whether he was walking into a trap. Luckily for him, he still held on to a scrap of his usual wit. "Not a word of it, Mrs. Adonis. I haven't the slightest idea of any venom cast in my direction, and therefore, have no reason for forgiveness or punishments as you claim. Rest assured; Rachel will be found."

Much to Lawrence's surprise, as he expected Angela to run off and leave him to his oath, she stayed for a moment, lingering on the promise of a kindness undeserved. Regardless of whether our dutiful manager openly recognized it, Angela had been rather terse with him earlier that morning. And while it is easy to say that the manager has a duty to the guest, ill-mannered or otherwise, his exuberance was heartfelt. He had great success in making her truly believe that all his energy belonged to her designs. And they did, whether he knew so or not.

When she finally tore her soft eyes from Lawrence, he turned with a stern, yet not unkind, "Aurelia!" The call to action.

As had been seen on many prior occasions wherein a guest found themselves lacking in some accommodation or other—the wayward drunk who needed help cleaning himself off the floor, the disgruntled old maid who felt that her stock of pillows was not quite up to the standard of the Genovie—Aurelia simply nodded and turned to take the reins of the impending solution. As it was in this particular case, Lawrence saw fit to halt her before the effort began.

Rather annoyed for the break in her silent and graceful momentum (and conceiving to make a disgruntled expression in order to convene that discontent), she stood awaiting further instruction.

"Please tell all members of staff to be on high alert for our honorable young guest, to check the nooks and crannies," Lawrence began.

Aurelia's face began to twist and contort even further, her eyes rolling to the back of her head at having to be told such an obvious directive. It was as if she painted her features to say, "Yes, yes, can I get on with it now, or would you like to explain how to tie one's shoes first?"

Lawrence, perceptibly picking up this coded message, continued. "And," he said with inflection, causing Aurelia to uncross her tightly folded arms, "please insist that not a living soul enter room 319." She gave him pause. Her eyes narrowed, her face softened and tilted. Lawrence knew that look of confusion; he knew her mind was beginning to race. It was precisely what he'd like to have avoided, had he had his own way.

He chose to ignore Aurelia's inquisitive stare. "In fact, it's best they avoid the third floor altogether. We have a very important guest staying with us that does not need to be disturbed. I will handle the search on that floor, rest assured."

Aurelia was not assured.

"That Kosorukov fellow," she said with the silence of her eyes.

The response Lawrence decided to give turned out to be nothing more than the weary wisp of an exhale. Rather than continue in her protest—a pastime she had grown rather comfortable with, and indeed, seemed to enjoy—she nodded her understanding. Though it was fleeting.

"Thank you," Lawrence whispered, before she changed her mind. As still as carved stone, he watched her prance out of sight. Before she turned the corner, Lawrence feared she might run straight into a guest standing idly by the marble wall where prior managers found their final immortal rest through the cast of their bronze busts lined in a row.

Instead, she walked straight through her.

Sonya Ivanovna stood still, her eyes fixed on Lawrence, holding her hand with one finger stretched out and pressed to her lips. "Silence," her form said. Silence for what was the question that was plaguing his own mind. Had he not assumed that Sonya would have basked in the glory of his undoing? What her motivation for that banal hatred was, he wasn't sure. However, he was sure that it was there. He was sure that whatever she wanted, whatever her desire was in making her presence known to him, it was not for his own benefit. So, what would his silence do in the effort to obtain his misery?

Perhaps he should confess.

Lawrence knew that his confession, guiltless though he thought himself, would certainly bring him nothing but discomfort to say the least. Yet was he not stooped in discomfort? What was the constant paranoia and delusions of the dead drifting through the hotel halls if not discomfort?

Perhaps her warning for silence was not in relation to Kosorukov. But what else? Just as the thought began to take form in his mind, it was disturbed by the grim haunt of an icy voice.

"What's this about a missing child?" Cyrus asked.

"What?"

"A child is missing? Lawrence, my dear, what a day this is turning out to be for you!"

"Aye, I am sure you are privy to just what a day I've had, aren't you?"

"Whatever do you mean?" Cyrus sneered with the hint of a smile. Lawrence had, earlier in the office, decided that same smile was Cyrus's own undoing. An admission of guilt. But he had since thought better of it. Had Cyrus not always given him that vicious smile whenever he thought he had the upper hand in a sparring match of wits? It was not vindictive or malevolent, only irksome.

"Nothing, nevermind."

"Well?" Cyrus asked.

"Well, what?"

"What's this about a child missing?" It was rare that Cyrus became impatient. Or at least, it was rare that he let his impatience seethe through his teeth when he spoke. Even rarer still was the occasion that circumstances in front of house were found to be so interesting to him that he troubled himself with moving from the office.

"One of the guests, er, the one from this morning."

"You mean that troubling business with the booking for a little one?"

"The very same," Lawrence confirmed.

"You aren't saying..." Cyrus feigned concern.

"I am."

"Well, this is troubling, quite troubling indeed. Perhaps the little miss thought better of it, thought she deserved her own room. After all, she had reserved one."

"Have your jokes, Cyrus. But I hope for your sake she is unharmed. There is a monstrous storm about, you know."

"Oh, I never joke, darling. And one needn't be worried about my sake. Not when yours so obviously takes precedence."

"What's your meaning?" Lawrence chided, turning to look at Cyrus.

"I'm not quite sure I have the luxury of meaning, my dear."

"You know what I mean."

"There's that word again. I think if we are to discuss the finer points of what it is *to mean*, I should like to have another cup of tea. Won't you join me, Lawrence? Oh, that's right. You have quite the little problem to solve. You'll forgive the play on words, darling; I didn't have any meaning by it. Ah, see, I've done it again. Meaning. Well, I'll leave you now before I begin to babel as I fear I am at risk of. Until you see fit, Lawrence."

Without the knowledge as to why, Lawrence felt a suspicious pang in his stomach to plead for Cyrus to stay. Perhaps it was the fear. Sonya Ivanovna turned his blood to icy sludge. At least when he was among company, he could pretend he didn't see her staring at him.

But when he was alone, he was alone with her.

And there it was. The singular thought that illuminated the dark sea of horrors splashing about in a terrifying storm in his mind. One fragile and terrible thought that, if left to obsess over, it might have proven to consume him in some fashion that would forever chain him to the shackles of a sanity no longer his own. Sonya Ivanovna had not been seen. Not by Aurelia, who walked straight through her without a care. Not by Cyrus, who stood next to Lawrence while Sonya curled her ashen smile and held her finger to her lips. Only by Lawrence.

In the realm of hotel haunts and lavish ghouls, Lawrence was alone.

XVII

Despite the manager's preconception of loneliness, and despite the shattering depth of its darkness, Lawrence knew well not to dwell for too long. Perhaps it is something not altogether easy for the writer to convey, but the object of a task, a problem to solve, was enough to pull him from the abyss. A soul shrouded in the dark thirsting for a drink of light.

That it was unavoidable, try though he might to push it from his consciousness, was the nature of the problem. The volatility of its danger. Not that Lawrence believed there was any real danger in the Adonis child going missing. Not for her life, that is to say. Plenty of young children had gotten lost in the maze of the Genovie over the years, each of them swiftly recovered.

Of course, there was that nasty business of that Kindelay boy back in '93. He had the misfortune to have trapped himself in a cohort of the attic, the existence of which the residing manager was not even aware. It was, if memory serves the writer, three days and three nights that the unfortunate soul was made to starve in, for all intents and purposes, a small black box. By the grace of his ingenuity in pounding upon the metal ducts his little hideaway had backed up against, the little sparrow was found in his nest, a rather regrettable pile of excrement fashioned in the corner. The writer might dare to say that he has never seen such shivering upon such a young pallor before or since.

The precariousness of the situation resided in the exact nature of where the little angel might have found a suitable hiding place. The attic, the bar, a broom closet, a flooded cellar, a room where a corpse had just mysteriously disappeared. It was the variety of it. The seemingly infinite areas where a child, a small child, might find worthy of hiding within.

Lawrence, in the span of an exhale, became overwhelmingly thankful for fate's decision to exclude such a "miracle" from his life. Nothing but liabilities and headaches, the way he saw it.

Still, he did enjoy seeing their beaming faces as they traversed through the hotel doors. The well-behaved ones, at least. He had thought Rachel was just such a child. Well-behaved. She had reminded him so much of Aurelia. So prim, so proper, so silent. If all children had seen fit to behave in the manner instilled in young Miss Adonis, Lawrence felt the world would be better for it.

Yet this one fooled him. She was cunning, sly. Masking her own store of chaos in the veil of propriety. Just long enough to catch him off-guard. Perhaps Sonya Ivanovna had something to do with this. Perhaps it was her toying with him, utilizing every whim at her disposal. That thought sat upon his chest with the weight of an immovable boulder, crushing his ribs until they snapped and penetrated his lungs.

If Sonya could direct the whims of a child, who else might she be able to intoxicate with her ghoulish seduction?

And if she were behind it all, as our unnerved manager had settled upon as the impenetrable truth, would she not direct the child precisely in the direction of the room he least wanted her to open? The room that buried itself tooth and claw into the recesses of his mind?

This was, of course, worrying to the young manager. Not only was he still desperately battling with the notion that somewhere in the hotel there was a body he had to get rid of, but now he had to contend with the possibility that a small child might be his undoing. Such was the nature of his vexation. He had two options, find the child before the child found the body; or, and perhaps the much more pressing given the implications outside of the wandering child—a hotel employee stumbling upon a lifeless Kosorukov amidst their desperate search for young Rachel—find the body before the child found it.

While he could certainly look for one while keeping an eye out for the other, Lawrence chose to focus his efforts on finding Kosorukov first. Rachel would have to be the priority of the hotel staff.

As it were, he saw fit to journey to the third floor, praying to a god he had never believed in that no soul would disobey his orders and carry out their search among those rooms. Kosorukov had to be there somewhere. No better place to begin than in the offending room itself.

Thankfully for Lawrence's sake—or, perhaps more precisely observed, thankful for Arthur's sake—the jam in the lift seemed to have dissolved with the right amount of sweat and elbow grease applied to its fixture. When questioned as to the nature of the jam, Arthur simply shrugged his shoulders and uttered a few worried syllables amounting to something along the lines of, "one never knows with these things, sir," Lawrence decided not to dwell and take the improvement as a positive sign.

Therein ended the positivity for our dear manager. When Mr. Erlik stepped foot upon the well-trodden carpet of the third floor, relieved to see that it was not a flooded river, Lawrence observed something that sent him into a momentary state of paralysis.

Turning his head to the right of the lift, Lawrence saw a shadow. Not just any shadow. This particular shade was in the shape and size of a young girl. Yes, in fact, upon a rubbing of the eyes and a few blinks with the rapidity to send one into a haze, Lawrence's worst fears became realized. The young girl, no doubt Rachel Adonis, was reaching out for the handle of the door whose hinges rested firmly in the frame of room 319.

"No!" he shouted, a little louder than he had anticipated. Ordinarily, the occasion would call for an even sharper tone and a higher volume, but not wanting to arouse further suspicion than had already been accumulated throughout the afternoon, Lawrence didn't want to shout so loud as to alert the other guests.

Just the same, Lawrence was not in any state to calculate risks. Instead, the only thing he knew to do in that moment was run. Run, lest the darling Rachel set her eyes upon a vision that would not only be his ruin, but perhaps steal away an innocence that ought to be held onto as if it were precious gemstones.

The only thing Lawrence could think of in that frantic moment as he sprinted down the hall, watching Rachel disappear into the room, was how he had been daft enough to forget to lock the door upon exiting his last visit. That and to wonder whether the hallway had stretched since the last time he was there.

Reaching the end of the hallway, swinging the door open with panting breath, Lawrence was met by nothing.

Not a little girl, not a corpse, not even a smirking specter.

Simply an empty room. Thinking of all the tricks that had been played on him up until this point, Lawrence swung around and locked the door. Not only the latch, but he made sure to hook the chain, thinking of how it was out of reach to a girl of Rachel's height.

If his eyes had not been playing tricks on him, which he wasn't entirely sure they weren't, Rachel would not be able to slip past him. And so, the search began.

Lawrence ripped up the bedroom first. Throwing pillows across the room, stripping the bed of the large comforter and, for no logical reason, removing the sheets as well. All the while, he labored under the illusion that he might be permitted to ignore the ghastly bit of script still painted on the bedroom wall. There was even the faintest inclination—one which Lawrence dutifully followed—to flip the mattress from its box spring. Were any child harboring underneath the weight of the mattress, he would be sure to know about it before leaving the room. As was the case for dead bodies. Any spot that a child might find suitable for hiding from hotel managers might have been a suitable spot for Roman Pavlovich Kosorukov to be stowed away.

But young Rachel was simply nowhere to be found. Not under the covers, not hiding between mattresses, not under the bed. Nor in the armoire, nor the closet, nor the exceptionally large dresser drawers that when one stretched one's imagination, one might envision a child managing to close after having crawled inside.

The master bathroom was found empty with nothing in the corners and nothing hiding behind the shower curtain. For all intents and purposes, the sleeping quarters were exceptionally vacant. Apart from an unnerved hotel manager, that was.

It wasn't until a giggle came from the parlor that Lawrence

had a renewed sense of spirit. Perhaps she was hiding in the coat closet, behind the leather couch, underneath the console table, wrapped in the velvet drapery. Perhaps. But they were all, to the detail, vacant.

Apart from Lawrence, not a soul resided in room 319. He stood in the center of the room, a heaving chest threatening to completely unfasten his already partially untucked shirt from his trousers. His waistcoat was so crumpled from moving around that the center of his stomach felt several degrees colder from the missing layer of protection. It was a sight to see. A man of perfection driven to such a disheveled state. A pity.

On top of it all, Lawrence now had to contend with the possibility that he was hearing things—a worrisome realization on its own. Such a thing becomes doubly unnerving when the sound in question is an isolated child's giggle, echoing in the vacancy of the very hotel room where one's sanity already began to unravel hours prior. It leaves one rather desperate. Suffice it to say, the chill creeping up his spine, resulting in a violent shudder as his eyes pleaded with the empty room to show him the solid form of a child, was well placed.

Lawrence turned to face the window, which, evidently, seemed to be in danger of crashing into the room from the howling wind and pounding rain. It was a funny thing—Lawrence turned so as to make himself decent in privacy, as if facing the door was a type of exposure to the world. A ridiculous notion, he thought, tugging on the waistcoat and pulling his messy hair back.

Right at the moment he started to feel put together again, he was interrupted by the commanding, yet paradoxically soothing, timbre of a voice he had grown rather fond of as of late.

"Hello, Mr. Erlik," the voice said, demanding that he turn around. However, in that moment, Lawrence's sense of want was altogether in direct contradiction with such a formidable command. In fact, he had more of a mind to sprint straight through the thin glass windowpane, welcoming the storm in to cleanse room 319 as he plummeted down the macabre facade of the Genovie. Perhaps for the first time in his life, he might just welcome death with open arms.

As if he had spent his life carved of stone, only to break free from the stationary nature that marble embodies, he began to turn. To twist, to slowly move himself in the direction of his speaker with a climbing temperature making its way from his stomach up through his neck and finding a suitable position to rest upon his cheeks, coloring them rosy. Like a child that had been caught stealing a slice of pie cooling from the windowsill, he faced his visitor. Angela Adonis.

Of course, he was well aware that it was Mrs. Adonis speaking to him. How could he mistake the coolness of her voice? But it was the question of precisely how it was that Mrs. Adonis came to be within the walls of 319. The door was locked, the chain was latched. That was more than the suspicion of a memory, for Lawrence glanced beyond the well-curved figure to confirm that the door remained in the very condition that he had left it. Locked.

But here she was. Though she was not in her former state; she was not the sniveling, groveling shell of a woman who had lost something dear to her. She was not...incidental. Rather, she stood with purpose, with design, with the intent of a woman who stands before a man with full knowledge of the shift in the dynamic of power between the two of them. For, as it related to Lawrence Erlik, Angela Adonis was a goddess, a Venus on earth.

"Madam," he managed to mutter, his eyes darting from her to the small pool of blood he stood in front of that had mysteriously managed to avoid soaking into the rug. "I apologize for the…mess."

Perplexed though it may have made Lawrence, the stunning figure of Angela Adonis made no quip of reply. Except to breeze toward him. Her eyes flashed like a wild cat on the hunt, her smirk was resolutely shining with red lipstick, and her dress was wound tightly around her waist. Lawrence began to babble like a madman, speaking much but saying very little, all the while she strode.

The feeling of her breath against his lips was the only thing that managed to still his stuttered speech. With little memory of how it came to be, Lawrence felt his arm wound around her waist in a warm snug.

What a mystery to the manager it was to find that her form was soft and resolute, warm and chilled to the bone, exciting and perilously dull, all at once. Chest burned of fire, frozen with ice. The quiver of a lip gave way to the sea of serenity. Would that he had her to himself, what happiness he would succumb to. What burden he would leave behind; that of the office, that of the dead, that of the damned.

Yet there she was, pressed into him as if they were two youths in the spring of life, yearning to know only themselves and one another. Breathing, panting, choking.

"Well, Mr. Erlik?" she whispered, her eyes bouncing from his eyes to his lip, back to his eyes once more. *Propriety be damned,* thought he, merciless though he knew the devil's trappings to be. *That I should perish with the wicked for the sin of my temptation, so shall it be.*

As his lips pressed fervently into hers, he heard the clock strike four from the lobby, though from the distance it might have been impossible. The thunder rolled, the rain poured, and something foreign and unbelonging found its way to crash to the window. Something with a flutter.

Yet her lips were not warm or filled with the passion he felt radiating from her breasts. She did not curl her arms around his neck and press him closer, beckoning him to continue with his gaiety. And when he opened his eyes he saw, not Angela Adonis yearning for a moment with Lawrence Erlik, but the black searching eyes of Sonya Ivanovna.

Lawrence collapsed in fright, falling straight backward and, only for the grace of the side table, avoided landing in the pool of Kosorukov's blood. As it took our dear manager more than the span of a single breath to collect himself from such a grizzly fright, one would be forgiven for sympathizing with his consternation of finding that he was alone in the room once more.

There he sat on the brink of madness, contemplating the futility in moving forward with his day. He would have been lying to himself if he had rejected the notion that he carried some small measure of desire to see an end to it. To lock himself up in room 319 and wait for the authorities. Indeed, as his plan to find and bury Kosorukov had failed so spectacularly, there was no doubt that such authorities would arrive any moment. Perhaps he would be permitted to make it through one last dinner service.

He did so enjoy the dinner services. And, if it was the case that he had in fact heard the tolling of the grandfather clock striking four, there was not very much time at all until the hour of service arrived. He so wanted to see an end to this business before then.

The longer he sat helplessly upon the floor, the more his memory began to refresh. Kosorukov, Sonya Ivanovna, the little note in his pocket, the message on the wall. Rachel.

That was it; he simply must have been seeing things. First Rachel, then Mrs. Adonis, then Sonya Ivanovna. All in the span of a few hours he had allowed himself to quite foolishly unravel. That was fixable. With a few tugs of the waistcoat and a proper measure of counting, Lawrence Erlik would be right as rain.

Rain. The storm had been hollering outside the windows for hours now. A pounding monsoon of contempt, or so it felt. Lawrence dared himself to step over the sticky mess he had so narrowly avoided only moments before and pulled the drapery from the window.

The rain had fallen for so long at such a demoralizing speed, that an incongruous body of water had formed in the gardens. More than a pooling of rainwater—a snake of a river wrapping around the hotel and flooding into the parking lot. If such a roaring monster of water were to continue in its growth, Lawrence feared it would endanger the very safety of the hotel.

It was at the moment when he began to worry about the safety of the hotel and, more specifically, the ability of the front doors to hold back what seemed to be an insurmountable amount of water, that he remembered the cellar. The hotel's very own growing bog of danger. And it was when the thought of the flooding of the cellar crossed his mind that the lights surrounding the manager began to flicker. It was not just that they were flickering, a worrisome thing for a hotel manager to witness alone, but that they all flickered together. In such a way, they were indicating a problem, a very grave problem. For if the lights were all flickering in this room, then it was not an insurmountable stretch that the lights may be malfunctioning in every room. And if they were so in every room, then there was something to be said for adorning the fear of what Lawrence now saw as the inevitable. The fear of a flooding cellar reaching the electrical panels and turning out the lights entirely.

As Lawrence, chided into action by just such a concern, turned around to rid room 319 of his presence, the fluttering returned to the window. A terrifyingly cold chill ran down his spine when he turned his head and saw through the streaks of rain slathering the windowpane, a rather haughty and exasperated raven attempting to peck his way into the room. When the veracity of the bird's aggression caused the glass to crack, Lawrence found the fear to be motivating enough to quickly undo the chain on the door, swing it open, turn the key on the other side and take a heavy breath as he heard the tumblers fall into place.

Three tugs of the waistcoat gave him enough strength to embark upon a search. Not for Kosorukov, nor for a young girl prancing about the hotel's most secret hiding spots. But for a hammer and a handful of nails.

XVIII

Conviction is a formidable maiden. Such is especially the case when she infects the blood of a man who has spent the better part of an afternoon rapidly approaching his wit's end. In such a case, the assuredness with which the poor creature conducts his or herself clashes with the safety and peace of what is happily considered the orthodox. One must be careful. If one allows conviction to blind one's ability to see facts and figures that are laid out in front of them, regrettable consequences could be determined as a result of one's actions. Our dear friend Lawrence was nervously balancing on the threads of just such a state of mind as he marched through the main hall in order to find Joel's broom closet.

The nature of a broom closet was one that demanded a man such as Lawrence to be unfamiliar with. In fact, the manager's lavender soap-scented hands had come into contact with the rusty brass of the broom closet perhaps three times in his time at the hotel. But on this particular occasion, after Lawrence had ignored the brimming faces of half of the hotel staff along the route to the closet door, his hand reached with a bit of a shake.

It was not the worrisome shiver of a man left out in the cold without a proper jacket for too long, nor the tremor of a man turned brittle after residing in the fruits of life for longer than expected. This was quite simply the type of shiver that only ever seems to come along when a man has been thoroughly plagued with a type of trepidation that finds itself seeping into his bones. An unquenchable fear.

For Lawrence, this fear was at war with itself. The truth of the matter was, as he continued to relentlessly mull over the idiosyncrasies of the dead, his mind might have been more perturbed by the splitting of fear into two monolithic pillars. In such a case, a man has little hope. When there is but one driving force behind one's fear, perhaps it could be deemed possible to face that fear head on. A struggle of the light against the wicked. But when one's fear takes the form of not one, but two ghastly configurations, one finds oneself to be rather outnumbered.

In the case of Lawrence's current disquietude, he was caught between the realization that not only do the dead linger beyond the grave, but one seemed to have attached herself to his very consciousness. There was also the pain of guilt. That guilt festered the longer he contemplated the letters scratched with ink on the scrap of paper burning a hole in his pocket.

It wasn't that he fancied himself a murderer. No, he was quite reasonably sure that the sender of the little scrap of paper had that particular detail wrong. Unconscionably wrong, in fact. However, there was the ever-inescapable problem of optics. But Lawrence was well on his way toward dealing with that unavoidable issue.

The broom closet was much the same as Lawrence remembered it amid his last unfortunate foray into the dreary vault. Dark, damp, and with an indescribably putrid scent that was slightly reminiscent of a piece of cheese. Cheese that had spoiled terribly in the sun, that is to say.

Lawrence's eyes scanned the small space in desperate search for the proper instrument to put an end to the whole affair. Well, perhaps not the whole affair. The rather troubling detail pertaining to the whereabouts of the plump old man's cold lump of a body was something else entirely inopportune. However, Lawrence had a particular idea in the back of his mind that most of his worries would begin to subside after the conclusion of this auspicious errand, if only he could find the hammer he was so desperately in search of.

Perhaps it is a silly notion to find in the mind of a hotel manager—perhaps even sillier still when one contemplates the incontrovertible lack of faith in this particular mind of this particular manager—but in the moment when his eyes gleaned the slight protrusion of the hammer's handle from a fold of peculiar fabric that had been balled and tossed about, Lawrence had the inclination to thank divine intervention. After all, as it was so well hidden from the untrained eye, it seemed rather like a miracle that he should find it. Further still, the miracle seemed to extend itself to the discovery of a handful of rusty looking nails rolling about the floor under the hammer's well-used head.

It is with a particular apprehension, dear reader, that the writer should see fit to expound upon the covetousness with which that troublesome smile curled around Lawrence's lips. One would be forgiven for having chills run down one's back at the mere sight. There was something in that very moment, as fate would have it, that twisted and contorted in the manager's chest as he reached for the hammer. Something deep, something not altogether saintly. The notion that Lawrence had clung to so vehemently up until that very point—that is, the notion that he was, in a whole and complete sense, incapable of killing—seemed to slip from his sweaty fingers as they curled around that hammer.

Thankfully for Lawrence, he had no one he felt was worth killing—at the moment. Sure, Angela was becoming a nuisance, and Cyrus had never done anything to keep from climbing under Lawrence's skin. But these were not murderable offenses, to say the least. There was, of course, the question of his tormentor. The writer has insisted on the anonymity that naturally wrapped itself around such a word as tormentor, for that is exactly as Lawrence saw it. And therein lay his problem. Anonymity. The one living being—one would do well to emphasize the word *living*, for Lawrence had a select few belonging to the world thereafter that he would have had some choice words and a proper swing of the hammer for—the one living being Lawrence would see fit to bash into a pulp was unknown to him.

But there it was, the fundamental change of a man's very nature. The nature to kill. The sensation filled the man like a bucket of ice water crashing through and replacing his organs with glaciers. With a new conviction, a maddening conviction, Lawrence walked with the tight-gripped hammer in his hand toward the lift.

The only problem of the whole affair was once Lawrence got back to room 319, he found that he had forgotten a very important aspect of his errand. That of the wooden plank.

Pesky, rotten, filthy things, wooden planks. *How are we to dispel ourselves from troubles such as these without the necessary instruments of our design?* Though, between friends, there is significant merit to the suspicion that he had fallen prone to muttering to himself rather than silently thinking. Muttering with not a negligible amount of spittle, at that. And the reader would do well to avoid posing the question of exactly what Lawrence's meaning was with the use of the word *we* in place of the much less troublesome *I,* for it is beyond the knowledge of the writer. Though, at the risk of breaking down the barriers of a professional narrative, the writer will concede the strangeness of the habit.

With forgiveness of the digression, it would serve the purpose of this record to return to Lawrence's exasperated fume, standing outside the door of room 319.

The nature of that exasperation was not simply that he found himself without wooden planks, but that in order to retrieve them and not cause further delay given the approaching dinner hour, he would have to do the one thing this very errand was concocted to avoid his ever having to do again. He would have to enter room 319.

Such a curious thing it was. For in that daunting moment, the trial that his better angels (or perhaps his hidden demons) hoisted upon the small of his back in order that he might once more turn that handle, Lawrence had a premonition. Little did he know what awaited him beyond the door, but a feeling in the air had returned. This feeling, this unnamed notion that had been so absent from Lawrence's immediate surroundings ever since the knife slid through the old Russian's jaw, was warmth.

Do not mistake the word. Not warmth in the sense of the room's temperature, for Lawrence had well experienced such in both room 319 and the office. Warmth of the spirit. The hope that everything was going to be alright, baseless though the claim may have been. But for a brief second, as the creak of the door resounded through the hallway and just before the appearance of the room was made visible, Lawrence felt relief.

But the shadows of torture are often darkest when the victim flirts with such a tantalizing word as hope.

It opens one's mind to all manner of deceptions and artifices. Indeed, the very interpretation of immutable fact might itself come into jeopardy in the mind of a man who has given himself to the intoxication of the word hope. A vile pursuit, no doubt.

Such was the case when Lawrence opened the door to room 319 to find the old sod—that is to say, Roman Pavlovich Kosorukov—sitting perched upon the tufted oxblood leather couch, snifter in hand. Not alive by some divine miracle, as Lawrence's heart inadvisably clung to, but stone dead. Drained of all color. Cold, stiff, spent.

It wasn't until Lawrence let drop the hammer on his toe in excitement, danced in a frightfully jumpy manner to rid himself of the pain of a possibly broken toe, and dashed over the chair to greet the Russian as an old friend that he realized his folly. And somehow, though Lawrence had been well aware of Kosorukov's fate up until the brief lapse of time that he had managed to fool himself that he was still living, his heart split in two. It was as if he had relived the whole affair. The brandy, the confession, the knife, the blood. All together rushing through his memory in a cacophony of the macabre.

Coming to the realization that the shell of a man sat in his midst, Lawrence found the urge to speak. Whether through madness or desperation (two forces often caught in the throes of a love affair), he found he was unable to control himself.

"Where have you been, Romik?" he shouted, throwing his hands in the air.

Romik sat still. Pensive, as if to say he had yet to conclude that for himself.

"Have you any idea what sort of panic you've set me under? Any idea at all?" The berating continued. "Why, I suppose you could have uncovered the whole of the affair through your discovery! Though I don't suppose you thought about that?"

The inquisition continued for about four or five minutes until Lawrence came to the unavoidable realization that he had in fact been speaking to a man that could not respond to him. A man that could not respond to anyone if he wanted to.

Of course, nothing could have sailed this point straight into the harbor of Lawrence's conscious mind more than the manner in which the old Russian slowly slumped toward his left side until he found a new vocation of lying on the couch.

"Put yourself together, man," Lawrence whispered to himself. But this was one of those rare instances where the action was easier done than it was said. For in this very moment, Lawrence realized the founded purpose of his design strengthened. Not only was he now able to ensure that no guest or staff member entered the room bearing the blood of Kosorukov, but now that same room bore Kosorukov himself.

With a revival of his former fervor, Lawrence set to work again.

Seeing as the whole of room 319 was no longer fit for accommodation (at least not to the standard of the Genovie), Lawrence set his eyes on the beautiful armoire that sat in the bedroom within view from where he stood. A tower to excellent craftsmanship; it was a pity to have to destroy it. But Lawrence felt a deep sense of piety in his purpose. So much so that he felt himself to be absolved of the means with which he chose to despoil himself of the heavy burden Kosorukov saw fit to bestow upon him.

However, when he turned to retrieve the hammer that was resting with the pile of nails in the hallway, he was made to realize that the door had closed. No matter, such was the nature of a hotel room door. When left open, they slowly creeped closed in order to protect the sanctity of a guest's privacy, however forgetful they may be in the art of closing of doors. What was particularly off-putting was the additional decoration of more smeared scribbling in a thick ruby-red ink, much akin to what Lawrence had awoken to in the bedroom only a few feet away.

But this writing was not there before—Lawrence was quite sure of that. This was now the fourth time he had found himself within the confines of the abominable apartment and on no other such occasion had his eyes caught the quite noticeable scribble that now ornamented the entryway. What's more, it still shined with the gloss of wetness, of freshness.

"You'd better run, Romik," he whispered to himself, reading each word aloud as if it were slicing through his throat.

Perhaps an ordinary man would be forgiven for utilizing the appearance of a gruesome letter such as that to put off his design. In fact, many men would likely burst through the room, forgetting all about the hammer and small collection of rusty nails, and run straight down the stairs and out of the hotel lobby. Lawrence, however, was no such ordinary man. Instead, it further invigorated his energies with the vehemence of inspired action.

The hammer was quickly collected, its sharp end turned at the ready, and its curved teeth soon found its way into splintering the wood of the armoire. With such gusto did the hammer fall, its blunt force biting into the beauty of a more civilized era. But all the more impressive was the imposing exertion of Mr. Erlik's arm winding back and falling loose, much like the ingenious design of the Springdale, employed by the mighty General Dionysius I of Syracuse as he rained hellfire upon the ever-frightened Motyans.

With each swing of the hammer, Lawrence grunted through gritted teeth. "Five keys, four visits to room 319, three caws of the crow, two black eyes. One. Blasted. Death." Upon the final syllable, Lawrence's hammer swung truer than it had up until that point, coming crashing toward the armoire with all the might and fury that our young manager had to offer. Only, when its head crashed down, it landed not on the mess of chipped wood and sharp splinters, but on flesh and bone. In fact, the vision of a young, emaciated woman with blood dripping from the corner of her lips flashed before Lawrence's very eyes.

He could see the fear in her eyes for the split second before the hammer came crashing down, its blunt force cracking through the young woman's skull and splattering bits of warm matter across the room. Lawrence knew that petrified face. It was the same face that had been finding merit in haunting him all afternoon. "Sonya Ivanovna," he yelped and let the handle of the hammer release from his fervent grip before tripping on his own feet and falling straight back.

Though one in Lawrence's position might have expected a body to fall to the floor, perhaps even finding itself landing upon the manager as he scrambled to get every limb to a clear sanctuary from the impending fall, something else entirely transpired. While Lawrence kept his eyes shut, inching across the carpet to remove himself from the bedroom, he heard a loud thud. But not the thud of a body—the thud of a tool. A metal tool. The head of a hammer.

When Lawrence opened his eyes, it was with a startling measure of bewilderment that he realized nothing lay upon the cold floor but his hammer. No body, no Sonya Ivanovna Kosorukov.

This seemed quite impossible to Lawrence, and not at all settling. That is, it was as far from the realm of possibilities that he was comfortable venturing in the present moment, though the day's journey had rather expanded the bounds of his own sane definition of the word. But the piece that had sent him to a new realm of spiraling was the question of the physical. He had felt that hammer crash through skull and brain. He'd felt bits of bone and blood splatter across his face. And while his arm was in the automated state of retracting from the previous blow, he felt the hammer become stuck in the victim's head to the point where it would only remove itself after the coaxing of a good bit of proper yanking.

He had felt every bit of it, and yet it hadn't happened.

But Lawrence was not altogether comforted with the sweet liquor of vindication. It hadn't mattered whether or not it had happened. The truth of it was, he experienced it. What worried him even more than the experience was the enjoyment thereof.

There was, mixed in with the horror and the sorrow, relief. The relief that perhaps that crashing blow might put a final end to Sonya's chicanery about the hotel. Yet as it turned out, the very harrowing happening was yet another example of her tormenting him.

If only for the desire to see to the end of his aims, Lawrence allowed himself to shake off the mysteries of the last thirty seconds and set back to work.

While the whole of the bashing of the armoire proved to be a rather messy business, he was able to find a few serviceable pieces with which to board the door. After collecting three or four splintered stretches of wood, Lawrence gathered the hammer and marched into the hallway. He dared not stop to glance at Kosorukov a final time, he dared not look at the script smeared across the interior side of the door. Time was of the essence.

It should be noted, and indeed has been touched upon, that a manager would do well to avoid causing a disturbance in the hallways of a hotel. It is especially inadvisable to pound nails through wood and plaster so close to the dining hour. But the urgency in the situation called for a certain break in decorum.

Lawrence quickly nailed four boards across the door frame, being sure to land a nail on each side of the frame as well as right through the center of every board, attaching it to the very oak of the door itself. In so doing, he began to feel a good deal lighter. However, as one can never overdo oneself in the art of "good measure," Lawrence collected the key from his pocket, inserted its head into the keyhole and turned it tightly until he heard the tumblers fall securely into place. Feeling it too precarious a position to leave his safety to the designs of an exposed lock and a couple of planks of wood, Lawrence left the key in the keyhole, raised his hammer with the tallest stretch of the arm he could, and brought it down faster than lady guillotine gliding her vicious teeth toward the pale neck of Madame Deficit.

The feeling of finality was at hand, resting in the pocket of a hotel manager in the form of half of a broken key. With this small comfort in mind, a smile formed on Lawrence's lips as he strode down the hall and made his way toward the lobby, where guests would no doubt be gathering for a refreshing cocktail before dinner, which would be promptly served at seven o'clock.

XIX

"Where have you been hiding?"

The words were not spoken, as Aurelia's quips and phrases seldom were, but were hinted at through the subtle raise of the brow just high enough to cause a suitably worrying wrinkle in her forehead. While Lawrence might have been able to ascertain the subject of the inquisition, the manner of the contempt with which she conveyed her inquiry was borne out through the hands fastened to the hips. A regular dressing down, as they say.

However, as has already been no doubt sufficiently relayed to the reader, Lawrence was in no mood to be trifled with. While his inner sympathies for Aurelia's charm might have ordinarily endowed her with a certain leniency in her silent speech toward him, on this particular occasion, she was met with nothing short of haughtiness.

"Do tell me when it was the order of the world changed such that I am now meant to explain my whereabouts to you rather than the reverse?" he huffed.

However, he was dealing with no ordinary spirited girl. Aurelia stood her ground, and stood it well.

"And what about the child?" her brow furrowed and eyes

narrowed to say.

"Perhaps you ought to ask yourself such a question and report back to me, Aurelia. Was I not only responsible for searching one floor of the hotel, when there are indeed four? One man searching a quarter of such a building while you were armed with the rest of the staff. And she looks at me as if I am to know. Tell me, have you not found her then?"

Aurelia moved her hands from her waist and kept them frozen in the space just in front of her stomach, signaling a second thought. However, all thoughts Lawrence had of victory in this little exchange were decidedly premature. Aurelia folded her arms in the ever-distressing checkmate of: you are the manager here, not I.

To this, Lawrence had little choice but to concede. Not that a concession did him or Aurelia any good, for there still remained the problem of a very much missing child running about the hotel.

What was most noticeable to Lawrence in this moment, however, was how little that bothered him. Not much at all, in fact. For now that he had boarded up his concerns into the confines of room 319, making it rather impossible to pass through that doorway without a good bit of strength and the help of a fireman's ax, there was little concern of Rachel causing any trouble for him. At least not in the unorthodox sense. That is to say, her roaming about the hotel would not lead to the inevitability of a murder conviction.

"Well," he said at the end of an exaggeratedly long exhale, "she could have only gotten so far. The storm would no doubt prevent her from leaving the hotel, so that rules out the question of searching the grounds." To this, Aurelia simply nodded, clearly delighted to be through with their sparring match. "Have you checked the vacancies, the closets, the launderer, the boiler room, the…" and as Lawrence continued to rattle off a list of possible hiding places that a young child might find herself crawling into in order to hide away from the world's evils, Aurelia continued to nod her head. Owing to the particularly contentious beginning of their current encounter, she fought hard to keep her eyes from rolling so as not to cause another stir. Oh, the sacrifices we make in the face of power.

But it was when Lawrence finally listed off the kitchens as a possibility that Aurelia's head stopped nodding, her brow furrowing in a slow and uncertain fashion. Her eyes screwed up toward Lawrence's and a look of remorse covered her blushed cheeks.

"The kitchens, Aurelia! The kitchens! Honestly, how have we managed to let that castle slip by our efforts?" How indeed? For there were all manners of nooks and crannies for little ones to stow away in hopes that the seekers would confound themselves in an exhaustive search for the hider's benefit.

And so, it was off to the kitchens!

If one were to witness the manner in which the pair, hotel manager and assistant hotel manager, stretched their stride toward the den of delicacies that was Mr. Anton Bakker's domain, they would have figured nothing was wrong. At least nothing out of the usual for a hotel. The guests of the Genovie simply sat idly by as Lawrence pushed passed, followed in toe by young Aurelia. The cardinal difference between their appearance rested in their gait, with Lawrence fumbling over his feet as Aurelia moved with the grace of the ballet.

Indeed, there were many a guest to witness the occasion. Senators and their sons, steel tycoons, railway owners, Wall Street men. Men of fortune and men of luck, those of inheritance and those who rose from the mud and excrement that their city threw in their direction when they had the audacity to have been born amongst the slums. And why were they all gathering in the lobby? To pay homage to the maiden of the hour, the principal languish of the broken hearted, and the relentless fire of the jubilant. In a word, the drink.

For as Lawrence and Aurelia weaved their way through the meandering crowd, the clock was striking the fifth hour of the second half of the day, cocktail hour.

But there were two worrisome faces one might pluck out of the hopeful crowd. The face of a matriarch in the making, accompanied by the whimsical, devil-may-care air of a man who had risen to a station far above what his propriety gave him the aptitude for. As a matter of fact, it was a curious thing that the face of this young man was in such a state of apathy for the moment's urgency, given the daughter that his wife had struggled so hard for so many years to conceive, was still missing.

"Mr. Erlik! Oh, Mr. Erlik! Pray, tell me. Have you found her? Have you found my darling Rachel?" And such was the cause of Lawrence and Aurelia coming to a screeching halt in their commission just as quickly as they had gotten started.

"Mrs. Adonis," Lawrence said, feeling quite the unnatural stir muddle amongst his loins. He realized, as he looked into her eyes, stained with tear smudged mascara, that this was the first moment he had caught a glimpse of her since they met in room 319. Or rather, it would be more prudent to discern the difference between reality and the fickleness of imagination. For Lawrence could not yet convince himself of the simple fact that he had not, in fact, seen Angela since that fateful moment when she had sent him about this quest. There was no scandalous visit to room 319, no pressing against his chest, and certainly no kiss in the throes of passion.

While it is quite simple for the reader to understand that fact, the truth of it was, Lawrence had yet to come to grips with it. Not until he had seen that look in her soft, perilous eyes had he accepted that fact.

"Mrs. Adonis," he repeated, taking on the persona of his former self and letting slip the hysterics of the psychotic. However, the necessary words did not flow freely from his chest.

"You have been trying, haven't you, good man?" Ah, so there *was* a hint of concern in Frederick's voice. Just enough to make it believable that it was there, but not too much to cause his wife to spiral into a sort of neurotic fever. Perhaps he wore apathy like a facade. A carefully crafted mask intended, after years of hardship, for the keeping of panic at bay. Especially those around him. "I mean to say, you have all your men…and women searching."

Just as Lawrence was beginning to gain an appreciation for the man, he had to mutter his last words in a manner of contempt with his eyes darting toward young Aurelia. The devil with him! It was one thing to accost the manager of the Hotel Genovie, but to set one's sights on the purity in human form known to the mortal world by the name of Aurelia was an altogether unforgivable sin!

"Yes," Lawrence said with spite seething like smoke through the gaps of his teeth. "Yes, Mr. Adonis, you may rest assured that all of our men and our women under the employ of the Genovie are searching dutifully for your daughter. It is my intention to find her, as we were presently making our way toward the kitchens to—"

"The kitchens!" Angela exclaimed. "Oh, but there are so many things she could hurt herself with, Frederick. Knives, forks, broken china, hot pans. Oh, what have we done, letting her out of our sight? I told you, Frederick, I told you we need to keep an eye

on her. To always know where she is!" Through the last few
syllables, Mrs. Adonis had taken up the pastime of beating her
balled up fist into her husband's chest. This labor was cut short,
much to Mr. Adonis's pleasure, by the keeling over of his wife in
wincing pain. Her hand clutched tightly to a soft spot on her
midsection while her other kept her balance through the use of her
fingertips touching the floor.

Lawrence, in a manner that might have been considered
suspicious to a husband that was even a bit more attentive than Mr.
Adonis, dove down in order to offer a helping hand. More than a
helping hand, in fact. His hand slipped, in a far too familiar fashion,
underneath her arm with a tender squeeze of compassion that
went far beyond the bounds of an employee-guest relationship.

Ah, but it was the look in the young woman's eye as she shot
a glance in his direction that was the most questionable factor of
the exchange. Red and puffy though her eyes were, the makeup
betraying the subterfuge of her age, there was a returning of
tenderness in her gaze. A simple gesture, yet a fruitful one.
Something Lawrence could hold onto, if for nothing else than for
the comfort of his own charm.

"Are you quite alright, madam?" The words came out in more
of a whisper than a full-throated inquiry. Such was the nature of
his tenderness in his approach, that a few strange heads had stilled
their muttering to turn at the scene.

"What?" Angela asked, still clutching her stomach as if her
intestines would spill onto the floor were she to let go. "What?
Oh, yes. Yes, I am quite alright, Mr. Erlik. You needn't be
concerned."

"She's had these nasty little fits ever since Rachel was born,"
Frederick offered, lowering to take over the responsibility of
hoisting his wife back to the surface of the standing crowd. "I keep

telling her to see Doctor Hempstead about it, but she just refuses."

"You are a doctor, darling."

"A surgeon! Not an, an, an obstetrician! Really, he ought to have a proper fix. It's been bothering you for years."

"Really, darling, it's nothing."

As Angela formed the word "darling" with her crimson painted lips, Lawrence couldn't help but notice that she'd flashed her eyes in his direction. Only for a moment, but enough to make his heart flutter.

"Might I offer the simple remedy of a glass of tonic? Perhaps a drop of gin, if it should suit your sensibility?" Lawrence offered, ignoring the stern look Aurelia's raised eyebrows were radiating in his direction at the mention of the word gin.

"You know, I think that is a capital idea, old man. What do you say, Angela? I fear this business of finding Rachel has worn you rather thin."

"But Frederick, we have to find—"

"You'll be no use to her if you are at your wit's end when she is finally found. I think we can rest assured with the search remaining in Mr.—"

"Erlik, sir. Lawrence, if you please."

"R-right. Mr. Erlik's capable hands."

"Oh...alright. Perhaps just one small drink. I do think it will settle the stomach rather well."

"That's the spirit," Lawrence interjected as Frederick was about to open his mouth, presumably—judging by the bewildered look stretched across his face—to utter the same words himself. "Come, I'll have a table set out for you in the Swan."

The Golden Swan was a thing of beauty, owing much to the brass details about the room that were polished to such a shine as to appear golden. She—for everyone in the hotel referred to the

Swan as if she were a member of the female sex—had been constructed fifteen years after the Gonovie first opened her doors in response to a portly old fellow, who had made the hotel somewhat of a permanent residence, continuously complaining that a proper bar was necessary for the enjoyment of a glass of brandy at eleven o'clock in the evening. There were simply too few dissenting voices to prevent the inevitable.

Lawrence—who had taken complete control as Angela's guide, leaving Frederick to follow along as a borzoi with its tail tucked curtly beneath its legs—ushered her along past the long stretch of the bar, where Monsieur Mino Perry was pounding away at a brick of ice, to land upon a table neatly tucked in the corner of the room. He slid Angela into the seat as one drops a handful of change into a jar and snapped his finger.

"Good evening, Madam, Monsieur," the fellow hailing from the French quarter of New Orleans greeted. Wearing his golden jacket snug above the waist, Gabriel DuPont was a man of the old manner. His right arm was tucked behind his back with the left held astutely in front of him at the perfect ninety-degree angle, ornamented with a freshly pressed stark white towel. "How may I be of service this evening? We have—"

But before our dear old DuPont was able to wrestle through his lisp to explain the specials of the hour, Lawrence interrupted him with a closed-eyed shaking of the head. "That won't be necessary, Gabriel. Simply a tonic with a splash of gin for the lady and for the gentleman…"

"Ah, I suppose I'll have…a sherry. Whatever you recommend, Mr.…."

"Er, DuPont, sir. At your service."

"Mr. DuPont, thank you."

Without another word, Gabriel clicked his heels before

giving a bow so low, his hair was in danger of greasing the edge of the table. He then walked briskly toward the bar for a bit of rabble rousing with the old bartender, who had exhausted himself with the battle of the iceberg.

All the while, Lawrence felt himself outstaying his welcome, evidenced more than anything by the sharp tug at his coattail by a rather perturbed Aurelia standing over his shoulder.

"Yes, well," he said without giving Aurelia any sign that he had received the message. "We shall leave you to it. In the meantime, Aurelia and I will continue our search."

"In the kitchens?" Angela said wistfully.

"In the kitchens," Lawrence confirmed.

After lingering at the side of their table for far too long, Lawrence bid his adieu and took a considerable number of steps before turning to Aurelia and whispering, "Perhaps we'd better pay Chef Anton a visit."

Aurelia raised her left eyebrow and tapped the tip of her heel as if to say, "Indeed, I should say so." In a way, Lawrence was happy for the distraction of Aurelia's impertinent disposition. Things were beginning to feel altogether normal.

As they exited the Golden Swan, Lawrence made sure to give a certain nod to Mino. Mino responded in turn with a knowing nod of his own, the kind that is only ever established between two souls connected through an eternal understanding of one another's natural temperaments, especially when those temperaments were on the verge of being disturbed.

Such was the case, as we well know, of the Genovie's manager. However, the distress that had been mounting within the manager's chest, and had for a moment begun to subside, began to reinforce itself to the tune of the most peculiar instrument. It was not the ivory of the piano that the Maestro had begun to tap along in order to bring about a much-needed sense of calm through the air of the hotel, but something with a rather airy, yet rich, tone. One that, though Lawrence had never heard echo through the halls of the hotel, he felt he knew better than his own hand. Yet still, it sent a shiver down his spine and his blood to a boil.

"Do you hear that?" he couldn't help but ask in a flippant manner.

Aurelia turned with a brow that seemed to convey the message, "What are you talking about?"

"That sound," Lawrence answered, knowingly. "That...music." Lawrence must have caught the worried glance on Aurelia's face, guessing its meaning when he replied, "No, not Maestro Ellis. There's a different, softer sound. Is someone playing a record?"

But Lawrence knew as soon as he spoke the words that it was not that some free-spirited guest had lugged a traveling phonograph with them. Nor had anyone the ability to put the lobby's ornate phonograph into action without the manager's admittance. More singularly to the point, only one instrument was sounding. An instrument of an older age with a rusty sound of nostalgia that brought one home to the summer evenings in a country far from the American shores. That brought one to Russia.

Lawrence had fixed on the early tune of a crank organ.

XX

Conceding the point that might be vigorously pursued as to the validity of a man's concern at hearing the low hums of a crank organ when he was nowhere near such an instrument, we instead turn to the appreciable understanding of the consternation of coming to the bottom of one's glass of brandy. Heightened further by the realization that one's bottle has done one the disservice of remaining in the hotel room where it was originally placed. Up on the top of the cabinet with a white doily keeping it from slipping and falling onto the glasses presented to its left. Such was the case for our previously introduced acquaintance, Don Cherry.

Just as the hotel's manager had wrapped up discussing the continued search for Miss Rachel in the corner of the Golden Swan, and just as Lawrence began to be plagued by the melodic whispers of the crank organ, Mr. Cherry had a thought. An innocent little thought. Why pay for a glass of brandy to hold one over until the dinner hour when one had a perfectly suitable bottle in one's room? "Perhaps this DuPont fellow won't mind if I just slip out and—"

"I expect he'll find that terribly troublesome."

It is not all that difficult to appreciate the start with which Mr. Cherry jumped in his seat at the presence of a stranger sitting starkly his opposite. After all, how often does a traveler look down at his glass only to look up and find that he is suddenly in company? Not altogether warm or welcoming company at that. The stranger with whom the radio newsman now shared his table was clad in the sharpest suit his eyes had ever seen. And that was saying something in Mr. Cherry's line of work. His hair was slicked tightly back, his eyes a smoldering brown, and the cologne wafting from his neck was intoxicating.

"Oh," Mr. Cherry said, stumbling over his words for the fervency of the stranger's gaze. "I don't believe we have ever had the pleasure," he grumbled, becoming a bit ruffled at the delay in his seeing to a proper refill. He waited for the stranger to insert his name, for how often does one intrude upon another's evening and not commence introductions? He was made uneasy by the stranger's abject silence. "Er, allow me to introduce myself. The name's—"

"Donald Cherry, born Donald Humphrey to Leanne and Harold Humphrey in 1862. But you decided you'd prefer something a little more Californian when you moved to Atlanta, isn't that right? Thought it would make you seem a bit more— how did you put it to yourself—apropos of the new age? Yes, I think that was it."

"I'm sorry, sir. I'm afraid I do not have the pleasure."

"Yes, you've said that."

Once this measly second attempt had been thwarted by the stranger, Cherry simply did what he knew best in times of fruitless consternation. A shrug of the shoulders and a sip of the drink. Only there was nothing left in the glass. Had his confounded memory not been so poor as to forget this unfortunate fact, he might not have made himself look the fool in raising an empty glass to his lip. But fate is a mysterious thing. Had he not lifted an empty glass, looking disappointed as he shook its limitless nothing about in an invisible swirl and set it back to the table, the mysterious stranger might not have raised his hand. Nor would he have spoken to DuPont the words every gentleman longs to hear, "Another for Mr. Cherry, on me."

"Most kind of you, er, sir."

"No need to thank me," the stranger exhaled, as if made to suffer through this conversation. *Take yourself out of your misery then, old boy. I didn't invite you.*

"I am not in the business of being invited by anyone at any time, Mr. Cherry. I simply am where I ought to be on any particular occasion."

The old devil can hear my thoughts! But he soon convinced himself he was mistaken. That he had fallen into that terrible habit he often had of speaking one's thoughts aloud after having consumed a splash too much to drink. That was a much more comforting explanation. Even if it meant a small amount of embarrassment on his behalf.

"Anything for you, sir?" DuPont asked with a stern expressionless face and perfect posture. *They really train these boys well here, no matter how ancient they are. Heh.*

After forming his hand into the universal sign for the number two, indicating to DuPont that he would have the same as Cherry, the stranger turned back to his host.

"Is that what you think I am, the Devil?" he asked, looking Cherry straight in his eyes.

"W-what?" Cherry croaked.

"Isn't that what you've just said?"

"What do you mean? Are you in my thoughts, old boy?"

"I haven't the slightest idea of what you are on about, Mr. Cherry."

Cherry mulled this over for a moment, but there was little time to consider. Here, sitting in front of him, was an injured man. It mattered very little how it was that this man had caught wind of his injury, what mattered is that the offense was given by Cherry's hand. However unintentional it may have been.

"Sorry, old boy," he chuckled in an unconvincing sort of way, "just an expression, you know. Something endearing even. The old devils." Nervous laughter followed his last word in hopes that the tension would break. But the stranger continued his grave-like stare. The blacks of his eyes seemed to widen, nearly blocking all the color out in a shimmering void.

"So," he continued, hoping to take the heat off himself for a moment, "now that I have the pleasure," though he distinctly did not, "to what do I owe it?"

"You've had quite the career, Mr. Cherry." There was a pause before Cherry was permitted to respond, owing to DuPont's reappearance and the donning of two freshly poured glasses of brandy.

"Ah! A fan of my old work, are you? Why, you should have said so! I would have been happy to give you my autograph! Thank you very much for the drink; it is too kind of you."

At this abject sign of dismissal, Cherry knew he was a bit too hopeful that he would be able to shoo this visitor away so easily. The stranger simply continued his staring. It was a contradiction in sight. The way he laid back in the booth, his arm resting on the tabletop, his posture slackened. But his eyes remained on Cherry, sizing him up. Or perhaps admiring.

"Do you have a lot of people admire you on a regular basis?"

"Er," Cherry stumbled uneasily, wondering how on earth this chap was able to guess his every thought. "I'm not sure what you would call regular, but..." he trailed off, looking guiltily away toward the lobby, which he could see through the Golden Swan's entrance not far off. It began to swell with guests who had decided to assuage their hunger with a quench of their thirst.

"But it is something you thirst for. More than that brandy."

"I don't know what you mean. This is highly irregular, sir."

"I do not have much interest in the regular. Neither do you, as I understand it. A man interested in the regular is not a man that moves to a new town with a new name that stinks of a place he's never been."

"I'm sorry, but—"

"I try to make it a habit never to apologize for something I do not feel sorry for. Perhaps you might find virtue in the same habit, Mr. Cherry."

"Er, perhaps. What is all this about?"

"What is all what about?"

"All this…mystery. What do you want from me?"

"Ah, mystery," the stranger opined. "Do we not find that life ceases to exist when the mystery has died out?"

"I do not know. I have never been one for—"

"Fine talk? Yes, I suppose I myself am just the same."

"It's just a bit fanciful, don't you find?"

"I do, and wasteful."

"Wasteful," Cherry considered the word as he spoke it. "Yes, yes, that's good. Wasteful."

"But back to the point, Mr. Cherry."

"What is that?"

"What is what?" the stranger asked, turning his head to look toward the corner of the room. Cherry's eyes naturally followed suit, only to land upon the intoxicating beauty of Angela Adonis sitting in the corner. It seemed rather odd to see her in such a state, as she was weeping into a glass of some kind of clear drink, tonic perhaps. And Frederick was with her. Cherry had only met Frederick once in the past. It was at the wedding that he was sure he was only invited to in order to appease his mother, Angela's aunt.

"The point," Cherry managed to mumble, his eyes still fixed on his weeping cousin. Somehow her distressed state made her even more of a beauty, even more desirous. "What is the point?"

"Ah," the stranger said, watching Cherry's eyes as they slowly returned to his visitor. "Yes. Well, I find you an interesting subject, Mr. Cherry."

"Me?"

"The very same. A man who would leave his life behind in chase of something new. What was it you were chasing, Donald?" The stranger pulled out a silver case filled with pre-rolled cigarettes; Cherry could smell the tobacco from his seat. It smelled sweet, with hints of vanilla. His mouth watered. "Please," the stranger said, offering him a tightly rolled cigarette and a matchbox.

"Thank you, sir," Cherry said, readily accepting the gift. "It seems I am digging myself deeper into your debt, ha! Always tried to kick the habit, you know. Never did much like the coughing fits. But the damned things are too sweet to free myself from. Don't you agree?" Cherry was trying everything he could think of to distract his guest from whatever the "point" was, as it was starting to make him uncomfortable. Perhaps Cherry could lull him into boredom with a proper dose of domineering small talk.

"So, what is it?" the stranger asked, raising the freshly lit match to his own cigarette. The way the light flashed in front of the man's face made his skin turn a sickly gray. For a moment, Cherry decided his vision must have been fooled by the flash of the flame. A man couldn't really have eyes as black as the night. Could he?

"I don't understand."

"It's rather simple, actually," the stranger continued as if he were a professor contemplating theory. "Men don't make drastic changes without reason as equally drastic. I find, and am curious if you will agree, that changing one's name could also be considered a higher plane of the...desperate."

"Now listen here," Cherry's voice turned from hospitable to hostile. Perhaps it would have been successful in intimidating the guest, had it not been interrupted by a nasty fit of coughing one could only surmise was brought on by the cigarette.

"Do not mistake me, sir. I am in no way hoping to cause you offense. Put down the glove, my good man. I am just an interested party looking to understand a fascinating subject. As I understand it, you had quite the career in New York. Why would one leave that all behind in chase of something new, in chase of Atlanta? Oh, again, I fear I may be misunderstood. No one understands the southern charm more than myself, but when one considers the allure, the majesty of New York City, it puts things into certain...considerations."

"I felt like a change."

"Yes, yes, a change. A capital thing, change can be. It can mend the heart, they say. Of course, nothing quite like home. One would need a good reason to leave home to mend one's heart. So, was it a question of money? No, I oughtn't be so vulgar. A man of your means doesn't chase silver. What do you chase? Power, influence? Ah, now we've hit on something," the stranger said with a curled smile as Cherry squirmed in his seat.

"Don't be rude, Mr. Cherry. Finish your brandy." Cherry forced himself to gulp a significant draught of the amber liquor. Many a connoisseur had scoffed at the way Cherry gulped at his brandy, but he had never found that the manner in which one drank affected the way it tickled the mind.

"I've never found that a proper measure of influence is very harmful," Cherry conceded, his wet lower lip forming a drip of spittle. "It's altogether very hard to get anything done without it, I find. Once one has it, I will admit, it is awfully hard to give it up."

"Now, you are a man of influence. Yes, that is easy to see. One doesn't enter the radio news business without a certain thirst for influence, I suppose. But tell me, did you not have influence in New York? One could argue there's no finer venue. Pah! So, it is out to the gutter with that theory." The stranger took an unimaginatively long drag from his cigarette, nearly turning the whole thing to ash before Cherry's eyes.

"I think I have it, sir. I think I have it!"

"What?" Cherry said, looking up. "I don't understand this interest in my...my...motivations."

"Motivations! What an excellent term. Your motivations. Well, I said I had it, so I ought to show you what it is. You were not running toward something, Mr. Cherry, but running away."

"I don't know what you mean."

"Aha! There it is, sir. You were running from something. It was guilt that made you run. But what could make one so guilty that one runs from their dream career in their dream city, leaving their name to rot in the dust of their tracks, hmm? It must have been some manner of sin."

"This is nonsense, sir! Why do you continue in this way? You come and interrupt my drinking for your fun! You haven't told me a word of who you are, and you come and try to size me up like a carnival attraction! I won't have it; I won't, I won't!"

"Calm, Mr. Cherry, calm. I have just as much reason to run

from the Devil as you do! What man hasn't found himself crawling in his most vile instincts from time to time, eh?" The stranger rolled his words around his mouth like a hard candy, slowly savoring the flavor rather than crushing it to a sticky dust. "But this puts us at a bit of an impasse. For I fear it is impossible for me to guess the nature of the sin."

"The sin…"

"Yes, sir. The sin that you ran away from. Oh, I have little doubt that you will give yourself away. Yes, Mr. Cherry, you will clue me in by some self-betrayal. Humans have an unmistakable proclivity toward confession. We see it etched with iron pen throughout the history of literature. The old man's beating heart pounding on the floorboards, the murderer sick in the bushes dreaming of a beaten horse, the mayor of Montreuil-sur-Mer who stole a loaf of bread. We are born to repent, just as we are born to sin."

"I haven't sinned," Cherry croaked, opting to look into his empty glass rather than brave the stranger's soulless eyes another second. But the words fell at a bit of a falter in the way a breathless man champions the air in his lungs. In an attempt to avoid the obvious, Cherry raised his hand toward DuPont, who dutifully rushed to the side of the table before the stranger had the opportunity to retort.

"I'll have another brandy please, and for my friend here…"

"Oh, I'll sit this round out, Mr. Cherry."

"You really like to keep me in your debt, ha! Very well, one refill it is. Oh, and Mr. DuPont…"

"Sir?"

"I would like to buy a round for the charming couple in the corner. I do not know what ails them, but my compliments all the same!"

"Straightaway, sir."

"I do not think you believe your own claim," the stranger continued as soon as DuPont was far from earshot.

"Which claim is that?"

"That you are without sin."

"Well, I suppose everyone is with sin. I simply mean to say there is not a specific sin that I run...ran from."

"And I do not believe you."

"Are you calling me a liar, sir?"

"Of the worst kind. Now calm down and let me make myself clear. I am calling you a liar, yes, but not because I think you are lying to me—though I will admit, I do harbor such a suspicion—but because you lie to yourself. That is right. I can see in your eyes that the veracity of your claim of sinlessness holds water only in that you believe it yourself. Because you have told yourself so, and now you tell me."

"You have insulted me...I do not know how many times. If it were not for the charity of your brandy and your cigarette, I should have excused myself from this conversation shortly after it started. However, as it seems your charity has now run dry and you have nothing with which to pay for your insults, I think I'd rather you leave."

"I will leave when I have come to the end of my investigation. You see, now that you are fluxed, the game is quite afoot." As the stranger began to pull out and light another cigarette, Mr. Cherry found it to be a capital idea to walk away himself, brandy be damned.

"Sit down, Cherry." This erasure of the moniker of respect the stranger had been showing him through the guise of a prefix left something hollow in Mr. Cherry's throat. Whatever it was, it served to pull him back to his seat and neatly fold his arms in a brace for what came next.

"I believe," the stranger continued, "we've come to the end of it. Don't worry, Cherry, it will all be over soon. Yes, you've given yourself away."

"What is that?"

"You've given yourself away. Just now. In the throes of an insult, while you were squirming and trying to avoid giving me any sort of hint of this sin that you've committed. Yes, that you *have* committed; I'll accept no further protest. Just when you divert, you could not help yourself but show the final clue."

"And what is that?" Cherry asked, settling into the game after seeing no way out. At least a glass of brandy was on its way.

"You've offered that young lady a drink at your expense."

"So?"

"So? So, the offense was made to her."

"What? How on earth do my sympathies toward the young creature mean anything other than——"

"Than charity?" the stranger finished. "Because, Mr. Cherry, you are not a charitable man. Further, and I hope you'll forgive the lack of propriety in my having overheard this little detail while you were discussing the nature of your relations with that young lady, she is your relative."

The stranger was interrupted for a brief moment by DuPont's voice chiming from behind Mr. Cherry to say, "By the compliments of the young lady and young gentlemen, Mr. Cherry."

"What? No, I wanted to buy *them* a round, you miserable fool!"

"I'm afraid they rather insisted, sir, said they'd like to repay the act in kind." Before Cherry could utter another word in protest, DuPont bowed and hastened off to take care of a snapping patron.

"Ah, very interesting," the stranger continued. "It was interesting enough that a man should see a relative in distress and *not* rise to the occasion to comfort their vexation in person. It is interesting that he should offer that same relative a drink without delivering it himself, and it is further interesting that such a relative would not be comfortable accepting such a small act of...charity, without repaying it on the spot. Yes, I believe I have it now. The sin was an offense to the young lady, a relative, that was so grave that you would rather run to Atlanta and change your name than live with the disgrace!"

To this, Cherry offered no response. At least not in the realm of the spoken word. He simply picked up the glass of brandy that had been resting on the edge of the table for all of five minutes, raised it to his lips, and kicked back the whole of its contents, noticing that it was a skosh different in the notes of its flavor than the others.

It appears the woman ordered a different label. Couldn't spring for the top-shelf stuff, eh? Come on then, you harried bastard. You seem to hear my thoughts, well, go on and hear them. Yes! Yes, I caused the lady offense. I sullied her precious reputation. But no one knows but her, not a soul. So I am without sin, for the offense never reddened the white of her wedding gown.

Every word of this was thought while Cherry stared into the eyes of his visitor. However, the stranger gave little signal that he had heard even a bit of it. Instead, he fixed his cigarette case and matchbox into his breast pocket and stretched a handout for Cherry as he rose.

"I want to thank you for your playing along, Mr. Cherry. It is a rare thing, meeting a man like you. I have rather enjoyed myself." His grip was firm, with his index finger reaching out and pressing into Cherry's wrist. *An odd thing.* But, as he saw it, there wasn't much about this man that was not aptly labeled as odd. "Please, enjoy the rest of your stay at the Genovie."

But Cherry could hardly hear these last words. He was too focused on the irregular taste of almonds that was flushing around his tongue. As the stranger walked away, Mr. Cherry felt a compounding confusion overtake him.

The writer might be wrong in giving the benefit of the doubt to Mr. Cherry when he says that if Cherry had been keen to a few pieces of information, perhaps that confusion might have been dulled slightly. The first of which was that when Mrs. Adonis had received his compliments from DuPont, a look of pale disgust drained the color from her face.

However, cunning as a viper, the young lady had fashioned for herself a plot in the recesses of her mind earlier that same afternoon. After having seen the unfortunate relative in the lobby, she stole away to her room where she found a little glass vial hidden away in her husband's medical bag. Not having direct understanding of her designs, she slid it neatly in her clutch, having the intuition it might prove useful.

Seeing her moment to strike, she directed the honorable waiter to fetch whatever it was the old fool had been drinking and bring it to her, under the excuse that she wanted to bring it to Mr. Cherry directly. Asking Frederick to continue on searching the lobby while she found herself in such a familial obligation, she slipped the contents of the vial into the glass and gave it a proper stir. This is, of course, the moment where she recalled DuPont and claimed that she had been stolen away by a phone call requiring the urgent attention of both her and her husband and said, "Would you please do the honors of delivering this to Mr. Cherry after all?"

Ever the dutiful servant, DuPont did as he was bid without reason of suspicion, leaving Mr. Cherry in the tight bind of a fast heart rate, difficulty drawing breath, and splotches of his skin turning such a shade of crimson that he began to resemble the appearance of the ironically chosen last name he had fitted himself with.

XXI

As was perfectly advisable by anyone who has had the opportunity and pleasure of serving as an employee of the Hotel Genovie during the stint of time between the years 1899 and 1935, Lawrence rather avoided any condition wherein he was required to enter the kitchens. The flavors that our good Chef Anton Bakker melded together always seemed to be fitted to the exact palate our guests were accustomed to. I once made the mistake of asking him the secret to his genius, only to be placed on light rations for a week. To this very day, I find it quite perplexing that he should have been offended by my astonishment in his craft and that I should be daft enough to ask him how it was done! According to the old grump, such a question was a challenge to his authority as an artist. I hadn't the slightest idea what that meant in the moment, nor do I understand his ravings now.

You see, Chef Bakker is a man of hot temper, leaving many among the staff to remain convinced that the poisoning of the Baron in '94 was by his hand. Such a gruesome way to go, choking on one's dinner through searing pain in one's throat. Yet still, our good Chef maintains a profile of innocence in the whole affair to this very day. It is his view that if the Baron wanted to make it through dinner to taste dessert, he oughtn't to have kept so many enemies before he sat for appetizers. I am inclined to believe him, though I may be biased for not wanting to be placed on light rations once again. So, take that as you will.

But it would be best not to get sidetracked. During the particular occasion that is addressed throughout the pages of this record, the conditions had boiled over the kettle and necessitated a visit to the culinary sanctuary—the artist's studio, if it should please.

One was always met with a scented veil of rendered fats and spices long before the clanging of cookware began to resound along one's ears. A false sense of comfort. Smells of home and mother's cooking, smells of summer when one was too cold or of winter when one was too hot. No matter the season, the day, or the hour, Chef Bakker's kitchen was an admirable concoction of delights. The trouble only ensued when one approached the old man himself.

"What is it you want, Erlik?" he began. "I've told you countless times not to bother my staff when prepping for dinner. Madness it is, working in these conditions! You want perfection? You want excellence? How is it you expect me to provide that for you while you incessantly interrupt my craft? Hmm?" If the berating shouts weren't enough to set one on one's toes, surely the waving and stabbing of Bakker's cleaver through the air would provide one with an appropriate amount of apprehension for stepping another foot further into the den of delectable delights.

"Now Anton," Lawrence began, his hands raised level with his shoulders, his face soft and unassuming, and his assistant manager standing fearlessly at full attention to his side.

"What. Did. You. Just. Call. Me?"

"My apologies, Chef."

"That's better. I think if we are to work properly together, it's best we show each other respect, no?"

"Of course," Lawrence conceded.

"A chef most especially ought to be shown respect. The way I see it, Erlik, if you have the gall to disrespect the man who handles your food, you are taking your life into your own hands, no?"

"Perfectly put."

"And respect for a chef begins with his title. For if a man of the kitchen has nothing else, he must be left with his title, no?" This final argument articulated, the round man clapped his hands together in an uproarious thunder that matched the exterior storm he no doubt had little knowledge of in his seclusion. At the sound of his clapping there was an equally ground shaking "YES, CHEF," hollered in perfect unison by every member of the kitchen staff.

"You see, Erlik? Respect."

"Yes, I see, Chef. I mean nothing but that, respect." Lawrence slowly lowered his hands while the rosy cheeks and nose of Chef Bakker lowered toward the table, where he picked up his knife and began to slice into a cut of lamb.

"Now that we can agree on one thing," Chef continued, not showing the manager the respect of his full attention and, perhaps most egregiously, his eye contact. "Perhaps we can agree that you are intruding on our efforts? Or is there something more pressing than the sustenance of our guests that precludes you from practicing the decorum of chef and manager that has been celebrated throughout the ages? Hmm?"

"I am afraid so, An—Chef. I would leave you to your masterwork if it weren't for the pesky little detail of a lost child."

"A child, you say?" Chef asked without looking up from his work. All around him a fluttering of cooks were obeying the orders of the Sous Chef who continued to bark about, pretending nothing out of the ordinary was unfolding. "Did you say a child?" the chef repeated when Lawrence found himself mesmerized by the perfection with which each component of the machine operated. He yearned for this level of cohesion among his staff. They were close, it's true, but Bakker's fortitude lent itself to perfection.

"Er, yes. Yes, a child. A young girl, answers to the name Rachel. I'm afraid her parents, as well as the front of house, have been looking for her for hours now. She is about ye high," Lawrence put his hand parallel to the ground just below the line of his waist. "Brown curly hair, quite quiet."

"Let me stop you right there, Erlik. There's been no children of any height or any hair color or any volume running through my kitchen."

"You're sure of this? Could she not have crawled into a pot or a pantry or—"

"Are you saying I don't know my kitchen?"

"No, of course you know your kitchen, Chef."

"Ah, just not to the detail, is all. Is that it?"

"No, Chef, I am quite sure you know your kitchen to the detail."

"Aye, I thank you for the vote of confidence. Now, it is like I said. There is no one in this kitchen, other than the two of you," Anton said, pointing his cleaver toward Lawrence and Aurelia in a stabbing fashion. Aurelia made a face at the violent indication that made even Chef Anton raise a brow and regret his own brutish nature. "Ah-hem," he coughed, regaining himself. "The only souls in this kitchen are my hounds, isn't that right, you dogs?"

"YES, CHEF."

"You see? Harmony breeds perfection, Erlik. Harmony.

Perfection. Not children."

"Indeed," Lawrence conceded, no longer attempting to veil the annoyance dripping from his tongue. "All the same, would you mind terribly if we were to...look about? For posterity, Chef. I'd hate to return to the poor mother and father and report that my own eyes did not search the place."

Lawrence had gotten used to reading sentences from the expressions of one's face, what with his famous communication style with Aurelia. It was this very talent that aided Lawrence in discerning the meaning behind Chef Bakker's raised eyebrows and cunning stare. It conveyed, in not so many words, that "if you dare take another step into my domain and rummage about the place while my hounds are busy at work, I will shove this cleaver so far up your prissy ass that you'll taste steel before you breathe your last."

"Right," Lawrence said. "Perhaps, in this smallest of instances, it might be best to adorn the practice of the white lie. Wouldn't you agree, Aurelia?"

Aurelia did not agree. However, given the circumstances of Chef's temper alongside Lawrence's heightened nerves, he thought it best to pull Aurelia to the side to further their plot.

"Well," he whispered as she listened attentively, tapping her toe to communicate her scrap of protest of their retreat. "Perhaps we'll find it best to continue our search for as long as possible before we deliver this crumb of unfortunate news. What do you say?" While Aurelia didn't say anything, her pondering stare toward the space just left of Lawrence's ear told him that she was not wholly against the proposition. "It might be best to take the triplets and search the vacant rooms and all the closets and corners of the main floor. Be sure to check with Margery in the library. Oh, and Aurelia—"

While there was certainly something worth breaking his train of thought over, in order to add emphasis to its charter, Lawrence was interrupted by the entirely different tone of Chef Anton.

"Erlik! You're looking rather…not quite alive. Have you eaten today?"

"What?"

"I said, what have you eaten today?"

"Well, I, er…"

"That's what I thought. Come, come. I'll have no word to the contrary now. I have a very special preparation for tonight's menu. Very special. You too, Miss Aurelia," he said in his gentlest of voices. "You are always welcome in my kitchen, mademoiselle! Grigory!"

When Chef clapped (causing Aurelia to jump) and shouted for his sous chef "Grigory!" The burly looking man procured two small white bowls and two forks of the finest polished silver. "Richard!" This call produced a slender kitchen boy carrying a pot that looked much too heavy for a young man of his stature. When it was placed on the center table and the help shooed away, Chef opened the lid. Steam bellowed and curled under the lantern, twisting under the nose and drawing up visions of stewed pork fat, mushrooms, and the softest onions ever to hit the tongue.

Chef ladled a healthy cut of meat into each bowl, followed by a second ladle of a deep red wine sauce with small vegetables bobbing for air among the steam.

"Coq au Vin," Chef said with a smile, pushing a bowl to each of his guests. All the hostility, all the righteousness, all the disdain ran from the Chef's cheeks at the opportunity to watch them eat. For, to this very day, does there exist a chef on this earth that does not enjoy the look of bliss on one's face when they are indulging in culinary delicacies? "Go on, go on! She's been braising all afternoon!"

Lawrence took a bite, closing his eyes and letting his head fall back. Truthfully, he would have feigned this simple sign of pleasure in order to curry favor with the haughty chef, but in this particular instance, the reaction was genuine. Lawrence could not remember a time in all his life when he had tasted something so rich, so smooth, so delicately balanced in savory flavors of garlic, wine, and onion. All melding together on the center of his tongue.

"Chef," Lawrence began. But the words didn't come. Aurelia came to the rescue, putting her bowl down in an instant and giving the Chef a round of applause.

"Ah! Merci, Mademoiselle! It is an honor to know the work shall be praised."

"You have my word, Chef, you'll run out of this before service is over. I'll see that it's recommended with the highest regards!"

"Merveilleux!" Chef smiled. However, that smile did not last long. The flickering of the lights brought it to an abrupt end. "My service had better not be interrupted by this hotel's ridiculous electricity problems!"

"I will speak with Joel immediately, Chef. It is the storm; I am afraid it is rather akin to the wrath of God."

"Storm?" Chef said. "There is not supposed to be a storm! Confound it all! Not on a night like tonight, with my chicken!"

"Rest assured, Chef, God will have to work a lot harder to put you out of work."

"Yes," Chef Bakker said absentmindedly. "Yes, well...what are you two still standing about for? Can you not see we have work to get done? Out with you, out, out!"

There could not have been a more opportune time for the chef to decide to pummel his guests out of the double swinging doors of the kitchen, for as Lawrence was dusting off his jacket and collecting his stature after being manhandled on his way out, a glimpse of a ghost flashed across the hall. Not only did he see a ghost, and the very same ghost he had been catching glimpses of all afternoon, but that same specter held to the hand of a small child. The child had brown locks, a bright blue dress, and pranced along, as if taking a stroll with her mother through the park.

"Aurelia," Lawrence breathed, barely catching enough air for his voice to break through the silence, "see to finding Joel for me, and then take up the search. I will dive into it myself."

XXII

While Mr. Erlik managed, in some manner, to ignore the acrid tang of sulfur singing his nostrils, it became impossible to put it out of his mind upon entering the lobby in his dire chase.

"Adrian!" he shouted as he stormed through, trying to keep his eyes fixed on the corner he had just witnessed Sonya Ivanovna lead young Rachel around. "What in heaven's name is that smell?"

"Smell, sir?" the boy stood, perplexion bending his face. "I don't smell anything. Unless you mean the kitchens, sir!"

"No, I don't mean the kitchens! You don't...never mind, move along Adrian. Aurelia will be looking for you."

Rage boiled along the tips of Lawrence's earlobes when Adrian enthusiastically said, "Yes, sir!" But it was soon abated by the fear of what he was following.

Seeing a ghost once is often enough to place one in a catatonic state, much less being made to see glimpses throughout the entirety of a day. While the storm raged in a thunderous applause, while ravens were found in the most unnatural of places, and while all the haunts and fears were climbing from the depths of his shaken soul, Lawrence was expected to continue in his life's pursuit to provide perfect accommodation for his guests. Little though that effort seemed to spare them. For all his labors, he had still managed to witness one die while being unable to find a second. A poor girl lost in the labyrinth of what he had always considered his paradise.

While racing through the halls of the grand hotel, a memory with the sharpness of a dagger pierced through his heart. One he could hardly recognize, but he knew was distinctly his. Though the people looked gruff and unfamiliar, the city street grey and foreign, and the winter chill biting, he felt at home.

"Come with me, my little sweet," a tender voice shot through the cold, wrapping him in a blanket of warmth. "We must go to the hotel; we will be staying here now, my dove."

Lawrence could remember the silk of the woman's skin as she took his hand in hers, pulling his dust-covered little body through glass doors. The light of candles brought more than vision, they brought warmth and comfort. He heard the buzz of busy people with busy lives. The flip of a rotary, the clang of a service bell, the clunk of heavy suitcases falling onto a trolley shining of fine gold.

Another world, not his. A world wherein he was vermin, a rat that people wished to stomp out and shoo back into the streets among the steaming piles of horseshit and cold slush spraying all over his thick pants as carriages raced past. But not anymore. Not now that Mama had gotten a post at the hotel. From now on it would be warm soups and adventures through the attics and expeditions in the gardens. "You'll stay here, my dove," she would say, placing him upon a squeaky cot in the corner of a barren room, the ceiling slanting with the pitch of the roof.

But that was so long ago, so very long. Now Lawrence ran through the hotel, not as a street rat, but as an elegant horse, a trotter, pulling the weight of decadence on his reins. Steering to avoid another catastrophe, willing to trample over every manner of spirit and ghoul to circumvent calamity. A rejuvenating concoction of bravery and perseverance fluttered in his stomach like a warm tonic, though his nerves were sharply severed as he caught glimpse of his hunt once more.

There was no doubt as to their destination. Sonya Ivanovna was guiding Rachel to the cellar.

A mad rush of panic washed over Lawrence as he took to running down the hall. He was able to round the corner just in time to see the cellar door open, and Sonya Ivanovna look over her shoulder to see if she was being followed. It was not a concern, but rather a wish. For when her eyes fell upon a panicked hotel manager, the most precarious smile twisted about her lips, dripping a ruby red liquid from the corner of her mouth.

Lawrence could nearly reach out and touch the door. He could almost grab ahold of its handle and hold it open just as Sonya Ivanovna slammed it shut, an echo shuffling down the hall in her wake.

Not wanting to waste a single second and risk the life of the child, Lawrence pulled his sweaty hand toward the iron handle and moved to pull the door open. But it did not budge. Not only in the manner of a door that had been shut with a bolt put into place, but in the manner of one that was nailed in place. Not a budge, not an inch.

There were few sights more chilling than that of a madman denied entry to the one door that held his exoneration on the other side. Lawrence threw himself into the solid oak, as if his small frame could act as a battering ram against Constantinople's heaviest gates. He was breathless, he was bruised, and he was persistent. His constant slamming into the door provided a steady beat for the resumption of the crank organ ringing in his ears. If he had not been driven to the brink of his newly welcomed madness that very moment, perhaps he would have been obliged to hear it.

Instead, he threw himself again and again, taking turns battering and pulling on the handle with all his weight. A sane man might have turned breathless long before Lawrence found that he was up against a brick wall. Unfortunately—or, depending how the reader might choose to look at it, fortunately—Lawrence was dancing back and forth along the lines of what it meant to be a sane man. Luck was on his side. It had to be, given the fair maiden had abandoned him all morning for some other suitor. Surely, she'd return to aid him in the prying of the door to hell!

But fortune can often tickle a man's heart in such a way that he deigns to give himself the illusion of success over the horizon. In fact, had it not been for the searing pain that accompanied a sudden crack in his left shoulder while he savagely thrust his body against the door, he might have continued on the route to madness until his body was beaten to a fresh pulp.

Clutching the throb of his injury, Lawrence turned his back to the door, pressed against it, and slid slowly down to seat himself upon the solid ice of the floor. It was then that his ears registered the organ. It was a tune that he knew, and knew well. As if the apse of his memory were mocking him with a parade of the buried, the grim of the grave. Lawrence sat and listened to a chilling polka while his eyes deceived him into seeing phantom hems of dresses swaying in a merry dance while trousers lifted them up and gracefully let them fall back down to the floor.

"Mr. Erlik!" The voice was rough, but it was not a gentle approach that would bring Lawrence out of his trance. It was said after the fact, dear reader, that when the owner of this burly voice came upon our good manager, his head had even begun to sway to some deaf rhythm. "I don' know what yer doin' spillin' yourself along the floor, but you best be getting up now!"

"How wonderful it is, Joel, to see them dancing. What a state of bliss it must be to hear the songs of the angels."

"Angels? I don' think angels have nothin' to do with it, sir. Yer knows I'm a man of God, bless me. Yer knows, but I tell you the whore is comin' on her scarlet beast, she is. I tell ye, all this," Joel paused for the inconvenience of a deep guttural hiccup, "all this luxurious news, she feeds off it, do you hear? Feeds off it!"

Lawrence, hearing the familiar sermon of the old handyman, began to come to. "Joel?"

"Mr. Erlik?"

"Joel, when did you get here?"

"Why...just now, of course. You was swayin' and such on the ground here. I came cause, er...what was it she said?"

"Who?"

"Why, Miss Aurelia! She said somefin about...eh...blast my memory, sir. It's hard when you're old."

"Joel?"

"Yessir?"

"Have you been drinking whiskey?"

"The devil's water, sir? How dare...I...that is a sin, sir, a right sin. I am a man of God and—"

"It's alright, Joel; I only wish for a drop myself."

"Oh...you only...well then. In that case, I s'pose I'd better..."

Joel reached behind his back and pulled from a sly little slit in his body suit a silver flask. One would be rather astute to find the contradiction in this fine piece of silver belonging to a humble man of God, just as Lawrence was questioning in his own mind. "Bit of a luxury, wouldn't you say?"

But Joel offered no answer. At least not in the way of propriety. He simply blushed in a manner that Lawrence had never seen before and shrugged his shoulders as his manager took a small swig of his father's recipe for home-distilled whiskey.

In any other circumstance, the bite of the fiery liquor would have thrown dear Lawrence into a fit of coughing that would make him fear for the likelihood of his lungs flying straight out of his throat. But on this day, during this particular hour, when the uncanny was rapping at the door of his fine establishment, it was precisely what Lawrence was in need of.

"Very good, Joel. Very good. Now, get me through that door."

"What do you mean, sir?"

"What do you mean, what do I mean? It's locked! Bolted from the other side!"

"Sir, it's a cellar door. There's no bolt on the other side."

"What?"

"Pardon me, sir, but why would there be a bolt on the other side of the cellar door?"

"I suppose that's a rather sensible inquiry, Joel."

"What?"

"Oh, never mind. Open the door."

"If you insist, sir."

Much to the embarrassment of the poor manager, the handyman was able to open the door simply by wrapping his pudgy fingers around the iron handle and placing the smallest amount of strength in his pull. The door swung open with the eeriness that befits all cellar doors in the middle of a harrowing thunderstorm. Perhaps it had something to do with the creak.

"Very good then. Have you a torch?"

"Yes, sir. Right here, sir."

While Lawrence wasn't practiced in the art of knowing exactly what to expect when a door that had refused to open suddenly decided to creak on its hinges—even less practiced in the art when one added a ghost and a missing child to the mix—he certainly didn't expect what was revealed. That is to say, absolutely nothing.

The whole of the cellar stairwell was bleak, dark, and dingy. But it was empty. A shaky step onto the top step of the case was met by an equally ominous creak and a moan from a rusted nail that was considering whether it was worth the effort to keep Lawrence's foot stable or if it should just give up the ghost and let him fall. Luckily for Lawrence, the nail chose the former.

Far more violently than when he had first traversed the cellar stairs several hours earlier, Lawrence heard the sloshing sound of running water.

"I thought you plugged the holes, Joel."

"I did, sir. God as my witness!"

But the evidence was stacked against our dear service man. For as they reached the bottom half of the stairs, the last four steps were completely submerged in water. Such that, in order to get any further in his search, Lawrence was going to have to drown his legs in the murky pool.

Perhaps propriety ought to have dictated a bit more preparation, beginning with the removal of his Oxford shoes, the discarding of his jacket, or even the safe placing of his timepiece. But all of this was lost on Lawrence. If not for the nobility of finding the lost child, then at least for the peace of mind of putting an end to it all. Putting an end to the whining of a grieving mother who hadn't yet truly lost, an end to the taunting of a woman's spirit that had other worldly business, an end to his torture.

Lawrence proceeded as if his feet were to be met with dry planks of wood, as if there was no storm. By the time his toe touched the cellar floor, his knees were submerged in the grey water. With Joel's torch in hand, large shadows turned small, dark corners brightened.

The water gnawed at his skin with its frigid bite the further he waded through. The light of the torch moved this way and that, slowly illuminating the cellar's secrets. An empty bottle stashed away next to a beam over here, an old stack of broken-down chairs there. But nothing promising the end of Lawrence's grand search.

"Are you coming, Joel?"

"Oh!" Joel exclaimed, making the sign of the cross. "There's devilry down there, Mr. Erlik. The old fiend is lurking in the corners. I dare not pass, sir. I dare not face the prince of darkness on his own turf!"

"What nonsense. This is your turf, Joel. Besides, Aurelia sent you to look at the electric panels. We've been flickering all afternoon upstairs. You'd better make sure this water doesn't—" but a guttural scream cut Lawrence short, echoing from around the bend. Its bellowing cut through the skin of his back like a rusty nail, pulling his shoulder blades up and back and his eyes squinted shut.

"Did you hear that, Joel?"

"Hear what, sir?" Joel asked, plunging into the cold water and making his way to Lawrence's left in order to inspect the electrical panel.

"That...scream?"

"God as my witness, sir, no one screamed down here. 'Course my old ears aren't what they used to be. No, sir."

"I must have been imagining things..." Lawrence's voice trailed off as he wasn't able to believe his own words. A man knows when he hears a scream like that; he knows what a scream like that meant.

But Lawrence was made braver by Joel's presence. After all,

Sonya Ivanovna seemed to have an aversion to appearing before him in the presence of others. Perhaps Joel was enough to ward her away from the young child and allow Lawrence to come away the hero. But hope is a dangerous prospect.

As Lawrence rounded the corner, his hope took a stab in the chest. Yet again, he was met with the deafening silence of an empty room. A very large room, encompassing about a quarter of the hotel's footprint, but empty, nonetheless.

Light from the torch revealed nothing but old storage boxes, the bottom few rows now soiled from the water. Their dismal state reminded Lawrence that his trousers were no doubt ruined from the knee down. But there was something in Lawrence's chest that kept his feet locked in place, not allowing him to give up the search. Where had they gone? Was there some sort of nook he was unaware of where she had hidden the child?

"Rachel?" he shouted, waving his light at a pace far too quick for his darting eyes to pick up any sign of her. "Rachel!" he cried again.

The only response was a faint, yet unmistakable giggle of a small child.

"Rachel, come on now, your mother is worried sick." Silence. "It will be dinner time soon, Rachel. I'm sure all of this hide and seek is getting tiring. Perhaps you'd better fancy a nice hearty meal." Silence.

The feeling that Lawrence had gotten on the landing in the stairwell returned. The feeling that someone, or something, was breathing down his neck. It felt rapacious, drooling in hunger for something not quite earthly. Something eternal.

"Rachel!" Lawrence gave way to impatience, his voice faltering in its attempt to be stern.

The icy chill that had hitherto kept to his legs, spread through his spine like a needle threading lace. His torch flickered and the chill grew so intense he felt as if he hadn't worn any clothes. Each breath escaped his lips in a thick fog. The surface of the water began to change in the corners of the room. Lawrence squinted and flashed his torch in its direction, disbelieving his own eyes. The water had begun to freeze. In the middle of summer. The water shouldn't have even been cold, a thought that hadn't occurred to him until he witnessed the absurdity of its freezing. It turned so quickly to ice that it was soon enveloped around his legs, locking him in place.

Then the torch illuminated no more.

In the pitch of darkness Lawrence stood shivering, banging the head of the torch in the palm of his hand, trying to beat it into submission. The cold became overwhelming. "Joel?" he called, but his voice was faint and there was no answer in return. "Joe— Jo— J—" Before long he could do nothing but shiver, wrapping his arms around his torso and shaking in the dark.

Thoughts of giving in to the cold began to squirm into his head. Perhaps it was a fitting end, lying beneath the heart of the Genovie for the rest of its days. Guests would clammer over him with their heels in giddy anticipation for the promised beauty of their stay. And for all eternity, he would be present to see to their accommodation. Yet as he was considering the merits of this fateful end, he felt a presence. Someone stood next to him, so close he could feel the fibers of their clothing graze his arm.

Then he felt two gentle hands rest on his shoulder, one atop the other, pressing just enough to give their owner balance as they leaned forward. Something cold and soft pressed up against his cheek, and he knew them to be lips.

He shuddered. Whimpered. Lawrence wanted nothing more than to have had the strength to reject that kiss. But he could not move.

Seconds later the light in the torch returned. The ice was gone, the water was turned from freezing to lukewarm. But Lawrence still felt cold.

"Joel!" he called, his voice having returned to his chest. "Joel!"

"Yes, sir!" Joel called, not a hint of care in his words.

"Joel, are you alright?"

"Perfectly fine, sir!"

The note in the old man's voice told Lawrence that he had not experienced any of the horror that had just enveloped him. But there was little to be done. Had he only seen Sonya guiding Rachel because she wanted him to? Was any of this real?

Just as he was turning to wade back toward the stairs, he saw something flicker in the reflection of the torch light. Something floating in the grey water about four or five strides from where he stood.

When he reached for it, he couldn't quite tell what he was looking at until he was able to pick it up and shine the torch directly at its surface. But his fingers had recognized what they were touching almost instantly. Feathers.

Gripped in the manager's hand was a large black bird, a raven, void of life.

His first instinct was to drop it in disgust. But a flash of color caught his eye as the animal plunged back into the water. When it reached the surface again, Lawrence pulled at the sting of color that snaked the water. A ribbon. It was a long blue ribbon, meant to tie around hair, though it had found itself tied around the raven's right leg.

Lawrence panted in horror, imagining what this message was meant to convey. Had Sonya Ivanovna claimed the child? Was he to tell Angela and Frederick Adonis that she had traversed into a realm beyond their world, a realm Lawrence didn't even believe in?

While he was stammering to himself on how he could possibly report this finding to the parents, his thoughts were interrupted by a panicked shout.

"Mr. Erlik, are you down here? Mr. Erlik?"

"What is it, Baptiste?" he called.

"Mr. Erlik, oh thank God. Yes, he's down there; I've just heard him."

"What is it, Baptiste?" he repeated, stuffing the ribbon in his pocket. He shuddered when the tip of his finger met the edge of the small slip of paper with his condemnation written in ink.

"Mr. Erlik, come quick! A guest...Mr. Cherry! Mr. Cherry has died!"

XXIII

"What did you say?" Lawrence felt the air leave his lungs and his stomach tear into four equal parts at the word. "What did you just say to me, boy?" The menace in his tone was unintended, but somehow felt righteous. What little shred of empowerment he might have left resided in the space of a breath, the mere minutes that stood between him and the body that was slumped over a booth in the Golden Swan, suffering the inquisitive poking from DuPont's perfectly manicured finger.

"You'd better come quick, sir! I told them I'd get you right away. What are you doing down there in the water?"

"Did you say…dead?"

"Yes, sir, stone cold! Oh, to think of it!"

"But…how?"

"We don't rightly know, sir, he just…keeled over." Lawrence was at the top of the stairs when the bellman finished muttering the sad excuse of an explanation.

"What about the other guests? Did any others see?"

"During cocktail hour at the Golden Swan? Naturally, sir. There were several guests, but their interest faltered when Milo told everyone he was just drunk. He shut down the bar and he and

DuPont shuffled everybody out. They mostly went to the dining hall to finish their drinks and listen to the Maestro."

"Yes, well...thank heavens for Milo."

What a dastardly deviant the floor squeak can be. Not only is it a deplorable, ghastly sound, but it can give away all manner of secrets and whereabouts. But most importantly, in the case of Mr. Lawrence Erlik, it provided a reminder that he was soaking wet, dripping small puddles of grey water all across the floor and creating a hazard for his guests.

"Baptiste, see to it that you mop this floor before we end up with another casualty on our hands, and make sure Joel does not repeat our error in tracking further puddles into the lobby. When you've done that, go into my office and collect a set of slacks for me to change into. I expect there will be a pair folded in the bottom left drawer of my desk. You won't need a key."

"But...sir," the young man began his inadvisable protest at the notion of not being permitted to further investigate what was assuredly the only dead body he had ever seen.

"Now, boy!" Lawrence snapped, the grey pallor of his face throwing Baptiste from his complaint and setting him off at a bit of a run rather than the gentlemanly stride Lawrence had so tried to instill through instruction and good example. But if one was going to lose one's temper, it was not just to continue to complain about how an example had been set on how to behave like a gentleman. Rather hypocritical, in fact. And Lawrence was nothing if not fair.

Lawrence had little idea as to what he expected when stepping into the Golden Swan. Panic, fanfare, a crowd of inquisitive guests gathering at the barrier of the Swan's seldomly closed doors, wondering why they had been cut short from their early evening cocktails. What he certainly hadn't expected was calm. Curiosity, perhaps, but not panic or distress.

In fact, those employees that had caught a glimpse of what they could were few in number, and only a fraction of that small sample had countenances that would suggest anything remote to unease. Margarette, for her part, was feverishly making the sign of the cross over her head and chest, as if the devil himself lay keeled over in that very booth. Perhaps there was some truth to that suspicion.

Aurelia also appeared in one of her glummer moods, a small shake of her head every thirty to forty-five seconds as she balanced herself on the heel of her foot. Milo, DuPont, Adrian, and Dorian all stood as if a matter of business that needed taking care of was in front of them. As if they were fully aware that this was not the Genovie's first death of the day.

"Has he choked?" Dorian whispered to his brother.

"Choked on what? The old man's been drinking like a fish all day. I don't think I saw him ingest anything solid since he's arrived," Adrian retorted.

"Now, he's had lunch with Mrs. Applebaum, hasn't he?"

"Surely, but did you see? He drank most of that too. It wouldn't surprise me if his blood could be served on the rocks at this point."

"So, what then?"

"Looks like it finally got the best of him, young sirs," DuPont saw fit to explain. "It's a nasty business, we take part in. One not fit for gentlemen. Once I saw a man have so much to drink in one sitting, he got up to do the waltz and fell to his death on the dance floor. The life simply fell out of him, as if he could shake it loose and forget to hold on to it. Poor chap, he was so full of it too. A lot of life to lose, sirs. Don't you two go and find yourselves in a similar pinch."

"I don't think it was the liquor, DuPont," Milo interjected. "He had a lot to drink, sure, but he was no belligerent drunk trading his last breath for another drink. I've seen some dark souls come through those doors; this was something different. He was plenty cheery, till he wasn't, I suppose. Beats me as to why, but I think this poor chap was poisoned."

"Poison!" Margarette made several signs of the cross as she walked out of the room in a hurry, as if merely standing next to a dead man might infect her with the same poison that caused his end. "Poison!" she repeated. "Bless me, poison, in this house! Hail Mary, full of grace, blessed art thou..." But she was gone and beyond earshot before the others could hear the rest of the Ave Maria.

"Poison," Lawrence whispered to himself, finally announcing his presence to the others in the room, causing a stir to ripple through the onlookers.

"Mr. Erlik, sir!" Milo began. "I'll tell you before you ask. Nothing deadly left my bar! At least nothing that can kill in seconds. He was fine, wasn't he DuPont? He was fine one moment and then the next...well."

"Calm, Milo. I do not think you are to blame for this. DuPont, do the guests know?" Every word left Lawrence through the side of his mouth; his eyes still fixed on the body that he knew for certain he was not the only one witnessing. There was a strange calm to that, being in it together. This was something he couldn't be blamed for, something that needn't haunt him. So long as the guests remained blissfully unaware.

"No, sir. At least we have little reason to suspect otherwise. The old chap hadn't made much fuss in his exit. I confess I had little idea of his state until I came to collect his glass."

"How did you clear the bar?" Lawrence asked, directing his gaze to Milo.

"After DuPont let me know, I admit I didn't know how to handle this. How often does one pass out stone-cold dead in your bar, sir? Sure, pass out drunk. But dead? I swear I've never seen the like of it. And to think, it could have been anyone, like that poor lady and her husband." Milo's voice began to shake and his eyes well with tears.

"Milo, Milo. Let us not allow our imaginations to run freely! You'll still be serving the guests for the evening; we cannot have you groveling all over the place over the thought of what might have been." Lawrence tugged at his waistcoat in order to prevent himself from falling into such a state. "Now, I'll ask again, and this time I want no disarray, do you understand?" Milo nodded, his eyes looking at the body. "Look at me, Milo." Lawrence stepped in front of Cherry's slouching remains. "That's good. How did you clear the bar?"

"I said there was a problem from the storm, sir. That we had flooding in the back, and we needed to call in help. I said we'd be open after dinner. Will we?"

"Will we what?"

"Will we be open after dinner, sir?"

"Of course we will, Milo. And with a little grace, we will all be in a better state by then, forgetting all about this mess."

"Yes, sir. Forgetting."

"Now, you have done well with your fast thinking, Milo. In the meantime, we will have to do something about...about Mr. Cherry here. The authorities will not be able to aid us this evening, I believe the storm has seen to that. Just the same, our guests will not be able to leave, negating the culprit's ability to escape. We'll be sure to get a call out to the police and ensure they are here in the morning, as soon as the storm clears. But we can't keep him here in the meantime." Lawrence put his fingers to his chin, cupping and rubbing the stubble that had begun to form. "Messrs. Berus?"

"Yes, sir?" Adrian and Dorian said in unison.

"I believe there is a wheelchair in the back closet, is there not?"

"Er, yes, sir." The look on Dorian's face was excessively worried when he answered his manager.

"Very good. What was Mr. Cherry's room? 410, I believe. Yes, that is quite right. I would ask the two of you to manage transporting Mr. Cherry to room 410. Aurelia? Eyes up, my dear, you will retrieve the key for them. I believe it best we keep his copy in his pocket for the time being. Thank you."

"Mr. Erlik?" The words were strong and resolute, coming from the old DuPont who stood straight with the posture of a gentleman of propriety.

"Yes, Mr. DuPont?"

"I would have a word...privately."

"Well, you heard the man. Scuttle off!"

"But Mr. Erlik!" Dorian began. "Are we sure it is such a good idea to touch a...a dead man? Isn't that bad luck?"

"Can you think of worse luck than the ruin of the Genovie? Because I believe it is not a stretch to say that the discovery of a murder would be just that!"

"Would it not be discovered regardless, sir?"

"Yes, it would. But there is a lot to be said for controlling the message, Dorian. Now snap to it!" Everyone dispersed with a spring in their step, no doubt wishing to avoid the malice hidden in Lawrence's voice. Everyone but Aurelia, who stood staring at the ground, muttering silently under her breath. "Aurelia!" Lawrence barked, regretting his harshness as soon as it left him.

The shock reverberated through her chest. But it was effective, nonetheless. When Aurelia sprung into action, heading for the front desk to provide the key in question, Lawrence turned his attention to DuPont.

"Over here, sir," DuPont said, shuffling to the far corner of the bar, standing next to the very table that housed a weeping mother and an apathetic father less than an hour before.

"Is this necessary?"

"The Genovie has many ears, sir, as I am sure you are well aware."

"Yes," Lawrence said. "I suppose you are right; carry on then. What is this word you wished to speak?"

"I believe I have some information as to the nature of Mr. Cherry's death that might be of interest, assuming that Mr. Milo is correct in his calculation that the death was caused by less than honest intentions."

"Very well," Lawrence said with intense interest, leaning in toward his informant. "Carry on."

"Mr. Cherry was drinking with Master Cyrus, sir."

"Cyrus?"

"The very same, sir."

"You saw this?"

"As clear as I can hear the rain against the window, sir."

"And you think?"

"It is not the business of waiters to think anything in particular, sir. But it might be prudent for me to tell you that he purchased Mr. Cherry a drink."

"Cyrus bought a guest a drink?"

"Indeed, he did, sir."

"But he never…"

"Not once, sir."

"Why the interest in Cherry?"

"I wish I knew, sir, but he had a hunger in his eyes. Flashing like a siren, they were."

"Alright," Lawrence said at the end of an exhale. "I'll talk to him presently."

"And there is something else you should know, sir."

"Something else?"

"Indeed."

"Well?" Lawrence felt his knuckles turn white as his fingers gripped at nothing in his fist.

"Well, it is not proper for men of my trade to delve in gossip, sir. But given the circumstances…"

"Yes, yes, what is it?"

"Before Master Cyrus left the table, Mr. Cherry ordered a drink for Mrs. Adonis, to be sent by me, of course."

"Interesting, but I don't see what…"

"Mrs. Adonis returned the gesture, sir. But her behavior was rather…strange."

"Strange?"

"Yes, sir?"

"Do continue!"

"Well, it is rather simple. She requested that I bring the drink to her first."

"What?" Lawrence asked at a volume close to a shout. "Why on Earth—"

But DuPont interrupted the tirade of questions by raising his hand and saying, "She claimed she wanted to bring it to him herself, sir."

"Strange, but…"

"Even stranger still, sir, she waved me over and requested that I bring it to him after all. Mentioned something about a call that her husband had to make that concerned her attention, sir." DuPont looked to the ground and shook his head before returning his gaze to Lawrence. "I only regret that I hadn't the foresight of what either party, Master Cyrus or Mrs. Adonis, might have wished to achieve, sir. But it is only my wish to serve, as you would have it."

"Do not linger on that, DuPont. Another man...or woman's scheme has little to do with your guilt or innocence. You have done right by yourself and by the Genovie to have come to me with this."

"I am ever the humble servant, sir!" DuPont said with a bow before he returned to aid Milo behind the bar at the behest of Lawrence's nod.

Prudence may be found in the clarification of Lawrence's mood upon gripping the reins of this unfortunate unfolding of events. It was not joy that prickled the back of his neck. The reader would do well not to confuse his comfort for such a vulgar emotion as that. No, not joy. Relief, perhaps, but not joy. Relief from the torment of having little control over the course of an afternoon's horrors when one is used to having control over all of life's trials, horrors, or pleasures.

Further clarification may be necessary in order to assuage the opinion of the reader in Lawrence's favor. The relief did not manifest over the realization that Mr. Cherry had died. Any soul lost while in the care of the staff of the Genovie reflected poorly on both those staff members who said guest came in contact with as well as the manager. Perhaps the latter's shame ought to be tenfold that of the former. However, Lawrence felt it wise to be charitable with himself, for he was not the direct cause. Instead, he was a first responder, a director of light amidst shadow. Simply put, it was nice to be of some use, even if that use was of little good to Mr. Cherry.

Now, to further that use for the benefit of the authorities. Perhaps he could solve the little mystery before they arrived and have the whole affair wrapped in a neat little package with a bright blue ribbon tied around it.

If DuPont's word was to be trusted (and there was little reason it should have been distrusted) the prime suspects of the murder were the small sum of two. Cyrus and Angela Adonis. However, such a weak case could be built around Cyrus. In fact, the mere idea of attempting to build it gave Lawrence a moment of humor. To imagine Cyrus playing with something as concrete as the end of life, it was too permanent for his tastes. Though it was a curious thing, going to the Golden Swan and having a drink with the man. Rather peculiar.

Lawrence tried to think back to all the time he had spent in the hotel, and he couldn't remember a single moment wherein Cyrus felt the obligation to dine with a guest. The thought was rather obscene. Cyrus felt it was best to blend in with the wallpaper, and he did a fine job of it. In fact, there were precious few instances where any staff member referred to Cyrus by name, as their run-ins with the old hound had been so few and far in between, there was little relevance in their duties and responsibilities. And so in he blended.

However, there was something peculiar about the way Mrs. Adonis's story fell from DuPont's lips. Had Lawrence been so clouded by his love—love, what a vile word to enter the mind of a manager of the Hotel Genovie! Infatuation, that was closer to the point, Lawrence would say. Even so, lust and desire are opaque temptresses. One hardly has the capability of seeing beyond one's nose when seduced by their gait. Had he been so blinded to not see the snake in the grass, the wolf in the woods?

But what would draw her to such a thing? To commit murder and stain the beauty of the Genovie, it was madness! A madness that must be stomped out! She, her husband, and her child.

Her child.

Lawrence reached into his pocket and pulled out the blue ribbon that had previously wrapped itself around the cold foot of a raven. Even earlier still, it had held those curly locks of innocent youth in place. Perhaps protecting her from the evils that surround the charmed and the pure. What would be left to protect her now, to protect her from Sonya Ivanovna? The Genovie? Would she be enough?

Lawrence stuffed his token reminder of a sworn duty to a mother before approaching Aurelia. "Find Cyrus for me, I wish to speak with him."

But the thing of it was, Aurelia's famous brow had already been raised to a certain peak before he spoke. By the time he got through with his order, the meaning was all too clear. "He is not in the office?"

A shake of the head.

"Well, have you seen him lurking about the lobby?"

A second shake. The old fool had made his escape. This certainly did not bode well for the optics of his involvement, but Lawrence clung to the reminder in his pocket that he was onto something of a bit more importance.

"Very well, keep an eye out for him. What of Mrs. Adonis, have you seen—"

But Aurelia had a way of interrupting Lawrence with that

brow. Currently, its arc combined with a nod of her head in the direction directly over Lawrence's shoulder. Lawrence was given sufficient warning to turn around before the Adonises were close enough to hear their breath.

"Mrs. Adonis, Dr. Adonis."

"Mister is fine. I like to keep a lower profile."

"Very well, Mr. Adonis."

"What is going on with all the commotion? Have you found Rachel?" the doctor asked. So, he didn't know. It wasn't in the words; any fool can fake a good show of ignorance. It was the hopeful look in his eye that it might be the case. Whether that hope stemmed from a desire to see his daughter safe again or to live peacefully with a content wife once more, Lawrence did not deign to guess.

"I'm...sorry. I'm afraid not. There has been an incident involving a guest, but it is being taken care of. There is little need for concern." These two had concern enough without being let on that they were suspected of murdering a radio personality. Something struck Lawrence in the way Angela held herself before him. She was no longer sniveling, no longer filled with an expression of sorrow, but of something Lawrence felt a strange familiarity with. Triumph. Not the sort of triumph that causes elation when one accomplishes a highly contested task. But the type of soft sweetness that comes at the end of years of suffering. The end that one has brought about with their very hands. Vengeance. In that moment, Lawrence let his empathy get the better of him, and he started to admire Mrs. Adonis for accomplishing whatever it was she had put an end to.

"But please," he said, staring into her eyes in a knowing way. She nodded for him to continue, but a glimmer in the eye told him her nod meant something altogether separate. Something only each other could understand, haunted by a horror all their own. At least one of them could break the shackle. "We'll find little darling Rachel soon enough. The two of you look famished. I suspect we'll have found her by the time you've had a moment to look at the menu. Oh, I insist. The staff is wrapping up their rounds and there are only a few places left to check where she might be. Aurelia here will escort her personally to your table."

Frederick seemed unnerved by the suggestion of sitting down to dine when they had yet to find their daughter. But Frederick was spineless. He looked to his wife for her answer to such an indecent suggestion, only to find that her stone face remained fixed on Lawrence's. There was a fire burning in both of their eyes. Perhaps if Lawrence were to have tested it, he could convince Mrs. Adonis to take her dinner in the gardens while the heavens poured down on her lap.

She nodded, the ice of her breath coming in an extended exhale. Lawrence bowed and showed the way.

Within the length of a few strides, they could hear the chattering of several guests gossiping about the "ordeal at the Swan," as it had been labeled. But the edges of their rumors' blades fell dull to the floor as he walked past. There was quite literally nothing that could change his stoic presence now as he walked through those large doors to the haven he had come to love with all of his being. The moment of bliss had finally arrived, the hour of the dinner service had begun.

A MEMORY

Waking up to the squeal of rats was the worst part of the war. Michael had spent the whole of it avoiding rats. He had nightmares of them gnawing into his belly to burrow for the winter, a problem that may very well materialize if they had to suffer much more of this god-forsaken war.

"Oi, Mikey! You got a light? Oi! Mikey!" The voice was a whisper, just loud enough to cut through the night's air, thick with leftover mustard gas and smoke from smoldering shell holes. They had been shelling all afternoon, in an attempt to disorient the German line. Phosphate and mustard gas shells whirled overhead. Michael thought of the misery they caused on impact.

"What?" Michael asked. The voice in the shadow belonged to David. Michael hadn't much want of war, only promising his mother that he would get in and get out as best he could. Nearly a year since, he still shivered in his tunic and trousers along the northeastern region of France. Meuse-Argonne, they called it. Michael could hardly pronounce it. He hadn't spent much time trying. Most of his days were spent hunkered down, haunted by the sounds of incoming shells, the rattling of machine guns, and—worst of all—the babbling roll of the Meuse River.

Take your clothes off. Take them off, Michael. Do as I say.

"A light!" David said.

"Oh, right." David lost his trench lighter in a nasty storm of berating shells from the other side of the river. Michael reached into his pocket and pulled his out. Stopping for a second, he inspected it, not knowing what he was looking for. A slow thumb flipped the lid and struck the wheel, igniting tiny sparks that rolled into a small flame. His face glowed orange from its luminance.

"Alright, alright. Nuff showin' off, toss it here!" Michael shook himself from his starry gaze and closed the lid of the lighter, tossing it over. David struck it alight again, just when Michael's eyes had readjusted to the darkness, sending him into a temporary whiplash of vision.

"Thanks, Mikey Ol' boy!" David said, not warning Michael of the incoming lighter that crashed into his chest. Now all that illuminated their presence were the stars and the tip of David's cigarette.

Michael never told David to call him Mikey, never told anyone to, in fact. He had always been Michael. But David was funny like that, just sort of taking you in under his wing and changing small things about you to make you more appealing in his eyes. Mikey. It had a nice ring to it, but only from David's lips. Michael told himself that when he dragged himself home after the war. From then on, it would be Michael.

The pair met in boot camp. They both joined up and found themselves in the 32nd division. The Red Arrow, as they called it. They had suffered through Alsace together only a few months ago. Back then, the heat of the sun baked the rotting corpses something awful. Filled the whole trench with the stench of death. Michael lost count of how many times it made him retch. At least now they had the cool September breeze and the feeling of the river's mist on windy nights.

We need to make you clean again. We need to make you clean.

"I swear," David said, unprompted, "these Huns ought to have a piece of my bayonet tomorrow. Dragging us out here to this shit country. I'll slit every throat I can get these mugs around. You just watch, Mikey, every throat."

"I believe you, David," Michael said, his eyes still closed. More than anything, he was worried about sleep. The night before going over was always the worst. Some men slept like logs; Michael might have been one of them if David hadn't decided they were best friends. David's nerves kept his mouth running, keeping Michael up all night.

However, Michael really did believe David. He was a fierce warrior when he was enraged; and when it came to the Germans, he was always enraged. For Michael's part, he had always fired his weapon slightly above his target's head. He had had enough killing in his lifetime. Just holding a rifle felt like a sin, felt like he was unclean.

To the River.

The morning came with a vulture's grunt. They probably smelt the younger soldiers shitting themselves. The fellows from the 42nd division that hadn't seen as much action. Hadn't come to grips with the fact that there was no making it home. They had seen the last of their winding roads, the final smile and tear of their dames, their terminal hug from their mothers. Many of them would weep and call for them before the sun took rest. No one but the vultures to hear them.

"Coffee?"

Michael was in too much of a daze to register the first offer. It was after the second that he saw David's outstretched arm holding a steaming mess tin with a liquid resembling latrine water after a surprise charge.

"No," Michael said, wiping the bits of mucus from his eyes. "Thanks, I just…"

"I get it," David said. "Don't want the runs when you're on the run? Ha! Pretty smart, if you ask me. I ought to take a bit of that advice myself. Course I love a bean like a sailor and his rum. I'd rather die with it in my hands than suffer to live without."

"Right, yeah." Michael's short mumbles were typical the morning of a fight. Vulgar though David's explanation was, Michael had refused the coffee for a different reason. Something about the fray woke him to the point of jitters already. Add a little caffeine to the mix and his finger might spasm over his trigger. "It's quiet," he said, stretching.

"Lieutenant's just marched past. He'll be barking soon enough, I expect. Trying to enjoy a little morning peace while I can. I hear there's going to be a bit of a scrap later. Some high-class fighters stepping into the ring. Like Willard and Johnson. Wouldn't want to miss it."

"Yeah," Michael forced himself to chuckle. "That'd be a shame."

"Come on," David said, rising as if on his way to the office. *How does he always manage? Just another day at work.*

There was an eerie sense of dread wafting throughout the trench, but none so eerie as the absence of any souls in the dugout. By the time they reached the fire bay, Michael could count on his gloved fingers the number of men he had seen. Some even did the decency of stopping their shivering to look him in the eye. More was said in those brief seconds of eye contact than an entire novel could communicate. The fear, the desperation, and—for some— the breathless acknowledgment that their end had already arrived.

They were the serene ones. A bullet couldn't break their spirit. Can anything break what's already been shattered into a thousand pieces?

Michael envied them. He envied the bliss of sitting against a trench wall and waiting to welcome the sting of the last moment. To hear the angels singing one home. But Michael was burdened with the irretrievable instinct to survive. An inconvenience.

"Where is everyone?"

"You overslept. They're all at the front, waiting to go over."

"Already?"

"Captain says we're to go over second, the first wave will be starting any minute now. I hear they have double rations for those who can get to the German line first. I got a buddy in the 42nd that says he'll gouge out the gunnery's eyes. Wouldn't that be a sight? These new boys always think war has so much glory."

"What glory is there in shit, piss, and blood?"

"You're in a lovely mood this morning. Something on your mind?"

"Yeah, I've got a date I've been meaning to skip out on. Any ideas?"

"I don't know much about skipping dates. I've always tried to get under every skirt I can. Ha! There she goes!"

The devil's whistle, as David liked to call it, preceded an earth-shattering quake and a thousand bits of rock and splinters flying through the air nearly twenty yards to their left. Michael ducked and covered his head when he heard the whistle.

He used to find the practice silly. *If a shell's going to drop down on my head, what good is my arm going to do?* That was his way of thinking until three nights into his first round of real fighting he watched a splinter the size of a butcher knife sever his friend Shelley's neck from lack of coverage. The captain gave a twenty-minute lecture on the importance of shell safety while the body was still warm.

"I guess the Kaiser caught wind of our little surprise party, eh?" Sometimes Michael detested David's light heart. Most times, actually. For some reason, this morning was different.

"We'll just have to pretend he was surprised then," he added with a grin. The closer they got to the front, the looser Michael began to feel, shaking off the jitter of his hand that he could never seem to keep steady since he first held a gun in his hand.

"Come on, first whistle, they're getting ready." Michael could hear the long-winded blow that usually meant for the first wave to line up and fix bayonets. He felt his side for his own, comforted to feel the cold of its steel, despite his lack of memory for how it got there.

By the time they reached the front line and found the men of their company, the first wave had gone over, and the day was scored by the music of battle screams, the rattling of machine guns, the bellowing of mortars, and the weeping of wounded. At every note, Michael's throat felt a bit drier.

"Get ready, Mikey," David whispered, jabbing him in the ribs with his elbow. Michael saw the bayonet in his hand as David fastened it to the end of his Springfield. The relief of the steel turned to dread as he did the same.

"Stick with me, Mikey. We'll get to the other side before these lazy dogs!"

"Who you calling lazy?" a stout man named Carmichael chuffed.

"Don't mind him, he just likes to bark to make us hounds think he can bite. Not an ounce of teeth in the little pup," another man named Sorkin said to the one called Carmichael.

"Shut it, both of you!" David retorted, turning back to

Michael. "Just follow me."

It sounded so simple when David said it, so calm. Michael could hardly be blamed for thinking they were somewhere else entirely by the sound of David's voice.

But the shell that blasted into their trench, splitting Carmichael into five large slippery chunks and knocking him five feet to the left served as an unwelcomed reminder. He was in hell.

The ringing was insufferable. For the span of a full minute, Michael couldn't hear a damned thing but its toll. He was seeing double as a figure approached him lying against the trench wall. It was trying to say something to him, grabbing him by the scruff of his collar. He was yelling. Michael knew that face, blood-soaked though it was. David.

"We have to move; we've been called over!" The sound came back like a second shell right to the ear. Michael felt around, finding the stock of his Springfield and the rim of his helmet with the tips of his fingers. "Let's go!"

Describing the rush of charging through no man's land is a futile effort. Michael would later go on to do everything he could to forget the details that haunted him so viciously. The torn arms pooled in old rainwater and fresh blood. The flying dirt and the whizzing sound of different-sized pieces of metal flying past his ear, some designed to kill him, some designed to obliterate him.

He tried to keep the distance between him and David short, but every quake of the earth, every thunder of God's anger served to knock him down. It was a wonder David was still standing.

In the span it took for them to get to the other side, Michael thought he counted eight men shot down in front of David, hundreds more to his right, hundreds more to his left. But eight in front. That left David in the open, that left him next.

"David!" Michael called, hoping he'd hear, hoping they could fall into a shell hole and wait out the morning. Of course, some said that falling into a shell hole was only worse. Even if you did manage to claw your way out when the heavy fighting was done, there were sharpshooters to contend with.

But David didn't hear Michael. He stormed the German front line like an iron-clad Ares swiping through the Achaeans. In a twisted way, it was a romantic sight. Watching David move through the field and coming up the other side with several men from the Red Arrow right behind, firing at the Germans like fish in a barrel. A poet could write an epic for his bravery.

"David!" Michael shouted, ten paces from his friend. Michael's worst fear was building. A German with a trench knife was creeping up from behind. "David!" Michael tried again, but his voice was drowned by the rhythm of war.

He raised his Springfield and readied himself to do the very act he swore he would get through the entire war without doing. He had the German in his sight, pulled his trigger, let the stock kick back into his shoulder, and felt the gunpowder plaster his cheeks. By the time his shell hit the ground, he could see the blood poor out of the German's flesh. Michael got him in the arm.

A minor wound, but enough to slow him, enough to make him squeal in pain and warn David. David turned and tried to swing his own rifle around and fire off a round. Michael's ears isolated the sound of the bullet leaving the chamber, but the German was quick to recover and bash the hilt of his knife into the rifle's handguard, throwing his aim off center.

He slashed at David. Michael tried to get a second shot, but before long the two soldiers were wrestling one another to the ground. Michael knew he wasn't an expert marksman, he never thought he'd have to be. The risk of hitting David was too great. He ran to help. Time seemed to slow on the journey over.

David bashed his fist into the soldier's jaw, which appeared to be made of stone. Blood poured down the German's face from his broken nose, but he swung like a madman with his knife, nearly slashing David in the face. The rolling of the river roared behind them. Michael was nearly within distance to land a blow on the German by the time the two soldiers rolled down a small hill, coming to a halt at the edge of the river, another several paces from Michael.

Time stopped with the stillness of David's body, resting on his knees. The German faced him with the tip of his knife breaking through the back of David's neck.

For the rest of Michael's days, he would remember the yellow shade of the bastard's teeth when he ran toward him. They gritted like a wolf baring at a predator.

Michael charged with his bayonet, but the German, anticipating the blow, knocked his rifle to the side and rounded over Michael, plunging his knife into the side of his thigh. Whatever grace may have been loaned to him in that moment to ease the pain, Michael would never understand. But he understood that death stood beside him, one hand on his shoulder, readying to offer him safe passage. It took the form of a man in a pristine tuxedo, unmarred from the blood and the dirt flying through the air.

Michael resisted and flung himself around, ignoring the phantom and throwing himself on top of the now defenseless German. They were so close to the water that the German stumbled and fell in. Michael kept him plunged under with the weight of his whole body pressed on his chest. His fingers wrapped around his neck, slowly pressing down, then letting go to try to force him to breathe on instinct. It worked. The soldier was choking up bubbles of air for a moment, and then...stillness.

Michael heaved and nearly retched. His fingers slipped freely from the now lifeless neck, and he couldn't help but fixate on the way the soldier's eyes bulged from their sockets.

The searing pain from the knife served as a reminder. David.

He took the knife from his leg and applied pressure with one hand and recovered his rifle with his other.

David was convulsing in a pool of his own blood by the time Michael made it back to him. Speaking was rendered impossible, but the infinity of the heavens might have been discerned from his eyes. His face was already ashen, his eyes bloodshot. Michael smelled sulfur rise in his nostrils and he began to fear gas.

"No, David! You can't go, you can't! I can't do this without you…" The tears fell from Michael's cheek down to David's blood-stained nose. "Don't go where I can't follow. Don't go, David, not there." Through the haze of watery eyes, Michael saw a pair of patent leather shoes tread on top of the sullen grass. He looked up to realize the oddity of the man dressed in a tuxedo on the field of battle. There was an age to his skin, yet youth was hinted at in key areas. The eyes, there was something wrong about his eyes.

"You won't take him! You won't!" Michael screamed, seeming only now to understand. "I just need to clean him. I need to make him clean! Come on," he said, turning back to David. "Come on, let's go to the river." Michael was delirious, hardly noticing the drum of battle happening behind him.

The Meuse-Argonne was filthy, but it would serve to cleanse the soul. "I can make you clean again, David. You'll hear the angels; they sound so pretty, don't they?" But Michael hadn't heard the angels since the night his father died. And he did not hear them now. But maybe David would.

He dipped his best friend's head in the water after dragging him across the mud. "That's better, isn't it?" Michael asked. "It's okay, David, it's okay." He dipped his head several more times, continuing the raucous chant: "We have to make you clean again. The angels will sing for you!"

But a hundred dips in the water would not serve to change those pale eyes staring to the heavens without an ounce of life in them. Michael sat, staring at his friend and fought the urge to scream and curse God and his angels. The thought of drowning himself in the river followed, and he plunged his whole torso and head in just to pay penance for such a thought.

There, in the tranquility of destruction, he sat surrounded by death.

XXIV

In the dregs of Lawrence's memory—behind the aching chill of a haunting ghost, behind the burden of a missing girl, and the scandal of a suspected murder occurring within those hallowed halls—remained a small fire in danger of burning out. That fire was, however insignificant it may seem to the reader, that he was still manager of the Hotel Genovie. And there were precious few aspects of management that Lawrence indulged in vanity over. One of those precious few was dinner service.

After all, there is a particular brand of solace in setting about one's way in the wild world and landing upon the fixings of a fine restaurant in a fine hotel. The type of restaurant where one finds the perfect suggestion of pairing a bottle of Domaine des Comtes Lafon, perhaps the 1909 vintage, with your poached salmon under hollandaise. The type of restaurant with lofty ceilings bearing crystal chandeliers that flickered to the notes of the Maestro's fingers pressing down the ivory of the grand piano in the back of the room. One with the opulence of a world long passed, left in an age that hadn't known the destruction of the modern wars, hadn't seen the production of the steam engine or the riches of the stock market. A restaurant with plush velvet drapes falling over windows so tall that one might dream of viewing the heavens and the earth all at once.

Tables were made to look as if fresh snow covered the green fields of France in white banks, with crisp linens constructing an elegant backdrop for gleaming silverware and meticulously arranged china and flutes of champagne at the ready.

The Seraphine was just such a restaurant.

Lawrence felt the air hit his lungs and warm his heart as he walked through the entryway and led Frederick and Angela Adonis toward the center of the room, where a table with three settings was at the ready. Pulling out a chair for Mrs. Adonis with his left hand while simultaneously snapping his finger with his right, three menus were brought before the couple could sit down. Two were placed in the hands of those present, while the third was neatly balanced on top of the place setting for the young miss who was due presently.

"You're sure you'll be finding her shortly then, Mr. Erlik?" Angela asked, ignoring the menu in front of her and resuming the ardent stare they had begun in the lobby moments ago.

"I am quite sure, madam. Worry needn't be vexing you anymore. I have little doubt that Aurelia will bring your beaming little one here any moment. In the meantime, Benjamin will be thrilled to take care of your every last whim. Benjamin?" Lawrence asked with a wave of his hand. Benjamin knew not to wait. With a bottle already in hand, the young waiter set about pouring the Adonises a glass of champagne each. Frederick ignored the gesture, but Angela picked up her glass and finished it in one impressive gulp, waving for a second as soon as its base hit the table.

While it was perfectly clear they were being left in the most capable of hands, Lawrence bowed to the Adonises and made his way to the front podium in order to employ the role of Maître D'hôtel.

"Mr. Erlik!" He was greeted as soon as he assumed his position. The charming Madam Applebaum's grin was so wide and folded at the seams that it stretched her face like a half-pitched tent.

"Mrs. Applebaum! How is the Genovie treating you?"

"Oh, I have not a single complaint for a charmer like you, Mr. Erlik. Though I would welcome an answer to a little curiosity, if it isn't too indecent to ask."

"Anything in my power to give will be yours, madam."

"You are too kind, you rascal. You'll forgive the absence of my protesting to your indulging ways. An old woman must find little pleasantries where she can."

"Nonsense, you don't look a day over twenty-five!" Such was the way of Lawrence Erlik when he forced tragedy from his mind long enough to transform into the service-obsessed manager that resided in the center of his burning chest. Charming, illustrative, welcoming, unforgettable. "What is it I can answer for you?"

"There was truth in my calling you a devil, I can see it in your eyes! Twenty-five! Oh, but I won't deny myself the temptation, you old flirt!" There was a sparkle ignited in the woman's eyes that Lawrence could clearly tell, given his talent for reading worn faces, had lost its spark years ago. Until she entered the Genovie. "Would you tell me what has happened with that wickedly charming man? Mr. Cherry. Yes, I knew you would know who I was talking about before I finished. It's a little thing—he said he would be in the lobby to meet me. We were to have dinner together. Shame me all you want, Mr. Erlik. An old woman ought to allow herself the odd indulgence."

There it was, the breaking of the glass. How he could be so

daft to think he could ignore the dismay that incessantly trailed him for the span of a dinner service was beyond him. Of course, the Genovie had ways of reminding one of the guilt that slid to the back of the throat. A lump that couldn't quite be swallowed whole. But perhaps there was still room to recover; perhaps he could reside in the breath of bliss for but another moment. He need only the aid of a lie.

"I am frightfully sorry, Mrs. Applebaum, but I'm afraid you've just reminded me. Mr. Cherry was called away for the evening on some important…family business. He meant to wait to give his apologies in person, but that was just not possible. I can tell you; he really did lament having to leave." The old woman deserved the comfort. For some reason beyond his own understanding, Lawrence was certain of that.

"Oh…yes. Well, how regrettable." Mrs. Applebaum gazed over the dining room before looking back at Lawrence. Perhaps she was surveying for a glimpse of a lie, waiting to find that Cherry had not been pulled away and was, in fact, dining with a younger beneficiary of his charm. When she found no evidence to confirm her suspicions, she returned to Lawrence. "He really looked upset?"

"Absolutely wretched, Mrs. Applebaum."

"Very well," she said on the breath of an exhale. And then she leaned in to whisper something in Lawrence's ear. It was something he did not at all expect, though surprises seemed to offer him little shock anymore. A request. A small and humble request, but one that might require a little charm of his own.

"Aye, Mrs. Applebaum. I can see to that."

"You really are a darling man, Mr. Erlik. A darling man."

"She asked for me?" Michael's voice was a great deal weaker than the last time Lawrence had met him for the luncheon hour.

"Indeed, she did. It appears you are rather popular among the guests today, Private Goodman."

"But...why?"

"I'm afraid I hadn't the slightest idea. It is not the business of a hotel manager to understand motivations. However, I suspect that it is all in the best of intentions. And I would feel rather complimented, lad. I hear rumor that Mrs. Applebaum does not offer her audience to just anyone," Lawrence lied. "She is a stickler for company and seems to be tickled by your presence."

"It seems one doesn't often dine alone in this hotel."

"I'm afraid not, Private. However, that is what the Genovie offers to her most deserving guests. Society."

"I'm not entirely sure that is a gift." Michael spoke in such a solemn tone and with such a melancholic look on his face as he looked out the window to the storm that Lawrence began to worry for his health.

"Private Goodman?"

"I'm sorry," the young soldier apologized, as if waking from an ill-timed doze. "Yes," he agreed. "I'd be honored to dine with the lady."

"She will be thrilled for it!" Lawrence exclaimed, taking note of the expression that communicated young Michael was not so thrilled.

But that was of little use to Lawrence. Walking through the Seraphine caused one to drift from the consciousness and droll of everyday ordinary life (even if one's day was far from ordinary,) providing Lawrence a bliss unparalleled. Setting the soldier down at the table with a "here you are," a menu, a snap of the finger, and a final bow to both Private Goodman and Mrs. Applebaum, Lawrence was free to roam about the tables and overhear curious goings on.

The clinking of glasses and rolling of poured champagnes created a perfect symphony with the accompaniment of Maestro Ellis and his floating fingers. The smell of the first amuse-bouche wafted through the air and filled one's nose with a sense of exciting journeys to lands with ripe tomatoes and bright green basil. The hum of interesting conversation, whether rumors about a man keeling over in the hotel bar or of the peculiar storm rolling through, creating a calming white noise.

Except, just then, Lawrence felt that familiar tickling of the ear as an uncomfortable reality seeped in; he noticed something perplexing. The notes of the waitstaff's feet sounded an octave lower than usual. The ring of the china was off-key. The beat of the rain's drum, with a bass of thunder, was off rhythm. Each note of the evening's symphony was a scratch in the wrong direction, and the timing of the few bars Lawrence was able to concentrate on, fell to shambles. At once, the beauty of a dinner at the Seraphine began to plunge into a depth of shadow that turned the blood flowing with fresh gusto in Lawrence's veins to icy cold.

He saw her.

She was sitting solo at a table in the far corner of the room, just past the set of steps of the platform that encompassed the second half of the restaurant floor, sipping on a glass of blood-red wine. Her grey fingers tapped out of time to the tune of Maestro's fingers.

Perhaps furthering Lawrence's dismay at having realized Sonya Ivanovna, now sitting in an elegant evening gown of pitch-black velvet, the key of the music changed. More to the point,

Maestro strayed from his usual sonatas that were gifted to the human ear by none other than Dominico Scarlatti and Joseph Haydn and was tempted by the damnable complexities of Berlioz. Berlioz on his darkest days, at that.

It is an entirely distressing consternation when one's mind has given way to the pounding of the Symphonie Fantastique, particularly when one arrives at the fourth movement. *A rather contestable piece for the piano,* Lawrence might have thought to himself, were his thoughts and sight not equally fixed upon the singularity of Mrs. Kosorukov's greyish disposition. In particular, his gaze was set upon her smile.

Were his attention a few inches higher, he might have found something altogether desperate in its possible meaning. Her eyes. They were not focused on him, as they had been when his attention had first been captured by the specter, but on a certain young soldier who was having a rather uncomfortable dinner with his newest patron, Mrs. Applebaum.

Aside from the usual chit-chat, the sort that makes one's eyes roll to the back of the head, Michael found that dining with a perfect stranger who had not made a career out of counseling the young and the destitute to be perfectly boring. There were plenty of dull, meandering questions like "Hello, my name is Doris and yours?" followed by the interminable "Yes, and how is your stay?" or "This is all rather splendid, isn't it?" or "It's been such a long time since I've last enjoyed the company of a young man for dinner."

It was shaping up to be an entirely dull affair until they caught onto the very subject that Michael was convinced was the sole

reason for any stranger wishing his company over anything from a
pint of beer all the way to a fine dinner at a mysterious hotel. The
substantially disquieting topic of the war.

The very one that Michael despised discussing most of all.
Not for the lack of stories, nor for the endless tirade of questions,
but for the question of valor. The truth of it was Michael could not
help but feel a deep sense of shame. Not only shame for what he
did, but shame for what he failed to do. Shame for David.

Nevertheless, the boy put on an admirable show in order to
avoid being found out for a coward, for a fraud, for anything other
than what everyone around him seemingly needed him to be: a
hero.

"Was it terribly frightening over there?" Mrs. Applebaum
spoke in a low tone, not nearly as congenial as it had been. There
was something in the way that tone fried, choked even, that bid
Michael to choose the honest path. Here was a friend, it said, not
a spectator looking for a glimpse of glory.

"Yes," he said, forcing the syllable through his throat. He
nearly coughed from the choke, excusing himself with the cover
of the stark white napkin he had unfolded onto his lap. One might
be forgiven for disbelieving he was brought up by modest means.

"Yes, I was afraid so," Mrs. Applebaum returned, taking a sip
of her wine. There was something funny about the way she spoke,
something that burrowed a hole into Michael's chest with a pain
quite familiar to his own abject misery. "Tell me, were there ever
moments of…well, I suppose there wouldn't be, would there?
But perhaps it wouldn't hurt to ask. Were there many moments
of solace? When it wasn't so frightening?"

"Yes," Michael said, not knowing how he had managed to
forget most of the English language, other than that fair syllable.
"Cards, books, cigarettes," he forced himself to say, "chocolate."

"Chocolate?"

"Yes, they gave us plenty of chocolate. It wasn't like anything you'd find in a place like this, I expect. But to a soldier…well, it tasted like…home."

"Yes, I suppose it would, wouldn't it?" The pair were made to leave their conversation at that, contemplating the validity of whether it would—or, in fact, wouldn't—remind one of home, given the abrupt interruption of the waiter.

Michael had never tasted salmon en croute, though he figured he'd rather like it. The smell brought him back to the days when Pa wasn't too drunk to take him fishing. They'd pile up on cod and fry them all dry, picking at them throughout the night till their bellies nearly burst open and poured them back into the river.

"Did you write to your mother often, like a good lad?"

"Aye…yes, Ma'am. I wrote to her every chance I got. She's a terrible worrier. We're all each other's got after Pa died."

"Oh, I'm so sorry, dear. How did he die?"

"Hunting accident."

"Ah, abominable habit, hunting. My husband used to go out for a month to hunt before he died. Every year. Truth be told, it was the most peace I ever found." Mrs. Applebaum seemed to carry on as if Michael weren't needed for the conversation. Truth be told, he was happy that nothing was expected of him.

"It's good that you wrote to your mother. Sensible. That way she didn't have to stay up late, worrying. Though I'm sure she still did. I don't think it would have made much difference if I had ever gotten a letter from my own son. I still would have lost him…in the end."

"I'm sorry, Ma'am. I hadn't realized you had a son who fought."

"It shocked us all, dear. His father pleaded with him not to go. Said a gentleman needn't fight in a war like this. That it was like going to his death, what with the way the fighting is done these days. To charge like that, it doesn't seem sensible, does it? When the other side is snug in their hole? I can't bear to think of it!

"But he was so adamant. When his father told him he wouldn't get a penny from the trust if he went away to fight Woodrow's war—a desperate attempt to coax him into staying, even I knew it wouldn't work—he simply said he'd renounce his entire fortune before he renounced his honor. There's bravery in that, I suppose. Tell me, why do men always choose bravery over sensibility?"

"I don't know, Ma'am—"

"Oh, Doris, please. You make me feel so old! Of course, you're right around the age of—oh, enough of my blubbering. You'll forgive an old woman. You were saying?"

"I don't know, Ma—Doris; I don't think we rightly have a choice."

"No, I suppose you don't. That's what he said, anyway. He went out the next day and joined up. The last I heard he was joining the 32nd division."

Michael dropped his fork and knife, causing an unpleasant clatter upon the china. Thunder rolled alongside its echo, causing several heads to turn and soften their own voices in an attempt to hear without making it too obvious they were listening in.

"What's the matter, dear?"

"Nothing, I just. It's nothing. That's the division I served in."

"Oh, well perhaps you know my David! Knew—I'm still getting used to the past tense. Of course, he didn't go by the name Applebaum when he enlisted. He changed his name to Reed. David Reed."

Michael's blood turned to ice at the sound of a gunshot.

XXV

After he had left Michael and Mrs. Applebaum to their dinner, and after he had returned to his podium in an effort to find solace in the evening's splendor, Lawrence gave himself to dismay at the realization that Sonya Ivanovna was there to remind him. Remind him of the evil, of the shadow, of the torment that was further enveloping the hotel with each strike of the grandfather clock.

What have you done with her? He tangled the blue ribbon around his fingers inside his trouser pocket. But Sonya Ivanovna had little concern for the whereabouts of the youngest member of the Adonis trio.

It was far too late by the time Lawrence took notice of the poor target of her malignant glare. His eyes were transfixed on the glass of wine, wondering how it had made its way to the table—had she ordered it? Did that mean another person had seen her, had they spoken to her?—when she rose from the table and began to walk toward Michael and Mrs. Applebaum.

Lawrence was frozen, unable to move even the joint on his big toe. Not that it made much of a difference. From where he stood, it would have been impossible to make it all the way across the room to intercept whatever it was Sonya intended to do. At least not without causing the very thing Lawrence had been trying to avoid all afternoon: a scene.

Though he tried, such a scene was about to transpire. It ought to be noted that at this very moment, the one wherein Lawrence witnessed Sonya Ivanovna stride with a gait beyond mortal grace, Michael was learning about the nature of Mrs. Applebaum's final relations with her son.

In fact, Sonya Ivanovna was standing right next to Michael while Mrs. Applebaum spoke. While her eyes were fixed on Lawrence, her deadpan stare furthering the freeze of the manager's bloodstream (it really did, so much so that the poor creature felt his heartbeat begin to slow to an unrecognizable pace), her hand found a place to rest on the young man's shoulder.

Just as a concerto finds its crescendo at the meeting of several instruments from their little parts to form a larger whole, so did the events of this explosive moment where Lawrence's hopes of coming back to a state of regularity were set in flames. For as Mrs. Applebaum was uttering the words, "He changed his name to Reed. David Reed." Sonya bent down to press her lips on Michael's cheek. At the exact second—yes, the exact second—that her lips touched his skin and the final syllable "Reed" lifted off from Mrs. Applebaum's tongue, a passing waiter suddenly felt the heavy silver tray suddenly jerk from his grip as if being stolen away. It fell with such a tumultuous BANG that it ought to have given anyone in the room a proper fright.

There were many comparisons one might have made, had one been in the room, to the sound of the precious metal clambering about the floor. The musically inclined may have been forgiven for thinking an accompaniment of cymbals had joined the maestro. A mechanic may have likened it to an engine backfire. One might, if one had sufficiently numbed the senses with a proper dose of red wine, have mistaken it for a particularly close strike of lighting. But to a soldier, none of these possibilities came to mind. For if one was a soldier on that very night, in the dim lighting of the Seraphine's crystal chandeliers floating overhead, that sound was mistaken for a gunshot.

"Down! Down, get down!" Michael screamed at the top of his lungs, gripping the handle of the knife that sat upon the table's freshly pressed linen. It was at this moment, and not a moment before nor after, that Lawrence regretted how sharp he always insisted the knives be kept.

His heart fell to the floor as he watched Michael overturn the table. The desire to yell at Mrs. Applebaum to back away, rather than reach out with comforting arms in an attempt to calm him, came in vain. Before he had the opportunity to utter a syllable, Michael's knife had made its cut across her forearm. The fresh linen had been profaned with the shade of an old woman's blood.

For Mrs. Applebaum's part, the reader would be forgiven for thinking her action to be the opposite of sensible. Indeed, in many ways it was. But the moment her young dining companion had seized into a fit of panic at the impending danger of the enemy front line closing in, she saw a face swap with his own. A very familiar face of a young man. It may be even more appropriate to say boy. As Michael's eyes began to dilate and contract, Mrs. Applebaum saw her son. David.

And so it would not be altogether accurate to say that her reaching out toward young Michael was an act of compassion for a desperately unwell soldier who had one too many things that continued to haunt him. Rather, it was a pleading. A pleading for her son to return to the warmth of her arms. Have we all not been deceived by such phantom illusions in the grip of an unforgiving and theatrical moment?

So, did it hurt? That is, had Mrs. Applebaum felt the bitter sting of the knife's edge slicing through the paper-thin skin one only cultivates from a lifetime of soft sheets and silk dresses? Indeed, but not in the way the reader might expect. In a way, the pain served to comfort her. It was a penance for the way she had left things with her son. How she had not intervened when her wickedly proud husband cut him off from the family fortune for the devilish desire to serve his country. But it was never about the fortune, she then came to understand in the glint of her ruby life-blood drip down her arm. It was about home. They had stolen from him a loving home.

For years she had felt shame. Perhaps now she could feel something physical rather than the dull ache within.

However, it would behoove the writer not to pontificate over the different nature of a parent's suffering amidst a young man's hellish delusion. For Michael saw the river flood the polished floors of the Seraphine. He heard through the roaring claps of thunder outside the rattling of machine gun fire. And across the room, staring back at him with a look of abject terror, was David.

"David! Please, David! Come on, we have to go back! We can't take them, there's too many! God, why did I come here, why?" Michael shouted so loud his face turned the color of ripe beets, his lips filled with spittle, and his nose drained of snot.

But, as the reader well knows, the figure Michael was screaming at was not David. Instead, he screamed his pleas toward Mr. Erlik, who was rushing toward him.

Perhaps this was the wrong thing to do, to rush toward a man who was clearly transporting his very consciousness back to the sight of the wretched war that had torn his soul from his body.

Perhaps it was doubly worse that Frederick, for once in his life, decided to act the bolder man and jump into the fray. After all, if he was to be useless in finding his daughter, he ought to at least find use in calming the dispirited antics of a damaged soldier.

Frederick's call to action would have been better served right where he was. For as soon as he had leaped "to the rescue" as he would later think of it, Mrs. Adonis was left alone with a pang in her stomach akin to what caused her to keel over in pain. It started seconds after she felt a curious sensation of frigid cold on her cheek as if something pressed into it. However, when she brushed her fingers against her skin, there was no evidence of anything earthly making contact with her face. At the table by herself, she muttered the phrase, "I need to get it out of me," to no one in particular. Perhaps Frederick could have been useful there, perhaps not. It is not for the writer to decide.

"Stay back! I mean it! Don't you come any closer, or I'll stick you!" Michael was leaning against the downed table, brandishing what he no doubt took to be a bayonet gathered off the corpse of a young sergeant.

"Michael!" Lawrence called out to try and get Michael to register the familiarity of his voice. It was to no avail. Michael continued to swing about in a rush, lunging forward if Lawrence or Frederick took a step in his direction. A member of the waitstaff rushed over to usher Mrs. Applebaum from the fray.

"Michael, it's alright. The war is over. You're in a hotel, Michael."

"What have I done? What have I done? Mama, what have I done?"

"Michael, you haven't done anything that can't be fixed." Lawrence found that his breath was sharp and hardly filled his lungs. He kept a palm raised toward Michael, not knowing what else to do to keep him from lunging.

A fraction of his mind veered from the present calamity in order to appreciate the likelihood of his never having been presented with the sudden outburst of a guest who thought he had been transported back in the thick of battle. And what were the odds that it was to happen this day? It was when he asked himself this question that the reality of the situation dawned on him. This day. This entire day was happening to him at the behest of a kiss from Sonya Ivanovna. Had she kissed Rachel? Had she kissed Mr. Cherry? Who would she kiss next? And as *that* question rolled around in the back of his mind, he descended into fear and panic at the realization that he too had been kissed.

But, as one can well see, this was no time for Lawrence to ponder the question of his own doom. He was far too busy with Michael's.

It seemed, at least for the moment, that Michael was finished with the absurd notion that anyone in the room was a German soldier and had moved from aggression to fear and remorse. That, however, did not aid in lowering the weapon clung tightly in his white-knuckled hands.

"I didn't mean it, Mama!" he shouted, looking at no one in particular. Owing to the great commotion, any guest, waitstaff, or bellmen who figured he may be of service had rushed to the scene.

"What do we do?" Baptiste asked, panting in Lawrence's direction.

"The poor lad's lost it," Adrian surmised.

"He thinks he's back," Dorian added.

"Keep back, boys," Lawrence warned, motioning for them to take a step back while he stepped forward. "Michael? Michael, can you hear me?"

"I...I killed a...I killed him. I strangled him. With my own hands."

"I know, lad," Lawrence lied. "I know. You did what you had to, son. You'll have to forgive yourself."

"I'll never forgive myself for what I've done! I was wrong, sir. I was so very wrong! There's blood, so much. Oh, Mama! Forgive me! I was wrong; they found me, Mama. They found me again."

"Who found you, son?" Frederick piped in, no doubt feeling his lack of use in this moment.

"My demons, they chased me to France. They followed me." Michael's knife-wielding hand began to shake, but he kept it well hoisted in the air, taking turns on which man he pointed it toward. It was a warning, to all those who approached, that death awaited their hubris.

"Point the knife at me, son," Lawrence said. "Point it here." The manager became something that, in all of his life, he had never quite been. Brave. "That's it, let's breathe together. I'm not going to hurt you, and you're not going to hurt anyone."

"Can you hear them, Mr. Erlik?"

"Can I hear who?"

"The devils. They're laughing at me."

"No one's laughing, Private." However—whether it was the planting of the idea or if it was actually happening—Lawrence could, very faintly, hear the sounds of a chuckle.

"I'm not clean," Michael said, as if not hearing Lawrence. "I need to be clean again. Mama, I need to get clean again! The river!"

"Son?"

"The river!" Michael screamed, shaking his knife in Lawrence's direction. "I need to go to the river; I need to be clean again! Forgive me for what I've done! I couldn't...I couldn't save him...I,"

Michael's tirade was cut short by something extraordinary, at least in Lawrence's mind. I dare admit that I, too, found it to be worthy of the name miracle.

She didn't even have to let the crowd know that she had arrived before they parted for her. There was a defined grace in the way the light reflected from her skin as she stepped next to Lawrence and placed her hand on his arm. Without a word, as was her usual way, Aurelia told Lawrence that she would handle it from there.

Michael's arm remained extended toward Lawrence, the point of his knife following him as he stepped back. But Aurelia had no fear of sharp knives and desperate men. Instead, she reached for its ivory handle, wrapping her warm fingers around Michael's. His eyes didn't break from Lawrence, though a visible shiver ran through his entire body as the knife fell from his grip into Aurelia's hand. By the time she handed it to Lawrence, Michael was curled into himself on the floor, stuttering as he repeated, "I need to go to the river. I have to get clean. I can hear them. I can hear them; I can hear them."

Aurelia stepped back, and with the nature of a mother, she wrapped her arm around his shoulders in a warm embrace. With her other hand, she held tightly to his shaking hands that slowed to a stillness in her grip.

"I need to go to the river," he said, now looking her in the eye. Now, there were not many who had the fortune of a proper view of Aurelia's face. But if they had, all those present would have seen a singular tear fall from her right eye as she nodded at the broken soldier's request.

To the river, her soft brow seemed to suggest.

Together, they rose.

Just as they had for Aurelia's arrival, and just as the Red Sea, the crowd parted for them. Lawrence followed not too closely behind as Aurelia led Michael out of the Seraphine.

Through all of this, Mrs. Adonis remained seated at her table, clutching her stomach, and muttering a curious phrase about removing something from it. She was now left completely alone. That is, aside from the few members of the waitstaff that were too stunned to move. Even a bloodied Mrs. Applebaum had followed the pair out of the room. It was a terrible circumstance, then, that the entire room which would have been witness to Mrs. Adonis's discovery of a small blue ribbon lying on the ground, doubtless having fallen from Mr. Erlik's pocket in the thick of the chaos, was empty. There was no one to hear her scream in fright, her mind parading her through the terrible scenarios that such a lost ribbon could mean. It can plainly be said, reader, that a mother's mind has the frightful capacity to travel to the darkest of places that others wouldn't dare dream of on their wildest of nights.

But alas, no one saw her spiral from the icy statue she had composed herself within for those past few hours. No one heard the frantic muttering of the phrase "Get it out, get it out!" as she knocked over chairs and even caused a glass to fall to the floor in a spritz of shattered crystal on her way to the lift. And no one saw her clutch the blue ribbon between her shaking fingers as she pressed her hand to the bottom of her stomach. Every soul in the hotel was too occupied with the conclusion of the young soldier's journey.

The crowd watched as Michael and Aurelia exited the large double doors, as they walked to the lobby, and as they, against all preconceived notions of sensibility, walked out the front door and into the raging storm.

It ought to be noted that every set of eyes that witnessed the young man and woman walk out and brave such a dangerous storm embracing tightly together understood. What was it they understood? Perhaps it cannot truly be described due to its inherent sadness. But if one were to put it into words, one might say there was an understanding that the end had come for them, and they were ready to meet it.

Of course, no one knew exactly what that entailed. They did not know that Aurelia walked young Private Goodman down into the gardens. Indeed, had they been aware, they may have been able to witness through the Seraphine's window as the young couple approached the swelling river that had formed through the gardens at the behest of the heaviest storm on record before or since. Only then would they have known that, as Aurelia walked him to the river's edge, and as he fell to his knees with a splash of the enveloping water, she kissed his forehead.

The water swelled ferociously as Michael felt it cleanse him of the evils of this world, of the world he had never found a proper place in. All the horror, all the pain, all the sorrow washed away in a manner he had never felt before. And for the first time since he was a little boy, he felt the warmth of an indescribable love. The type of love a poet curses himself for his inability to master.

"I can hear them, Mama," he cried, letting the rain pound on his face with joy. "I can hear them singing! I can hear them again!"

While Aurelia stood by his side, he laid down and let the river flow over him. It didn't hurt. Or if it had, Michael was too busy listening to what he knew was the singing of the angels, sent by his mother. And then as the water rushed into his lungs, there was nothing.

Though the rain hid any signs from her cheeks, Aurelia wept.

A MEMORY

The air felt thinner without her woolen dress and stockings to keep her warm. That was the queer thing about it. Not colder, just thinner. Angela had been waiting for this moment ever since Frederick had placed that shining rock upon her finger, declaring to all the world that she would be an Adonis. But the world had other plans for her.

A trial, many trials. One after the other. Some making it a month, others making it three or four. But they all died. Tiny little coffins. Of course, they were empty of anything resembling flesh and bone, but the symbolism was still there. It was a funny word, symbolism.

Where was the symbolism in trying over and over again only to have a piece of life ripped out of you as if a beast fixed her claws into your stomach? Where was the lesson? Where was the romance? But now her time was here; now she could be whole.

Angela placed a hand on her enlarged stomach, feeling warmth radiate from her skin, feeling life. There it was, inches from her fingers. Life. No more pain, no more sorrow, no more tiny wooden boxes buried in the backyard, underneath rose bushes. Her little rose bushes. Life.

But she wouldn't forget them, not with the success of this little angel. She couldn't forget. This one would bear the weight of the lives never lived in her grace, and Angela would teach her how. It wasn't fair, Angela knew that, but she also knew that fairness had little to do with it. She would raise a viper, ready to lunge at the world. A proud gait, a soft chin, a sharp eye. An Adonis.

"How are you feeling, my love?"

Poor Frederick. Flawed, complicated, loving Frederick. Angela had plenty of reasons to spite the handsome carving of a man, but she didn't. After all, he had stood by her through thick and thin. He had stayed up with her through grueling nights. The ones when she woke up screaming in pain. Sometimes physical, sometimes the feeling of those sharp black claws carving up her belly would be there. But mostly she wailed and wept for the loss.

The dreams were the worst, the ones where they would come to her. They would kiss her on the cheek and smile at their mother. But whenever Angela would reach out to touch them, to hold them in her arms, they would float away. Angela didn't know which had been more painful, the losses or the dreams.

But Frederick was always there. Always awoken with a fright, quick to wrap his arms around her, to rock her to sleep, to gather a glass of tonic on the easier nights, gin on the harder ones. Sweet, ignorant Frederick.

What would the poor darling think if he knew it was his fault? If all the loss, all the pain and misery, were due to his own inadequacies. Of course, the thought had never occurred to him. Why should the plights of women hinder the triumph of men?

"Yes, dear, I'm feeling fine. Just fine. Would you make sure the doctor is coming?"

"He's on his way presently, ma'am." The soft tinny, almost

apologetic voice came from a nurse standing in the corner. Not apologetic in the sense that she was sorry for the inconvenience of the wait, but sorry for suffering the listener to hear her voice. Weakness. That's how Angela saw it, and a good measure of disdain formed in her chest every time she heard its intonations.

"Yes, well, alright then," Angela said, eyeing the nurse with the flame of a raging fire. The pain was unlike anything she'd imagined. She had heard stories, sure, but nothing like this. It felt like waves of knives slowly pressing into her uterus and twisting around. It felt like the claws had returned.

But it was worth it, it was worth all of the pain to get to this point. And it was worth the means. The grimy, cigarette smoke-filled studio where her cousin worked. The way he smiled and showed his ridiculous gold-plated tooth. His breath tasted of stale whiskey and old peanuts. Why had he insisted on kissing her? Why couldn't they just have gotten it over with? Like a business deal, nothing personal, nothing sensual about it. Cold, black and white, firm paper. The kind that made a full resonating sound when you rubbed two fingers together.

But Don couldn't have it that way. He'd had his filthy eyes on her since childhood, since she was old enough that her mother didn't want her alone with boys, or even men for that matter. Family or not. It wasn't safe, she had always said. It wasn't safe. Don wasn't safe.

Don was the only one who wouldn't tell. The only one that was so desperate for a taste, he would agree to anything just to have one memory. How funny it was that the same five minutes can be remembered by one to be filled with riches, as if surrounded by gold and diamonds reflecting on the skin. But the other remember it with utter darkness, ash. Ash to fertilize the tiny rose bushes, ash to harbor a change for the better. Ash mixing with cheap liquor to make a harrowing soot. That's how the memory tasted in Angela's mouth, like warm whiskey-flavored soot.

"Well, happy to see you've all felt the need to grace me with a visit. To what do I owe the pleasure?"

Dr. Hampstead. The black knight, the one that was honest with her, didn't bother with the nonsense of telling her she could keep trying. He knew as well as she did that there was no hope. Such as that was, Angela quite enjoyed the look on his face when she told him she was pregnant. She made sure to wait three months to tell him, to make a real show of it. With Dr. Hampstead, none of her priors had made it past two months.

She wasn't used to seeing him so...radiant. So happy. A year ago, she would put any price on seeing this side of his office. Indeed, she had put a price on it and paid the piper on a storm-filled night.

It was always a storm-filled night with these sorts of things. The devil likely had something to do with it. Had she sold her soul? In the stories there's always some cartoonish figure with his hand held out, dirty nails sharpened to a point. Yellow teeth. There was always a contract. Sign on the crimson line if you dare. Sign with blood.

Angela signed with whiskey. With thick, grubby, sausage-like hands curling around her waist. Her perfect, milky skin. Tainted with the stain of the unwashed.

Does your brilliant husband know you're here?

What a sick thing to ask, but that was Don's way. He got off on the scandal, probably more than he got off on her. She didn't know which made her sicker. Perhaps that's why he had hardly loosened his buckle before it was all over.

But the worst of it wasn't that it had happened, it was that she was glad it had happened. And Frederick would never know. No one would ever know. And with enough time, even Angela would forget the deal she made with the devil, the deal for her child.

"Alright, that's it. Ten centimeters! Angela." The doctor took her hand, her soft, shaking hand, and rubbed the top of it with his practiced thumb as he squeezed. It felt rehearsed, like he had done it a million times. Angela was happy to be a million and one, so long as she got her due. His touch warmed her, brought weight back to the air. "Angela, I'm going to need you to work with me, alright? We're a team, you and I. Been through a lot together haven't we, dear? Never thought we'd make it; well, you showed them, didn't you?"

The pain shot through her pelvis and traveled up her back only to clog her throat with an unmanageable lump. But she was able to nod. She showed them, she showed all of them. No more whispering at dinner parties when Angela walked in the room. No more of those little hens clucking, "Oh, but she's such a sweet girl. What a tragedy she's been through." "Poor Frederick. I hear she throws herself down the stairs. The thought of raising his child sickens her." "Oh, what a wicked thing to say! It is rotten luck is all. Such rotten luck."

Not anymore.

"What are we, dear?" Doctor Hampstead insisted, squeezing her palm to coax the response.

"A team." Angela barely understood how she got the words out, how she was even able to breathe. The pain was intolerable. Perhaps she should have included a comfortable delivery in her little deal with the devil. No matter, none of it mattered.

"Alright, that's quite right, Angela. Quite right. Now, I'm going to place my hands at the ready—"

"Oh, I think this is my call to step out. Good luck, my love.

Be my little soldier now. You can do this. You can take on the
world with your wrath. Let it burn; let it light!" Frederick kissed
the top of her forehead and stepped into the hall, hardly waiting
for Angela to respond. He was replaced by two nurses. One
offered her a hand to squeeze, as well as a strap of leather to bite
down on. Angela welcomed that; she felt like her teeth would
shatter if they kept grinding.

The leather tasted like salt. Like the last poor girl to clamp
down on it had exhausted all of her sweat into the grain. Once she
got over the crudity of the thought, it turned rather romantic. An
army of women suffering to bring little ones into the world, each
to their own degree. Each reminded the one to come after that it
could be done, it had been done, and will continue to be done. It
comforted her more than the tender hand she was nearly breaking
with her grip.

The pain brought her away from it all, like a drug that was
sending her out of her body and into the stratosphere. Her vision
faded to black as she heard the doctor tell her to push. She pushed,
and limitless pain filled her entire body. It felt like a dream, like
the pain was a vessel, a ferry drifting across the river Styx. And
her ferryman was Dr. Hampstead.

No, not Dr. Hampstead, but a dark, cloaked figure. A man,
tall and aged, dressed in polished satin, the lines of his tuxedo
sharp and well-tailored. Who was this man, and how had he come
to collect her? Had she died? Had she come all this way, offered
up all this struggle, sacrificed herself on the altar of the
unobtainable only to be brought to the final moment and hung to
dry?

She reached for the ferryman, his cloak hung over his head,
his arms stretching out to the top of a wooden pole, grabbing the
rocky surface of the bottom of the river and then pulling them

closer to the other side. Pulling them closer to the end.

"No," she said, but her voice gurgled, as if she had plunged under the surface of the water at the family lake house. The lake she and her friends would go diving in on hot summer afternoons. Memories of her father bringing out fresh lemonade her mother had made. Small cut sandwiches and slices of hefty oranges. Safety.

But here she wasn't safe.

"No," she shouted, pulling at the sleeve of the ferryman, yanking at his hood. "No, I'm not ready." He was probably used to hearing that. But he had to believe her. He slowed in his efforts, a sly grin poking through shadow.

Enraged, Angela grabbed ahold of his hood, yanking it from the ferryman's head. "No," she demanded, "take me back."

She wasn't sure what she was expecting. Some forlorn wrinkled creature with brown skin and long hair, perhaps a furry beast, perhaps the devil himself. But instead, the ferryman was debonair, his hair greased back, and his visage polished and friendly. The friendly gaze as intoxicating as the cologne wafting from his stubbled neck. Kindness. An expression beckoning her to trust him, to come with him, to rest.

It wasn't safe.

"Take me back," she demanded. "I want to go back!"

Angela Adonis was not going to go gently to the underworld. Whether that of Dante or Homer, she would not go. Not before the devil upheld his end of the deal. Whiskey and blood, ash and soot. Angela Adonis was not done with the world of the living.

"Will she be alright, doctor?" She knew that voice as it echoed across the dark cavern. The ferryman began to turn around, to bring her back. What was it to him? She would pay the two coins eventually. She would cross sooner or later.

"I expect she will be fine, though it will be difficult to bear.

Frederick, sometimes these things…sometimes these things break us. They are hard to come back from."

"But she will come back."

"I expect, with a good deal of effort, she will heal from this."

"You don't understand my wife, Dr. Hampstead. Angela is not an ordinary woman. She is stronger, stronger than man, stronger than ten men."

"I do not doubt. We have a fighter on our hands."

Angela felt the black claws scrape at her stomach.

"A fighter," the doctor repeated.

Angela opened her eyes. It was unclear how long it had been since she heard the doctor speak, but he was no longer there. The room was empty, void of all life except hers and her darling Frederick folded into himself on an uncomfortable-looking chair, sound asleep.

"Fre—" she tried to say his name, but with her voice the pain returned.

"Freder—" she tried again, and again she failed. But not entirely, for her darling woke up. They made it through, it was over, and they could carry on together. As a family. What was a little pain, a little healing when gifted with the miracle of life and love?

"Oh my god. Oh my god. My love, oh I thought I had lost you. Oh my god, does it hurt? Are you quite alright? Oh, Angela, it's so good to see you awake. Oh, I love you, I love you, I love you!"

"I lo—"

"Don't speak, darling. It's alright, don't speak."

"Ra—"

"I'll get the doctor." As soon as Frederick was able to leave the room, Angela was able to speak her first word. She spoke as her eyes met a brightly colored bassinet sitting next to the chair that Frederick had been sleeping in.

"Rachel." A single tear fell down her cheek. Not for the pain, but for the love of that sweet little bassinet.

"Well, I will have to admit I am surprised to see you awake. They told me you'd be awake this soon. I simply said it was impossible. Yet here you are."

Dr. Hampstead, she'd never been happier to see his old, warm face. But there was something to his voice. A change in timbre, a hollowness to his words.

"Doctor," she choked out.

"Oh, you mustn't overburden yourself, dear. You've lost a lot of blood and are no doubt in a lot of pain."

But Angela insisted. "Doctor," she said. Hampstead looked worriedly at Frederick and, seeing there was no use in protesting, looked back at Angela. "How is she? How is my Rachel?"

"Darling," Frederick began. His voice was grim, choked, soot. "Darling, I'm afraid it didn't go so well."

"What?"

"Well, you see. The doctor came to me and explained everything. It was bad luck, is all. Could have happened to anyone. It was the umbilical cord, it seems." Frederick stumbled over his words, evidently not knowing which word to choose to follow the former.

"Angela," Dr Hampstead began. "It's called prolapse. Sometimes, well, sometimes when we are trying to push the baby out, the umbilical cord precedes the baby, and well. Sometimes when that happens..." The doctor paused, looking between Frederick and Angela.

"I told you, doctor, stronger than ten men."

But Angela didn't hear Frederick's endorsement of her

strength. Instead, her eyes darted to the opposite end of the room. The corner with the chair, with the bassinet. There sat the ferryman. Grim, pale, smiling. His legs were crossed in a gentlemanly fashion, one hand perched upon his kneecap. His other hand rested on the handle of the bassinet, rocking it back and forth. But his eyes remained fixed on her. His flaring orange and yellow eyes. What had she done?

"Right," Dr. Hamstead said, sitting beside Angela and taking her hand in that same tender fashion. He rubbed the top with his thumb. "Angela, when that happens, sometimes the baby can lose oxygen and blood flow. And while we are often able to deliver in enough time to avoid any further complications, I'm afraid you fell incapacitated." Angela could tell he didn't want to say it, wanted to run from the woman whom he had stood side by side for so many long and tortuous months.

"Tell...me," she reassured him. Why was it always she that had to do the reassuring?

"Angela, I'm afraid Rachel lost oxygen for too long. By the time we were able to deliver, by the time...Angela, Rachel didn't make it."

XXVI

"Are you quite alright, madam? I am terribly sorry; I cannot begin to—"

"Oh, nonsense, Mr. Erlik! It's only a scratch. I only wish that poor boy didn't have to suffer in that way. Where do you suppose they went?"

"I don't know, ma'am. I was wondering that myself, truth be told. But Aurelia will take care of him. I expect they are walking it off in the rain. Not that I would advise it—it's looking rather biblical out there, wouldn't you say?"

"I would. I think that's absolutely the word. Biblical. You know, I think he knew my son?"

"Is that right?"

"Yes, I think it is. My David served with him, or so it seems. I didn't get to talk to him much about it, that damned clatter seemed to set him off right when we were getting to the point. What do you suppose is wrong?"

"Well, Ma'am, he is on his way to find out himself, I expect. Though it isn't the business of the Genovie to pry in such cases."

"Whatever help he needs, I hope he receives it well."

"Yes, I would say we are aligned in that wish, ma'am. There

you are; how is that?"

The bandage, tightly wound and expertly placed, impressed even Lawrence himself. Regrettably, given the storm, there was little chance of having a proper professional tend to Mrs. Applebaum's care, but the manager's efforts were suitable in a pinch. It allowed his mind to be occupied, but it was fleeting. There was little to be done to avoid the pressing urgency of Sonya Ivanovna, who was now extending her ploys beyond Lawrence and spreading into the consciousness of the guests.

This deeply worried him.

And why shouldn't it? After all, it was concerning enough when he thought it was only him that she was after. But now, it seemed, she had a new thirst.

"Will you be alright, ma'am?" Lawrence asked, more so in a tone that would communicate, in the politest possible way, that Mrs. Applebaum's lingering had become a nuisance.

"Oh, yes. I shall be just fine."

"Perhaps a spot of sherry? The Golden Swan—"

"Yes, yes. I'll find it myself, Mr. Erlik. Thank you, you have been most helpful. And…if there is anything I can do for the poor boy…"

"I'll know where to find you, ma'am."

"Excellent!" Lawrence couldn't believe his relief at leaving, but she was quickly replaced. Standing in front of Lawrence in the manner of a cod as it's pulled from the water, were the brothers Berus. Adrian, Dorian, and Baptiste (in no particular order, as they would remind all who dared list their names). "Enough standing about; there is plenty to do. I am sure you can find work helping clean up in the Seraphine! Some of our guests would surely like to continue their dinner, and they don't need the place a mess, do they? And haven't we a young lady that needs searching for?

And where the devil is Cyrus? I swear I asked for him an hour ago!"

The wrath in his voice was enough to send a quake through all three brothers before they stood mumbling to each other, each hoping one of the others could surmise an answer to one of Mr. Erlik's questions. To little avail.

"Well?" Lawrence insisted.

"We haven't seen Mr. Cyrus, sir. Not since this morning." Dorian was the one to answer, though the other two nodded along in moral support. Shaky ground needed a little encouragement from time to time.

"Well, I saw him last when I was with you, sir. You know, while we were discussing the fire," Baptiste added.

"There was a fire?" Adrian inquired.

"When?" Dorian added.

"Not today, lads. Old news, happened years ago in room—"

"That is quite enough, Baptiste! Run along, all of you, before I have a mind to see to it that you've swept your last."

Following a chorus of "Yes sirs," Lawrence found that he didn't feel any better for having rid himself of the nuisance. Instead, he watched solemnly as they scuttled off toward endeavors doubtless intended to make them look busier than they were.

There was little time for discovery as to which endeavors each chose, for Lawrence heard the next horror at the exact moment that Sonya Ivanovna rounded the corner leading to the Seraphine with a raven as black as coal perched on her shoulder. Somehow her smile looked blacker than that wicked bird.

It was a scream. A man's desperate and exasperated scream. Lawrence could tell from the way it came to his ears, hollow, that it was far away, floors above him. But somewhere, someone in his grand hotel had witnessed such a horror that he was unable to contain any shred of composure. While his first thought might have been to assume that this terrified character had witnessed Sonya Ivanovna in the flesh—and, it must be said, Lawrence would do little in the ways of blaming anyone who had such a reaction to realizing that a ghost was standing in from of him, it was all he could do to keep himself from doing the same—that notion quickly left him. After all, she was standing right here. And while her mere existence was enough to make a man as resolute as Lawrence Erlik question a great deal, he was rather certain she was not capable of multiplicity.

What was capable of duplication, as Lawrence was quickly made to realize, was that desperate scream. All sense of warmth, whatever Sonya Ivanovna had allowed him to maintain throughout the day, left him in an instant. Still, sweat poured down his forehead. His bones rattled as he fought the urge to curl into a ball right in the center of the lobby and ignore whatever the source of that hellish sound was.

But there Sonya Ivanovna stood. A beacon, she was. A reminder that—though Lawrence struggled to understand precisely why—he was being tormented. No matter what he did to hide, to stow himself away and attempt to dissolve into the ether, she would pull him back out and drag him to the scream.

"Aurelia," Lawrence croaked, keeping his eyes fixed on those black eyes. "Aurelia!" he managed to shout. But, for perhaps the first time in all of Lawrence Erlik's shaded memory, there came no answer from his most faithful partner. Silence of a kind that was foreign and unfamiliar.

Lawrence would simply have to tread this path himself.

While the screaming had subsided, Lawrence felt he could still hear the ghost of its echo in the back of his thoughts. Stepping toward the lift, he shuddered at the recollection of its bellow. His blood curdled when it sounded, twisted his heart into oblivion.

"What was that?" a few meandering guests had asked, likely only thinking it a creak in the floorboard or a clap of thunder that continued to pound in a fiendish rage. Though many others would have heard it for what it was. Those in the surrounding rooms would hear the death of innocence and gaiety.

Had Rachel been found? Had she been strangled? Mangled? Had another guest been poisoned by her blood-ravenous mother?

Each question boiled in his chest as he thought of which floor it must have sounded from. But that question needed little guesswork. Before he could reach the lift, a quivering figure of an old man began to plead to his manager.

"Mr. Erlik, Mr. Erlik! Come quick! Oh, heavens, what could have driven her to it?"

"Driven who to what? Arthur! Calm yourself, man. Take a breath and tell me what's going on! Are you talking about that scream?"

"So, you've heard it, sir? Oh, it's terrible, terrible. I heard it as I was sitting waiting for my next guest, sir. I had just lifted Mr. Adonis, said he was looking for his wife. Well, I told him, I said, 'Hullo! I just lifted her to go back to your room' and I offered to take him as well. I stayed on the fourth floor; in case they'd be fast about coming back. Watched him go into his room even. I don't know why; I just like to make sure everyone is safe, you know? It's my nature, sir. I don't mean anything by it."

"Arthur!" Lawrence insisted. "What has this got to do with anything? Tell me what has happened!"

Before he could continue, Arthur murmured something under his breath as his entire body convulsed in a violent shiver. The pallor of his visage proved to be the sort that covers the man who has seen too much of the world to carry on with their prior bliss.

"He was covered in blood, sir."

Arthur slowly moved his face from the grandfather clock to Mr. Erlik's eyes. Lawrence saw an ocean of horror storming in those eyes. Great waves plundered the rippling surface.

"Who?" Lawrence dared to inquire.

"The doctor, sir. He called from the hallway. He screamed for me to find help. I came straight down, Mr. Erlik." The old man removed his cap to run his shriveled fingers through his hair, moist from the day's sweat. "There was just so much blood," he croaked, shaking his head.

"Come on, then," Lawrence said, unable to come up with an appropriate excuse to stay where he was. "Adrian, you'll come with me."

"Sir…I," Adrian stammered, unlucky enough to have chosen a spot nearby to make himself seem busy. He was cursing the luck of his brothers.

"Now, Adrian!" Lawrence thundered, abandoning all preconditioned tendencies to keep his voice from raising enough for the guests to hear.

True to Arthur's word, there was an unfathomable amount of blood. But let's not get ahead of ourselves. The first aspect of room 419 (yes, the room directly above that very one that has been the focus of this narrative) was the acrid taste that bit one's tongue upon entering. It came in through the nose, smelling of burning hair, and stabbed the tastebuds in the back of the throat. Lawrence almost gave in to a violent heave and a retch, though caught himself in time. Adrian was not so graceful.

The second feature that caught one's attention was the

desolate wailing. It sounded of a deeper sense of desperation than anything Lawrence—or, especially, Adrian—had ever had the misfortune to hear. Loss of sense, loss of purpose, loss of self. But more acutely, there was a realization in its bellow, as if the man screaming realized that the prize that he had lost had been taken for granted. Does it not often happen that way? Man surrenders himself to the throes of life, taking his spoils as God-given and sacrosanct, only to realize the fragility of his station once it has been ripped from him.

In a way, Lawrence was experiencing much of the same phenomenon, though he had yet to realize it.

Everything else about the room was as one might expect. Ordinary.

The couches remained undisturbed, an armchair held a black coat draped over its back, the luggage was propped, still unopened, on a carrier in the back corner, and the bed was unspoiled in any way. The only piece of furniture that could reasonably be described as askew might have been the writing desk, whose chair was pulled out and set at an angle.

There was but one fracture in the room's pristine condition, and that was the blood soiling the floor. The irony of two rooms stacked on top of one another with bloodied floors was not lost on Lawrence, though he didn't know what to make of it.

The blood in room 419 didn't take the form of a collected pool. Rather, there were several neatly pressed prints of feet. Not just any prints, but a pair telling two separate stories of two separate states of mind. The first were heading from the main bedroom toward the front door. These were smeared and hardly the shape of a full shoe. They told the story of a man frantically running in order to find help, a man in a desperate panic, a man who still believed that something ought to be done.

The second set of prints were obviously the returning set, leading from the front room back toward the bedroom. These were a different sort, a solemn footing. Neatly pressed in the ground, they told the story of a man who gave up any ounce of frantic hope, any scrap of confidence that anything could be done at all. Fate was sealed. It had a habit of doing that. Men are often bold enough to believe they can shape fate, mold it into the future they so desire. All the more painful it then becomes when fate shows her hand with the sharpest of pains.

"Mr. Adonis? Mrs. Adonis?" Lawrence called, keeping the shake in his voice at bay, if only for a little while. Nothing came in return but the soft whimper of a man who hadn't heard his name called for the simple fact that all sound was dead to him.

"Mr. Erlik, should we call the police?"

"Yes, Adrian, but we'd better get a little more information first. They can't get here any quicker, the storm will see to that. It's best we have everything—"

"Why? What have you done? Why did you do it?"

"What was that?" Adrian whispered.

"Pull yourself together and stand up straight! This is not how a man of the Genovie behaves, creeping about." While Adrian would likely struggle to come up with the exact reason why, he had actually begun to crouch as they walked closer to the bedroom.

The voice he had heard, one that sent enough of a shiver down his spine to quite literally pull him toward the ground in that abominable crouch that Lawrence so despised, was Frederick Adonis.

Lawrence discovered him upon turning into the bedroom. It ought to be pointed out for posterity that Lawrence (or any other member of staff, for that matter) did not make it a habit of entering a guest's bedroom uninvited. However, the extenuating circumstances being so…well, extenuating, he made an exception.

For the rest of his days, he would wish he hadn't.

Not that there was much avoiding it; he would have had to enter the room eventually. But there are many actions that are regrettably unavoidable, yet they come to be repented as if they were made by choice. A sinner who knew better.

And it wasn't entering the bedroom that sent the darkness shooting through Lawrence's veins. Seeing with a light coming from the master bathroom, Lawrence and Adrian found the horror that had awaited them.

Perhaps it was the smell of so much blood that made Adrian keel over and evacuate every ounce from his stomach. Or maybe it was just the sight of it. After all, how often does one traverse into a bathroom to find a woman lying in the bathtub filled with her own blood? The sight is enough to send a man to the brink of madness, even without the addition of the pitiful husband holding her head to his chest, adding a river of his tears to the hellish bath.

It is a certain kind of perdition, bathing in one's own blood, and it is not one to be sought after. That was, however, exactly what it turned out Angela Adonis had done. Sought this precise end.

That may be a bit unfair, and the reader will certainly be asking themselves how exactly it came to be that the pristine porcelain had come to be tainted by such a morbid filling. It was not altogether clear to those in the room either, but the details were eventually worked out.

The letter that was sitting on the ground, nearly blotted out with the sticky red ink that was splattered about the floor, clued Lawrence in just as it had clued Frederick when he had discovered it resting atop the writing desk. The stationary Lawrence recognized easily enough, having provided it to her as a complimentary addition to her stay when it was requested earlier that morning.

Her writing was superb. That is to say, the style of her penmanship. It was practiced, elegant—regal, even—giving all the more ghastliness to the words.

I regret not the drop of the poison in his glass, but his poison in my womb.

I had to get it out.

I'm sorry for the way I am to leave you, darling, but I can bear it no longer.

I had to get it out.

I shall soon be with our darling Rachel.

I had to get it out.

I breathe with solace at the prospect of finally meeting her.

All my love,

Your Darling Angela

"Suicide," Lawrence couldn't help but whisper. But the manner in which it was enacted was too much to bear. Not a soul that stood in that room would ever be the same. Lawrence stepped lightly in the direction of the sobbing husband, debating whether to reach out a hand.

For the benefit of the reader, I would like to step back in time to when we last saw Angela.

Crippling over a panged stomach, Angela made quite a show of exiting the Seraphine with the crashing of glasses and the spilling of chairs. The only thing was there was no one to watch. It is true that the pains that enveloped Angela's midsection were gradually growing worse throughout the day, but it was at the particular discovery of the long stretch of blue ribbon lying on the floor that she remembered exactly why she had come to feel such agonizing horror. There was, by her own estimation, something growing inside of her that did not belong.

Now, one might be hard-pressed to come to such a conclusion through the simplicity of stomach pain, no matter how heavily that pain pressed into one's abdomen. That, however, was the secret to Angela's intuition. The pain was something more than a mortal wound. She knew it well. It was an immortal reminder of a past sin. The very same sin for which our former radio newsman had run to Atlanta. A shared misjudgment, so to speak.

While the reader may approach Angela's transgressions with a proper measure of sympathy that ought not to be afforded to Mr. Cherry—indeed, it is the writer's opinion that she might be deserving of the honor—the pain remained all the same. It appeared she had not felt the soothing calm of forgiveness. Rather, she felt claws. Sharp ones, black ones, the kind that form in the womb of a great depravity of spirit. And they were tearing away at her.

So it was that Angela had, nearly crawling from the pain, made her way to the room she had avoided staying within to remove the ghastly growth she had convinced herself was residing in her stomach.

As to the question of the removal of said parasite, it dawned on Angela that it was best to see to it immediately. Without exchanging so much as a word with our poor lift operator who was to very shortly undergo the shock of his life, Angela rose to the fourth floor and entered room 419.

Of course, all of this happened—it is prudent to remind the reader—after she had experienced a rather frigid press into her cheek on the right side. While that remained a mystery to Angela Adonis, those reading this record will doubtless conclude the nature of that infelicitous sensation.

It was upon entering room 419 that Angela Adonis directly approached the writing desk wherein she had previously stashed the stack of stationary alongside the Parker Duofold pen—which, she was reluctant to admit, wrote like a dream. The words which have already been recorded flowed out of her without so much as a breath or a pause.

Something with a bit more of a point also rested in the drawer of the writing desk that Angela was not altogether prepared for. A knife. Not just any knife, but one so ornate that it dazzled the eye. A silver hilt with several precious gemstones inlaid in the handguard and pommel.

Such a piece of smith work often speaks to each viewer in a unique fashion. For Angela, as she laid eyes upon its intoxicating glimmer, she heard soft and comforting whispers telling her to *come home*. And for the span of a moment, she knew precisely what that meant.

Rising to the occasion, and without taking her eyes from the dagger that she held aloft as she twisted in the direction of the main bedroom, Angela Adonis made her way toward the bathtub in order to take her grim bow from this world.

All the while, she wept for what ought to have been, what she had deserved, what she had made a deal for. Robbed of her reward, her penitence was swift and unyielding. Climbing into the bathtub, without removing so much as a single sleek black stiletto, she continued to mutter, "I need to get it out."

Over and over again. "I need to get it out." As she lowered herself and propped her legs on the porcelain rim. "I need to get it out." As she wiped a stray tear from her cheek that was in danger of plunging itself into the red sheen of her lipstick. "I need to get it out." And just before the point of the blade plunged into the soft sea of her belly, she cried, "I need to get her out."

And so, the summation of her self-imposed perdition was set on display for Lawrence to see, Frederick to weep, and Adrian to retch. Lawrence, having stepped close enough to see the resulting misfortune, felt the same instinct as the young bellman. It was particularly strong when he saw the carving of a large U starting from the side of her mid-belly, coming down below her waist to her lower abdomen, and back up to her mid-belly on the opposite side.

"Adrian, open the window. Now, Adrian!" Lawrence demanded, unable to think of anything but the smell. It wasn't until the breeze of the rain-filled air crept over to his profaned nostrils that he was able to settle the dizzy spell he suffered. Then his mind began to tackle questions.

What did she have to get out? Clearly, she had attempted to carve something from her stomach, only to end in a pool of the resulting blood, a pale, lifeless face staring at the ceiling. The memory of Mrs. Adonis keeling over in the lobby shot into him like a bullet in the chest. How he wished for that very sensation in that moment. Perhaps then he wouldn't be saddled with such a tragic end to his career. No doubt any manager, even one as qualified as Lawrence Erlik, would see the end of his hotel managing days at the behest of three deaths in one day.

"Mr. Adonis," Lawrence whispered, unable to clear enough phlegm from his throat to make the proper sounds. "Doctor," he choked. Frederick stopped his whimpering for a moment and raised his head toward the worried manager. Bloodshot eyes, snot-run nose, and drooling bottom lip were a few of the harrowing symptoms stretched about this wretched man's face. "I'm going to have to ask you to...accompany me...down to my office. We'll need to...grab a full account to...alert the authorities."

Lawrence found it quite difficult to get through his statement without retching, though he managed it just the same. Frederick, for his part, proved remarkably amenable for a man in his position, rising before the manager had concluded his request. "Adrian," Lawrence said. "Run along ahead and ensure there are no guests to gawk at us!"

Adrian, for reasons too obvious to mention, ran along with a gusto.

"Now," Lawrence began, looking at the sniveling shell of the doctor he had, for reasons well forgotten by this point, come to loathe. "How about a change of clothing, hm? I suppose you'll have—"

Lawrence was cut short at the reflection of light coming from inside the tub. What he had failed to realize upon initial inspection was the instrument of Mrs. Adonis' surgery was still propped in her right hand, partially drowned by the red sea. He recognized the protruding handguard immediately as the very weapon that ran through the chin of Roman Pavlovich Kosorukov earlier that same morning.

Unable to utter so much as a sentence in response to this discovery, Lawrence turned to find Frederick standing in the bedroom just outside the door, unable to keep his eyes from the bathtub. Standing next to him, looking directly at Lawrence, was Sonya Ivanovna.

She was smiling, similar to that grim grin that had twisted her face in the Seraphine. And just as she had leaned over to Michael, Sonya rose herself to the tips of her toes in order to press her ice-cold lips to the cheek of the mourning doctor.

"No!" Lawrence called with as much volume as his chest could muster. Unfortunately, he found his plea fell on deaf ears. Without so much as a second thought, Frederick turned around and marched straight toward the window. Lawrence rushed toward him as he climbed onto the windowsill. It may have been possible, had Frederick Adonis paused but for a moment of brief hesitation, for Lawrence to have extended his arm just enough to grab onto the doctor's braces and pull him back into the safety of the Genovie (whatever that "safety" hitherto been reduced to).

But as it was, Frederick was imbued with the confidence of the damned. Without a second's delay, he propelled himself into the abyss with a swift and resounding kick from the hotel's outer stone facade.

Lawrence met the scene with utter contempt for its origin. He whirled around just after witnessing the man fall to his end. What had he expected to see? Sonya Ivanovna staring back triumphantly? Perhaps it was a defense mechanism brought on through fear of her having the thought to push him next. She had already kissed him, after all. But when he turned around in a desperate heave of a breath, he found a solitary space, abandoned by all living, even those living after death.

Though he wished to do the opposite, to walk passively down the hall, into the lift, through the lobby, and into his office where he could rest a piping hot kettle over the fire and await Cyrus's assured tirade of abuses, he forced himself to view the morbid reality he had come to confront.

It might be said that it was for the benefit of the poor doctor that the hotel's base just below the window of room 419 was outfitted with a number of large, jagged looking boulders. They made for a quick end. What poor devil would wish to abide by the torments of a slow fading after a quick drop? But for Lawrence, they made for a messy, mangled view.

Of course, his focus would have remained on the tragedy of death—a fourth death, under his watch, no less—were it not for the malevolence of Sonya Ivanovna. She stood, impervious to the rain, on top of the tallest boulder, looking down at her handiwork.

Lawrence had given up questioning how she moved great distances in the span of a second, that much was a secret kept beyond the grave. But something in the way she cocked her head up to look at him while two ravens flew through the storm to land on her shoulders, sent him into a fit of passion and rage.

That was the moment the kiss did its job. That was the moment Lawrence snapped.

XXVII

Consequently, the very moment Sonya Ivanovna's kiss took hold of her victim, Lawrence began to hear the unbearable drum of a malicious pounding. The sound came, first with the accompaniment of thunder, and then with the rhythm of the crank organ. Lawrence could hear both, the pounding and the organ, as clear as if they were in the room with him.

"Stop!" he shouted to himself for no apparent reason other than a descent into the darkness. "Make it stop!"

But his pleas quickly turned into something else. When he closed his eyes, he saw Sonya's. When he opened them, he could see her lurking in the shadows. One thing became a certainty: she would not let it stop. That was up to him.

The pounding doubled in volume as he stepped with purpose into the sitting room and toward the door. There was no denying its origin as he reached for the handle; it was coming right below where he stood. Someone was pounding on the door to room 319.

And so, it was confirmed—after running out of the room, through the hall, and down the stairwell in a manner that suggested to the neutral observer that he had lost himself—the door was shaking.

A violent, petulant shake. There was someone on the other

side, someone that Lawrence had inadvertently nailed into the room without knowledge and was pleading to get out. For a moment, Lawrence forgot about the anger and rage, locking them in the recesses of his mind, and became engrossed in the desire to free the girl on the other side.

I mention the girl on the other side, as that is precisely what Lawrence had assumed. Rachel. The missing piece had always been Rachel. Specifically what Sonya Ivanovna had done to her. Surely, she had done something. She had trapped her in room 319 with his help. Hidden her in a dark corner where Lawrence had not noticed and drove him to nail it shut.

Luckily, he had left the hammer on the floor after having secured room 319.

"It's okay!" he shouted. "I'll get you out! I'll...get...you...out!" But the pounding only quickened in pace and increased in power as Lawrence set to work prying off the scrap boards he had fashioned from beautiful furniture.

What a sight it was had the reader the pleasure of seeing it! The proper, pristine manager of the Hotel Genovie swung maddeningly toward the barred door. Sweat poured down his beet-red face, hair fell in greasy locks in front of his eyes, and his coat tore at the seams as he swung with all his strength. Had the majority of guests not remained on the main floor in order to reseat themselves after the unfortunate disturbance to the Seraphine's service, Lawrence would have aroused quite the commotion.

Yet, without an audience, the commotion was contained to the depths of his soul. Each swing of the hammer, each pull of a nail, he felt his spirit weaken in one place and strengthen in another. A grand shift of alignment threw him off kilter, yet kept him prodding at the abyss that lay beyond the heavy panel of oak that served as a gateway into his own personal hell.

And still, it shook. It pounded, it groaned, it wept. Lawrence tried to ignore the drumming of its taunt, but each landing of a fist onto the opposite side of the wood drove him a width of a strand of hair further into madness. Flashes of faces sprang into vision, faces that were obliterated by the smashing of his hammer. Mr. Cherry, Private Goodman, Angela Adonis, Frederick Adonis. Rachel.

The child's face appeared at the final blow of the last board. It splintered and shattered under the weight of his swing. Lawrence nearly jumped from fright, the child's innocent eyes serving to pull him from his frenzy. Perhaps some small fraction of his soul was residing yet undisturbed in the vacuous void he had found himself.

And then the pounding resumed. It pulled him from his momentary trance like a bucket of ice water yanks a soldier from unearned sleep.

Finding the lock jammed by his own doing, Lawrence had to resort once more to the instrument of the hammer. As it rose high above his head, the music of the crank organ came to a height that blocked out the sound of the hammer coming down on the brass of the handle. One, two, three times it took, and three times he did not hear the echo of his swing for the rage of the music.

His breath was made of needles, stabbing holes into his lungs until they deflated. The strength he had found for the span of a moment in order to rip those boards to pieces seemed fleeting. He used the last of it to hurl himself, shoulder first into the door, the edge of its wood splitting into splinters large enough to impale a man.

The music stopped, the pounding ceased, and, as if it had a mind of its own, the door creaked open. It was slow, the same slowness of the door to the bedroom that worked its way open in order to produce Sonya Ivanovna only seconds after Kosorukov fell lifeless to the floor. And, just as it had then, this door opened to reveal her once again.

Sonya stood, her hands clasped in front of her waist, in the center of the room. Aside from her, there was no sign of the room ever having been disturbed. There was no bottle of brandy, no pair of snifters, no box of cigars, no pool of blood, no dead body perched upon the tufted leather couch.

Only Sonya.

The sight of her brought Lawrence to a boiling rage. He gripped the hammer tight in his hand, nearly rubbing his skin raw as he moved it around. He could measure the weight of it, the way the head would bear down like a mortar with the right force. A yearning burned in his chest. A yearning to wipe the smile from her grey lips, to put an end to the misery she caused Cherry, the Adonises, Goodman. The misery she caused him. The thought tasted sweet on his tongue, like a freshly plucked strawberry. How does one refuse such a bite when the mouth waters from such a tantalizing invitation?

Three steps and one swing, I think it was. It was swift, like the fleeting, fragile note of the violin before getting lost in the crescendo.

Sonya's smile did not break the entire time he rushed, not as his hammer split through the air like an ax. He heard the crack of her skull only a fraction of a second before he tasted the blood that splashed against his face. It was warm; it was coppery with a pinch of salt; it was real.

Lawrence caught his breath, heaving out of control. No matter how long he drew in air, those little holes he had imagined being poked into his lungs seemed to curse him. While his eyes remained facing forward, he could no longer see the specter that had followed him all afternoon. He could no longer feel her breath on his neck, nor her lips on his cheek. With the heavy thud as she crashed to the floor, he felt the tension wash away from his shoulders. Drunk with the poison of his endeavors, laughter left him like a flock of geese sounding in the mid-morning flight. Air tasted sweeter on his tongue, and again, his mind's eye turned to strawberries. He could live on this feeling forever, succumbing to its seduction until the rapture pulled him from his gaiety.

But fate is a formidable charlatan. Once she removes one ounce of grief, she replaces it with two. Such was the case when the wave of despair flooded through Lawrence's blood, run cold with contempt and repentance.

"Sonechka!" he gasped, throwing himself to the floor without a care for the world that had crashed around him in a burning flame. The sweetness of the air disappeared; the lightness of his chest vanished. Sulfur returned to his nose as he scooped her into his arms. The body was limp, heavy, and very much real. As real as it had felt in his dream. Sonya Ivanovna was dead, and Lawrence had swung the hammer that bludgeoned her.

"What have I done? What have I done to you, my love?" And for the second time that day, his voice did not sound his own. It sounded old and dusty, the way an old, neglected binding croaks with decades of disuse as it is opened once again. "I've ruined you; I have! I didn't mean it; I didn't mean it. Oh God, I am so sorry. Forgive me, Sonechka!"

"Hello, Romik." The words sent a volley of arrows to pierce his spine, one at a time until he could hardly take in an ounce of air. He held Sonya Ivanovna tight to his chest, the blood from her wound soaking his stark white shirt as Angela's had soaked Frederick's. It took all the strength that remained in his body to turn his head and face his discoverer.

"Cyrus?" he said, seeing the old man's warm features gazing down on him in his usual, condescending way. He looked as if nothing was out of the ordinary, as if Lawrence had stepped into the office and slumped into his chair, awaiting his cup of tea.

But there was something about his presence that had never been there before, at least not in a way that Lawrence could recall. There was warmth, welcoming. Standing over the dilapidated figure of a once proud hotel manager, Cyrus seemed to be a knight of honor and repute.

"Cyrus! You must understand, I—she was—this isn't—" but the words hit him before he could get an explanation out. "What did you call me?"

"I must say, it is very nice to see you...feeling yourself again."

"What is this? What do you mean, feeling myself? What's happened?" He clung tighter to Sonya, and as he did, she burst into a pile of ash, burying his knees in the soot.

"Roman Pavlovich Kosorukov. I've always preferred the name. Don't mistake me, darling, Lawrence Erlik has quite the nice ring to it, but it pays to be accurate, don't you find? It pays to be...honest."

"Honest about what? Why are you calling me by that name?"

"Don't pretend to carry on with this charade, darling, I've only seen you just now! You know as well as I do!"

"Know what?" Lawrence shouted, his face turning bright red.

"Who you are! My dear, haven't you seen that this is what it's all been about?"

"I don't understand. I'm not—Kosorukov came to the hotel. He...he told me about his wife. She died of consumption, and he couldn't get her help. He couldn't stop drinking. He...he...he was haunted by her."

"Sonya Ivanovna didn't die of consumption, did she, Romik?"

"Why do you keep calling me that? I don't know any more than what he told me. I—" he paused and nearly choked on his own breath. His eyes dilated and retracted while a pain shot through his head. He blinked and looked around the room as if he had never seen it in his life.

"You said you were going to America," Cyrus said. "That's what you told her."

"To America, yes...yes, that's what I said, isn't it?"

"Why?"

"Why what?"

"Why were you going to America, Romik?"

"Her father...she was...her father was going to take her away from me. We were going to get married, and he was going to put an end to our happiness before it had even begun. You must understand I—" But Romik was interrupted at the midpoint of his explanation with a halt of Cyrus's hand and a closed-eyed shake of his head.

"It isn't my place to understand, my dear."

"She told me that night. I paid for a room..."

"Why did you choose the Genovie?"

"It was...where my mother worked. I lived here for—"

"A while," Cyrus aided, finding the words that Romik could not.

"She told me she was going to go back, that she couldn't leave her father. I couldn't, I just couldn't let her go. She was all that I had, all that I loved. I couldn't let her go, I couldn't! But she kept trying to leave. I got so...so angry. I couldn't do anything to keep her. I could see that, and it made me so angry. So, I—" but Romik choked.

"So, you bludgeoned her with a hammer."

"I loved her. Why couldn't she see that I loved her? Could she not see?" His voice failed him, coming out at more of a rusty croak than his usual timbre. "It wasn't the way it should be..." he pushed from his breath, clutching his chest with a tightened grip.

"She comes to visit me, you know..."

"Yes, Romik, I have known for a while."

"She was here just a moment ago. Here with me. I can still feel her breath on my neck, the warmth of her embrace. I really do think there was a time that she loved me."

"Perhaps, though time winds in its own fashion, leaving us in its wake."

"The flames..." Romik continued, "they were so beautiful that night, weren't they? The way the reflections danced within the shine of the marble."

"I'm afraid I have resigned my eyes from the grace of beauty a long time ago. In a different life."

"Yes, yes, I do think they were. You know, I've really been considering beauty as of late."

"What a charming pastime."

"Don't laugh, Cyrus. Thirsting for a little brightness, that's all. Thirsting for her." He paused and looked about the room, climbing to his feet and dusting himself off. He tugged at his waistcoat and stood straight for the first time in the past few hours. "You know, I dream of them every night? The flames. They envelop all that surrounds me, devour all the evils in the world in their wake. Such beautiful little things, they are. Don't you think? Oh, you've already answered that haven't you? I always wake before they reach me. But that was not the way of it...that night, was it, Cyrus?"

"No, my dear, that was not the way of it."

"Tell me, did it hurt much?"

"Does it matter, darling? Would it comfort you to know that it didn't?"

"Yes, I think it should."

"Very well, Romik, it did not hurt. Like fading into a daydream on a summer afternoon."

"I think you lie to me, friend."

"Perhaps."

"Perhaps, he says. Tell me, Cyrus, how long have we been here?"

"A long time, Romik. A very long time."

All of this was spoken without an inch of movement between either man, though something looked as if it were about to break in Romik. He began to see things a bit clearer. His memory—or lack thereof, as I should say—returned to him of never having left the hotel's glass doors. The busts of previous managers all seem to take on the same likeness, only the dates changing at the bottom of their brass necks. How long had he been there? A very long time.

"And...what about the others?"

"The others?"

"The others, the guests. Mr. and Mrs. Adonis. Private Goodman."

"They were here for a short spell, but they have been ferried to their final destination, my friend. You see, the hotel is a fine thing. Man's greatest invention, I might suggest. It offers itself up as an intermediary, a place of quiet reflection between states. Our friends have left us, yes, but their time with us was short because they reflected on their prior existence with a quick burn. Awfully impressive, if you ask me. You, on the other hand...you've needed a bit more."

"A bit more what?"

"Reflecting."

"What is this place?"

"Why, it is the Hotel Genovie."

"I mean…is this—"

"Hell? Why, do you mean to tell me you were expecting fire and brimstone? Little demons with hooks and souls burning in little stone boxes with a hole in the lid to keep the fire going? I must say, I did have a good laugh when I first read Mr. Alighieri's works. Such an imaginative one, he was. I always wondered why he bothered himself with worrying about the physics of keeping the flame going and stopped there. Truly—"

"Cyrus."

"Alright, this is not what I would call 'Hell', but if it makes it easier for you to see it that way, I don't see the harm."

"This was all your doing!" Romik spat, a vein popping from his forehead, his index finger pointed like a small dagger in the direction of Cyrus's heart. "You've tortured me relentlessly! You…you snuck notes in my pocket, you had her following me, you sent ravens to mock me! I've been on the brink of madness!"

"I?"

"You!"

"I'm afraid most of that work would be better attributed to your darling Sonya. And are you so quick to assume you are not deserving of her every whim? Did you not beat her to death? Did you not risk the lives of others when you set room 319 into flames? Really, Romik, I thought we had moved past this self-centered behavior by now. You are like a little boy who reaches out for candy before supper. You must get ahold of yourself!"

Kosorukov stood still for a moment, contemplating everything that had led him to this point. Could he remember a moment in time before that very morning? Try as he did, not a whisper of a memory could be found. He kept reverting back to that discussion with Kosorukov, the old wretched Kosorukov—a mirror image of himself, of his guilt and contempt for his own image. He painted with a brush covered in blood the figure of an old man weathered with pain and infamy. Had that image admitted to the murder of Sonya Ivanovna? In its own way, Romik supposed it had.

The mirage of a life he never lived evaporated the longer he contemplated. All the while, Cyrus waited patiently for him to come to a proper understanding. He was Kosorukov, and Kosorukov was him.

That leaves the question—the one that most assuredly must be addressed—of who exactly was Mr. Lawrence Erlik? Romik nearly fell to the floor in shock as a vivid memory compounded in his chest, fluttering before him as if it were in front of his very eyes.

"Romusha, Romusha!" the fair, nervous voice called. "Come, Romusha, meet Mama's new employer. He is the manager of the hotel, little darling; he is in charge around here. You be sure to say your pleases and thank yous from here on out. This is a very special hotel, you know. And we are very lucky to be here! I expect you will give the staff no trouble!" Roman shivered at the memory of the cold streets of St. Petersburg he had so freshly escaped. His heart pounded as his neck cranked up to see the man standing before him.

"It is a pleasure to make your acquaintance, Roman Pavlovich, a real pleasure, young sir!" The man was young, too young for his station, but stood well within it. His black hair was slicked back with oil, his perfume radiant, and his waistcoat fit snug underneath his jacket.

He extended a white gloved hand for little Romik to grasp with his small, dirty fingers. "That's a good lad," he spoke in Russian, though in an accent Roman had never heard before. "A good strong lad! I am Lawrence Erlik the Third, but you can call me Lawrence."

"Romik?" Cyrus called in a gentle nudge. "Romik, are you here with me, darling?"

"What? What?"

"Come, now, you really are looking dreadful." Roman Pavlovich nearly fell to the floor from a weakness in the knees. And how can one blame him? It is not everyday you find you have been living in the echo of an illusion!

But, albeit slowly, he began to accept the reality of his situation. His mind jumped from thoughts of Aurelia, the Berus brothers, and all those that had served the grand illusion. But his mouth could only form the words of a single question.

"What now?"

"I'm afraid we are coming up very close to the end, my dear."

"How will it happen?"

"First will be the flames."

"First." It was more of a statement than a question.

"First."

"Will it hurt?"

"Only a little."

"Yes, I suppose it ought to." Roman nodded at the conjecture. "Then what?"

"Well…then we do it over again, I fear."

"For how long?"

"Until your old man tells the proper story, I expect."

"He'll tell it next time," Roman said with the conviction of a man who had never known the concept he was pontificating. Like a young man speaking of glory but having never seen death.

"You've said that before, Romik."

"I have? When? How many times have we done this?"

"I told you, a very long time." Cyrus let the words sink in before finally saying, "I'm afraid we are running out of time." As he spoke these words, Lawrence could smell the smoke tickling his nose, scratching at his eyes. The room began to feel hotter and his mind harkened back to the broken radiator that was never really broken at all.

By the time the flames touched his pant leg, Roman was alone in the room, alone except one figure, that of Sonya Ivanovna.

"I'm so sorry," he said, weeping madly. "I'm so very sorry. Forgive me, Sonechka, forgive the evil I did to you." The phantom stared, only she was a phantom no longer. As Romik's understanding of his damnation compounded, he noticed that the color had returned to her cheeks, her gown was neatly pressed in the fashion of a councilor's daughter—in the fashion that Roman Pavlovich could never have afforded to maintain. And her smile, her smile was filled with warmth and tenderness. It confused Romik, for how could such tenderness be given to him? A louse, vermin under her shoe.

"Do not shed a tear for me, my love," he opined, feeling the heat crawl beneath his skin. "I am a louse who never deserved you. This is the fate I have reaped. I hope I never tell myself the correct story, such that I shall stay in this hotel for eternity in order to better serve you. Burn me, let me perish in the squalor of my sins. But know that all that I was, every scrap of it no matter how vile, was in worship of you."

Somewhere in the pining of our good friend Kosorukov's, Sonya faded from his vision. Whether she disintegrated with the heat of the flames, or simply walked out the door, he would never know.

With Sonya Ivanovna's disappearance came a final flicker of the lights. The cellar, Romik had then assumed, finally reached the point of fully flooding. The guests would likely see water trickle into the lobby. That is, if the Berus brothers would have the sense to light enough candles to show the way until the power could be restored. But of course, they would have enough sense. The Berus brothers were the best bellmen a hotel like the Genovie could ask for. And even if they hadn't thought of it, Aurelia would be there to direct them silently yet effectively, cutting a wave of her brow at the slightest groan.

But then Romik remembered it was all a dream—a wicked, tortured dream. He needn't worry about the guests any longer; he needn't consider the attributes of his members of staff. Not at least until the fire burned through his flesh, until his bones were charred black, and he awoke in the morning anew.

Romik shivered in the flame, muttering something under his breath that even he could not decipher. When the flame began to burn his skin, true to Cyrus' word, it only hurt a fraction of what Lawrence expected.

"Five guests of the Hotel Genovie," he choked through the smoke. "Four deaths, moving on from our hospitality. Three caws of the raven, two cracks of the hammer. One phantom paramour, one silent assistant, one blue ribbon, one murderer, one bow in flame."

.

EPILOGUE

What a pity that the previous manager under the employ of the Hotel Genovie lost his head. Granted, it was only in a manner of speaking, though lost it was just the same. I do hope the reader will forgive the theatrics. You see, it is imperative, not only to the narrative but to the—shall we say—rehabilitation of the subject in question.

We, at the Genovie, take an illustrious amount of pride in ensuring that our guests and admirers are treated to the highest experience that the world of accommodation has to offer. I dare say, with a skosh of humility on my own part, that this record has shown just that. We have even gone so far out of our way as to put a guest at the helm of the ship. (While I oversaw his every move, of course. What kind of manager would I be if I were to just let a guest prance about the deck without great care in supervision? You ought to know better by now!)

Anyway, I'm afraid I've given myself to the abominable habit of the digression.

The Genovie is a precious gem. It was correctly said that it is the great intermediary. For Lawrence—or, perhaps it would do better to call him by his proper name, Romik—the transition between states, so to speak, took a little more time than the average guest. But, as I have told the staff from the very beginning, we are the ferrymen crossing our guests over the grey river that might, with good reason, cause them quite a bit of fear and dismay.

And why shouldn't it? It is not every day that one breaks the threshold of home only to find oneself in foreign surroundings. And to think that some do not see it coming! It is a tragedy in the making.

That is where we come into play.

I would challenge the reader, before judging our humble promises of providing the most luxurious of transitions before our guests reach their final destination, to harken back upon their own journeys. Has fear not been relieved at the behest of a warm blanket and a soft pillow? Has a proper dinner service never been the cure for a case of homesickness?

A hotel is never what it seems, though a proper one does all it can to become so. We, at the Genovie, have worked hard to be our guests' home away from the life they left behind. Not an easy task, I'm afraid. But sometimes it can be a bit more than that. Oftentimes, we are expected to provide our guests with an experience very much the opposite of the life they led. Decadence in the face of poverty, honor in the face of shame, health in the face of sickness. Even if only for a moment, the Genovie is here to serve.

All this talk of life and the great intermediation leaves me pondering a simple question. How does one measure the worth of a man? I must admit, my time with Romik has left me holding on to this question with a tight grip. We are, after all, pulled screaming into the frigid cold of the world and sent about our way to make something of ourselves. The proverbial we, you understand. I would not dare to harken upon the experiences of the staff; it would not be...proper.

But back to the question at hand. Are we to take the whole life, pulling instances of good and evil and placing them on scales to decide the balance? Or ought we judge by the greatest good and the greatest evil? I haven't the capacity to see the answer clearly.

For Romik's part, one might be hard pressed to see past his greatest sin. I daresay, though it is admittedly not my place, that I would find it hard to blame them. But there was something in Sonya Ivanovna's eyes each night before she watched her lover burn. A twinkle, if you will. That look has caught me in a bind, dear reader. The very woman who ought to have festered the highest level of contempt for the soul of a man so overwrought with jealousy, he would rather see her in a pool of her own blood than watch her walk out the door of room 319. A troubling thought. This very woman had *warmth* left over for him. So, I ask myself again, over and over, how do we judge the worth of a man?

Perhaps it was the love he had for her that nurtured that warmth. After all, his greatest blunder was, in a twisted sort of way, an act of love. But brutality is love's ugly cousin. It contorts the mind and warps the soul. So much does it distort love, evil takes its place.

It's been a secondary interest of mine to understand that love. Surely, Romik burned with passion for Sonya Ivanovna. I confess there have been moments in my time with them that even I might have begun to feel the tinge of love for her in my own way, were I able to feel such a vulgar sensation. But as it is, my time with them has passed, making it prudent for me to record their foray into the next phase.

Why have I seen fit for such an endeavor? The undertaking may seem odd to those on the outside, I will admit, but to one such as I, nothing seems more natural. I have said on the outset of this record that we are in the business of life and have tried to dissuade the reader from believing that we are in the business of death. While that may seem, in hindsight, to have been dishonest, I beseech the reader not to fall prey to such a misunderstanding. It is precisely life that we concern ourselves with. We give no interest to how a person has died, but how a soul lived their life. I believe the Kosorukovs are exemplary of such a statement.

I also put forth that we often have the opportunity to change our guests, but that it is rare to see a guest change the staff. While I admittedly misled the reader into focusing on the changes that "Lawrence" underwent, it was I who was changed by him.

Perhaps we won't see another of his like for centuries, perhaps we will tomorrow. It is not for me to know. What I do know, as proprietor, is that it is imperative to take in the change that is offered by such a rare guest.

Until the next one,

Your Affectionate Manager of the Hotel Genovie,
Cyrus

THE END

Please, if you finished and enjoyed The Hotel Genovie, I would appreciate you leaving a review on Goodreads or wherever you purchased.

/

ACKNOWLEDGMENTS

I once heard it said that the Russian Novel is all you need. While this may be reductive, not giving some of my favorites through the history of written word their due, I cannot deny the life changing shift that overcame my sense of self after having read my first piece of Russian Literature, The Brothers Karamazov by the immortal genius of Fyodor Dostoevsky. An interest turned to an obsession, and an obsession turned into an idea—a bold idea. The concept that plagued my mind being that it was possible to write something resembling, even in a fraction of a sense, the style of the Russian novel. The result, after many late nights, tireless mornings, and constant reconsidering, was The Hotel Genovie.

It is, in a sense, a love letter. Sure, that letter could easily be addressed to Alyosha Karamazov, Rodion Raskolnikov, or even Woland from Mikhail Bulgakov's version of genius in the Master and the Margarita. After all, Romik and Sonya are very much crafted in order to thank these giants for their hours and hours of entertainment, challenge, and reflection. But, the truth is, it is a love letter to many people in my own life who have fostered my love for the written word.

First, my eighth grade English teacher, Mr. Hume, was the first person to show me the depth of what a novel can achieve. That education was furthered throughout my student career with Mrs. Larson, Mrs. Bronski, and Ms. Kevonian, all building with kindling and log the flame that has yet to extinguish in my chest. And, most importantly, my wife, Kayla.

For listening to the ravings of an overly-inspired reader, for holding my hand along the journey of doubt and remorse, for reading every scrap of terrible writing in the beginning, to supporting me in publishing the work within these pages. I thank you.

Finally, I would like to thank you, dear reader, for blessing me with your time. If I could beg one final act of kindness from you, it would be in the form of a review. Please, if you finished and enjoyed The Hotel Genovie, I would appreciate you leaving a review on Goodreads or wherever you purchased.

ABOUT THE AUTHOR

Shane Ryan is a debut author out of Metro-Detroit, Michigan. He has spent many years writing for sport and honing his craft and is excited to announce his debut novel, The Hotel Genovie! The Hotel Genovie is a gothic literature novel based around the esteemed hotel and its mysterious guests. It is a project he has put all his passion into and is thrilled to share it with the world.

www.ingramcontent.com/pod-product-compliance
Lightning Source LLC
Chambersburg PA
CBHW030230120726
47903CB00005B/1426